© Gasper Tringale

JEFFREY EUGENIDES was born in Detroit and attended Brown and Stanford Universities. His first novel, *The Virgin Suicides,* was published by FSG to great acclaim in 1993, and he has received numerous awards for his work. In 2003, Eugenides received the Pulitzer Prize for his novel *Middlesex.* (FSG, 2002), which was also a finalist for the National Book Critics Circle Award, the International IMPAC Dublin Literary Award, and France's Prix Médicis.

Also by Jeffrey Eugenides

Middlesex

The Virgin Suicides

My Mistress's Sparrow Is Dead (editor)

Additional Praise for *The Marriage Plot*

NAMED A BEST BOOK OF THE YEAR BY
The Seattle Times • *The New Republic* • *The Telegraph*
Salon • NPR • *The New York Times Book Review*
Publishers Weekly • *Houston Chronicle* • *The Miami Herald*

"Layered with exactly the kinds of things that people who love novels will love." —*Los Angeles Times*

"Acutely captures what it's like to be a conflicted twentysomething. Eugenides . . . has managed to reinvigorate the classic coming-of-age genre." —*W* magazine

"*The Marriage Plot*'s characters are wonderfully imagined, and its deconstruction of the marriage plot . . . in a modern-day setting is an irresistible setup for any reader who loves books the way Madeleine loves them. . . . Eugenides infuses his prose with intelligence, humor, and the happy knowledge that there's a reason readers return to familiar stories so often: They tell us more about ourselves and about what we really want than we'd care to admit." —Connie Ogle, *The Miami Herald*

"Eugenides steers effortlessly through the intertwining tales of his three protagonists. . . . His prose is smooth but never flashy, and his eye for the telling detail or gesture is keen. . . . *The Marriage Plot* is fun to read and ultimately affirming." —Associated Press

"Eugenides has declined to moan in public about the plight of the novel, as Franzen has, or to make bold statements about his intention to revive it. He has simply proceeded to his own project of renovation, without making a fuss over it. . . . His experimentation is subtle: no Wallacian footnotes or typographical tricks. But he has reinvented himself with each book. He is genuinely original." —Ruth Franklin, *The New Republic*

"A prodigiously absorbing novel . . . Brilliant."   —*The Kansas City Star*

"Eugenides is especially adept at capturing the struggles, the good sense, and the nonsense of emerging adults in contemporary America. . . . The members of Eugenides's ménage remain compelling, and touchingly 'real.' . . . He has provided them, and us, with survival kits for an existential world, insights about life and love, and, let's hope, an enduring appreciation for works of fiction, those 'hard-won, transcendent things.'"
                                                    —*The Philadelphia Inquirer*

"Eugenides has always shown faith in stories and the people who live them. *The Marriage Plot* puts that on the line, giving us the most fully realized characters Eugenides has drawn. Upon reaching Eugenides's modest and modern twist on the Victorian ending, one is ready to say 'I do.'"   —*Milwaukee Journal Sentinel*

"Eugenides's prose is as lush, unassuming, and addictive as ever in his newest novel, *The Marriage Plot*, an Austenesque tale of love and imminent adulthood."   —*Time Out* (New York)

"Eugenides speaks truly, in prose that perfectly evokes the complexities of the heart. . . . The workings of each character's mind are laid bare, and each endears the reader more and more deeply with the turn of each page."   —*Wisconsin State Journal*

"A comic, rueful, compelling dissection of a young love triangle and the hard lessons of that 'last period of total freedom,' the college years . . . Read *The Marriage Plot* as contemporary love fable, as elegiac nostalgia, as a writer's celebration of writers and his own roots—or just read it because you too still carry a torch first kindled by all those fine books you fell for in college."   —*Bloomberg*

"Eugenides has mastered the pattering through which the finest novels build their power, repeating ideas and themes with nuanced variations until every detail seems to reinforce the logic of the whole. . . . No one combines Eugenides's broadness of imagination with his technical mastery of the novel form."   —*The New Republic*

"As his protagonists confront the hard realities of adulthood, Eugenides captures the electric atmosphere of early-'80s, postmodernist-influenced Ivy League academia in gorgeous prose. . . . The beauty and intelligence of Eugenides's writing make *Plot* a rewarding read."   —*People*

"There's a coaxing ease to the prose, which carries both intellectual rigor and sheer storytelling verve. The novel's humor disarms the reader, opening us to a serious accounting of the troubled human search for love and truth."   —*Detroit Free Press*

"*The Marriage Plot* is part cultural anthropology, part relationship drama, and part dare: They say the marriage plot is dead?—Well, this novel aims to prove otherwise. . . . [Eugenides] gives us a tale with all the perverse, vertiginous pull of his earlier books. . . . Can the marriage plot survive in modern fiction? *The Marriage Plot* suggests not only that it can, but that it's as good a way as ever to tell a story that matters."   —*The Boston Globe*

"*The Marriage Plot* [is] a gently self-referential take on the question of whether the love novel still works in a postmodern world. Turns out the answer is unequivocally: Yes."   —*GQ's "The Year in Reading"*

"Jeffrey Eugenides has too much fun with *The Marriage Plot*, a smart, sly gloss of literary theory that's populated by flesh-and-blood characters, a deconstruction of the love story that is a love story, a roman à clef that opens the door to a wider world. . . . Funny, moving, insightful, generous, and possessed of one of the most surprising and satisfying endings I've come across in many a volume, *The Marriage Plot* wants you, dear reader."   —*St. Petersburg Times*

"*The Marriage Plot* is wonderfully written. It's an apt, canny, capacious portrait of three individuals finding their way, wherever that may lead. Meanwhile, if we have to wait a decade between Eugenides books, then wait we will. The payoff is worth it."   —*Popmatters.com*

"Captivating . . . A compulsive read . . . Humorously honest."   —*Richmond Times-Dispatch*

Jeffrey Eugenides

The Marriage Plot

Picador   Farrar, Straus and Giroux   New York

For the roomies,
Stevie and Moo Moo

www.picadorusa.com
www.twitter.com/picadorusa • www.facebook.com/picadorusa
www.picadorbookroom.tumblr.com

Picador® is a U.S. registered trademark and is used by Farrar, Straus and Giroux under license from Pan Books Limited.

For book club information, please visit www.facebook.com/picadorbookclub or e-mail marketing@picadorusa.com

Excerpts from The Marriage Plot originally appeared, in slightly different form, in The New Yorker.

Grateful acknowledgment is made for permission to reprint lyrics from "Once in a Lifetime," by David Byrne, Chris Frantz, Jerry Harrison, Tina Weymouth, and Brian Eno. Copyright © 1981 Index Music, Inc., Bleu-Disque Music Co., and E.G. Music Ltd. All rights on behalf of Index Music, Inc., Bleu-Disque Co., Inc., administered by WB Music Corp. All rights reserved. Used by permission. Warner Brothers Publications, U.S. Inc., Miami, Florida 33014.

The Library of Congress has cataloged the Farrar, Straus and Giroux edition as follows:

Eugenides, Jeffrey.
    The marriage plot / Jeffrey Eugenides. — 1st ed.
        p. cm
    ISBN 978-0-374-20305-4
    1. Triangles (Interpersonal relations)—Fiction.   2. Literature—Appreciation—
Fiction.   3. Self-actualization—Fiction.   I. Title.

PS3555.U4M37 2011
813'.54—dc23

                                                                                    2011022099

Picador ISBN 978-1-250-01476-4

First published in the United States by Farrar, Straus and Giroux

First Picador Edition: September 2012

10   9   8   7   6   5   4   3   2   1

The author would like to thank the following individuals for their assistance in providing and verifying factual material used in The Marriage Plot: Dr. Richard A. Friedman, director of psychopharmacology at the Payne Whitney Manhattan psychiatric clinic and professor of clinical psychiatry at the Weill Cornell Medical College; Professor David Botstein, director of the Lewis-Sigler Institute for Integrative Genomics at Princeton University; and Georgia Eugenides, local Madeline expert. In addition, the author would like to cite the following article, from which he drew information on yeast genetics: "The Mother-Daughter Mating Type Switching Asymmetry of Budding Yeast Is Not Conferred by the Segregation of Parental HO Gene DNA Strands," by Amar J. S. Klar.

People would never fall in love if they hadn't heard love talked about.
—François de La Rochefoucauld

And you may ask yourself, Well, how did I get here? . . .
And you may tell yourself,
This is not my beautiful house.
And you may tell yourself,
This is not my beautiful wife.

—Talking Heads

A Madman in Love

To start with, look at all the books. There were her Edith Wharton novels, arranged not by title but date of publication; there was the complete Modern Library set of Henry James, a gift from her father on her twenty-first birthday; there were the dog-eared paperbacks assigned in her college courses, a lot of Dickens, a smidgen of Trollope, along with good helpings of Austen, George Eliot, and the redoubtable Brontë sisters. There were a whole lot of black-and-white New Directions paperbacks, mostly poetry by people like H.D. or Denise Levertov. There were the Colette novels she read on the sly. There was the first edition of *Couples*, belonging to her mother, which Madeleine had surreptitiously dipped into back in sixth grade and which she was using now to provide textual support in her English honors thesis on the marriage plot. There was, in short, this mid-size but still portable library representing pretty much everything Madeleine had read in college, a collection of texts, seemingly chosen at random, whose focus slowly narrowed, like a personality test, a sophisticated one you couldn't trick by anticipating the implications of its questions and finally got so lost in that your only recourse was to answer the simple truth. And then you waited for the result, hoping for "Artistic," or "Passionate," thinking you could live with "Sensitive," secretly fearing "Narcissistic" and "Domestic," but finally being presented with an outcome that cut both ways and made you feel different depending on the day, the hour, or the guy you happened to be dating: "Incurably Romantic."

These were the books in the room where Madeleine lay, with a pillow over her head, on the morning of her college graduation. She'd read each and every one, often multiple times, frequently underlining passages, but that was no help to her now. Madeleine was trying to ignore the room and everything in it. She was hoping to drift back down into the oblivion where she'd been safely couched for the last three hours. Any higher level of wakefulness would force her to come to grips with certain disagreeable facts: for instance, the amount and variety of the alcohol she'd imbibed last night, and the fact that she'd gone to sleep with her contacts in. Thinking about such specifics would, in turn, call to mind the reasons she'd drunk so much in the first place, which she definitely didn't want to do. And so Madeleine adjusted her pillow, blocking out the early morning light, and tried to fall back to sleep.

But it was useless. Because right then, at the other end of her apartment, the doorbell began to ring.

Early June, Providence, Rhode Island, the sun up for almost two hours already, lighting up the pale bay and the smokestacks of the Narragansett Electric factory, rising like the sun on the Brown University seal emblazoned on all the pennants and banners draped up over campus, a sun with a sagacious face, representing knowledge. But this sun—the one over Providence—was doing the metaphorical sun one better, because the founders of the university, in their Baptist pessimism, had chosen to depict the light of knowledge enshrouded by clouds, indicating that ignorance had not yet been dispelled from the human realm, whereas the actual sun was just now fighting its way through cloud cover, sending down splintered beams of light and giving hope to the squadrons of parents, who'd been soaked and frozen all weekend, that the unseasonable weather might not ruin the day's festivities. All over College Hill, in the geometric gardens of the Georgian mansions, the magnolia-scented front yards of Victorians, along brick sidewalks running past black iron fences like those in a Charles Addams cartoon or a Lovecraft story; outside the art studios at the Rhode Island School of Design, where one painting major, having stayed up all night to work, was blaring Patti Smith; shining off the instruments (tuba and trumpet, respectively) of the two members of the Brown marching band who had arrived early at the meeting point and were nervously looking around, wondering where everyone else was; brightening the cobblestone side streets that led downhill to the polluted river, the sun was shining on every brass doorknob, insect wing, and blade of grass. And, in concert with the suddenly flooding light, like a starting gun for all the activity, the doorbell in Madeleine's fourth-floor apartment began, clamorously, insistently, to ring.

The pulse reached her less as a sound than as a sensation, an electric shock shooting up her spine. In one motion Madeleine tore the pillow off her head and sat up in bed. She knew who was ringing the buzzer. It was her parents. She'd agreed to meet Alton and Phyllida for breakfast at 7:30. She'd made this plan with them two months ago, in April, and now here they were, at the appointed time, in their eager, dependable way. That Alton and Phyllida had driven up from New Jersey to see her graduate, that what they were here to celebrate today wasn't only her achievement but their own as parents, had nothing wrong or unexpected about it. The problem was that Madeleine, for the first time in her life, wanted no part of it. She wasn't proud of herself. She was in no mood to celebrate. She'd lost faith in the significance of the day and what the day represented.

She considered not answering. But she knew that if she didn't answer, one of her roommates would, and then she'd have to explain where she'd disappeared to last night, and with whom. Therefore, Madeleine slid out of the bed and reluctantly stood up.

This seemed to go well for a moment, standing up. Her head felt curiously light, as if hollowed out. But then the blood, draining from her skull like sand from an hourglass, hit a bottleneck, and the back of her head exploded in pain.

In the midst of this barrage, like the furious core from which it emanated, the buzzer erupted again.

She came out of her bedroom and stumbled in bare feet to the intercom in the hall, slapping the SPEAK button to silence the buzzer.

"Hello?"

"What's the matter? Didn't you hear the bell?" It was Alton's voice, as deep and commanding as ever, despite the fact that it was issuing from a tiny speaker.

"Sorry," Madeleine said. "I was in the shower."

"Likely story. Will you let us in, please?"

Madeleine didn't want to. She needed to wash up first.

"I'm coming down," she said.

This time, she held down the SPEAK button too long, cutting off Alton's response. She pressed it again and said, "Daddy?" but while she was speaking, Alton must have been speaking, too, because when she pressed LISTEN all that came through was static.

Madeleine took this pause in communications to lean her forehead against the door frame. The wood felt nice and cool. The thought struck her that, if she could keep her face pressed against the soothing wood, she might be able to cure her headache, and if she could keep her forehead pressed against the door frame for the rest of the day, while somehow still being able to leave the apartment, she might make it through breakfast with her parents, march in the commencement procession, get a diploma, and graduate.

She lifted her face and pressed SPEAK again.

"Daddy?"

But it was Phyllida's voice that answered. "Maddy? What's the matter? Let us in."

"My roommates are still asleep. I'm coming down. Don't ring the bell anymore."

"We want to see your apartment!"

"Not now. I'm coming down. Don't ring."

She took her hand from the buttons and stood back, glaring at the intercom as if daring it to make a sound. When it didn't, she started back down the hall. She was halfway to the bathroom when her roommate Abby emerged, blocking the way. She yawned, running a hand through her big hair, and then, noticing Madeleine, smiled knowingly.

"So," Abby said, "where did *you* sneak off to last night?"

"My parents are here," Madeleine said. "I have to go to breakfast."

"Come on. Tell me."

"There's nothing to tell. I'm late."

"How come you're wearing the same clothes, then?"

Instead of replying, Madeleine looked down at herself. Ten hours earlier, when she'd borrowed the black Betsey Johnson dress from Olivia, Madeleine had thought it looked good on her. But now the dress felt hot and sticky, the fat leather belt looked like an S&M restraint, and there was a stain near the hem that she didn't want to identify.

Abby, meanwhile, had knocked on Olivia's door and entered. "So much for Maddy's broken heart," she said. "Wake up! You've got to see this."

The path to the bathroom was clear. Madeleine's need for a shower was extreme, almost medical. At a minimum, she had to brush her teeth. But Olivia's voice was audible now. Soon Madeleine would have two roommates interrogating her. Her parents were liable to start ringing again any minute. As quietly as possible, she inched back down the hall. She stepped into a pair of loafers left by the front door, crushing the heels flat as she caught her balance, and escaped into the outer corridor.

The elevator was waiting at the end of the floral runner. Waiting, Madeleine realized, because she'd failed to close the sliding gate when she'd staggered out of the thing a few hours earlier. Now she shut the gate securely and pressed the button for the lobby, and with a jolt the antique contraption began to descend through the building's interior gloom.

Madeleine's building, a Neo-Romanesque castle called the Narragansett that wrapped around the plunging corner of Benefit Street and Church Street, had been built at the turn of the century. Among its surviving period details—the stained-glass skylight, the brass wall sconces, the marble lobby—was the elevator. Made of curving metal bars like a giant birdcage, the elevator miraculously still functioned, but it moved slowly, and as the car dropped, Madeleine took the opportunity to make herself more presentable. She ran her hands through her hair, finger-combing it. She polished her front teeth with her index finger. She rubbed mascara crumbs from her eyes and moistened her lips with her tongue. Finally, passing the balustrade on the second floor, she checked her reflection in the small mirror attached to the rear panel.

One of the nice things about being twenty-two, or about being Madeleine Hanna, was that three weeks of romantic anguish, followed by a night of epic drinking, didn't do much visible damage. Except for puffiness around her eyes, Madeleine looked like the same pretty, dark-haired person as usual. The symmetries of her face—the straight nose, the Katharine Hepburn–ish cheekbones and jawline—were almost mathematical in their precision. Only the slight furrow in her brow gave evidence of the slightly anxious person that Madeleine felt herself, intrinsically, to be.

She could see her parents waiting below. They were trapped between the lobby door and the door to the street, Alton in a seersucker jacket, Phyllida in a navy suit and matching gold-buckled purse. For a second, Madeleine had an impulse to stop the elevator and leave her parents stuck in the foyer amid all the college-town clutter—the posters for New Wave bands with names like Wretched Misery or the Clits, the pornographic Egon Schiele drawings by the RISD kid on the second floor, all the clamorous Xeroxes whose subtext conveyed the message that the wholesome, patriotic values of her parents' generation were now on the ash heap of history, replaced by a nihilistic, post-punk sensibility that Madeleine herself didn't understand but was perfectly happy to scandalize her parents by pretending that she did—before the elevator stopped in the lobby and she slid open the gate and stepped out to meet them.

Alton was first through the door. "Here she is!" he said avidly. "The college graduate!" In his net-charging way, he surged forward to seize her in a hug. Madeleine stiffened, worried that she smelled of alcohol or, worse, of sex.

"I don't know why you wouldn't let us see your apartment," Phyllida said, coming up next. "I was looking forward to meeting Abby and Olivia. We'd love to treat them to dinner later."

"We're not staying for dinner," Alton reminded her.

"Well, we might. That depends on Maddy's schedule."

"No, that's not the plan. The plan is to see Maddy for breakfast and then leave after the ceremony."

"Your father and his plans," Phyllida said to Madeleine. "Are you wearing that dress to the ceremony?"

"I don't know," Madeleine said.

"I can't get used to these shoulder pads all the young women are wearing. They're so mannish."

"It's Olivia's."

"You look pretty whacked out, Mad," Alton said. "Big party last night?"

"Not really."

"Don't you have anything of your own to wear?" Phyllida said.

"I'll have my robe on, Mummy," Madeleine said, and, to forestall further inspection, headed past them through the foyer. Outside, the sun had lost its battle with the clouds and vanished. The weather looked not much better than it had all weekend. Campus Dance, on Friday night, had been more or less rained out. The Baccalaureate service on Sunday had proceeded under a steady drizzle. Now, on Monday, the rain had stopped, but the temperature felt closer to St. Patrick's than to Memorial Day.

As she waited for her parents to join her on the sidewalk, it occurred to Madeleine that she hadn't had sex, not really. This was some consolation.

"Your sister sends her regrets," Phyllida said, coming out. "She has to take Richard the Lionhearted for an ultrasound today."

Richard the Lionhearted was Madeleine's nine-week-old nephew. Everyone else called him Richard.

"What's the matter with him?" Madeleine asked.

"One of his kidneys is petite, apparently. The doctors want to keep an eye on it. If you ask me, all these ultrasounds do is find things to worry about."

"Speaking of ultrasounds," Alton said, "I need to get one on my knee."

Phyllida paid no attention. "Anyway, Allie's *devastated* not to see you graduate. As is Blake. But they're hoping you and your new beau might visit them this summer, on your way to the Cape."

You had to stay alert around Phyllida. Here she was, ostensibly talking about Richard the Lionhearted's petite kidney, and already she'd managed to move the subject to Madeleine's new boyfriend, Leonard (whom Phyllida and Alton hadn't met), and to Cape Cod (where Madeleine had announced plans to cohabitate with him). On a normal day, when her brain was working, Madeleine would have been able to keep one step ahead of Phyllida, but this morning the best she could manage was to let the words float past her.

Fortunately, Alton changed the subject. "So, where do you recommend for breakfast?"

Madeleine turned and looked vaguely down Benefit Street. "There's a place this way."

She started shuffling along the sidewalk. Walking—moving—seemed like a good idea. She led them past a line of quaint, nicely maintained houses bearing historical placards, and a big apartment building with a gable roof. Providence was a corrupt town, crime-ridden and mob-controlled, but up on College Hill this was hard to see. The sketchy downtown and dying or dead textile mills lay below, in the grim distance.

Here the narrow streets, many of them cobblestone, climbed past mansions or snaked around Puritan graveyards full of headstones as narrow as heaven's door, streets with names like Prospect, Benevolent, Hope, and Meeting, all of them feeding into the arboreous campus at the top. The sheer physical elevation suggested an intellectual one.

"Aren't these slate sidewalks lovely," Phyllida said as she followed along. "We used to have slate sidewalks on our street. They're *much* more attractive. But then the borough replaced them with concrete."

"Assessed us for the bill, too," Alton said. He was limping slightly, bringing up the rear. The right leg of his charcoal trousers was swelled from the knee brace he wore on and off the tennis court. Alton had been club champion in his age group for twelve years running, one of those older guys with a sweatband ringing a balding crown, a choppy forehand, and absolute murder in his eyes. Madeleine had been trying to beat Alton her entire life without success. This was even more infuriating because she was better than he was, at this point. But whenever she took a set from Alton he started intimidating her, acting mean, disputing calls, and her game fell apart. Madeleine was worried that there was something paradigmatic in this, that she was destined to go through life being cowed by less capable men. As a result, Madeleine's tennis matches against Alton had assumed such outsize personal significance for her that she got tight whenever she played him, with predictable results. And Alton still gloated when he won, still got all rosy and jiggly, as if he'd bested her by sheer talent.

At the corner of Benefit and Waterman, they crossed behind the white steeple of First Baptist Church. In preparation for the ceremony, loudspeakers had been set up on the lawn. A man wearing a bow tie, a dean-of-students-looking person, was tensely smoking a cigarette and inspecting a raft of balloons tied to the churchyard fence.

By now Phyllida had caught up to Madeleine, taking her arm to negotiate the uneven slate, which was pushed up by the roots of gnarled plane trees that lined the curb. As a little girl, Madeleine had thought her mother pretty, but that was a long time ago. Phyllida's face had gotten heavier over the years; her cheeks were beginning to sag like those of a camel. The conservative clothes she wore—the clothes of a philanthropist or lady ambassador—had a tendency to conceal her figure. Phyllida's hair was where her power resided. It was expensively set into a smooth dome, like a band shell for the presentation of that long-running act, her face. For as long as Madeleine could remember, Phyllida had never been at a loss for words or shy about a point of etiquette. Among her friends Madeleine liked to make fun of her mother's formality, but she often found herself comparing other people's manners unfavorably with Phyllida's.

And right now Phyllida was looking at Madeleine with the proper expression for *this* moment: thrilled by the pomp and ceremony, eager to put intelligent questions to any of Madeleine's professors she happened to meet, or to trade pleasantries with fellow parents of graduating seniors. In short, she was available to everyone and everything and in step with the social and academic pageantry, all of which exacerbated Madeleine's feeling of being out of step, for this day and the rest of her life.

She plunged on, however, across Waterman Street, and up the steps of Carr House, seeking refuge and coffee.

The café had just opened. The guy behind the counter, who was wearing Elvis Costello glasses, was rinsing out the espresso machine. At a table against the wall, a girl with stiff pink hair was smoking a clove cigarette and reading *Invisible Cities*. "Tainted Love" played from the stereo on top of the refrigerator.

Phyllida, holding her handbag protectively against her chest, had paused to peruse the student art on the walls: six paintings of small, skin-diseased dogs wearing bleach-bottle collars.

"Isn't this fun?" she said tolerantly.

"*La Bohème,*" Alton said.

Madeleine installed her parents at a table near the bay window, as far away from the pink-haired girl as possible, and went up to the counter. The guy took his time coming over. She ordered three coffees—a large for her—and bagels. While the bagels were being toasted, she brought the coffees over to her parents.

Alton, who couldn't sit at the breakfast table without reading, had taken a discarded *Village Voice* from a nearby table and was perusing it. Phyllida was staring overtly at the girl with pink hair.

"Do you think that's comfortable?" she inquired in a low voice.

Madeleine turned to see that the girl's ragged black jeans were held together by a few hundred safety pins.

"I don't know, Mummy. Why don't you go ask her?"

"I'm afraid of getting poked."

"According to this article," Alton said, reading the *Voice*, "homosexuality didn't exist until the nineteenth century. It was invented. In Germany."

The coffee was hot, and lifesavingly good. Sipping it, Madeleine began to feel slightly less awful.

After a few minutes, she went up to get the bagels. They were a little burned, but she didn't want to wait for new ones, and so brought them back to the table. After examining his with a sour expression, Alton began scraping it punitively with a plastic knife.

Phyllida asked, "So, are we going to meet Leonard today?"

"I'm not sure," Madeleine said.

"Anything you want us to know about?"

"No."

"Are you two still planning to live together this summer?"

By this time Madeleine had taken a bite of her bagel. And since the answer to her mother's question was complicated—strictly speaking, Madeleine and Leonard weren't planning on living together, because they'd broken up three weeks ago; despite this fact, however, Madeleine hadn't given up hope of a reconciliation, and seeing as she'd spent so much effort getting her parents used to the idea of her living with a guy, and didn't want to jeopardize that by admitting that the plan was off— she was relieved to be able to point at her full mouth, which prevented her from replying.

"Well, you're an adult now," Phyllida said. "You can do what you like. Though, for the record, I have to say that I don't approve."

"You've already gone on record about that," Alton broke in.

"Because it's still a bad idea!" Phyllida cried. "I don't mean the propriety of it. I'm talking about the practical problems. If you move in with Leonard—or any young man—and *he's* the one with the job, then you begin at a disadvantage. What happens if you two don't get along? Where are you then? You won't have any place to live. Or anything to do."

That her mother was correct in her analysis, that the predicament

Phyllida warned Madeleine about was exactly the predicament she was already in, didn't motivate Madeleine to register agreement.

"You quit your job when you met me," Alton said to Phyllida.

"That's why I know what I'm talking about."

"Can we change the subject?" Madeleine said at last, having swallowed her food.

"Of course we can, sweetheart. That's the last I'll say about it. If your plans change, you can always come home. Your father and I would love to have you."

"Not me," Alton said. "I don't want her. Moving back home is always a bad idea. Stay away."

"Don't worry," Madeleine said. "I will."

"The choice is yours," Phyllida said. "But if you *do* come home, you could have the loft. That way you can come and go as you like."

To her surprise, Madeleine found herself contemplating this proposal. Why not tell her parents everything, curl up in the backseat of the car, and let them take her home? She could move into her old bedroom, with the sleigh bed and the Madeline wallpaper. She could become a spinster, like Emily Dickinson, writing poems full of dashes and brilliance, and never gaining weight.

Phyllida brought her out of this reverie.

"Maddy?" she said. "Isn't that your friend Mitchell?"

Madeleine wheeled in her seat. "Where?"

"I think that's Mitchell. Across the street."

In the churchyard, sitting Indian-style in the freshly mown grass, Madeleine's "friend" Mitchell Grammaticus was indeed there. His lips were moving, as if he was talking to himself.

"Why don't you invite him to join us?" Phyllida said.

"Now?"

"Why not? I'd love to see Mitchell."

"He's probably waiting for his parents," Madeleine said.

Phyllida waved, despite the fact that Mitchell was too far away to notice.

"What's he doing sitting on the ground?" Alton asked.

The three Hannas stared across the street at Mitchell in his half-lotus.

"Well, if you're not going to ask him, I will," Phyllida finally said.

"O.K.," Madeleine said. "Fine. I'll go ask him."

The day was getting warmer, but not by much. Black clouds were massing in the distance as Madeleine came down the steps of Carr House and crossed the street into the churchyard. Someone inside the church was testing the loudspeakers, fussily repeating, "Sussex, Essex, and Kent. Sussex, Essex, and Kent." A banner draped over the church entrance read "Class of 1982." Beneath the banner, in the grass, was Mitchell. His lips were still moving silently, but when he noticed Madeleine approaching they abruptly stopped.

Madeleine remained a few feet away.

"My parents are here," she informed him.

"It's graduation," Mitchell replied evenly. "Everyone's parents are here."

"They want to say hello to you."

At this Mitchell smiled faintly. "They probably don't realize you're not speaking to me."

"No, they don't," Madeleine said. "And, anyway, I am. Now. Speaking to you."

"Under duress or as a change of policy?"

Madeleine shifted her weight, wrinkling her face unhappily. "Look. I'm really hungover. I barely slept last night. My parents have been here about ten minutes and they're already driving me crazy. So if you could just come over and say hello, that would be great."

Mitchell's large emotional eyes blinked twice. He was wearing a vintage gabardine shirt, dark wool pants, and beat-up wingtips. Madeleine had never seen him in shorts or tennis shoes.

"I'm sorry," he said. "About what happened."

"Fine," Madeleine said, looking away. "It doesn't matter."

"I was just being my usual vile self."

"So was I."

They were quiet a moment. Madeleine felt Mitchell's eyes on her, and she crossed her arms over her chest.

What had happened was this: one night the previous December, in a state of anxiety about her romantic life, Madeleine had run into Mitchell on campus and brought him back to her apartment. She'd needed male attention and had flirted with him, without entirely admitting it to herself. In her bedroom, Mitchell had picked up a jar of deep-heating gel on her desk, asking what it was for. Madeleine had explained that people who were *athletic* sometimes got sore muscles. She understood that Mitchell might not have experienced this phenomenon, seeing as all he did was sit in the library, but he should take her word for it. At that point, Mitchell had come up behind her and wiped a gob of heating gel behind her ear. Madeleine jumped up, shouting at Mitchell, and wiped the gunk off with a T-shirt. Though she was within her rights to be angry, Madeleine also knew (even at the time) that she was using the incident as a pretext for getting Mitchell out of her bedroom and for covering up the fact that she'd been flirting with him in the first place. The worst part of the incident was how stricken Mitchell had looked, as if he'd been about to cry. He kept saying he was sorry, he was just joking around, but she ordered him to leave. In the following days, replaying the incident in her mind, Madeleine had felt worse and worse about it. She'd been on the verge of calling Mitchell to apologize when she'd received a letter from him, a highly detailed, cogently argued, psychologically astute, quietly hostile four-page letter, in which he called her a "cocktease" and claimed that her behavior that night had been "the erotic equivalent of bread and circus, with just the circus." The next time they'd run into each other, Madeleine had acted as if she didn't know him, and they hadn't spoken since.

Now, in the churchyard of First Baptist, Mitchell looked up at her and said, "O.K. Let's go say hello to your parents."

Phyllida was waving as they came up the steps. In the flirtatious voice she reserved for her favorite of Madeleine's friends, she called out, "I thought that was you on the ground. You looked like a swami!"

"Congratulations, Mitchell!" Alton said, heartily shaking Mitchell's hand. "Big day today. One of the milestones. A new generation takes the reins."

They invited Mitchell to sit down and asked him if he wanted anything to eat. Madeleine went back to the counter to get more coffee, glad to have Mitchell keeping her parents occupied. As she watched him, in his old man's clothes, engaging Alton and Phyllida in conversation, Madeleine thought to herself, as she'd thought many times before, that Mitchell was the kind of smart, sane, parent-pleasing boy she should fall in love with and marry. That she would never fall in love with Mitchell and marry him, precisely because of this eligibility, was yet another indication, in a morning teeming with them, of just how screwed up she was in matters of the heart.

When she returned to the table, no one acknowledged her.

"So, Mitchell," Phyllida was asking, "what are your plans after graduation?"

"My father's been asking me the same question," Mitchell answered. "For some reason he thinks Religious Studies isn't a marketable degree."

Madeleine smiled for the first time all day. "See? Mitchell doesn't have a job lined up, either."

"Well, I sort of do," Mitchell said.

"You do not," Madeleine challenged him.

"I'm serious. I do." He explained that he and his roommate, Larry Pleshette, had come up with a plan to fight the recession. As liberal-arts degree holders matriculating into the job market at a time when unemployment was at 9.5 percent, they had decided, after much consideration, to leave the country and stay away as long as possible. At the end of the summer, after they'd saved up enough money, they were going to backpack through Europe. After they'd seen everything in Europe there was to see, they were going to fly to India and stay there as long as their money held out. The whole trip would take eight or nine months, maybe as long as a year.

"You're going to India?" Madeleine said. "That's not a job."

"We're going to be research assistants," Mitchell said. "For Prof. Hughes."

"Prof. Hughes in the theater department?"

"I saw a program about India recently," Phyllida said. "It was terribly depressing. The poverty!"

"That's a plus for me, Mrs. Hanna," Mitchell said. "I thrive in squalor."

Phyllida, who couldn't resist this sort of mischief, gave up her solemnity, rippling with amusement. "Then you're going to the right place!"

"Maybe I'll take a trip, too," Madeleine said in a threatening tone.

No one reacted. Instead Alton asked Mitchell, "What sort of immunizations do you need for India?"

"Cholera and typhus. Gamma globulin's optional."

Phyllida shook her head. "Your mother must be worried sick."

"When I was in the service," Alton said, "they shot us up with a million things. Didn't even tell us what the shots were for."

"I think *I'll* move to Paris," Madeleine said in a louder voice. "Instead of getting a job."

"Mitchell," Phyllida continued, "with your interest in religious studies, I'd think India would be a perfect fit. They've got everything. Hindus, Muslims, Sikhs, Zoroastrians, Jains, Buddhists. It's like Baskin and Robbins! I've always been fascinated by religion. Unlike my doubting-Thomas husband."

Alton winked. "I doubt that doubting Thomas existed."

"Do you know Paul Moore, *Bishop* Moore, at the Cathedral of Saint John the Divine?" Phyllida said, keeping Mitchell's attention. "He's a great friend. You might find it interesting to meet him. We'd be happy to introduce you. When we're in the city, I always go to services at the cathedral. Have you ever been there? Oh. Well. How can I describe it? It's simply—well, simply *divine!*"

Phyllida held a hand to her throat with the pleasure of this bon mot, while Mitchell obligingly, even convincingly, laughed.

"Speaking of religious dignitaries," Alton cut in, "did I ever tell you about the time we met the Dalai Lama? It was at this fund-raiser at the Waldorf. We were in the receiving line. Must have been three hundred people at least. Anyway, when we finally got up to the Dalai Lama, I asked him, 'Are you any relation to Dolly Parton?'"

"I was mortified!" Phyllida cried. "Absolutely mortified."

"Daddy," Madeleine said, "you're going to be late."

"What?"

"You should get going if you want to get a good spot."

Alton looked at his watch. "We've still got an hour."

"It gets really crowded," Madeleine emphasized. "You should go now."

Alton and Phyllida looked at Mitchell, as if they trusted him to advise them. Under the table, Madeleine kicked him, and he alertly responded, "It does get pretty crowded."

"Where's the best place to stand?" Alton asked, again addressing Mitchell.

"By the Van Wickle Gates. At the top of College Street. That's where we'll come through."

Alton stood up from the table. After shaking Mitchell's hand, he bent to kiss Madeleine on the cheek. "We'll see *you* later. Miss Bacca-laureate, 1982."

"Congratulations, Mitchell," Phyllida said. "*So* nice to see you. And remember, when you're on your Grand Tour, be sure to send your mother *loads* of letters. Otherwise, she'll be frantic."

To Madeleine, she said, "You might change that dress before the march. It has a visible stain."

With that, Alton and Phyllida, in their glaring parental actuality, all seersucker and handbag, cuff links and pearls, crossed the beige-and-brick space of Carr House and went out the door.

As though to signal their departure, a new song came on: Joe Jackson's high-pitched voice swooping above a synthesized drumbeat. The guy behind the counter cranked up the volume.

Madeleine laid her head on the table, her hair covering her face.

"I'm never drinking again," she said.

"Famous last words."

"You have no idea what's been going on with me."

"How could I? You haven't been speaking to me."

Without lifting her cheek from the table, Madeleine said in a pitiful voice, "I'm homeless. I'm graduating from college and I'm a homeless person."

"Yeah, sure."

"I am!" Madeleine insisted. "First I was supposed to move to New York with Abby and Olivia. Then it looked like I was moving to the Cape, though, so I told them to get another roommate. And now I'm *not* moving to the Cape and I have nowhere to go. My mother wants me to move back home but I'd rather kill myself."

"I'm moving back home for the summer," Mitchell said. "To *Detroit*. At least you're near New York."

"I haven't heard back from grad school yet and it's *June*," Madeleine continued. "I was supposed to find out over a month ago! I could call the admissions department, but I don't because I'm scared to find out that I've been rejected. As long as I don't know, I still have hope."

There was a moment before Mitchell spoke again. "You can come to India with me," he said.

Madeleine opened one eye to see, through a whorl in her hair, that Mitchell wasn't entirely joking.

"It's not even about grad school," she said. Taking a deep breath, she confessed, "Leonard and I broke up."

It felt deeply pleasurable to say this, to name her sadness, and so Madeleine was surprised by the coldness of Mitchell's reply.

"Why are you telling me this?" he said.

She lifted her head, brushing her hair out of her face. "I don't know. You wanted to know what was the matter."

"I didn't, actually. I didn't even ask."

"I thought you might care," Madeleine said. "Since you're my friend."

"Right," Mitchell said, his voice suddenly sarcastic. "Our wonderful friendship! Our 'friendship' isn't a real friendship because it only works on your terms. *You* set the rules, Madeleine. If you decide you don't want to talk to me for three months, we don't talk. Then you decide you *do* want to talk to me because you need me to entertain your parents—and now we're talking again. We're friends when you want to be friends, and we're never *more* than friends because you don't want to be. And I have to go along with that."

"I'm sorry," Madeleine said, feeling put-upon and blindsided. "I just don't like you that way."

"Exactly!" Mitchell cried. "You're not attracted to me physically. O.K., fine. But who says I was ever attracted to you *mentally*?"

Madeleine reacted as if she'd been slapped. She was outraged, hurt, and defiant all at once.

"You're such a"—she tried to think of the worst thing to say—"you're such a *jerk!*" She was hoping to remain imperious, but her chest was stinging, and, to her dismay, she burst into tears.

Mitchell reached out to touch her arm, but Madeleine shook him off. Getting to her feet, trying not to look like someone angrily weeping, she went out the door and down the steps onto Waterman Street. Confronted by the festive churchyard, she turned downhill toward the river. She wanted to get away from campus. Her headache had returned, her temples were throbbing, and as she looked up at the storm clouds massing over downtown like more bad things to come, she asked herself why everyone was being so mean to her.

Madeleine's love troubles had begun at a time when the French theory she was reading deconstructed the very notion of love. Semiotics 211 was an upper-level seminar taught by a former English department renegade. Michael Zipperstein had come to Brown thirty-two years earlier as a New Critic. He'd inculcated the habits of close reading and biography-free interpretation into three generations of students before taking a Road to Damascus sabbatical, in Paris, in 1975, where he'd met Roland Barthes at a dinner party and been converted, over cassoulet, to the new faith. Now Zipperstein taught two courses in the newly created Program in Semiotics Studies: Introduction to Semiotic Theory in the fall and, in the spring, Semiotics 211. Hygienically bald, with a seaman's mustacheless white beard, Zipperstein favored French fisherman's sweaters and wide-wale corduroys. He buried people with his reading lists: in addition to all the semiotic big hitters—Derrida, Eco, Barthes—the students in Semiotics 211 had to contend with a magpie nest of reserve reading that included everything from Balzac's *Sarrasine* to issues of *Semiotext(e)* to photocopied selections from E. M. Cioran, Robert Walser, Claude Levi-Strauss, Peter Handke, and Carl Van Vechten. To get into the seminar, you had to submit to a one-on-one interview with Zipperstein during which he asked bland personal questions, such as what your favorite food or dog breed was, and made enigmatic Warholian remarks in response. This esoteric probing, along with Zipperstein's guru's dome and beard, gave his students a sense that they'd been spiritually vetted and were now—for two hours on Thursday afternoons, at least—part of a campus lit-crit elite.

Which was exactly what Madeleine wanted. She'd become an English major for the purest and dullest of reasons: because she loved to read. The university's "British and American Literature Course Catalog" was, for Madeleine, what its Bergdorf equivalent was for her roommates. A course listing like "English 274: Lyly's Euphues" excited Madeleine the way a pair of Fiorucci cowboy boots did Abby. "English 450A: Hawthorne and James" filled Madeleine with an expectation of sinful hours in bed not unlike what Olivia got from wearing a Lycra skirt and leather blazer to Danceteria. Even as a girl in their house in Prettybrook, Madeleine wandered into the library, with its shelves of books rising higher than she could reach—newly purchased volumes such as *Love Story* or *Myra Breckinridge* that exuded a faintly forbidden air, as well as venerable leather-bound editions of Fielding, Thackeray, and Dickens—and the magisterial presence of all those potentially readable words stopped her in her tracks. She could scan book spines for as long as an hour. Her cataloging of the family's holdings rivaled the Dewey decimal system in its comprehensiveness. Madeleine knew right where everything was. The shelves near the fireplace held Alton's favorites, biographies of American presidents and British prime ministers, memoirs by warmongering secretaries of state, novels about sailing or espionage by William F. Buckley, Jr. Phyllida's books filled the left side of the bookcases leading up to the parlor, *NYRB*-reviewed novels and essay collections, as well as coffee-table volumes about English gardens or chinoiserie. Even now, at bed-and-breakfasts or seaside hotels, a shelf full of forlorn books always cried out to Madeleine. She ran her fingers over their salt-spotted covers. She peeled apart pages made tacky by ocean air. She had no sympathy for paperback thrillers and detective stories. It was the abandoned hardback, the jacketless 1931 Dial Press edition ringed with many a coffee cup, that pierced Madeleine's heart. Her friends might be calling her name on the beach, the clambake already under way, but Madeleine would sit down on the bed and read for a little while to make the sad old book feel better. She had read Longfellow's "Hiawatha" that way. She'd read James Fenimore Cooper. She'd read *H. M. Pulham, Esquire* by John P. Marquand.

And yet sometimes she worried about what those musty old books were doing to her. Some people majored in English to prepare for law school. Others became journalists. The smartest guy in the honors program, Adam Vogel, a child of academics, was planning on getting a Ph.D. and becoming an academic himself. That left a large contingent of people majoring in English by default. Because they weren't left-brained enough for science, because history was too dry, philosophy too difficult, geology too petroleum-oriented, and math too mathematical—because they weren't musical, artistic, financially motivated, or really all that smart, these people were pursuing university degrees doing something no different from what they'd done in first grade: reading stories. English was what people who didn't know what to major in majored in.

Her junior year, Madeleine had taken an honors seminar called The Marriage Plot: Selected Novels of Austen, Eliot, and James. The class was taught by K. McCall Saunders. Saunders was a seventy-nine-year-old New Englander. He had a long, horsey face and a moist laugh that exposed his gaudy dental work. His pedagogical method consisted of his reading aloud lectures he'd written twenty or thirty years earlier. Madeleine stayed in the class because she felt sorry for Professor Saunders and because the reading list was so good. In Saunders's opinion, the novel had reached its apogee with the marriage plot and had never recovered from its disappearance. In the days when success in life had depended on marriage, and marriage had depended on money, novelists had had a subject to write about. The great epics sang of war, the novel of marriage. Sexual equality, good for women, had been bad for the novel. And divorce had undone it completely. What would it matter whom Emma married if she could file for separation later? How would Isabel Archer's marriage to Gilbert Osmond have been affected by the existence of a prenup? As far as Saunders was concerned, marriage didn't mean much anymore, and neither did the novel. Where could you find the marriage plot nowadays? You couldn't. You had to read historical fiction. You had to read non-Western novels involving traditional societies. Afghani novels, Indian novels. You had to go, literarily speaking, back in time.

Madeleine's final paper for the seminar was titled "The Interrogative Mood: Marriage Proposals and the (Strictly Limited) Sphere of the Feminine." It had impressed Saunders so much that he'd asked Madeleine to come see him. In his office, which had a grandparental smell, he expressed his opinion that Madeleine might expand her paper into a senior honors thesis, along with his willingness to serve as her advisor. Madeleine smiled politely. Professor Saunders specialized in the periods she was interested in, the Regency leading into the Victorian era. He was sweet, and learned, and it was clear from his unsubscribed office hours that no one else wanted him as an advisor, and so Madeleine had said yes, she would love to work with him on her senior thesis.

She used a line from Trollope's *Barchester Towers* as an epigraph: "There is no happiness in love, except at the end of an English novel." Her plan was to begin with Jane Austen. After a brief examination of *Pride and Prejudice*, *Persuasion*, and *Sense and Sensibility*, all comedies, essentially, that ended with weddings, Madeleine was going to move on to the Victorian novel, where things got more complicated and considerably darker. *Middlemarch* and *The Portrait of a Lady* didn't end with weddings. They began with the traditional moves of the marriage plot—the suitors, the proposals, the misunderstandings—but after the wedding ceremony they kept on going. These novels followed their spirited, intelligent heroines, Dorothea Brooke and Isabel Archer, into their disappointing married lives, and it was here that the marriage plot reached its greatest artistic expression.

By 1900 the marriage plot was no more. Madeleine planned to end with a brief discussion of its demise. In *Sister Carrie*, Dreiser had Carrie live adulterously with Drouet, marry Hurstwood in an invalid ceremony, and then run off to become an actress—and this was only in 1900! For a conclusion, Madeleine thought she might cite the wife-swapping in Updike. That was the last vestige of the marriage plot: the persistence in calling it "wife-swapping" instead of "husband-swapping." As if the woman were still a piece of property to be passed around.

Professor Saunders suggested that Madeleine look at historical sources. She'd obediently boned up on the rise of industrialism and the nuclear family, the formation of the middle class, and the Matrimonial Causes Act of 1857. But it wasn't long before she'd become bored with the thesis. Doubts about the originality of her work nagged at her. She felt as if she was regurgitating the arguments Saunders had made in his marriage plot seminar. Her meetings with the old professor were dispiriting, consisting of Saunders shuffling the pages she'd given him, pointing out various red marks he'd made in the margins.

Then one Sunday morning, before winter break, Abby's boyfriend, Whitney, materialized at their kitchen table, reading something called *Of Grammatology*. When Madeleine asked what the book was about, she was given to understand by Whitney that the idea of a book being "about" something was exactly what this book was against, and that, if it was "about" anything, then it was about the need to stop thinking of books as being about things. Madeleine said she was going to make coffee. Whitney asked if she would make him some, too.

College wasn't like the real world. In the real world people dropped names based on their renown. In college, people dropped names based on their obscurity. Thus, in the weeks after this exchange with Whitney, Madeleine began hearing people saying "Derrida." She heard them saying "Lyotard" and "Foucault" and "Deleuze" and "Baudrillard." That most of these people were those she instinctually disapproved of— upper-middle-class kids who wore Doc Martens and anarchist symbols— made Madeleine dubious about the value of their enthusiasm. But soon she noticed David Koppel, a smart and talented poet, also reading Derrida. And Pookie Ames, who read slush for *The Paris Review* and whom Madeleine *liked*, was taking a course with Professor Zipperstein. Madeleine had always been partial to grandiose professors, people like Sears Jayne who hammed it up in the classroom, reciting Hart Crane or Anne Sexton in a gag voice. Whitney acted as though Professor Jayne was a joke. Madeleine didn't agree. But after three solid years of taking literature courses, Madeleine had nothing like a firm critical methodology to apply to what she read. Instead she had a fuzzy, unsystematic way of talking about books. It embarrassed her to hear the things people said in class. And the things she said. I felt that. It was interesting the way Proust. I liked the way Faulkner.

And when Olivia, who was tall and slim, with a long, aristocratic nose like a saluki, came in one day carrying *Of Grammatology*, Madeleine knew that what had been marginal was now mainstream.

"What's that book like?"

"You haven't read it?"

"Would I be asking if I had?"

Olivia sniffed. "Aren't *we* a little bitchy today?"

"Sorry."

"Just kidding. It's great. Derrida is my absolute god!"

Almost overnight it became laughable to read writers like Cheever or Updike, who wrote about the suburbia Madeleine and most of her friends had grown up in, in favor of reading the Marquis de Sade, who wrote about anally deflowering virgins in eighteenth-century France. The reason de Sade was preferable was that his shocking sex scenes weren't about sex but politics. They were therefore anti-imperialist, anti-bourgeois, anti-patriarchal, and anti-everything a smart young feminist should be against. Right up through her third year at college, Madeleine kept wholesomely taking courses like Victorian Fantasy: From *Phantastes* to *The Water-Babies*, but by senior year she could no longer ignore the contrast between the hard-up, blinky people in her Beowulf seminar and the hipsters down the hall reading Maurice Blanchot. Going to college in the moneymaking eighties lacked a certain radicalism. Semiotics was the first thing that smacked of revolution. It drew a line; it created an elect; it was sophisticated and Continental; it dealt with provocative subjects, with torture, sadism, hermaphroditism—with sex and power.

Madeleine had always been popular at school. Years of being popular had left her with the reflexive ability to separate the cool from the uncool, even within subgroups, like the English department, where the concept of cool didn't appear to obtain.

If Restoration drama was getting you down, if scanning Wordsworth was making you feel dowdy and ink-stained, there was another option. You could flee K. McCall Saunders and the old New Criticism. You could defect to the new imperium of Derrida and Eco. You could sign up for Semiotics 211 and find out what everyone else was talking about.

Semiotics 211 was limited to ten students. Of the ten, eight had taken Introduction to Semiotic Theory. This was visually apparent at the first class meeting. Lounging around the seminar table, when Madeleine came into the room from the wintry weather outside, were eight people in black T-shirts and ripped black jeans. A few had razored off the necks or sleeves of their T-shirts. There was something creepy about one guy's face—it was like a baby's face that had grown whiskers—and it took Madeleine a full minute to realize that he'd shaved off his eyebrows. Everyone in the room was so spectral-looking that Madeleine's natural healthiness seemed suspect, like a vote for Reagan. She was relieved, therefore, when a big guy in a down jacket and snowmobile boots showed up and took the empty seat next to her. He had a cup of take-out coffee.

Zipperstein asked the students to introduce themselves and explain why they were taking the seminar.

The boy without eyebrows spoke up first. "Um, let's see. I'm finding it hard to introduce myself, actually, because the whole idea of social introductions is so problematized. Like, if I tell you that my name is Thurston Meems and that I grew up in Stamford, Connecticut, will you know who I am? O.K. My name's Thurston and I'm from Stamford, Connecticut. I'm taking this course because I read *Of Grammatology* last summer and it blew my mind." When it was the turn of the boy next to Madeleine, he said in a quiet voice that he was a double major (biology and philosophy) and had never taken a semiotics course before, that his parents had named him Leonard, that it had always seemed pretty handy to have a name, especially when you were being called to dinner, and that if anyone wanted to call him Leonard he would answer to it.

Leonard didn't make another comment. During the rest of the class, he leaned back in his chair, stretching out his long legs. After he finished his coffee, he dug into his right snowmobile boot and, to Madeleine's surprise, pulled out a tin of chewing tobacco. With two stained fingers, he placed a wad of tobacco in his cheek. For the next two hours, every minute or so, he spat, discreetly but audibly, into the cup.

Every week Zipperstein assigned one daunting book of theory and one literary selection. The pairings were eccentric if not downright arbitrary. (What did Saussure's *Writings in General Linguistics*, for instance, have to do with Pynchon's *The Crying of Lot 49*?) As for Zipperstein himself, he didn't run the class so much as observe it from behind the one-way mirror of his opaque personality. He hardly said a word. He asked questions now and then to stimulate discussion, and often went to the window to gaze in the direction of Narragansett Bay, as if thinking about his wooden sloop in dry dock.

Three weeks into the course, on a February day of flurries and gray skies, they read Zipperstein's own book, *The Making of Signs*, along with Peter Handke's *A Sorrow Beyond Dreams*.

It was always embarrassing when professors assigned their own books. Even Madeleine, who found all the reading hard going, could tell that Zipperstein's contribution to the field was reformulative and second-tier.

Everyone seemed a little hesitant when talking about *The Making of Signs*, so it was a relief when, after the break, they turned to the literary selection.

"So," Zipperstein asked, blinking behind his round wire-rims. "What did you make of the Handke?"

After a short silence, Thurston spoke up. "The Handke was totally dank and depressing," he said. "I loved it."

Thurston was a sly-looking boy with short, gelled hair. His eyebrow-lessness, along with his pale complexion, gave his face a superintelligent quality, like a floating, disembodied brain.

"Care to elaborate?" Zipperstein said.

"Well, Professor, here's a subject dear to my heart—offing yourself." The other students tittered as Thurston warmed to his topic. "It's purportedly autobiographical, this book. But I'd contend, with Barthes, that the act of writing is itself a fictionalization, even if you're treating actual events."

Bart. So that was how you pronounced it. Madeleine made a note, grateful to be spared humiliation.

Meanwhile Thurston was saying, "So Handke's mother commits suicide and Handke sits down to write about it. He wants to be as objective as possible, to be totally—remorseless!" Thurston stifled a smile. He aspired to be a person who would react to his own mother's suicide with high-literary remorselessness, and his soft, young face lit up with pleasure. "Suicide is a trope," he announced. "Especially in German literature. You've got *The Sorrows of Young Werther*. You've got Kleist. Hey, I just thought of something." He held up a finger. *"The Sorrows of Young Werther."* He held up another finger. *"A Sorrow Beyond Dreams.* My theory is that Handke felt the weight of all that tradition and this book was his attempt to break free."

"How do you mean 'free'?" Zipperstein said.

"From the whole Teutonic, Sturm-und-Drang, suicidal thing."

The flurries swirling outside the windows looked like either flakes of soap or flecks of ash, like something either very clean or very dirty.

"The Sorrows of Young Werther is an apt reference," Zipperstein said. "But I think that's more the translator's doing than Handke's. In German the book's called *Wunschloses Unglück.*"

Thurston smiled, either because he was pleased to be receiving Zipperstein's full attention or because he thought German sounded funny.

"It's a play on a German saying, *wunschlos glücklich,* which means being happier than you could ever wish for. Only here Handke makes a nice reversal. It's a serious and strangely wonderful title."

"So it means being unhappier than you could ever wish for," Madeleine said.

Zipperstein looked at her for the first time.

"In a sense. As I said, something is lost in translation. What was your take?"

"On the book?" Madeleine asked, and immediately realized how stupid this sounded. She fell silent, the blood beating in her ears.

People blushed in nineteenth-century English novels but never in contemporary Austrian ones.

Before the silence became uncomfortable, Leonard came to her rescue. "I have a comment," he said. "If I was going to write about my mother's suicide, I don't think I'd be too concerned about being experimental." He leaned forward, putting his elbows on the table. "I mean, wasn't anybody put off by Handke's so-called remorselessness? Didn't this book strike anyone as a tad cold?"

"Better cold than sentimental," Thurston said.

"Do you think? Why?"

"Because we've read the sentimental, filial account of a cherished dead parent before. We've read it a million times. It doesn't have any power anymore."

"I'm doing a little thought experiment here," Leonard said. "Say my mother killed herself. And say I wrote a book about it. Why would I want to do something like that?" He closed his eyes and leaned his head back. "First, I'd do it to cope with my grief. Second, maybe to paint a portrait of my mother. To keep her alive in my memory."

"And you think your reaction is universal," Thurston said. "That because you'd respond to the death of a parent a certain way, that obligates Handke to do the same."

"I'm saying that if your mother kills herself it's not a literary trope."

Madeleine's heart had quieted now. She was listening to the discussion with interest.

Thurston was nodding his head in a way that somehow didn't suggest agreement. "Yeah, O.K.," he said. "Handke's *real* mother killed herself. She died in a *real* world and Handke felt *real* grief or whatever. But that's not what this book's about. Books aren't about 'real life.' Books are about other books." He raised his mouth like a wind instrument and blew out bright notes. "My theory is that the problem Handke was trying to solve here, from a literary standpoint, was how do you write about something, even something real and painful—like suicide—when all of the writing that's been done on that subject has robbed you of any originality of expression?"

What Thurston was saying seemed to Madeleine both insightful and horribly wrong. It was maybe true, what he said, but it shouldn't have been.

"'Popular Literature,'" Zipperstein quipped, proposing an essay title. "'Or, How to Beat a Dead Horse.'"

A spasm of mirth traveled through the class. Madeleine looked over to see that Leonard was staring at her. When the class ended, he gathered up his books and left.

She started seeing Leonard around after that. She saw him crossing the green one afternoon, hatless in winter drizzle. She saw him at Mutt & Geoff's, eating a messy Buddy Cianci sandwich. She saw him, one morning, waiting for a bus on South Main. Each time, Leonard was alone, looking forlorn and uncombed like a great big motherless boy. At the same time, he appeared somehow older than most guys at school.

It was Madeleine's last semester of senior year, a time when she was supposed to have some fun, and she wasn't having any. She'd never thought of herself as hard up. She preferred to think of her current boyfriendless state as salutary and head-clearing. But when she found herself wondering what it would be like to kiss a guy who chewed tobacco, she began to worry that she was fooling herself.

Looking back, Madeleine realized that her college love life had fallen short of expectations. Her freshman roommate, Jennifer Boomgaard, had rushed off to Health Services the first week of school to be fitted for a diaphragm. Unaccustomed to sharing a room with anybody, much less a stranger, Madeleine felt that Jenny was a little too quick with her intimacies. She didn't want to be shown Jennifer's diaphragm, which reminded her of an uncooked ravioli, and she certainly didn't want to feel the spermicidal jelly that Jenny offered to squirt into her palm. Madeleine was shocked when Jennifer started going to parties with the diaphragm already in place, when she wore it to the Harvard-Brown game, and when she left it one morning on top of their miniature fridge. That winter, when the Rev. Desmond Tutu came to campus for an anti-apartheid rally, Madeleine asked Jennifer on their way to see the great cleric, "Did you put your diaphragm in?" They lived the next four months in an eighteen-by-fifteen room without speaking to each other.

Though Madeleine hadn't arrived at college sexually inexperienced, her freshman learning curve resembled a flat line. Aside from one makeout session with a Uruguáyan named Carlos, a sandal-wearing engineering student who in low light looked like Che Guevara, the only boy she'd fooled around with was a high school senior visiting campus for Early Action weekend. She found Tim standing in line at the Ratty, pushing his cafeteria tray along the metal track, and visibly quivering. His blue blazer was too big for him. He'd spent the entire day wandering around campus with no one speaking to him. Now he was starving and wasn't sure if he was allowed to eat in the cafeteria or not. Tim seemed to be the only person at Brown more lost than Madeleine. She helped him negotiate the Ratty and, afterward, took him on a tour of the university. Finally, around ten-thirty that night, they ended up back in Madeleine's dorm room. Tim had the long-lashed eyes and pretty features of an expensive Bavarian doll, a little prince or yodeling shepherd boy. His blue blazer was on the floor and Madeleine's shirt unbuttoned when Jennifer Boomgaard came through the door. "Oh," she said, "sorry," and proceeded to stand there, smiling at the floor as if already relishing how this juicy bit of gossip would play along the hall. When she finally did leave, Madeleine sat up and readjusted her clothes, and Tim picked up his blazer and went back to high school.

At Christmas, when Madeleine went home for vacation, she thought the scale in her parents' bathroom was broken. She got off to recalibrate the dial and got back on, whereupon the scale again registered the same weight. Stepping in front of the mirror, Madeleine encountered a worried chipmunk staring back. "Am I not getting asked out because I'm fat," the chipmunk said, "or am I fat because I'm not getting asked out?"

"I never got the freshman fifteen," her sister gloated when Madeleine came down to breakfast. "But I didn't pig out like all my friends did." Accustomed to Alwyn's teasing, Madeleine paid no attention, quietly slicing and eating the first of the fifty-seven grapefruits she subsisted on until New Year's.

Dieting fooled you into thinking you could control your life. By January, Madeleine was down five pounds, and by the time squash season ended she was back in great shape, and still she didn't meet anyone she liked. The boys at college seemed either incredibly immature or prematurely middle-aged, bearded like therapists, warming brandy snifters over candles while listening to Coltrane's *A Love Supreme*. It wasn't until her junior year that Madeleine had a serious boyfriend. Billy Bainbridge was the son of Dorothy Bainbridge, whose uncle owned a third of the newspapers in the United States. Billy had flushed cheeks, blond curls, and a scar on his right temple that made him even more adorable than he already was. He was soft-spoken and nice-smelling, like Ivory soap. Naked, his body was nearly hairless.

Billy didn't like to talk about his family. Madeleine took this as a sign of good breeding. Billy was a legacy at Brown and sometimes worried that he wouldn't have gotten in on his own. Sex with Billy was cozy, it was snuggly, it was perfectly fine. He wanted to be a filmmaker. The one film he made for Advanced Filmmaking, however, was a violent, unbroken twelve minutes of Billy throwing fecal-looking brownie mix at the camera. Madeleine began to wonder if there was a reason he never talked about his family.

One thing he did talk about, however, with increasing intensity, was circumcision. Billy had read an article in an alternative health magazine that argued against the practice, and it made a big impression on him. "If you think about it, it's a pretty weird thing to do to a baby," he said. "Cut off part of its dick? What's so different about a tribe in, like, Papua New Guinea putting bones through their noses and cutting off a baby's foreskin? A bone through the nose is a lot less invasive." Madeleine listened, trying to look sympathetic, and hoped Billy would drop the subject. But as the weeks passed he kept returning to it. "The doctors just do it automatically in this country," he said. "They didn't ask my parents. It's not like I'm Jewish or anything." He derided justifications on the basis of health or hygiene. "Maybe that made sense three thousand years ago, out in the desert, when you couldn't take a shower. But now?"

One night, as they were lying in bed, naked, Madeleine noticed Billy examining his penis, stretching it.

"What are you doing?" she asked.

"I'm looking for the scar," he said somberly.

He interrogated his European friends, Henrik the Intact, Olivier the Foreskinned, asking, "But does it feel supersensitive?" Billy was convinced that he'd been deprived of sensation. Madeleine tried not to take this personally. Plus there were other problems with their relationship by then. Billy had a habit of staring deeply into Madeleine's eyes in a way that was somehow controlling. His roommate situation was odd. He lived off campus with an attractive, muscular girl named Kyle who was sleeping with at least three people, including Fatima Shirazi, a niece of the shah of Iran. On the wall of his living room Billy had painted the words *Kill the Father*. Killing the father was what, in Billy's opinion, college was all about.

"Who's *your* father?" he asked Madeleine. "Is it Virginia Woolf? Is it Sontag?"

"In my case," Madeleine said, "my father really is my father."

"Then you have to kill him."

"Who's your father?"

"Godard," he said.

Billy talked about renting a house in Guanajuato with Madeleine over the summer. He said she could write a novel while he made a film. His faith in her, in her writing (even though she hardly wrote any fiction), made Madeleine feel so good that she started going along with the idea. And then one day she came up onto Billy's front porch and was about to rap on his window when something told her to look in the window instead. In the storm-tossed bed, Billy lay curled, John Lennon–style, against the spread-eagled Kyle. Both were naked. A second later, in a puff of smoke, Fatima materialized, also naked, shaking baby powder over her gleaming Persian skin. She smiled at her bedmates, her teeth seed-like in purple, royal gums.

Maddy's next boyfriend wasn't strictly her fault. She would never have met Dabney Carlisle if she hadn't taken an acting class, and she would never have taken an acting class if it hadn't been for her mother. As a young woman, Phyllida had wanted to be an actress. Her parents had been opposed, however. "Acting wasn't what people in our family, especially the ladies, did," was the way Phyllida put it. Every so often, in reflective moods, she told her daughters the story of her one great disobedience. After graduating from college, Phyllida had "run away" to Hollywood. Without telling her parents, she'd flown out to Los Angeles, staying with a friend from Smith. She'd found a job as a secretary in an insurance company. She and the friend, a girl named Sally Peyton, moved into a bungalow in Santa Monica. In six months Phyllida had three auditions, one screen test, and "loads of invitations." She'd once seen Jackie Gleason carrying a chihuahua into a restaurant. She'd developed a lustrous suntan she described as "Egyptian." Whenever Phyllida spoke about this period in her life, it seemed as if she was talking about another person. As for Alton, he became quiet, fully aware that Phyllida's loss had been his gain. It was on the train back to New York, the next Christmas, that she'd met the straight-backed lieutenant colonel, recently returned from Berlin. Phyllida never went back to L.A. She got married instead. "And had you two," she told her daughters.

Phyllida's inability to realize her dreams had given Madeleine her own. Her mother's life was the great counterexample. It represented the injustice Madeleine's life would rectify. To come of age simultaneously with a great social movement, to grow up in the age of Betty Friedan and

ERA marches and Bella Abzug's indomitable hats, to define your identity when it was being redefined, this was a freedom as great as any of the American freedoms Madeleine had read about in school. She could remember the night, in 1973, when her family gathered before the television in the den to watch the tennis match between Billie Jean King and Bobby Riggs. How she, Alwyn, and Phyllida had rooted for Billie Jean, while Alton had pulled for Bobby Riggs. How, as King ran Riggs back and forth across the court, outserving him, hitting winners he was too slow to return, Alton began to grumble. "It's not a fair fight! Riggs is too old. If they want a real test, she should play Smith or Newcombe." But it didn't matter what Alton said. It didn't matter that Bobby Riggs was fifty-five and King twenty-nine, or that Riggs hadn't been an especially great player even in his prime. What mattered was that this tennis match was on national television, during prime time, billed for weeks as "The Battle of the Sexes," and that the woman was winning. If any single moment defined Madeleine's generation of girls, dramatized their aspirations, put into clear focus what they expected from themselves and from life, it was those two hours and fifteen minutes when the country watched a man in white shorts get thrashed by a woman, pummeled repeatedly until all he could do, after match point, was to jump feebly over the net. And even that was telling: you were supposed to jump the net when you won, not lost. So how male was that, to act like a winner when you'd just been creamed?

At the first meeting of Acting Workshop, Professor Churchill, a bald bullfrog of a man, asked the students to say something about themselves. Half the people in the class were theater majors, serious about acting or directing. Madeleine mumbled something about loving Shakespeare and Eugene O'Neill.

Dabney Carlisle stood up and said, "I've done a little modeling work, down in New York. My agent suggested I should take some acting lessons. So here I am."

The modeling he'd done consisted of a single magazine ad, showing a group of Leni Riefenstahl–ish athletes in boxer briefs, standing in a receding line on a beach whose black volcanic sand steamed around their marble feet. Madeleine didn't see the photograph until she and Dabney were already going out, when Dabney gingerly took it out of the bartending manual where he kept it safely pressed. She was inclined to make fun of it but something reverential in Dabney's expression stopped her. And so she asked where the beach had been (Montauk) and why it was so black (it wasn't) and how much he'd gotten paid ("four figures") and what the other guys were like ("total a-holes") and if he was wearing the underpants right now. It was sometimes difficult, with boys, to take an interest in the things that interested them. But with Dabney she wished it had been curling, she longed for it to be the model UN, anything but male modeling. This, anyway, was the authentic emotion she now identified herself as having felt. At the time—Dabney cautioned her against touching the ad before he got it laminated—Madeleine had rehearsed in her mind the standard arguments: that though objectification was de facto bad, the emergence of the idealized male form in the mass media scored a point for equality; that if men started getting objectified and started worrying about their looks and their bodies, they might begin to understand the burden women had been living with since forever, and might therefore be sensitized to these issues of the body. She even went so far as to admire Dabney for his courage in allowing himself to be photographed in snug little gray underpants.

Looking the way Madeleine and Dabney did, it was inevitable that they would be cast as romantic leads in the scenes the workshop performed. Madeleine was Rosalind to Dabney's wooden Orlando, Maggie to his brick-like Brick in *Cat on a Hot Tin Roof.* To rehearse the first time, they met at Dabney's fraternity house. Merely stepping through the front door reinforced Madeleine's aversion to places like Sigma Chi. It was around ten on a Sunday morning. The vestiges of the previous evening's "Hawaiian Night" were still there to see—the lei hanging from the antlers of the moose head on the wall, the plastic "grass" skirt trampled on the beer-sodden floor, a skirt that, should Madeleine succumb to the outrageous good looks of Dabney Carlisle, she might, at a minimum, have to watch some drunken slut hula in to the baying of the brothers, or, at a maximum (for mai tais made you do crazy things), might even don herself, up in Dabney's room, for his pleasure alone. On the low-slung couch two Sigma Chi members were watching TV. At Madeleine's appearance, they stirred, rising out of the gloom like openmouthed carp. She hurried to the back stairs, thinking the things she always thought when it came to frats and frat guys: that their appeal stemmed from a primitive need for protection (one thought of Neanderthal clans banding together against other Neanderthal clans); that the hazing the pledges underwent (being stripped and blindfolded and left in the lobby of the Biltmore Hotel with bus fare taped to their genitals) enacted the very fears of male rape and emasculation that membership in the fraternity promised protection against; that any guy who longed to join a frat suffered from insecurities that poisoned his relationships with women; that there was something seriously wrong with homophobic guys who centered their lives around a homoerotic bond; that the stately mansions maintained by generations of dues-paying fraternity members were in reality sites for date rape and problem drinking; that frats always smelled bad; that you didn't ever want to shower in one; that only freshman girls were stupid enough to go to frat parties; that Kelly Traub had slept with a Sigma Delt guy who kept saying, "Now you see it, now you don't, now you see it, now you don't"; that such a thing wasn't going to happen to her, to Madeleine, ever.

What she hadn't expected when it came to a fraternity was a sunny-haired silent type like Dabney, learning his lines in a folding chair, in parachute pants, shoeless. Looking back on their relationship, Madeleine figured she'd had no choice. Dabney and she had been selected for each other in a Royal Wedding kind of way. She was Prince Charles to his Princess Di. She knew he couldn't act. Dabney had the artistic soul of a third-string tight end. In life Dabney moved and said little. Onstage he moved not at all but had to say a lot. His best dramatic moments came when the strain on his face from remembering his lines resembled the emotion he was trying to simulate.

Acting opposite Dabney made Madeleine more stiff and nervous than she already was. She wanted to do scenes with the talented kids in the workshop. She suggested interesting bits from *The Vietnamization of New Jersey* and Mamet's *Sexual Perversity in Chicago*, but got no takers. Nobody wanted to lower his or her average by acting with her.

Dabney didn't let it bother him. "Bunch of little shits in that class," he said. "They'll never get any print work, much less movies."

He was more laconic than she liked her boyfriends to be. He had the wit of a store mannequin. But Dabney's physical perfection pushed these realities out of her mind. She'd never been in a relationship where she wasn't the more attractive partner. It was slightly intimidating. But she could handle it. At three a.m., while Dabney lay sleeping beside her,

Madeleine found she was up to the task of inventorying each abdominal cord, every hard lump of muscle. She enjoyed applying calipers to Dabney's waist to measure his body fat. Underwear modeling was all about the abs, Dabney said, and the abs were all about sit-ups and diet. The pleasure Madeleine got from looking at Dabney was reminiscent of the pleasure she'd gotten as a girl from looking at sleek hunting dogs. Underneath this pleasure, like the coals that fed it, was a fierce need to enfold Dabney and siphon off his strength and beauty. It was all very primitive and evolutionary and felt fantastic. The problem was that she hadn't been able to allow herself to enjoy Dabney or even to exploit him a little, but had had to go and be a total girl about it and convince herself that she was in love with him. Madeleine required emotion, apparently. She disapproved of the idea of meaningless, extremely satisfying sex.

And so she began to tell herself that Dabney's acting was "restrained" or "economical." She appreciated that Dabney was "secure about himself" and "didn't need to prove anything" and wasn't a "showoff." Instead of worrying that he was dull, Madeleine decided he was gentle. Instead of thinking he was poorly read, she called him intuitive. She exaggerated Dabney's mental abilities in order not to feel shallow for wanting his body. To this end she helped Dabney write—O.K., she wrote—English and anthro papers for him and, when he got A's, felt confirmed of his intelligence. She sent him off to modeling auditions in New York with good-luck kisses and listened to him complain bitterly about the "faggots" who hadn't hired his services. It turned out that Dabney wasn't so beautiful. Among the truly beautiful he was only so-so. He couldn't even smile right.

At the end of the semester, the acting students met separately with the professor for a critical review. Churchill welcomed Madeleine with a wolfish yellow grin, then sat back jowly and deliberate in his chair.

"I've enjoyed having you in the class, Madeleine," he said. "But you can't act."

"Don't hold back," Madeleine said, chastened but laughing. "Give it to me straight."

"You have a good feel for language, for Shakespeare especially. But your voice is reedy and you look worried onstage. Your forehead has a perpetual crease. A vocal coach could go a long way toward helping your instrument. But I worry about your worrying. You've got it right now. The crease."

"It's called thinking."

"Which is fine. If you're playing Eleanor Roosevelt. Or Golda Meir. But those parts don't come around very often."

Churchill, steepling his fingers, continued, "I'd be more diplomatic if I thought this meant a lot to you. But I get the feeling you don't want to be a professional actress, do you?"

"No," Madeleine said.

"Good. You're lovely. You're bright. The world is your oyster. Go with my blessings."

When Dabney returned from his review with Churchill, he looked even more self-contented than usual.

"So?" Madeleine asked. "How did it go?"

"He says I'm perfect for soaps."

"Soap commercials?"

Dabney looked peeved. "*Days of Our Lives. General Hospital.* Ever heard of those?"

"Did he mean that as a compliment?"

"How else could he mean it? Soap actors have it made! They work every day, make great money, and never have to travel. I've been wasting my time trying to get all this advertising work. Screw that. I'm going to tell my agent to start lining up some auditions for soaps."

Madeleine was silent at this news. She'd assumed Dabney's enthusiasm for modeling was temporary, a tuition-earning scheme. Now she realized he was in earnest. She was, in fact, dating a model.

"What are you thinking?" Dabney asked her.

"Nothing."

"Tell me."

"Just that—I don't know—but I doubt Prof. Churchill has that high of an opinion of the acting on *Days of Our Lives.*"

"What did he tell us the first class? He said he was giving a workshop in acting. For people who wanted to work in the theater."

"In the theater doesn't mean . . ."

"What did he tell *you*? Did he say you were going to be a movie star?"

"He told me I couldn't act," Madeleine said.

"He did, huh?" Dabney put his hands in his pockets, leaning back on his heels as if relieved not to have to deliver this verdict himself. "Is that why you're so pissed off? And have to tear down my crit?"

"I'm not tearing down your crit. I'm just not sure you got Churchill's meaning, exactly."

Dabney let out a bitter laugh. "I wouldn't get it right, would I? I'm too dumb. I'm just some dumb jock you have to write English papers for."

"I don't know. You seem to have a pretty good grasp of sarcasm."

"Man, am I ever lucky," Dabney said. "What would I do if you weren't around? You have to catch all the subtleties for me, don't you? You and your flair for catching subtleties. It must be nice to be rich and sit around all day catching subtleties. What do you know about needing to make a living? It's fine for you to make fun of my ad. You didn't get into college on a football scholarship. And now you have to come in here and run me down. You know what? This is bullshit. This is total bullshit. I'm sick of your condescension and your superiority complex. And Churchill's right. You can't act."

In the end Madeleine had to admit that Dabney was far more fluent than she'd ever expected. He was capable of portraying a range of emotions, too, anger, disgust, wounded pride, and of simulating others, including affection, passion, and love. He had a great career in the soaps ahead of him.

Madeleine and Dabney had broken up in May, right before summer, and there was no better time than summer to forget about somebody. She'd gone straight down to Prettybrook the day she finished her last exam. For once she was glad to have such sociable parents. With all the cocktail parties and convivial dinners on Wilson Lane there was little time to dwell on herself. In July, she got an internship at a nonprofit poetry organization on the Upper East Side and began riding the train into the city. Madeleine's job was to oversee submissions for the annual New Voices award, which involved making sure that the submissions were complete before sending them off to the judge (Howard Nemerov, that year). Madeleine wasn't particularly technical, but because everyone else in the office was even less so, she ended up being the go-to person whenever the copier or the dot-matrix printer malfunctioned. Her coworker Brenda would come up to Madeleine's desk at least once a week and ask in a babyish voice, "Can you help me? The printer's not being nice." The only part of the day Madeleine enjoyed was her lunch hour, when she got to walk around the muggy, stinking, thrilling streets, eat quiche in a French bistro as narrow as a bowling alley, and stare at the styles women her age or a little older were wearing. When the one straight guy at the nonprofit asked her to have a drink after work, Madeleine cooly answered, "Sorry, I can't," trying not to feel bad about hurting his feelings, trying to think about her own feelings for a change.

She arrived back at college for her senior year, then, intent on being studious, career-oriented, and aggressively celibate. Casting a wide net, Madeleine sent away for applications to Yale grad school (English Language and Literature), an organization for teaching English in China, and an advertising internship at Foote, Cone & Belding, in Chicago. She studied for the GRE using a sample booklet. The verbal section was easy. The math required brushing up on her high school algebra. The logic problems, however, were a defeat to the spirit. "At the annual dancers' ball a number of dancers performed their favorite dance with their favorite partners. Alan danced the tango, while Becky watched the waltz. James and Charlotte were fantastic together. Keith was magnificent during his foxtrot and Simon excelled at the rumba. Jessica danced with Alan. But Laura did not dance with Simon. Can you determine who danced with whom and which dance they each enjoyed?" Logic wasn't something Madeleine had been expressly taught. It seemed unfair to be asked about it. She did as the book suggested, diagramming the problems, placing Alan, Becky, James, Charlotte, Keith, Simon, Jessica, and Laura on the dance floor of her scrap paper, and pairing them according to the instructions. But their complicated transit wasn't a subject Madeleine's mind naturally followed. She wanted to know why James and Charlotte were fantastic together, and if Jessica and Alan were going out, and why Laura wouldn't dance with Simon, and if Becky was upset, watching.

One afternoon, on the bulletin board outside Hillel House, Madeleine noticed a flyer announcing the Melvin and Hetty Greenberg Fellowship for summer study at Hebrew University in Jerusalem, and she applied for that. Using contacts of Alton's in the publishing world, she put on a business suit and went down to New York for an informational interview with an editor at Simon and Schuster. The editor, Terry Wirth, had once been a bright, idealistic English major just like Madeleine, but she found him that afternoon, in his tiny, manuscript-piled office look-ing onto the gloomy canyon of Sixth Avenue, a middle-aged father of two with a salary far below the median of his former classmates and a nasty, hour-and-fifteen-minute commute to his split-level in Montclair, New Jersey. On the prospects of a book he was publishing that month, the memoir of a migrant farmer, Wirth said, "Now's the calm before the calm." He gave Madeleine a stack of manuscripts from the slush pile to critique, offering to pay her fifty bucks a pop.

Instead of reading the manuscripts, Madeleine took the subway down to the East Village. After buying a bag of pignoli cookies at De Robertis, she plunged into a hair salon, where, on a whim, she allowed a butch woman with a short, rat-tailed haircut to go to work on her. "Cut it close on the sides, higher on top," Madeleine said. "You sure?" the woman said. "I'm sure," Madeleine answered. To show her resolve, she took off her glasses. Forty-five minutes later, she put her glasses back on, horror-struck and elated at the transformation. Her head was really quite enormous. She had never fathomed its true size. She looked like Annie Lennox, or David Bowie. Like someone the hairdresser might be dating.

The Annie Lennox look was O.K., however. Androgyny was just the thing. Once she was back at school, Madeleine's haircut proclaimed her serious frame of mind, and by the end of the year, when her bangs had grown out to a maddening length she didn't know what to do with, she remained firm in her renunciations. (Her only slip-up had been the night in her bedroom with Mitchell, but nothing had happened.) Madeleine had her thesis to write. She had her future to figure out. The last thing she needed was a boy to distract her from her work and disturb her equi-librium. But then, during spring semester, she met Leonard Bankhead and her resolve went out the window.

He shaved irregularly. His Skoal had a menthol scent, cleaner, more pleasant than Madeleine expected. Whenever she looked up to find Leonard staring at her with his St. Bernard's eyes (the eyes of a drooler, maybe, but also of a loyal brute who could dig you out of an avalanche), Madeleine couldn't help staring back a significant moment longer.

One evening in early March, when she went to the Rockefeller Li-brary to pick up the reserve reading for Semiotics 211, she found Leonard there as well. He was leaning against the counter, speaking animatedly to the girl on duty, who was unfortunately rather cute in a busty Bettie Page way.

"Think about it, though," Leonard was saying to the girl. "Think about it from the point of view of the fly."

"O.K., I'm a fly," the girl said with a throaty laugh.

"We move in slow motion to them. They can see the swatter coming from a million miles away. The flies are like, 'Wake me when the swatter gets close.'"

Noticing Madeleine, the girl told Leonard, "Just a sec."

Madeleine held out her call order slip, and the girl took it and went off into the stacks.

"Picking up the Balzac?" Leonard said.

"Yes."

"Balzac to the rescue."

Normally, Madeleine would have had many things to say to this, many comments about Balzac to make. But her mind was a blank. She didn't even remember to smile until he'd looked away.

Bettie Page came back with Madeleine's order, sliding it toward her and immediately turning back to Leonard. He seemed different than he did in class, more exuberant, supercharged. He raised his eyebrows in a crazed, Jack Nicholson way and said, "My housefly theory is related to my theory about why time seems to go faster as you get older."

"Why's that?" the girl asked.

"It's proportional," Leonard explained. "When you're five, you've only been alive a couple thousand days. But by the time you're fifty, you've lived around twenty thousand days. So a day when you're five seems longer because it's a greater percentage of the whole."

"Yeah, sure," the girl teased, "that follows."

But Madeleine had understood. "That makes sense," she said. "I always wondered why that was."

"It's just a theory," Leonard said.

Bettie Page tapped Leonard's hand to get his attention. "Flies aren't always so fast," she said. "I've caught flies in my bare hands before."

"Especially in winter," Leonard said. "That's probably the kind of fly I'd be. One of those knucklehead winter flies."

There was no good excuse for Madeleine to hang around the reserve reading room, and so she put the Balzac into her bag and headed out.

She began to dress differently on the days she had semiotics. She took out her diamond studs, leaving her ears bare. She stood in front of the mirror wondering if her Annie Hall glasses might possibly project a New Wave look. She decided not and wore her contacts. She unearthed a pair of Beatle boots she'd bought at a church basement sale in Vinalhaven. She put up her collar, and wore more black.

In Week Four, Zipperstein assigned Umberto Eco's *The Role of the Reader*. It hadn't done much for Madeleine. She wasn't all that interested, as a reader, in the reader. She was still partial to that increasingly eclipsed entity: the writer. Madeleine had a feeling that most semiotic theorists had been unpopular as children, often bullied or overlooked, and so had directed their lingering rage onto literature. They wanted to demote the author. They wanted a *book*, that hard-won, transcendent thing, to be a *text*, contingent, indeterminate, and open for suggestions. They wanted the reader to be the main thing. Because *they* were readers.

Whereas Madeleine was perfectly happy with the idea of genius. She wanted a book to take her places she couldn't get to herself. She thought a writer should work harder writing a book than she did reading it. When it came to letters and literature, Madeleine championed a virtue that had fallen out of esteem: namely, clarity. The week after they read Eco, they read portions of Derrida's *Writing and Difference*. The week after that, they read Jonathan Culler's *On Deconstruction*, and Madeleine came to class ready to contribute to the discussion for the first time. Before she could do so, however, Thurston beat her to it.

"The Culler was passable at best," Thurston said.

"What didn't you like about it?" the professor asked him.

Thurston had his knee up against the edge of the seminar table. He pushed his chair up on its back legs, scrunching up his face. "It's readable and everything," he said. "And well argued and all that. But it's just a question of whether you can use a discredited discourse—like, say, reason—to explicate something as paradigmatically revolutionary as deconstruction."

Madeleine searched along the table for mutual eye-rolling but the other students seemed eager to hear what Thurston had to say.

"Care to elaborate?" Zipperstein said.

"Well, what I mean is, first off, reason is just a discourse like any other, right? It's only been imbued with a sense of absolute truth because it's the privileged discourse of the West. What Derrida's saying is that you have to use reason because, you know, reason is all there is. But at the same time you have to be aware that language is by its very nature *un*reasonable. You have to reason yourself out of reasonableness." He pulled up the sleeve of his T-shirt and scratched his bony shoulder. "Culler, on the other hand, is still operating in the old mode. Mono as opposed to stereo. So from that point of view, I found the book, yeah, a little bit disappointing."

A silence ensued. And deepened.

"I don't know," Madeleine said, glancing at Leonard for support. "Maybe it's just me, but wasn't it a relief to read a logical argument for once? Culler boils down everything Eco and Derrida are saying into a digestible form."

Thurston turned his head slowly to gaze across the seminar table at her. "I'm not saying it's *bad*," he said. "It's fine. But Culler's work is of a different order than Derrida. Every genius needs an explainer. That's what Culler is for Derrida."

Madeleine shrugged this off. "I got a lot better idea of what deconstruction is from reading Culler than from reading Derrida."

Thurston took pains to give her point of view full consideration. "It's the nature of a simplification to be simple," he said.

Class ended shortly after that, leaving Madeleine fuming. As she was coming out of Sayles Hall, she saw Leonard standing on the steps, holding a Coke can. She went right up to him and said, "Thanks for the help."

"Excuse me?"

"I thought you were on my side. Why didn't you say anything in class?"

"First Law of Thermodynamics," Leonard said. "Conservation of energy."

"Didn't you agree with me?"

"I did and I didn't," Leonard said.

"You didn't like the Culler?"

"The Culler's good. But Derrida's a heavyweight. You can't just write him off."

Madeleine looked dubious, but Derrida wasn't who she was mad at. "Considering how Thurston's always going on about how much he *worships* language, you'd think he wouldn't parrot so much jargon. He used the word *phallus* three times today."

Leonard smiled. "Figures if he says it it'll be like having one."

"He drives me crazy."

"You want to get some coffee?"

"And *fascist*. That's another of his favorites. You know the dry cleaners on Thayer Street? He called *them* fascist."

"Must have gone extra heavy on the starch."

"Yes," Madeleine said.

"Yes, what?"

"You just invited me for coffee."

"I did?" Leonard said. "Yes, I did. O.K. Let's go get coffee."

Leonard didn't want to go to the Blue Room. He said he didn't like to be around college students. They headed through Wayland Arch up to Hope Street, in the direction of Fox Point.

As they walked, Leonard spat into his Coke can every so often. "Pardon my disgusting habit," he said.

Madeleine wrinkled up her nose. "Are you going to keep doing that?"

"No," Leonard said. "I don't even know why I do it. It's just something I picked up from my rodeo days."

At the next trash can they came to, he tossed the Coke and spat out his wad of tobacco.

Within a few blocks pretty campus plantings of tulip and daffodil gave way to treeless streets lined by working-class houses painted in cheerful hues. They passed a Portuguese bakery and a Portuguese fish store selling sardines and cuttlefish. The kids here had no yards to play in but seemed happy enough, wheeling back and forth along the blank sidewalks. Nearer the highway, there were a few warehouses and, on the corner of Wickenden, a local diner.

Leonard wanted to sit at the counter. "I need to be close to the pies," he said. "I need to see which one is talking to me."

As Madeleine took a stool next to him, Leonard stared at the dessert case.

"Do you remember when they used to serve slices of cheese with apple pie?" he asked.

"Vaguely," Madeleine said.

"They don't seem to do that anymore. You and I are probably the only two people in this place who remember it."

"Actually, I don't remember it," Madeleine said.

"You don't? Never had a little slice of Wisconsin cheddar with your apple pie? I'm sorry to hear that."

"Maybe they'll put a slice of cheese on a piece if you ask them."

"I didn't say I *liked* it. I'm just mourning its passage."

The conversation lapsed. And suddenly, to her surprise, Madeleine was flooded with panic. She felt the silence like a judgment against her. At the same time, her anxiety about the silence made it even harder to speak.

Though it didn't feel nice to be so nervous, it did feel nice, in a way. It had been a while since Madeleine had been that way around a guy.

The waitress was down at the end of the counter talking to another customer.

"So why are you taking Zipperstein's class?" she asked.

"Philosophical interest," Leonard said. "Literally. Philosophy's all about theory of language right now. It's all linguistics. So I figured I'd check it out."

"Aren't you a biology major, too?"

"That's what I really am," Leonard said. "The philosophy's just a sideline."

Madeleine realized that she'd never dated a science major. "Do you want to be a doctor?"

"Right now all I want to do is get the waitress's attention."

Leonard waved his arm a few times to no avail. Suddenly he said, "Is it hot in here?" Without waiting for an answer, he reached into the back pocket of his jeans and pulled out a blue bandanna, which he proceeded to put over his head, tying it in back and making a number of small, precise adjustments until he was satisfied. Madeleine watched this with a slight feeling of disappointment. She associated bandannas with hacky sack, the Grateful Dead, and alfalfa sprouts, all of which she could do without. Still, she was impressed with Leonard's sheer size on the stool next to her. His largeness, coupled with the softness—the delicacy, almost—of his voice, gave Madeleine a strange fairy-tale feeling, as if she were a princess sitting beside a gentle giant.

45

"The thing is, though," Leonard said, still staring in the waitress's direction, "I didn't get interested in philosophy because of linguistics. I got interested for the eternal verities. To learn how to die, et cetera. Now it's more like, 'What do we *mean* when we say we die?' 'What do we *mean* we mean when we say we die?'"

Finally, the waitress came over. Madeleine ordered the cottage cheese plate and coffee. Leonard ordered apple pie and coffee. When the waitress left, he spun his stool rightward, so that their knees briefly touched.

"How very female of you," he said.

"Sorry?"

"Cottage cheese."

"I like cottage cheese."

"Are you on a diet? You don't look like someone on a diet."

"Why do you want to know?" Madeleine said.

And here, for the first time, Leonard appeared rattled. Beneath the line of the bandanna, his face colored, and he spun away, breaking eye contact. "Just curious," he said.

In the next second, he spun back, resuming the previous conversation. "Derrida's supposed to be a lot clearer in French," he said. "Rumor has it his prose in French is limpid."

"Maybe I should read it in French, then."

"You know French?" Leonard said, sounding impressed.

"I'm not great. I can read Flaubert."

It was then that Madeleine made a big mistake. Things were going so well with Leonard, the mood was so promising—even the weather lending a hand because, after they finished their food and left the diner, walking back to campus, a March drizzle forced them to share Madeleine's collapsible umbrella—that a feeling came over her like those she'd had as a girl when treated to a pastry or a dessert, a happiness so fraught by an awareness of its brevity that she took the tiniest bites, making the cream puff or éclair last as long as possible. In this same way, instead of seeing where the afternoon led, Madeleine decided to check its progress, to save some for later, and she told Leonard she had to go home and study.

They didn't kiss goodbye. They didn't come close to it. Leonard, hunching under the umbrella, abruptly said "Bye" and hurried off through the rain, keeping his head down. Madeleine went back to the Narragansett. She lay down on her bed, and didn't move for a long time.

The days dragged until the next meeting of Sem 211. Madeleine arrived early, choosing a seat at the seminar table next to Leonard's usual spot. But when he showed up, ten minutes late, he took an available chair next to the professor. He didn't say anything in class or glance in Madeleine's direction even once. His face looked swollen and there was a line of blemishes running down one cheek. When the class ended, Leonard was the first one out the door.

The next week he missed class entirely.

And so Madeleine was left to contend with semiotics, and with Zipperstein and his disciples, all by herself.

By now they had moved on to Derrida's *Of Grammatology*. The Derrida went like this: "In that sense, it is the *Aufhebung* of other writings, particularly of hieroglyphic script and of the Leibnizian characteristic that had been criticized previously through one and the same gesture." In poetic moods, the Derrida went like this: "What writing itself, in its nonphonetic moment, betrays, is life. It menaces at once the breath, the spirit, and history as the spirit's relationship with itself. It is their end, their finitude, their paralysis."

Since Derrida claimed that language, by its very nature, undermined any meaning it attempted to promote, Madeleine wondered how Derrida expected her to get his meaning. Maybe he didn't. That was why he deployed so much arcane terminology, so many loop-de-looping clauses. That was why he said what he said in sentences it took a minute to identify the subjects of. (Could "the access to pluridimensionality and to a delinearized temporality" really be a subject?)

Reading a novel after reading semiotic theory was like jogging empty-handed after jogging with hand weights. After getting out of Semiotics 211, Madeleine fled to the Rockefeller Library, down to B Level, where the stacks exuded a vivifying smell of mold, and grabbed something—anything, *The House of Mirth*, *Daniel Deronda*—to restore herself to sanity. How wonderful it was when one sentence followed logically from the sentence before! What exquisite guilt she felt, wickedly enjoying narrative! Madeleine felt safe with a nineteenth-century novel. There were going to be people in it. Something was going to happen to them in a place resembling the world.

Then, too, there were lots of weddings in Wharton and Austen. There were all kinds of irresistible gloomy men.

The next Thursday, Madeleine came to class wearing a Norwegian sweater with a snowflake design. She'd gone back to her glasses. For the second week in a row, Leonard didn't show up. Madeleine worried that he'd dropped the class, but it was too late in the semester to do that. Zipperstein said, "Has anybody seen Mr. Bankhead? Is he sick?" Nobody knew. Thurston arrived with a girl named Cassandra Hart, both of them sniffly and heroin-pale. Taking out a black Flair pen, Thurston wrote on Cassandra's bare shoulder, "Not Real Skin."

Zipperstein was in a lively mood. He'd just returned from a conference in New York, dressed differently than usual. Listening to him talk about the paper he'd given at the New School, Madeleine suddenly understood. Semiotics was the form Zipperstein's midlife crisis had taken. Becoming a semiotician allowed Zipperstein to wear a leather jacket, to fly off to Douglas Sirk retrospectives in Vancouver, and to get all the sexy waifs in his classes. Instead of leaving his wife, Zipperstein had left the English department. Instead of buying a sports car, he'd bought deconstruction.

He sat at the seminar table now and started speaking:

"I hope you read the *Semiotext(e)* for this week. Apropos of Lyotard, and in homage to Gertrude Stein, let me suggest the following: the thing about desire is that there is no there there."

That was it. That was Zipperstein's prompt. He sat before them, blinking, waiting for somebody to reply. He appeared to have all the patience in the world.

Madeleine had wanted to know what semiotics was. She'd wanted to know what the fuss was about. Well, now she felt she knew.

But then, in Week Ten, for reasons that were entirely extracurricular, semiotics began making sense.

It was a Friday night in April, just past eleven, and Madeleine was in bed, reading. The assigned text for that week was Roland Barthes' *A Lover's Discourse*. For a book purportedly about love, it didn't look very romantic. The cover was a somber chocolate brown, the title turquoise. There was no author photograph and only a sketchy bio, listing Barthes' other works.

Madeleine had the book in her lap. With her right hand she was eating peanut butter straight from the jar. The spoon fit perfectly against the curve of her upper palate, allowing the peanut butter to dissolve creamily against her tongue.

Opening to the introduction, she began to read:

The necessity for this book is to be found in the following consideration: that the lover's discourse is today of an extreme solitude.

Outside, the temperature, which had remained cold through March, had shot up into the fifties. The resulting thaw was alarming in its suddenness, drainpipes and gutters dripping, sidewalks puddling, streets flooded, a constant sound of water rushing downhill.

Madeleine had her windows open on the liquid darkness. She sucked the spoon and read on:

What we have been able to say below about waiting, anxiety, memory is no more than a modest supplement offered to the reader to be made free with, to be added to, subtracted from, and passed on to others: around the figure, the players pass the handkerchief which sometimes, by a final parenthesis, is held a second longer before handing it on. (Ideally, the book would be a cooperative: "To the United Readers and Lovers.")

It wasn't only that this writing seemed beautiful to Madeleine. It wasn't only that these opening sentences of Barthes' made immediate sense. It wasn't only the relief at recognizing that here, finally, was a book she might write her final paper on. What made Madeleine sit up in bed was something closer to the reason she read books in the first place and had always loved them. Here was a sign that she wasn't alone. Here was an articulation of what she had been so far mutely feeling. In bed on a Friday night, wearing sweatpants, her hair tied back, her glasses smudged, and eating peanut butter from the jar, Madeleine was in a state of extreme solitude.

It had to do with Leonard. With how she felt about him and how she couldn't tell anyone. With how much she liked him and how little she knew about him. With how desperately she wanted to see him and how hard it was to do so.

In recent days, from her solitude, Madeleine had sent out feelers. She talked about Semiotics 211 with her roommates, mentioning Thurston, Cassandra, and Leonard. It turned out that Abby knew Leonard from her freshman year.

"What was he like?" Madeleine asked.

"Sort of intense. Really smart, but intense. He used to call me all the time. Like every day."

"Did he like you?"

"No, he just wanted to talk. He'd keep me on the phone for an hour."

"What did you guys talk about?"

"Everything! His relationship. My relationship. His parents, my parents. Jimmy Carter getting attacked by that swamp rabbit, which he was obsessed about. He'd go on and on."

"Who was he going out with?"

"Some girl named Mindy. But then they broke up. That's when he *really* started calling me. He'd call like six times a day. He was always going on about how good Mindy smelled. She had this smell that was supposedly perfectly compatible to Leonard, *chemically*. He was worried no girl would ever smell right to him again. I told him it was probably her moisturizer. He said no, it was her *skin*. It was *chemically perfect*. That's what he's like." She paused and gave Madeleine a searching look. "Why are you asking? Do you like him?"

"I just know him from class," Madeleine said.

"Do you want me to invite him for dinner?"

"I didn't say that."

"I'll invite him to dinner," Abby said.

The dinner had been on Tuesday night, three days ago. Leonard had come politely bearing a gift, a set of dish towels. He'd dressed up, wearing a white shirt with a skinny necktie, his long hair gathered in a masculine ponytail like a Scottish warrior. He was touchingly sincere, saying hello to Abby, handing her the wrapped gift and thanking her for the invitation.

Madeleine tried not to seem overeager. At dinner, she paid attention to Brian Weeger, whose breath had a dog-food smell. A couple of times, when she looked over at Leonard, he stared back, fixedly, appearing almost upset. Later, when Madeleine was in the kitchen, rinsing dishes, Leonard came in. She turned to find him inspecting a bump on the wall.

"This must be an old gas main," he said.

Madeleine looked at the bump, which had been painted over many times.

"They used to have gas lamps in these old places," Leonard went on. "They probably used to pump the gas up from the basement. If anybody's pilot blew out, on any floor, you'd have a leak. Gas didn't have an odor back then, either. They didn't start adding methyl mercaptan until later."

"Good to know," Madeleine said.

"This place must have been a powder keg." Leonard tapped the jutting object with his fingernail, turned, and looked Madeleine meaningfully in the face.

"I haven't been going to class," he said.

"I know."

Leonard's head was way up above her, but then he bent down, in a peaceful, leaf-eater motion, and said, "I haven't been feeling well."

"Were you sick?"

"I'm better now."

In the living room Olivia called out, "Who wants some Delamain? It's yummy!"

"I want some," Brian Weeger said. "That stuff's killer."

Leonard said, "Were the dish towels all right?"

"What?"

"The dish towels. I bought you some dish towels."

"Oh, they're great," Madeleine said. "They're perfect. We'll use them! Thank you."

"I would have brought wine, or scotch, but that's the kind of thing my father would do."

"You don't want to do anything your father would do?"

Leonard's face and voice remained solemn as he replied, "My father is a depressive who self-medicates with alcohol. My mother is more or less the same."

"Where do they live?"

"They're divorced. My mother still lives in Portland, where I'm from. My dad's in Europe. He lives in Antwerp. Last time I heard."

This interchange was encouraging, in a way. Leonard was sharing personal information. On the other hand, the information indicated that

51

he had a troubled relationship with his parents, who were themselves troubled, and Madeleine made a point of going out only with guys who liked their parents.

"What does *your* father do?" Leonard asked.

Caught off guard, Madeleine hesitated. "He used to work at a college," she said. "He's retired."

"What was he? Professor?"

"He was the president."

Leonard's face twitched. "Oh."

"It's just a small college. In New Jersey. It's called Baxter."

Abby came in to get some glasses. Leonard helped her get them off the top shelf. When she was gone, he turned back to Madeleine and said, as if in pain, "There's a Fellini film playing at the Cable Car this weekend. *Amarcord*."

Madeleine gazed encouragingly up at him. There were all kinds of outmoded, novelistic words to describe how she was feeling, words like *aflutter*. But she had her rules. One rule was that the guy had to ask her out, not the other way around.

"I think it's playing on Saturday," Leonard said.

"This Saturday?"

"Do you like Fellini?"

To reply to this question did not, in Madeleine's view, compromise her rule. "You want to know something embarrassing?" she said. "I've never seen a Fellini film."

"You should see one," Leonard said. "I'll call you."

"All right."

"Do I have your number? Oh, right, I have it. It's the same as Abby's number."

"Do you want me to write it down?" Madeleine asked.

"No," Leonard said. "I have it."

And he rose, brontosaurus-like, to his place among the treetops.

For the rest of the week, Madeleine stayed in every night, waiting for Leonard to call. When she came back from classes in the afternoon she interrogated her roommates to find out if he had called while she was out.

"Some guy called yesterday," Olivia said, on Thursday. "When I was in the shower."

"Why didn't you tell me?"

"Sorry, I forgot."

"Who was it?"

"He didn't say."

"Did it sound like Leonard?"

"I didn't notice. I was dripping wet."

"Thanks for taking a message!"

"Sor-ree," Olivia said. "God. It was just a two-second call. He said he'd call back later."

And so now it was Friday night—Friday night!—and Madeleine had declined to go out with Abby and Olivia in order to stay in and wait by the phone. She was reading *A Lover's Discourse* and marveling at its relevance to her life.

Waiting
attente / *waiting*

Tumult of anxiety provoked by waiting for the loved being, subject to trivial delays (rendezvous, letters, telephone calls, returns).

. . . *Waiting is an enchantment: I have received* orders not to move. *Waiting for a telephone is thereby woven out of tiny, un-avowable interdictions* to infinity: *I forbid myself to leave the room, to go to the toilet, even to telephone (to keep the line from being busy)* . . .

She could hear the television going in the apartment below. Madeleine's bedroom faced the State Capitol dome, brightly lit against the dark sky. The heat, which they couldn't control, was still on, the radiator wastefully knocking and hissing.

The more she thought about it, the more Madeleine understood that extreme solitude didn't just describe the way she was feeling about Leonard. It explained how she'd always felt when she was in love. It explained what love was like and, just maybe, what was wrong with it.

The telephone rang.

Madeleine sat up in bed. She dog-eared the page she was reading. She waited as long as she could (three rings) before answering.

"Hello?"

"Maddy?"

It was Alton, calling from Prettybrook.

"Oh. Hi, Daddy."

"Don't sound so excited."

"I'm studying."

In his usual way, without niceties, he got to the matter at hand. "Your mother and I were just discussing graduation plans."

For a moment, Madeleine thought Alton meant that they were discussing her future. But then she realized it was just logistics.

"It's April," she said. "Graduation's not until June."

"My experience with college towns is that the hotels get booked up months in advance. So we have to decide what we're doing. Now, here are the options. Are you listening?"

"Yes," Madeleine said, and began, at that instant, to tune out. She stuck the spoon back into the peanut butter jar and brought it to her mouth, this time just licking it.

In the phone Alton's voice was saying, "Option one: Your mother and I come up the night before the ceremony, stay in a hotel, and we see you for dinner the night of graduation. Option two: We come up the morning of the ceremony, have breakfast with you, and then leave after the ceremony. Both proposals are acceptable to us. It's your choice. But let me explain the pros and cons of each scenario."

Madeleine was about to answer when Phyllida spoke up on another extension.

"Hi, dear. I hope we didn't wake you."

"We didn't wake her," Alton barked. "Eleven o'clock's not late at college. Especially on a Friday night. Hey, what are you doing *in* on a Friday night? Got a pimple?"

"Hi, Mummy," Madeleine said, ignoring him.

"Maddy, sweetie, we're redoing your bedroom and I wanted to ask you—"

"You're redoing my bedroom?"

"Yes, it needs freshening up. I—"

"*My* room?"

"Yes. I was thinking about recarpeting it in green. You know, a *good* green."

"No!" Madeleine cried.

"Maddy, we've kept your room the way it is for four years now—you'd think it was a shrine! I'd like to be able to use it as a guest room, occasionally, because of the en suite bathroom. You can still have it when you come home, don't worry. It'll always be your room."

"What about my wallpaper?"

"It's old. It's peeling."

"You can't change my wallpaper!"

"Oh, all right. I'll leave the wallpaper alone. But the carpet—"

"Excuse me," Alton said in a peremptory tone. "This call is about graduation. Phyl, you're hijacking my agenda. You two sort out the redecorating some other time. Now, Maddy, let me go over the pros and cons. When your cousin graduated from Williams, we all had dinner *after* the ceremony. And, if you'll remember, Doats complained the whole time that he was missing all the parties—and he left halfway through the meal. Now, your mother and I are willing to stay the night—or two nights—if we're going to see you. But if you're going to be busy, maybe the breakfast option makes more sense."

"Graduation's two months away. I don't even know what's happening yet."

"That's what I told your father," Phyllida said.

It occurred to Madeleine that she was tying up the line.

"Let me think about it," she said abruptly. "I have to go. I'm studying."

"If we're going to stay the night," Alton repeated, "I'd like to make reservations soon."

"Call me later. Let me think about it. Call me Sunday."

Alton was still speaking when she hung up, so when the phone rang again, twenty seconds later, Madeleine picked up and said, "Daddy, stop it. We don't have to decide tonight."

There was silence on the line. And then a male voice said, "You don't have to call me Daddy."

"Oh, God. Leonard? Sorry! I thought you were my father. He's freaking out about graduation plans already."

"I was just having a little freak-out myself."

"About what?"

55

"About calling you."

This was good. Madeleine ran a finger along her lower lip. She said, "Have you calmed down or do you want to call back later?"

"I'm resting comfortably now, thank you."

Madeleine waited for more. None came. "Are you calling for a reason?" she asked.

"Yes. That Fellini film? I was hoping you might, if you're not too, I know it's bad manners calling so late, but I was at the lab."

Leonard did sound a little nervous. That *wasn't* good. Madeleine didn't like nervous guys. Nervous guys were nervous for a reason. Up until now Leonard had seemed more the tortured type than the nervous type. Tortured was better.

"I don't think that was a complete sentence," she said.

"What did I leave out?" Leonard asked.

"How about, 'Would you like to come with me?'"

"I'd be happy to," Leonard said.

Madeleine frowned into the receiver. She had a feeling that Leonard had set up this exchange, like a chess player thinking eight moves ahead. She was going to complain when Leonard said, "Sorry. Not funny." He comically cleared his throat. "Listen, would you like to go to the movies with me?"

She didn't answer right away. He deserved a little punishment. And so she put the screws to him—for another three seconds.

"I'd love to."

And there it was already, that word. She wondered if Leonard had noticed. She wondered what it meant that *she* had noticed. It was just a word, after all. A way of speaking.

The next night, Saturday, the fickle weather turned cold again. Madeleine was chilled in her brown suede jacket as she walked to the restaurant where they'd agreed to meet. Afterward, they made their way to the Cable Car and found a sagging couch among the other mismatched sofas and armchairs that furnished the art-house cinema.

She had a hard time following the movie. The narrative cues weren't as crisp as those of Hollywood, and the film had a dream-like quality, lush but discontinuous. The audience, being a college audience, laughed knowingly during the risqué European moments: when the huge-titted woman stuffed her huge tit into the young hero's mouth; or when the old man up in the tree cried out, "I want a woman!" Fellini's theme appeared to be the same as Roland Barthes'—love—but here it was Italian and all about the body instead of French and all about the mind. She wondered if Leonard had known what *Amarcord* was going to be about. She wondered if it was his way of getting her in the mood. As it so happened, she was in the mood, but no thanks to the movie. The movie was pretty to look at but confused her and made her feel naïve and suburban. It seemed both overly indulgent and overly male.

After it was over, they made their way out onto South Main. They had no stated destination. Madeleine was pleased to realize that Leonard, though tall, wasn't too tall. If she wore heels, the top of her head came up higher than his shoulders, almost to his chin.

"What did you think?" he said.

"Well, at least now I know what Felliniesque is."

The downtown skyline was on their left, across the river, the spire of the Superman building visible against the unnaturally pink city sky. The streets were empty except for other people leaving the cinema.

"My goal in life is to become an adjective," Leonard said. "People would go around saying, 'That was so Bankheadian.' Or, 'A little too Bankheadian for my taste.'"

"Bankheadian has a ring," Madeleine said.

"It's better than Bankheadesque."

"Or Bankheadish."

"*Ish* is terrible all around. There's Joycean, Shakespearean, Faulknerian. But *ish*? Who *is* there who's an *ish*?"

"Thomas Mannish?"

"Kafkaesque," Leonard said. "Pynchonesque! See, Pynchon's already an adjective. Gaddis. What would Gaddis be? Gaddisesque? Gaddisy?"

"You can't really do it with Gaddis," Madeleine said.

"Yeah," Leonard said. "Tough luck for Gaddis. Do you like him?"

"I read a little of *The Recognitions*," Madeleine said.

They turned up Planet Street, climbing the slope.

"Bellovian," Leonard said. "It's extra nice when they change the spelling slightly. Nabokovian already has the *v*. So does Chekhovian. The Russians have it made. Tolstoyan! That guy was an adjective waiting to happen."

"Don't forget Tolstoyanism," Madeleine said.

"My God!" Leonard said. "A noun! I've never even dreamed of being a noun."

"What would Bankheadian mean?"

Leonard thought for a second. "'Of or related to Leonard Bankhead (American, born 1959), characterized by excessive introspection or worry. Gloomy, depressive. See *basket case*.'"

Madeleine was laughing. Leonard stopped walking and took hold of her arm, looking at her seriously.

"I'm taking you to my place," he said.

"What?"

"All this time we've been walking? I've been leading you back to my place. This is how I do it, apparently. It's shameful. Shameful. I don't want it to be like that. Not with you. So I'm telling you."

"I figured we were going back to your place."

"You did?"

"I was going to call you on it. When we got closer."

"We're already close."

"I can't come up."

"*Please.*"

"No. Not tonight."

"*Hannaesque*," Leonard said. "Stubborn. Given to ironclad positions."

"*Hannarian*," Madeleine said. "Dangerous. Not to be messed with."

"I stand warned."

They stood looking at each other on cold, dark Planet Street. Leonard took his hands out of his pockets to tuck his long hair behind his ears.

"Maybe I'll come up just for a minute," Madeleine said.

"Special Days"
fête / *festivity*
The amorous subject experiences every meeting
with the loved being as a festival.

1. The Festivity is what is waited for, what is expected. What I expect of the promised presence is an unheard-of totality of pleasures, a banquet; I rejoice like the child laughing at the sight of

the mother whose mere presence heralds and signifies a pleni-
tude of satisfactions: I am about to have before me, and for
myself, the "source of all good things."

"I am living through days as happy as those God keeps for his
chosen people; and whatever becomes of me, I can never say that
I have not tasted the purest joys of life."

It was debatable whether or not Madeleine had fallen in love with Leonard the first moment she'd seen him. She hadn't even known him then,
and so what she'd felt was only sexual attraction, not love. Even after
they'd gone out for coffee, she couldn't say that what she was feeling was
anything more than infatuation. But ever since the night when they went
back to Leonard's place after watching *Amarcord* and started fooling
around, when Madeleine found that instead of being turned off by
physical stuff, the way she often was with boys, instead of putting up
with that or trying to overlook it, she'd spent the entire night worrying
that *she* was turning Leonard off, worrying that her body wasn't good
enough, or that her breath was bad from the Caesar salad she'd unwisely
ordered at dinner; worrying, too, about having suggested they order martinis because of the way Leonard had sarcastically said, "Sure. Martinis.
We can pretend we're Salinger characters"; after having had, as a consequence of all this anxiety, pretty much no sexual pleasure, despite the
perfectly respectable session they'd put together; and after Leonard
(like every guy) had immediately fallen asleep, leaving her to lie awake
stroking his head and vaguely hoping she didn't get a urinary tract infection, Madeleine asked herself if the fact that she'd just spent the
whole night worrying wasn't, in fact, a surefire sign that she was falling
in love. And certainly after they'd spent the next three days at Leonard's
place having sex and eating pizza, after she'd relaxed enough to be able
to come at least once in a while and finally to stop worrying so much
about having an orgasm because her hunger for Leonard was in some
way satisfied by his satisfaction, after she'd allowed herself to sit naked
on his gross couch and to walk to the bathroom knowing he was staring
at her (imperfect) ass, to root for food in his disgusting refrigerator, to
read the brilliant half-page of philosophy paper sticking up out of his
typewriter, and to hear him pee with taurine force into the toilet bowl,

certainly, by the end of those three days, Madeleine knew she was in love.

But that didn't mean she had to tell anyone. Especially Leonard.

Leonard Bankhead had a studio apartment on the third floor of a low-rent student building. The halls were full of bikes and junk mail. Stickers decorated the other tenants' doors: a fluorescent marijuana leaf, a silk-screen Blondie. Leonard's door, however, was as blank as the apartment inside. In the middle of the room, a twin mattress lay beside a plastic milk crate supporting a reading lamp. There was no desk, no bookcase, not even a table, only the nasty couch, with a typewriter on another milk crate in front of it. There was nothing on the walls but bits of masking tape and, in one corner, a small portrait of Leonard, done in pencil. The drawing showed Leonard as George Washington, wearing a tricorne hat and sheltering under a blanket at Valley Forge. The caption read: "You go. I like it here."

Madeleine thought the handwriting looked feminine.

A ficus tree endured in the corner. Leonard moved it into the sun whenever he remembered to. Madeleine, taking pity on the tree, began to water it, until she caught Leonard looking at her one day, his eyes narrowed with suspicion.

"What?" she said.

"Nothing."

"Come on. What?"

"You're watering my tree."

"The soil's dry."

"You're taking care of my tree."

She stopped doing it after that.

There was a tiny kitchen where Leonard brewed and reheated the gallon of coffee he drank every day. A big greasy wok sat on the stove. The most Leonard did in the way of preparing a meal, however, was to pour Grape Nuts into the wok. With raisins. Raisins satisfied his fruit requirement.

The apartment had a message. The message said: I am an orphan. Abby and Olivia asked Madeleine what she and Leonard did together and she never had an answer. They didn't *do* anything. She came to his apartment and they lay down on the mattress and Leonard asked her how she was doing, really wanting to know. What did they do? She talked; he listened; then he talked and she listened. She'd never met anyone, and certainly not a guy, who was so receptive, who took everything in. She guessed that Leonard's shrink-like manner came from years of seeing shrinks himself, and though another of her rules was to never date guys who went to shrinks, Madeleine began to reconsider this prohibition. Back home, she and her sister had a phrase for serious emotional talks. They called it "having a heavy." If a boy approached during one, the girls would look up and give warning: "We're having a heavy." And the boy would retreat. Until it was over. Until the heavy had passed.

Going out with Leonard was like having a heavy all the time. Whenever she was with him, Leonard gave her his full attention. He didn't stare into her eyes or smother her the way Billy had, but he made it clear he was available. He offered little advice. Only listened, and murmured, reassuringly.

People often fell in love with their shrinks, didn't they? That was called transference and was to be avoided. But what if you were already sleeping with your shrink? What if your shrink's couch was already a bed?

And plus it wasn't all heavy, the heavies. Leonard was funny. He told hilarious stories in a deadpan voice. His head sank into his shoulders, his eyes filled with rue, as his sentences drawled on. "Did I ever tell you I play an instrument? The summer my parents got divorced, they sent me to live with my grandparents in Buffalo. The people next door were Latvian, the Bruverises. And they both played the kokle. Do you know what a kokle is? It's sort of like a zither, but Latvian.

"Anyway, I used to hear Mr. and Mrs. Bruveris playing their kokles over in the next yard. It was an amazing sound. Sort of wild and over-stimulated on the one hand, but melancholy on the other. The kokle is the manic-depressive of the string family. Anyway, I was bored to death that summer. I was sixteen. Six foot one. One hundred and thirty-eight pounds. A major reefer smoker. I used to get high in my bedroom and blow the smoke out the window, and then I'd go out to the porch and listen to the Bruverises playing next door. Sometimes other people came over. Other kokle players. They set up lawn chairs in the backyard and they'd all sit there playing together. It was an orchestra! A kokle orchestra. Then one day they saw me watching and invited me over. They gave me potato salad and a grape Popsicle and I asked Mr. Bruveris how you played a kokle and he started giving me lessons. I used to go over there every day. They had an old kokle they let me borrow. I used to practice five, six hours a day. I was into it.

"At the end of that summer, when I had to leave, the Bruverises gave me the kokle. To keep. I took it on the plane with me. I got a separate seat for it, like I was Rostropovich. My father had moved out of the house by then. So it was just me, my sister, and my mother. And I kept on practicing. I got good enough that I joined this band. We used to play at ethnic festivals and Orthodox weddings. We had these traditional costumes, embroidered vests, puffy sleeves, knee-high boots. Me and all the adults. Most of them were Latvian, some Russians, too. Our big number was 'Otchi Tchornyia.' That's the only thing that saved me in high school. The kokle."

"Do you still play?"

"Hell no. Are you kidding? The kokle?"

Listening to Leonard, Madeleine felt impoverished by her happy childhood. She never wondered why she acted the way she did, or what effect her parents had had on her personality. Being fortunate had dulled her powers of observation. Whereas Leonard noticed every little thing. For instance, they spent a weekend on Cape Cod (partly to visit Pilgrim Lake Laboratory, where Leonard was applying for a research fellowship), and as they were driving back, Leonard said, "What do you do? Just hold it?"

"What?"

"You just hold it. For two days. Until you get back home."

As his meaning seeped in, she said, "I can't believe you!"

"You have never, ever, taken a dump in my presence."

"In your presence?"

"When I am present. Or nearby."

"What's wrong with that?"

"What's wrong with it? Nothing. If you're talking about I-sleep-over-and-go-off-to-class-the-next-morning and then you go and take a dump, that's understandable. But when we spend two, almost three days together, eating surf and turf, and you do not take a dump the entire time, I can only conclude that you are more than a little anal."

"So what? It's embarrassing!" Madeleine said. "O.K.? I find it embarrassing."

Leonard stared at her without expression and said, "Do you mind when I take a dump?"

"Do we have to talk about this? It's sort of gross."

"I think we do need to talk about it. Because you're obviously not very relaxed around me, and I am—or thought I was—your boyfriend, and that means—or should mean—that I'm the person you're most relaxed around. Leonard equals maximum relaxation."

Guys weren't supposed to be the talkers. Guys weren't supposed to get you to open up. But this guy was; this guy did. He'd said he was her "boyfriend," too. He'd made it official.

"I'll try to be more relaxed," Madeleine said, "if it'll make you happy. But in terms of—excretion—don't get your hopes up."

"This isn't for me," Leonard said. "This is for Mr. Lower Intestine. This is for Mr. Duodenum."

Even though this kind of amateur therapy didn't exactly work (after that last conversation, for instance, Madeleine had more, not less, trouble going Number 2 if Leonard was within a mile), it affected Madeleine deeply. Leonard was examining her closely. She felt handled in the right way, like something precious or immensely fascinating. It made her happy to think about how much he thought about her.

By the end of April, Madeleine and Leonard had gotten into a routine of spending every night together. On weeknights, after Madeleine finished studying, she headed over to the biology lab, where she'd find Leonard staring at slides with two Chinese grad students. After she finally got Leonard to leave the lab, Madeleine then had to cajole him into sleeping at her place. At first, Leonard had liked staying at the Narragansett. He liked the ornate moldings and the view from her bedroom. He charmed Olivia and Abby by making pancakes on Sunday mornings. But soon Leonard began to complain that they *always* stayed at Madeleine's place and that he *never* got to wake up in his own bed. Staying at Leonard's place, however, required Madeleine to bring a fresh set of clothes each night, and since he didn't like her to leave clothes at his place (and, to be honest, she didn't like to, either, because whatever she left picked up a fusty smell), Madeleine had to carry her dirty clothes around to classes all day. She preferred sleeping at her own apartment, where she could use her own shampoo, conditioner, and loofah, and where it was "clean-sheet day" every Wednesday. Leonard never changed his sheets. They were a disturbing gray color. Dust balls clung to the edges of the mattress. One morning, Madeleine was horrified to see a calligraphic smear of blood that had leaked from her three weeks earlier, a stain she'd attacked with a kitchen sponge while Leonard was sleeping.

"You never wash your sheets!" she complained.

"I wash them," Leonard said evenly.

"How often?"

"When they get dirty."

"They're always dirty."

"Not everyone can drop off their laundry at the cleaners every week. Not everybody grew up with 'clean-sheet day.'"

"You don't have to drop them off," Madeleine said, undeterred. "You've got a washer in the basement."

"I use the washer," Leonard said. "Just not every Wednesday. I don't equate dirt with death and decay."

"Oh, and I do? I'm obsessed with death because I wash my sheets?"

"People's attitudes to cleanliness have a lot to do with their fear of death."

"This isn't about death, Leonard. This is about crumbs in the bed. This is about the fact that your pillow smells like a liverwurst sandwich."

"Wrong."

"It does!"

"Wrong."

"Smell it, Leonard!"

"It's salami. I don't like liverwurst."

To a certain extent, this kind of arguing was fun. But then came nights when Madeleine forgot to pack a change of clothes and Leonard accused her of doing this on purpose in order to force him to sleep at her place. Next, more worryingly, came nights when Leonard said he was going home to study and would see her tomorrow. He began pulling all-nighters. One of his philosophy professors offered Leonard the use of his cabin in the Berkshires and, for an entire rainy weekend, Leonard went there, alone, to write a paper on Fichte, returning with a typescript 123 pages long and wearing a bright orange hunter's vest. The vest became his favorite item of clothing. He wore it all the time.

He started finishing Madeleine's sentences. As if her mind was too slow. As if he couldn't wait for her to gather her thoughts. He riffed on the things she said, going off on strange tangents, making puns. Whenever she told him he needed to get some sleep, he got angry and didn't call her for days. And it was during this period that Madeleine fully understood how the lover's discourse was of an extreme solitude. The solitude was extreme because it wasn't physical. It was extreme because you felt it while in the company of the person you loved. It was extreme because it was in your head, that most solitary of places.

The more Leonard pulled away, the more anxious Madeleine became. The more desperate she became, the more Leonard pulled away. She told herself to act cool. She went to the library to work on her marriage-plot thesis, but the sex-fantasy atmosphere—the reading-room eye contact, the beckoning stacks—made her desperate to see Leonard. And so against her will her feet began leading her back across campus through the darkness to the biology department. Up to the last moment, Madeleine had the crazy hope that this expression of weakness might in fact be strength. It was a brilliant strategy because it lacked all strategy. It involved no games, only sincerity. Seeing such sincerity, how could Leonard fail to respond? She was almost happy as she came up behind the lab table and tapped Leonard on the shoulder, and her happiness lasted until he turned around with a look not of love but of annoyance.

It didn't help that it was spring. Every day, people seemed more and more unclothed. The magnolia trees, budding on the green, looked positively enflamed. They sent out a perfume that drifted through the windows of Semiotics 211. The magnolia trees hadn't read Roland Barthes. They didn't think love was a mental state; the magnolias insisted it was natural, perennial.

On a beautiful warm May day, Madeleine showered, shaved her legs with extra care, and put on her first spring dress: an apple-green babydoll dress with a bib collar and a high hem. With this, she wore Buster Browns, cream and rust, and went sockless. Her bare legs, toned from a winter of squash-playing, were pale but smooth. She kept her glasses on, left her hair loose, and walked over to Leonard's apartment on Planet Street. On the way, she stopped at a market to buy a hunk of cheese, some Stoned Wheat Thins, and a bottle of Valpolicella. Coming down the hill from Benefit toward South Main, she felt the warm breeze between her thighs. The front door of Leonard's building was propped open with a brick, so she went up to his apartment and knocked. Leonard opened the door. He looked like he'd been napping.

"Niiiiice dress," he said.

They never made it to the park. They picnicked on each other. As Leonard pulled her toward the mattress, Madeleine dropped her packages, hoping the wine bottle didn't break. She slipped her dress over her head. Soon they were naked, raiding, it felt like, a huge basket of goodies. Madeleine lay on her stomach, her side, her back, nibbling all the treats, the nice-smelling fruit candies, the meaty drumsticks, as well as more sophisticated offerings, the biscotti flavored with anise, the wrinkly truffles, the salty spoonfuls of olive tapenade. She'd never been so busy in her life. At the same time, she felt strangely displaced, not quite her usual tidy ego but merged with Leonard into a great big protoplasmic, ecstatic thing. She thought she'd been in love before. She *knew* she'd had sex before. But all those torrid adolescent gropings, all those awkward backseat romps, the meaningful, performative summer nights with her high school boyfriend Jim McManus, even the tender sessions with Billy where he insisted they look into each other's eyes as they came—none of that prepared her for the wallop, the all-consuming pleasure, of this.

Leonard was kissing her. When she could bear no more, Madeleine grabbed him savagely by his ears. She pulled Leonard's head away and held it still to show him the evidence of how she felt (she was crying now). In a hoarse voice edged with something else, a sense of peril, Madeleine said, "I love you."

Leonard stared back at her. His eyebrows twitched. Suddenly, he rolled sideways off the mattress. He stood up and walked, naked, across the room. Crouching, he reached into her bag and pulled out *A Lover's Discourse*, from the pocket where she always kept it. He flipped the pages until he found the one he wanted. Then he returned to the bed and handed the book to her.

I Love You
je-t'aime / I-love-you

As she read these words, Madeleine was flooded with happiness. She glanced up at Leonard, smiling. With his finger he motioned for her to keep going. *The figure refers not to the declaration of love, to the avowal, but to the repeated utterance of the love cry.* Suddenly Madeleine's happiness diminished, usurped by the feeling of peril. She wished she weren't naked. She narrowed her shoulders and covered herself with the bedsheet as she obediently read on.

Once the first avowal has been made, "I love you" has no meaning whatever . . .

Leonard, squatting, had a smirk on his face.

It was then that Madeleine threw the book at his head.

•

Beyond the bay window of Carr House, the graduation traffic was now steady. Roomy parental vehicles (Cadillacs and S-Class Mercedeses, along with the occasional Chrysler New Yorker or Pontiac Bonneville) were making their way from the downtown hotels up College Hill for the ceremony. At the wheel of each car was a father, solid-looking and determined but driving a bit tentatively owing to Providence's many one-way streets. In the passenger seats sat mothers, released from domestic duties nowhere else but here, in the husband-chauffered family car, and therefore free to stare out at the pretty college-town scenery. The cars carried entire families, siblings mostly, but here and there a grandparent picked up in Old Saybrook or Hartford and brought along to see Tim or Alice or Prakrti or Heejin collect a hard-won sheepskin. There were city taxis, too, and livery cabs spewing blue exhaust, and little scarab-like rental cars scurrying between lanes as though to avoid being squashed. As the traffic crossed the Providence River and began to climb Waterman Street, some drivers tooted their horns upon seeing the huge Brown banner above the entrance of First Baptist Church. Everyone had been hoping for beautiful weather for graduation. But, as far as Mitchell was concerned, the gray skies and unseasonably cool temperatures were fine with him. He was glad Campus Dance had gotten rained out. He was glad the sun wasn't shining. The sense of bad luck that hung over everything accorded perfectly with his mood.

It was never much fun to be called a jerk. It was worse to be called a jerk by a girl you particularly liked, and it was especially painful when the girl happened to be the person you secretly wanted to marry.

After Madeleine had stormed out of the café, Mitchell had remained at the table, paralyzed with regret. They'd made up for all of twenty minutes. He was leaving Providence that night and, in a few months, the country. There was no telling when or if he would ever see her again.

Across the street, the bells began to chime nine o'clock. Mitchell had to get going. The commencement march started in forty-five minutes. His cap and gown were back at his apartment, where Larry was waiting for him. Instead of getting up, however, Mitchell moved his chair closer to the window. He pressed his nose nearly to the glass, taking his last look at College Hill, while silently repeating the following words:

Lord Jesus Christ, have mercy on me, a sinner.
Lord Jesus Christ, have mercy on me, a sinner.
Lord Jesus Christ, have mercy on me, a sinner.
Lord Jesus Christ, have mercy on me, a sinner.
Lord Jesus Christ, have mercy on me, a sinner.
Lord Jesus Christ, have mercy on me, a sinner.
Lord Jesus Christ, have mercy on me, a sinner.
Lord Jesus Christ, have mercy on me, a sinner.
Lord Jesus Christ, have mercy on me, a sinner.
Lord Jesus Christ, have mercy on me, a sinner.
Lord Jesus Christ, have mercy on me, a sinner.
Lord Jesus Christ, have mercy on me, a sinner.
Lord Jesus Christ, have mercy on me, a sinner.
Lord Jesus Christ, have mercy on me, a sinner.
Lord Jesus Christ, have mercy on me, a sinner.
Lord Jesus Christ, have mercy on me, a sinner.
Lord Jesus Christ, have mercy on me, a sinner.
Lord Jesus Christ, have mercy on me, a sinner.
Lord Jesus Christ, have mercy on me, a sinner.
Lord Jesus Christ, have mercy on me, a sinner.
Lord Jesus Christ, have mercy on me, a sinner.

Mitchell had been reciting the Jesus Prayer for the past two weeks. He did this not only because it was the prayer Franny Glass repeated to herself in *Franny and Zooey* (though this was certainly a recommendation). Mitchell approved of Franny's religious desperation, her withdrawal from life, and her disdain for "section men." He found her book-length nervous breakdown, during which she never once moved from the couch, not only thrillingly dramatic but cathartic in a way Dostoyevsky was *supposed* to be but wasn't, for him. (Tolstoy was a different matter.) Still, even though Mitchell was undergoing a similar crisis of meaning, it hadn't been until he'd come across the Jesus Prayer in a book called *The Orthodox Church* that he'd decided to give it a try. The Jesus Prayer, it turned out, belonged to the religious tradition into which Mitchell had been obscurely baptized twenty-two years earlier. For this reason he felt entitled to say it. And so he'd been doing just that, while walking around campus, or during Quaker Meeting at the Meeting House near Moses Brown, or at moments like this when the inner tranquillity he'd been struggling to attain began to fray, to falter.

Mitchell liked the chant-like quality of the prayer. Franny said you didn't even have to think about what you were saying; you just kept repeating the prayer until your heart took over and started repeating it for you. This was important because, whenever Mitchell stopped to think about the words of the Jesus Prayer, he didn't much like them. "Lord Jesus" was a difficult opener. It had a Bible Belt ring. Likewise, asking for "mercy" felt lowly and serf-like. Having made it through "Lord Jesus Christ, have mercy on me," however, Mitchell was confronted with the final stumbling block of "a sinner." And this was hard indeed. The gospels, which Mitchell didn't take literally, said you had to die to be born again. The mystics, whom he took as literally as their metaphorical language allowed, said the self had to be subsumed in the Godhead. Mitchell liked the idea of being subsumed in the Godhead. But it was hard to kill your self off when you liked so many things about it.

He recited the prayer for another minute, until he felt calmer. Then he got up and went out of the café. Across the street, the side doors of the church were open now. The organist was warming up, the music drifting out over the grass. Mitchell looked down the hill in the direction that Madeleine had disappeared. Seeing no sign of her, he started down Benefit on the way back to his apartment.

Mitchell's relationship with Madeleine Hanna—his long, aspirational, sporadically promising yet frustrating relationship—had begun at a toga party during freshman orientation. It was the kind of thing he instinctively hated: a keg party based on a Hollywood movie, a capitulation to the mainstream. Mitchell hadn't come to college to act like John Belushi. He hadn't even seen *Animal House*. (He was an Altman fan.) The alternative, however, would have been to sit in his room alone, and so finally, in a spirit of refusal that didn't include boycotting the party outright, he'd attended in his regular clothes. As soon as he arrived in the basement recreation room, he knew he'd made a mistake. He'd thought that not wearing a toga would make him seem too cool for such jejune festivities, but as he stood in the corner, drinking a plastic cup of foamy beer, Mitchell felt just as much like a misfit as he always did at parties full of popular people.

It was at this point that he noticed Madeleine. She was in the middle of the floor, dancing with a guy whom Mitchell recognized as an RA. Unlike most girls at the party, who looked dumpy in their togas, Madeleine had tied a cord around her waist, fitting her sheet to her body. Her hair was piled on top of her head, Roman-style, and her back was alluringly bare. Other than her exceptional looks, Mitchell noticed that she was an uninspired dancer—she held a beer and talked to the RA, barely paying attention to the beat—and that she kept leaving the party to go down the hall. The third time she was going out, Mitchell, emboldened by alcohol, went up to her and blurted out, "Where do you keep going?"

Madeleine wasn't startled. She was probably used to strange guys trying to talk to her. "I'll tell you, but you'll think I'm weird."

"No, I won't," Mitchell said.

"This is my dorm. I figured since everyone was going to the party, the washers would be free. So I decided to do my laundry at the same time."

Mitchell took a sip of foam without taking his eyes off her. "Do you need help?"

"No," Madeleine said, "I can handle it." As if she thought this sounded mean, she added, "You can come watch, if you want. Laundry's pretty exciting."

She started down the cinder-block hallway and he followed at her side.

"Why aren't you wearing a toga?" she asked him.

"Because it's dumb!" Mitchell said, nearly shouting. "It's so stupid!"

This wasn't the best move, but Madeleine didn't appear to take it personally. "I just came because I was bored," she said. "If this wasn't my dorm, I probably would have bagged."

In the laundry room, Madeleine began pulling her damp underthings out of a coin-operated washer. For Mitchell, this was titillating enough. But in the next second, something unforgettable occurred. As Madeleine reached into the washer, the knot at her shoulder loosened and the bedsheet fell away.

It was amazing how an image like that—of nothing, really, just a few inches of epidermis—could persist in the mind with undiminished clarity. The moment had lasted no more than three seconds. Mitchell hadn't been entirely sober at the time. And yet now, almost four years later, he could return to the moment at will (and it was surprising how often he wanted to do this), summoning all of its sensory details, the rumbling of the dryers, the pounding music next door, the linty smell of the dank basement laundry room. He remembered exactly where he'd been standing and how Madeleine had stooped forward, tucking a strand of hair behind her ear, as the sheet slipped and, for a few exhilarating moments, her pale, quiet, Episcopalian breast exposed itself to his sight.

She quickly covered herself, glancing up and smiling, possibly with embarrassment.

Later on, after their relationship became the intimate, unsatisfying thing it became, Madeleine always disputed Mitchell's memory of that night. She insisted that she hadn't worn a toga to the party and that even if she had—and she wasn't saying that she had—it had never slipped off. Neither on that night, nor on any of the thousand nights since, had he ever seen her naked breast.

Mitchell replied that he'd seen it that once and was very sorry it hadn't happened again.

In the weeks following the toga party, Mitchell began appearing at Madeleine's dorm unannounced. After his afternoon Latin class, he walked through the cool leaf-smelling air to Wayland Quad and, his head still throbbing with Vergil's dactylic hexameter, climbed the stairs to her third-floor room. Standing in Madeleine's doorway or, on luckier days, sitting at her desk, Mitchell did his best to be amusing. Madeleine's roommate, Jennifer, always gave him a look indicating that she knew exactly why he was there. Fortunately, she and Madeleine didn't seem to get along, and Jenny often left them alone. Madeleine always seemed happy he'd dropped by. She immediately started telling him about whatever she was reading, while he nodded, as though he could possibly pay attention to her thoughts on Ezra Pound or Ford Madox Ford while standing close enough to smell her shampooed hair. Sometimes Madeleine made him tea. Instead of going for an herbal infusion from Celestial Seasonings, with a quotation from Lao Tzu on the package, Madeleine was a Fortnum & Mason's drinker, her favorite blend Earl Grey. She didn't just dump a bag in a cup, either, but brewed loose leaves, using a strainer and a tea cozy. Jennifer had a poster of Vail over her bed, a skier waist-deep in powder. Madeleine's side of the room was more sophisticated. She'd hung up a set of framed Man Ray photographs. Her bedspread and cashmere sham were the same serious shade of charcoal gray as her V-neck sweaters. On top of her dresser lay exciting womanly objects: a monogrammed silver lipstick, a Filofax containing maps of the New York Subway and the London Underground. But there were also semiembarrassing items: a photograph of her family wearing color-coordinated clothing; a Lilly Pulitzer bathrobe; and a decrepit stuffed bunny named Foo Foo.

Mitchell was prepared, considering Madeleine's other attributes, to overlook these details.

Sometimes when he stopped by, he found other guys already there. A sandy-haired prepster wearing wingtips without socks, or a large-nosed Milanese in tight pants. On these occasions Jennifer acted even less hospitable. As for Madeleine, she was either so used to male attention that she didn't notice it anymore, or so guileless that she didn't suspect why three guys might park themselves in her room like the suitors of Penelope. She didn't appear to be sleeping with the other guys, as far as Mitchell could tell. This gave him hope.

Little by little, he went from sitting at Madeleine's desk to sitting on the windowsill near her bed, to lying on the floor in front of her bed while she stretched out above him. Occasionally, the thought that he'd already seen her breast—that he knew exactly what her areola looked like—was enough to give him a hard-on, and he had to turn over on his stomach. Still, on the few times when Madeleine went on anything resembling a date with Mitchell—to a student theater production or poetry reading—there was a tightness around her eyes, as though she was registering the downside, socially and romantically, of being seen with him. She was new at college, too, and finding her way. It was possible she didn't want to limit her options too soon.

A year went by like this. An entire blue-balled year. Mitchell stopped dropping by Madeleine's room. Gradually, they drifted into different circles. He didn't forget about her so much as decide that she was out of his league. Whenever he ran into her, she was so talkative and touched his arm so often that he began to get ideas again, but it wasn't until sophomore year that anything came close to happening. In November, a few weeks before Thanksgiving, Mitchell mentioned that he was planning to stay on campus over break rather than fly back to Detroit, and Madeleine surprised him by inviting him to celebrate the holiday with her family in Prettybrook.

They arranged to meet at the Amtrak station, on Wednesday at noon. When Mitchell got there, lugging a prewar suitcase with some dead person's fading gold initials on it, he found Madeleine waiting for him on the platform, wearing glasses. They were large tortoiseshell frames and, if it was possible, they made him like her even more. The lenses were badly scratched and the left temple was slightly bent. Otherwise, Madeleine was as well put together as always, or even more so, since she was on her way to see her parents.

"I didn't know you wore glasses," Mitchell said.

"My contacts were hurting my eyes this morning."

"I like them."

"I only wear them sometimes. My eyes aren't that bad."

As he stood on the platform, Mitchell wondered if Madeleine's wearing her glasses indicated that she felt comfortable around him, or if it meant that she didn't care about looking her best for him. Once they were on the train, amid the crowd of holiday travelers, it was impossible to tell either way. After they found two seats together, Madeleine took her glasses off, holding them in her lap. As the train rolled out of Providence, she put them on again to watch the passing scenery, but quickly snatched them off, shoving them into her bag. (This was the reason her glasses were in the shape they were in; she'd lost the case long ago.)

The trip took five hours. Mitchell wouldn't have minded if it had taken five days. It was thrilling to have Madeleine captive in the seat beside him. She'd brought volume one of Anthony Powell's *A Dance to the Music of Time* and, in what appeared to be a guilty traveling habit, a thick copy of *Vogue*. Mitchell stared out at the warehouses and body shops of Cranston before pulling out his *Finnegans Wake*.

"You're not reading that," Madeleine said.

"I am."

"No way!"

"It's about a river," Mitchell said. "In Ireland."

The train proceeded along the Rhode Island coast and into Connecticut. Sometimes the ocean appeared, or marshland, then just as suddenly they were passing along the ugly backside of a manufacturing town. In New Haven the train stopped to switch engines before proceeding to Grand Central. After taking the subway to Penn Station, Madeleine led Mitchell down to another set of tracks to catch the train for New Jersey. They arrived at Prettybrook just before eight at night.

The Hannas' house was a hundred-year-old Tudor, fronted by London plane trees and dying hemlocks. Inside, everything was tasteful and half falling apart. The Oriental carpets had stains. The brick-red kitchen linoleum was thirty years old. When Mitchell used the powder room, he saw that the toilet paper dispenser had been repaired with Scotch tape. So had the peeling wallpaper in the hallway. Mitchell had encountered shabby gentility before, but here was Wasp thrift in its purest form. The plaster ceilings sagged alarmingly. Vestigial burglar alarms sprouted from the walls. The knob-and-tube wiring sent flames out of the lighting sockets when you unplugged anything.

Mitchell was good with parents. Parents were his specialty. Within an hour of arriving Wednesday night, he had established himself as a favorite. He knew the lyrics to the Cole Porter songs Alton played on the "hi-fi." He allowed Alton to read excerpts from Kingsley Amis's *On Drink* aloud, and seemed to find them just as hilarious as Alton did. At dinner, Mitchell talked about Sandra Day O'Connor with Phyllida and about Abscam with Alton. To top it off, Mitchell put in a dazzling performance later that night at Scrabble.

"I didn't know *groszy* was a word," Phyllida said, greatly impressed.

"It's Polish currency. A hundred groszy are worth one zloty."

"Are all your new friends at college this worldly, Maddy?" Alton said.

When Mitchell glanced at Madeleine, she was smiling at him. And that was when it had happened. Madeleine was wearing a bathrobe. She had her glasses on. She was looking both homey and sexy, completely out of his league and, at the same time, within reach, by virtue of how well he seemed to fit into her family already, and what a perfect son-in-law he would make. For all of these reasons Mitchell suddenly thought, "I'm going to marry this girl!" The knowledge went through him like electricity, a feeling of destiny.

"Foreign words are disallowed," Madeleine said.

He spent Thanksgiving morning moving chairs for Phyllida, and drinking Bloody Marys and playing pool with Alton. The billiard table had braided leather pockets instead of a ball return. Lining up a shot, Alton said, "A few years ago, I noticed this table wasn't level. The man the company sent out said it was warped, probably from one of the kids' friends sitting on it. He wanted me to buy a whole new base. But I put a piece of wood under one leg. Problem solved."

Soon company arrived. A mellow-voiced cousin named Doats, wearing tartan pants, his wife, Dinky, a frosted blonde with late–de Kooning teeth, and their young children and fat setter, Nap.

Madeleine got down on her knees to greet Nap, ruffling his fur and hugging him.

"Nap's gotten so fat," she said.

"You know what I think it is?" Doats said. "It's because he's fixed. Nap's a eunuch. And eunuchs were always famously plump, weren't they?"

Madeleine's sister, Alwyn, and her husband, Blake Higgins, showed up around one. Alton fixed the cocktails while Mitchell made himself helpful by building a fire.

Thanksgiving dinner proceeded in a blur of wine refills and jesting toasts. After dinner, everyone repaired to the library, where Alton began serving port. The fire was dying, and Mitchell stepped outside to get more wood. By this time he was feeling no pain. He stared up at the starry night sky, through the branches of the white pines. He was in the middle of New Jersey but it might have been the Black Forest. Mitchell loved the house. He loved the whole big, genteel, boozy Hanna operation. Returning with firewood, he heard music playing. Madeleine was at the piano, while Alton sang along. The selection was something called "Til," a family favorite. Alton's voice was surprisingly good; he'd been in an a capella singing group at Yale. Madeleine was a little slow with the chord changes, plunking them out. Her glasses slid down her nose as she read the sheet music. She'd kicked off her shoes to press the pedals with bare feet.

Mitchell stayed through the weekend. On his last night in Prettybrook, as he was lying in his attic guest room, reading, he heard the hallway door open and feet begin climbing the stairs. Madeleine knocked softly on his door and came in.

She was dressed in a Lawrenceville T-shirt and nothing else. Her upper thighs, level with Mitchell's head as she entered, were a little fuller than he'd expected.

She sat on the edge of the bed.

When she asked what he was reading, Mitchell had to look to remember the title. He was wonderfully and fearfully aware of his nakedness beneath the thin bedsheet. He felt that Madeleine was aware of this, too. He thought about kissing her. For a moment he thought that Madeleine might kiss him. And then, because Madeleine didn't, because he was a houseguest and her parents were sleeping downstairs, because, in that glorious moment, Mitchell felt that the tide had turned and he had all the time in the world to make his move, he did nothing. Finally, Madeleine got up, looking vaguely disappointed. She descended the stairs and switched off the light.

After she was gone, Mitchell replayed the scene in his mind, seeking a different outcome. Worried about soiling the bedding, he headed for the bathroom, bumping into an old box spring, which fell over with a clatter. When all was quiet again, he continued to the bathroom. In the tiny attic sink, he shot his load, turning on the tap to rinse away the least curd of evidence.

The next morning, they took the train back to Providence, walked together up College Hill, hugged, and parted. A few days later, Mitchell stopped by Madeleine's room. She wasn't there. On her message board was a note from someone named Billy: "Tarkovsky screening 7:30 Sayles. Be there or be □." Mitchell left an unsigned quotation, a bit from the Gerty MacDowell section of *Ulysses*: "Then the Roman candle burst and it was like a sigh of O! and everyone cried O! O! in raptures and it gushed out of it a stream of rain gold hair threads . . ."

A week went by and he didn't hear from Madeleine. When he called he got no answer.

He went back to her dorm. Again she was out. On her message board someone had drawn an arrow pointing to his Joyce quotation along with the note "Who's the perv?"

Mitchell erased this. He wrote, "Maddy, give me a call. Mitchell." Then he erased this and wrote, "Permit a colloquy. M."

Back in his own room, Mitchell examined himself in the mirror. He turned sideways, trying to see his profile. He pretended to be talking to someone at a party to see what he was really like.

After another week passed without his hearing from Madeleine, Mitchell stopped calling or dropping by her room. He became fierce about his studies, spending heroic amounts of time ornamenting his English papers, or translating Vergil's extended metaphors about vineyards and women. When he finally did run into Madeleine again, she was just as friendly as always. For the rest of the year they continued to be close, going to poetry readings together and occasionally eating dinner in the Ratty, alone or with other people. When Madeleine's parents visited in the spring, she invited Mitchell to have dinner with them at the Bluepoint Grill. But he never went back to the house in Prettybrook, never built a fire in their hearth, or drank a G & T on the deck overlooking the garden. Little by little, Mitchell managed to forge his own social life at school and, though they continued to be friends, Madeleine drifted off into hers. He never forgot his premonition, however. One night the following October, almost a year from the time he'd gone to Prettybrook, Mitchell saw Madeleine crossing campus in the purple twilight. She was with a curly-headed blond guy named Billy Bainbridge, whom Mitchell knew from his freshman hall. Billy took women's studies courses and referred to himself as a feminist. Presently, Billy had one hand sensitively in the back pocket of Madeleine's jeans. She had her hand in the back pocket of his jeans. They were moving along like that, each cupping a handful of the other. In Madeleine's face was a stupidity Mitchell had never seen before. It was the stupidity of all normal people. It was the stupidity of the fortunate and beautiful, of everybody who got what they wanted in life and so remained unremarkable.

•

In Plato's Phaedrus, *the speeches of Lysias the Sophist and of the early Socrates (before the latter makes his recantation) rest on*

this principle: that the lover is intolerable (by his heaviness) to
the beloved.

In the weeks after breaking up with Leonard, Madeleine spent most of her time at the Narragansett, lying on her bed. She dragged herself to her final classes. She lost much of her appetite. At night, an invisible hand kept shaking her awake every few hours. Grief was physiological, a disturbance in the blood. Sometimes a whole minute would pass in nameless dread—the bedside clock ticking, the blue moonlight coating the window like glue—before she'd remember the brutal fact that had caused it.

She expected Leonard to call. She fantasized about him appearing at her front door, asking her to come back. When he didn't, she became desperate and dialed his number. The line was often busy. Leonard was functioning just fine without her. He was calling people, other girls, probably. Sometimes Madeleine listened to the busy signal so long she found herself trying to hear Leonard's voice beneath it, as if he was just on the other side of the noise. If she heard his phone ring, the thought that Leonard might answer it at any second made Madeleine exhilarated, but then she panicked and slammed down the receiver, always thinking that she heard his voice say "Hello" at the last moment. In between calls, she lay on her side, thinking about calling.

Love had made her intolerable. It had made her heavy. Sprawled on her bed, keeping her shoes from touching the sheets (Madeleine remained fastidious despite her misery), she reviewed all the things she'd done to drive Leonard away. She'd been too needy, crawling up into his lap like a little girl, wanting to be with him all the time. She'd lost track of her own priorities and had become a drag.

Only one thing remained from her relationship with Leonard: the book she'd thrown at his head. Before storming out of Leonard's apartment that day—and while he lay in lordly nakedness on the bed, calmly repeating her name with the suggestion that she was overreacting—Madeleine had noticed the book lying open on the floor like a bird that had knocked itself out against a windowpane. To pick it up would prove Leonard's point: that she had an unhealthy obsession with *A Lover's Discourse*; that, contrary to dispelling her fantasies about love, the book had served to reinforce those fantasies; and that, in evidence of all this, she wasn't only a sentimentalist but a lousy literary critic besides.

On the other hand, to leave *A Lover's Discourse* on the floor—where Leonard could later pick it up and inspect the passages she'd highlighted, as well as her marginal notes (including, on page 123, in a chapter titled "In the Loving Calm of Your Arms," a single, exclamatory "Leonard!")—wasn't possible. So, after gathering up her bag, Madeleine in one fluid motion had snatched up the Barthes as well, not daring to check if Leonard had noticed. Five seconds later she'd slammed the door behind her.

She was glad she'd taken the book. Now, in her morose condition, the elegant prose of Roland Barthes was her one consolation. Breaking up with Leonard hadn't lessened the relevance of *A Lover's Discourse* one bit. There were more chapters about heartbreak than happiness, in fact. One chapter was called "Dependency." Another, "Suicide." Still another, "In Praise of Tears." *The amorous subject has a particular propensity to cry . . . The slightest amorous emotion, whether of happiness or of disappointment, brings Werther to tears. Werther weeps often, very often, and in floods. Is it the lover in Werther who weeps, or is it the romantic?*

Good question. Since breaking up with Leonard, Madeleine had been crying more or less all the time. She cried herself to sleep at night. She cried in the morning, brushing her teeth. She tried very hard not to cry in front of her roommates and for the most part succeeded.

A Lover's Discourse was the perfect cure for lovesickness. It was a repair manual for the heart, its one tool the brain. If you used your head, if you became aware of how love was culturally constructed and began to see your symptoms as purely mental, if you recognized that being "in love" was only an idea, then you could liberate yourself from its tyranny. Madeleine knew all that. The problem was, it didn't work. She could read Barthes' deconstructions of love all day without feeling her love for Leonard diminish the teeniest little bit. The more of *A Lover's Discourse* she read, the more in love she felt. She recognized herself on every page. She identified with Barthes' shadowy "I." She didn't want to be liberated from her emotions but to have their importance confirmed. Here was a book addressed to lovers, a book about being in love that contained the word *love* in just about every sentence. And, oh, how she loved it!

In the world outside, the semester, and thus college itself, was quickly speeding toward its end. Her roommates, art history majors both, had already found entry-level positions in New York, Olivia at Sotheby's, Abby at a gallery in Soho. A startling number of her friends and acquaintances were doing campus interviews with investment banks. Others had gotten scholarships or fellowships or were moving to L.A. to work in television.

The most Madeleine could muster in the way of preparing for the future was to peel herself out of bed once a day to check her P.O. box. In April, she'd been too distracted by work and love to notice that the fifteenth came and went without a letter from Yale arriving. By the time she did notice, she was too depressed about her breakup to bear another rejection. For two weeks, Madeleine didn't even go to the post office. Finally, when she forced herself to go and empty her overstuffed mailbox, there was still no letter from Yale.

There was news, however, about her other applications. The ESL organization sent her a gushing acceptance letter ("Congratulations, Madeleine!") along with a teacher enrollment form and the name of the Chinese province, Shandong, where she would be teaching. There was also an information packet containing various bold-faced sentences that leapt out at her:

Sanitation facilities (showers, toilets, etc.) may take some getting used to, but the majority of our teachers come to enjoy "roughing it."

The Chinese diet is quite varied, especially as compared to American standards. Don't be surprised if, after a few months in your host village, you find yourself eating snake with pleasure!

She didn't return the enrollment form.

Two days later, she received a rejection letter through campus mail from the Melvin and Hetty Greenberg Foundation informing her that she would not be receiving the Greenberg fellowship to study Hebrew in Jerusalem.

Back at her apartment, Madeleine confronted the cluster of shipping boxes. A week before they'd broken up, Leonard had received positive word from Pilgrim Lake Laboratory. In what had seemed a significant gesture at the time, he'd suggested that they live together in the free apartment that came with his fellowship. If Madeleine got into Yale, she could come up on weekends; if she didn't, she could live at Pilgrim Lake over the winter, and reapply. In short order, Madeleine had canceled her other plans and had begun packing boxes of books and clothes to ship to the lab ahead of their arrival. Since Madeleine had been questioning the intensity of Leonard's feelings for her, his invitation to live together made her blissful, and this, in turn, had played a strong part in Madeleine's avowal of love a few days later. And now, as a cruel reminder of that disaster, the boxes were sitting in her room, going nowhere.

Madeleine ripped off the address labels and shoved the boxes into the corner.

Somehow, she turned in her honors thesis. She handed in her final paper for Semiotics 211 but failed to pick it up after the exam period to see Zipperstein's comments and her grade.

By the time graduation weekend rolled around, Madeleine was doing her best to ignore it. Abby and Olivia had tried to get her to go to Campus Dance, but the thunderstorms that rolled through town, bringing winds that blew over cocktail tables and ripped down the strings of colored lanterns, caused the festivities to be moved inside to some gym, and nobody they knew went. Needing to occupy their families, Abby and Olivia had persisted in going to the clambake with President Swearer on Saturday afternoon, but after a half hour they sent their parents back to their hotel. On Sunday, all three roommates skipped the Baccalaureate ceremony at First Baptist Church. By nine o'clock that night, Madeleine was in her bedroom, curled up with *A Lover's Discourse*, not reading it, just keeping it nearby.

It wasn't clean-sheet day. It hadn't been clean-sheet day for a long time.

There was a knock at her bedroom door.

"Just a sec." Madeleine's voice was raspy from crying. She had mucus in her throat. "Come in," she said.

The door opened to reveal Abby and Olivia, shoulder-to-shoulder, like a delegation.

Abby came quickly forward and snatched the Roland Barthes away.

"We're confiscating this," she said.

"Give it back."

"You're not reading that book," Olivia said. "You're wallowing in it."

"I just wrote a paper on it. I was checking something."

Abby held the book behind her and shook her head. "You can't just lie around moping. This weekend's been a total bummer. But there's a party tonight at Lollie and Pookie's and you have to come. Come on!"

Abby and Olivia thought it was the romantic in Madeleine who wept. They thought she was delusional, ridiculous. She would have felt the same, if it had been one of them, pining away. Heartbreak is funny to everyone but the heartbroken.

"Give me my book," she said.

"I'll give it back if you come to the party."

Madeleine understood why her roommates trivialized her feelings. They'd never been in love, not really. They didn't know what she was dealing with.

"We're graduating tomorrow!" Olivia pleaded. "This is our last night at college. You can't stay in your room!"

Madeleine looked away and rubbed her face. "What time is it?" she asked.

"Ten."

"I haven't showered."

"We'll wait."

"I don't have anything to wear."

"You can borrow a dress from me," Olivia said.

They stood there, obliging and pestering all at once.

"Give me the book," Madeleine said.

"Only if you come."

"O.K.!" Madeleine relented. "I'll come."

Reluctantly, Abby handed Madeleine the paperback.

Madeleine stared at the cover. "What if Leonard's there?" she asked.

"He won't be," Abby said.

"What if he is?"

Abby looked away and repeated, "Trust me. He won't."

Lollie and Pookie Ames lived in a ramshackle house on Lloyd Avenue. As Madeleine and her roommates approached along the sidewalk, under the dripping elms, they could hear throbbing bass and alcohol-loosened voices coming from inside. Candles flickered behind the steamed-up windows.

They stashed their umbrellas behind the bikes on the porch and entered the front door. Inside, the air was warm and moist, like a beer-scented rain forest. The flea-market furniture had been pushed against the walls so that people could dance. Jeff Trombley, who was DJ-ing, was using a flashlight to see the turntable, the beam spilling onto a poster of Sandino on the wall behind him.

"You guys go first," Madeleine said. "Tell me if you see Leonard."

Abby looked annoyed. "I told you, he won't be here."

"He might."

"Why would he be? He doesn't like people. Look, I'm sorry, but now that you're broken up, I have to say it. Leonard's not exactly normal. He's weird."

"He is not," Madeleine objected.

"Will you please just get over him? Will you at least *try*?"

Olivia lit a cigarette and said, "God, if I worried about running into old boyfriends, I couldn't go anywhere!"

"O.K., forget it," Madeleine said. "Let's go in."

"Finally!" Abby said. "Come on. Let's have fun tonight. It's our last night."

Despite the loud music, not many people were dancing. Tony Perotti, in a Plasmatics T-shirt, was pogoing, all alone, in the middle of the floor. Debbie Boonstock, Carrie Mox, and Stacy Henkel were dancing in a ring around Marc Wheeland. Wheeland was wearing a white T-shirt and baggy shorts. His calves were massive. So were his shoulders. As the three girls pranced in front of him, Wheeland stared at the floor, stomping around and, every so often (this was the dancing part), minimally lifting his muscle-bound arms.

"How long before Marc Wheeland takes off his shirt?" Abby said as they headed down the hall.

"Like two minutes," Olivia said.

The kitchen resembled something in a submarine movie, dark, narrow, with pipes snaking overhead and a wet floor. Madeleine stepped on bottle caps as she squeezed through the throng of people.

They attained the open space at the kitchen's far end only to realize it was unoccupied due to the presence of a reeking litter box.

"Gross!" Olivia said.

"Don't they ever clean that thing?" Abby said.

A guy in a baseball hat was standing proprietarily in front of the refrigerator. When Abby opened it, he informed them, "The Grolsch are mine."

"Excuse me?"

"Don't take the Grolsch. They're mine."

"I thought this was a party," Abby said.

"Yeah, it is," the guy said. "But everyone always brings domestic beer. I brought imported."

Olivia rose to full Scandinavian height to cast him a withering look. "As if we even wanted beer," she said.

She bent to look into the refrigerator herself and said with distaste, "God, it's *all* beer."

Standing up again, she looked commandingly around the room until she saw Pookie Ames, and called to her over the noise.

Pookie, who normally had an afghan scarf wrapped around her head, tonight had on a black velvet dress and diamond earrings, in which she looked absolutely at home. "Pookie, save us," Olivia said. "We can't drink beer."

"Honey," Pookie said, "there's Veuve Clicquot!"

"Where?"

"In the crisper."

"Fabulous!" Olivia pulled out the tray and found the bottle. "Now we can celebrate!"

Madeleine wasn't much of a drinker. But her situation tonight called for traditional remedies. She took a plastic glass from the stack and allowed Olivia to fill it.

"Enjoy your Grolsch," Olivia said to the guy.

To Abby and Madeleine, she said, "I'll bring the bottle," and marched away.

Carefully, they shepherded their full champagne glasses back through the throng.

In the living room, Abby proposed a toast. "You guys? To a great year living together!"

The plastic glasses didn't clink, only flexed.

By this time, Madeleine was fairly sure that Leonard wasn't at the party. The thought that he was somewhere else, however, at another graduation party, opened a hole in her chest. She wasn't sure if vital fluids were leaking out or poisons being pumped in.

On the near wall a Halloween skeleton was kneeling before a life-size cutout of Ronald Reagan, as if going down on him. Near the president's beaming face someone had scrawled: "I've got a stiffy!"

Just then the dance floor shifted, kaleidoscopically, to reveal Lollie Ames and Jenny Crispin dancing. They were putting on a show, grinding their pelvises together and feeling each other up, while also laughing and passing a joint.

Nearby, Marc Wheeland, now officially "too hot," pulled off his T-shirt and tucked it into his back pocket. Bare-chested, he kept on dancing, doing the beefcake, the bench press, the love muscle. The girls around him danced closer.

Since breaking up with Leonard, Madeleine had been beset, on an almost hourly basis, by the most overpowering sexual urges. She wanted it all the time. But Wheeland's gleaming pectorals did nothing for her. Her desires were nontransferable. They had Leonard's name on them.

She'd been doing her best not to seem completely pathetic. Unfortunately, her insides were beginning to betray her. Her eyes were welling. The sucking hole at her center grew larger. Quickly, she climbed the front stairs, finding the bathroom and locking the door behind her.

For the next five minutes, Madeleine cried over the sink while the music downstairs shook the walls. The bath towels hanging on the door didn't look clean, so she dabbed at her eyes with wadded toilet paper.

When she'd stopped crying, Madeleine composed herself before the mirror. Her skin looked blotchy. Her breasts, of which she was normally proud, had withdrawn into themselves, as if depressed. Madeleine knew that this self-appraisal might not be accurate. A bruised ego reflected its own image. The possibility that she didn't look quite so much like shit as she appeared to was the only thing that got her to unlock the door and come out of the bathroom.

In a bedroom at the end of the hall, two girls with ponytails and pearl necklaces were lying across the bed. They paid no attention as Madeleine entered.

"I thought you hated me," the first girl said to the other. "Ever since Bologna I thought you hated me."

"I didn't say I didn't hate you," the second girl said.

The bookshelves held the usual Kafka, the obligatory Borges, the point-scoring Musil. Just beyond, a small balcony beckoned. Madeleine walked out.

The rain had paused. There was no moonlight, only the glow of street-lights, sickly purple. A broken kitchen chair stood before an upside-down trash can being used as a table. On the trash can lay an ashtray and a rain-soaked *Vanity Fair*. Vines hung shaggily down from an unseen trellis.

Madeleine leaned over the rickety railing, looking at the lawn.

It must have been the lover in her who wept, not the romantic. She had no desire to jump. She wasn't like Werther. Besides, the drop was only fifteen feet.

"Beware." A voice suddenly spoke behind her. "You are not alone."

She turned. Leaning against the house, half obscured in the vines, was Thurston Meems.

"Did I scare you?" he asked.

Madeleine considered a moment. "You're not exactly scary," she said.

Thurston accepted this good-naturedly. "Right, more like scared. Actually, I'm hiding."

Thurston's eyebrows were growing in, framing his wide eyes. He was leaning on the heels of his high-tops, his hands in his pockets.

"Do you usually come to parties to hide?" Madeleine asked.

"Parties bring my misanthropy into focus," Thurston said. "Why are *you* out here?"

"Same reason," Madeleine said, and surprised herself by laughing.

To give them room, Thurston moved the trash can aside. He picked up the book, brought it close to his face to see what it was, and violently flung it off the balcony. It made a thud in the damp grass.

"I guess you don't like *Vanity Fair*," Madeleine said.

"'Vanity of vanities, saith the prophet,'" Thurston said, "and all that shit."

A car stopped in the street, then backed up. People carrying six-packs got out and approached the house.

"More revelers," Thurston said, staring down at them.

A silence ensued. Finally, Madeleine said, "So what did you do your term paper on? Derrida?"

"*Naturellement*," Thurston said. "What about you?"

"Barthes."

"Which book?"

"*A Lover's Discourse.*"

Thurston squeezed his eyes shut, nodding with pleasure. "That's a great book."

"You like it?" Madeleine said.

"The thing about that book," Thurston said, "is that, ostensibly, it's a deconstruction of love. It's supposed to cast a cold eye on the whole romantic enterprise, right? But it reads like a diary."

"That's what my paper's on!" Madeleine cried. "I deconstructed Barthes' deconstruction of love."

Thurston kept nodding. "I'd like to read it."

"You would?" Madeleine's voice rose half an octave. She cleared her throat to bring it back down. "I don't know if it's any good. But maybe."

"Zipperstein's sort of brain-dead, don't you think?" Thurston said.

"I thought you liked him."

"Me? No. I like semiotics, but—"

"He never says anything!"

"I know," Thurston agreed. "He's inscrutable. He's like Harpo Marx without the horn."

Madeleine found herself, unexpectedly, liking Thurston. When he asked if she wanted to get a drink, she said yes. They returned to the kitchen, which was even louder and more crowded than before. The guy with the baseball cap hadn't moved.

"You're going to guard your beer all night?" Madeleine asked him.

"Whatever's necessary," the guy said.

"Don't take any of this guy's beer," Madeleine said to Thurston. "He's very particular about his beer."

Thurston had already opened the refrigerator and was reaching inside, his leather biker's jacket hanging open. "Which beer is yours?" he asked the guy.

"The Grolsch," the guy said.

"Ah, a Grolsch man, eh?" Thurston said, moving bottles around. "Lover of the old-school, Teutonic, rubber-stopper and ceramic-cap thingy. I understand your preference for that. The thing is, I wonder if the Grolsch family ever intended for those rubber-stoppered bottles to cross the ocean. You know what I mean? I've had more than a few Grolsch go skunky on me. I wouldn't drink it if you paid me." Thurston now held up two cans of Narragansett. "These only had to travel about a mile and a half."

"Narragansett tastes like piss," the guy said.

"Well, you'd be the one to know."

And with that, Thurston took Madeleine away. He led her out of the kitchen and back through the front hall, motioning for her to follow him outside. When they reached the porch he opened his biker jacket to reveal two bottles of Grolsch stashed inside.

"We better make a getaway," Thurston said.

They drank the beers while walking along Thayer Street, passing bars full of other graduating seniors. When the beers were gone they went to the Grad Center bar, and from the Grad Center bar, they went downtown, via taxi, to an old man's bar Thurston liked. The bar had a boxing theme, black-and-white photos of Marciano and Cassius Clay on the walls, a pair of autographed Everlast gloves in a dusty case. For a while they drank vodka with healthful juices. Next Thurston got nostalgic about something called a sidecar, which he used to have on skiing trips with his father. He pulled Madeleine by the hand down the street and across the plaza into the Biltmore Hotel. There the bartender didn't know how to make a sidecar. Thurston had to instruct him, grandly announcing, "The sidecar is the perfect winter drink. Brandy to warm the innards, and citrus to ward off colds."

"It isn't winter," Madeleine said.

"Let's pretend it is."

Sometime later, as Thurston and Madeleine were swaying down the sidewalk arm in arm, she felt him lurch sideways into yet another bar.

"A cleansing beer is in order," he said.

Over the next few minutes Thurston explained his theory—but it wasn't a theory, it was the wisdom of experience, tested and corroborated by Thurston and his Andover roommate, who, after downing vast quantities of "spirits," bourbon, mostly, but scotch, too, gin, vodka, Southern Comfort, whatever they could get their hands on, basically, whatever they could filch from "the parental cellars," Blue Nun, for a period, during the "Winter of Liebfraumilch," when they had the run of a friend's ski chalet in Stowe, and Pernod, once, because they'd heard it was the closest thing available to absinthe and they wanted to be writers and needed absinthe in the worst way— But he was getting off the point. He was allowing his fondness for digressions to run away with him. And so Thurston, hopping up on a bar stool and signaling to the bartender, explained that in each of these cases, with each and every one of these "intoxicants," a beer or two, afterward, always lessened the severity of the murderous hangover that inevitably followed.

"A cleansing beer," he said again. "That's what we need."

Being with Thurston wasn't at all like being with Leonard. Being with Thurston was like being with her family. It was like being with Alton, so punctilious about his snifters, superstitious about drinking grape after grain.

Whenever Leonard talked about his parents' drinking, it was all about how alcoholism was a disease. But Phyllida and Alton drank a lot and seemed relatively undamaged and responsible.

"O.K.," Madeleine agreed. "A cleansing beer."

And wouldn't that have been nice? The belief that a cold Budweiser— they had the longnecks in here; Thurston had fallen into this bar for a reason—could rinse away the effects of an entire night's binge had a certain magic to it. Given that magic, why stop at just one? It was the after-hours time of the night when it became incumbent on two people to get change from the bartender and pore over jukebox selections, their heads touching as they read the song titles. It was that timeless part of the night when it became absolutely necessary to play "Mack the Knife" and "I Heard It Through the Grapevine" and "Smoke on the Water" and to dance together among the tables in the otherwise empty bar. A cleansing beer might drown out thoughts of Leonard and anesthetize Madeleine from feelings of abandonment and unattractiveness. (And wasn't Thurston's nuzzling her further balm?) The beer seemed to be working, anyway. Thurston ordered two last Budweisers, sneaking them out in the pockets of his leather jacket, and they drank them as they walked back up College Hill to Thurston's place. Madeleine's awareness was wonderfully restricted to things that had no power to hurt her: the scraggly urban shrubs, the floating sidewalk, the jingling of the chains on Thurston's jacket.

She entered his room without having registered the stairs that led to it. Once there, however, Madeleine was clear about the protocol, and began taking off her clothes. She lay on her back, laughingly trying to grasp her shoes, and finally kicked them off. Thurston, by contrast, was instantaneously naked except for his underwear. He lay completely still, blending into his white sheets like a chameleon.

When it came to kissing, Thurston was a minimalist. He pressed his thin lips against Madeleine's and, just as she parted her own, he moved his mouth away. It was as if he were wiping his lips on hers. This hide-and-seek was a little off-putting. But she didn't want to be unhappy. Madeleine didn't want things to go badly (she wanted the cleansing beer to cleanse) and so she forgot about Thurston's mouth and started kissing him elsewhere. On his Ric Ocasek neck, his vampire-white belly, the front of his boxer shorts.

He remained silent in the midst of all this, Thurston who was so voluble in class.

It wasn't clear to Madeleine what she was seeking when she pulled Thurston's underpants down. She stood apart from the person doing this. Certain spring-loaded doorstops made a twanging sound when re-leased. Madeleine felt compelled to do what she did next. The wrong-ness of it was immediate. It went beyond the moral, straight to the biological. Her mouth just wasn't the organ nature had designed for this function. She felt orally overextended, like a dental patient waiting for a cast to dry. Plus, this cast wouldn't stay still. Whose idea was this, any-way? Who was the genius who thought pleasure and choking went to-gether? There was a better place to put Thurston, but already, influenced by physical cues—Thurston's unfamiliar smell, the faint frog-kicking of his legs—Madeleine knew she would never allow him into that other place. So she had to go on doing what she was doing, lowering her face over Thurston as he inflated like a stent to widen the artery of her throat. Her tongue began defensive movements, became a shield against deeper penetration, her hand that of a traffic cop, signaling, Stop! Out of one eye, she saw that Thurston had propped up his head with a pillow in or-der to watch.

What Madeleine was seeking here, with Thurston, wasn't Thurston at all. It was self-abasement. She wanted to demean herself, and she'd done so, though she wasn't clear on why, except that it had to do with Leonard and how much she was suffering. Without finishing what she'd started, Madeleine lifted her head, sat back on her heels, and began to softly weep.

Thurston made no complaint. He just blinked rapidly, lying still. In case the evening could be rescued.

She awoke, the next morning, in her own bed. Lying on her stomach, with her hands behind her head, like the victim of an execution. Which might have been preferable, under the circumstances. Which might have been a big relief.

In its horror her hangover was seamless with the horror of the night before. Here, emotional turbulence achieved physiological expression: the sick vodka-soaked taste in her mouth the very flavor of regret; her nausea self-reflexive, as if she didn't want to expel the contents of her stomach but her own personhood. Madeleine's only comfort came from knowing that she'd remained—technically—inviolate. It would have been so much worse to have the reminder of Thurston's come inside her, trickling, leaking out.

This thought was interrupted by the ringing of the doorbell, and by the realization that it was graduation day and her parents were downstairs.

•

In the sexual hierarchy of college, freshman males ranked at the very bottom. After his failure with Madeleine, Mitchell had spent a long, frustrating year. He spent many nights with guys in the same situation, looking through the class directory known as the Pig Book and picking out the prettiest girls. **Tricia Parkinson, Cleveland, OH** had big Farrah Fawcett hair. In her gingham blouse **Jessica Kennison, Old Lyme, MA** looked like a dream of a farmer's daughter. **Madeleine Hanna, Prettybrook, NJ** had sent in a black-and-white snapshot of herself, squinting into the sun with the wind blowing her hair across her forehead. It was a casual picture, neither calculated nor conceited, but also not her best. Most guys passed right over it, focusing on the better-lit and more obvious beauties. Mitchell didn't alert them to their mistake. He wanted to keep Madeleine Hanna his little secret and, to that end, pointed out **Sarah Kripke, Tuxedo Park, NY**.

As for his own photograph in the Pig Book, Mitchell had mailed in a picture cut out of a Civil War history book, showing a lean-faced Lutheran minister with a white shock of hair, tiny spectacles, and an expression of moral outrage. The editors had obediently printed this above the caption **Mitchell Grammaticus, Grosse Pointe, MI**. Using the old man's portrait relieved Mitchell of having to send an actual photo of himself, and of thereby entering into the beauty pageant that the Pig Book inevitably became. It was a way to erase his bodily self and replace it with a mark of his wit.

If Mitchell had hoped that his female classmates might see his joke photo and become interested in him, he was sadly disappointed. No one paid much attention. The boy whose photograph aroused feminine interest was **Leonard Bankhead, Portland, OR**. Bankhead had submitted a curious photo of himself standing in a snowy field, wearing a comically tall stocking cap. To Mitchell, Bankhead didn't look particularly handsome or unhandsome. As freshman year progressed, however, stories of Bankhead's sexual successes began to make their way into the zones of deprivation that served as Mitchell's habitat. John Kass, who'd gone to high school with Bankhead's roommate, claimed that Bankhead had made his friend sleep elsewhere so often that he'd finally applied for a single. One night Mitchell saw the legendary Bankhead at a party at West Quad, staring into a girl's face as if attempting a mind-meld. Mitchell didn't understand why girls couldn't see through Bankhead. He thought that his Lothario reputation would decrease his appeal, but it had the opposite effect. The more girls Bankhead slept with, the more girls wanted to sleep with him. Which made Mitchell uncomfortably aware of how little he knew about girls in the first place.

Mercifully, freshman year finally came to an end. When Mitchell returned the following fall, there was a whole new crop of freshman girls, one of whom, a redhead from Oklahoma, became his girlfriend during spring term. He forgot about Bankhead. (Except for a reli. stu. course they were both in sophomore year, he hardly saw him for the remainder of college.) When the Oklahoman broke up with him, Mitchell went out with other girls, and slept with still others, leaving the zones of deprivation behind. Then, senior year, two months after the heating-gel incident, he heard that Madeleine had a new boyfriend and that the lucky guy was Leonard Bankhead. For two or three days Mitchell remained numb, dealing with the news and not dealing with it, until he awoke one morning swamped by such raw feelings of diminishment and hopelessness that it was as if his entire self-worth (as well as his dick) had shriveled to the size of a pea. Bankhead's success with Madeleine revealed the truth about Mitchell. He didn't have the goods. He hadn't posted up the numbers. This was where he ranked. Out of contention.

His loss had a monumental effect. Mitchell retreated into obscurity to lick his wounds. His interest in quietism had been present beforehand, and so, with this fresh defeat, there was nothing keeping him from withdrawing within himself completely.

Like Madeleine, Mitchell had started out intending to be an English major. But after reading *The Varieties of Religious Experience* for a psychology course, he changed his mind. He'd expected the book to be clinical and cold, but it wasn't. William James described "cases" of all kinds, women and men he'd met or corresponded with, people suffering from melancholia, from nervous maladies, from digestive complaints, people who had yearned for suicide, who'd heard voices and changed their lives overnight. He reported their testimonies without a shred of ridicule. In fact, what was noteworthy about these stories was the intelligence of the people giving them. With apparent honesty, these voices described in detail how they'd lost the will to live, how they'd become ill, bedridden, abandoned by friends and family until suddenly a "New Thought" had occurred to them, the thought of their true place in the universe, at which point all their suffering had ended. Along with these testimonies, James analyzed the religious experience of famous men and women, Walt Whitman, John Bunyan, Leo Tolstoy, Saint Teresa, George Fox, John Wesley, and even Kant. There was no evident proselytizing motive. But the effect, for Mitchell, was to make him aware of the centrality of religion in human history and, more important, of the fact that religious feeling didn't arise from going to church or reading the Bible but from the most private interior experiences, either of great joy or of staggering pain.

Mitchell kept coming back to a paragraph about the neurotic temperament he'd underlined that seemed to describe his own personality and, at the same time, to make him feel better about it. It went:

Few of us are not in some way infirm, or even diseased; and our very infirmities help us unexpectedly. In [this] temperament we have the emotionality which is the *sine qua non* of moral perception; we have the intensity and the tendency to emphasis which are the essence of practical moral vigor; and we have the love of metaphysics and mysticism which carry one's interests beyond the surface of the sensible world. What, then, is more natural than that this temperament should introduce one to regions of religious truth, to corners of the universe, which your robust Philistine type of nervous system, forever offering its biceps to be felt, thumping its breast, and thanking Heaven that it hasn't a single morbid fiber in its composition, would be sure to hide forever from its self-satisfied possessors?

If there were such a thing as inspiration from a higher realm, it might well be that the neurotic temperament would furnish the chief condition of the requisite receptivity.

The first religious studies class Mitchell had taken (the one Bankhead had been in) was a trendy survey course on Eastern religion. Next he enrolled in a seminar on Islam. From there Mitchell graduated to stronger stuff—a course on Thomistic ethics, a seminar on German Pietism—before moving on, in his last semester, to a course called Religion and Alienation in 20th Century Culture. At the first class meeting, the professor, a severe-looking man named Hermann Richter, surveyed with suspicion the forty or so students packed into the classroom. Lifting his chin, he warned in a stern tone, "This is a rigorous, comprehensive, analytical course in twentieth-century religious thought. Any of you who think a little something in alienation *might do* should think otherwise."

Glowering, Richter handed out the syllabus. It included Max Weber's *The Protestant Ethic and the Spirit of Capitalism*, *Auguste Comte and Positivism: The Essential Writings*, Tillich's *The Courage to Be*, Heidegger's *Being and Time*, and *The Drama of Atheist Humanism* by Henri de Lubac. Around the room, students' faces fell. People had been hoping for *The Stranger*, which they'd already read in high school. At the next class meeting, fewer than fifteen kids remained.

Mitchell had never had a professor like Richter before. Richter dressed like a banker. He wore gray chalk-striped suits, conservative ties, button-down shirts, and polished brogues. He had the reassuring attributes of Mitchell's own father—the diligence, the sobriety, the masculinity—while leading a life of unfatherly intellectual cultivation. Every morning Richter had the *Frankfurter Allgemeine* delivered to his department mailbox. He could quote, in the French, the Vérendrye brothers' reaction upon seeing the Dakota badlands. He seemed worldlier than most professors and less ideologically programmed. His voice was low, Kissingerian, minus the accent. It was impossible to imagine him as a boy.

Twice a week they met with Richter and looked unflinchingly at the reasons why the Christian faith had, around the year 1848, expired. The fact that many people thought it was still alive, that it had never been sick at all, was dismissed outright. Richter wanted no fudging. If you couldn't answer the objections of a Schopenhauer, then you had to join him in pessimism. But this was by no means the only option. Richter insisted that unquestioning nihilism was no more intellectually sound than unquestioning faith. It was possible to pick over the corpse of Christianity, to pound its chest and blow into its mouth, to see if the heart started beating again. *I'm not dead. I'm only sleeping.* Stiff-backed, never sitting, his gray hair closely barbered but with hopeful signs about his person, a thistle in his buttonhole or a gift-wrapped present for his daughter protruding from the pocket of his overcoat, Richter asked the students questions and listened to their answers as if it might happen here today: in Room 112 of Richardson Hall, Dee Michaels, who played the Marilyn Monroe part in a campus production of *Bus Stop,* might throw a rope ladder across the void. Mitchell observed Richter's thoroughness, his compassionate revelation of error, his undimmed enthusiasm for presiding over the uncluttering of the twenty or so minds gathered around the seminar table. Getting these kids' heads in working order even now, so late in the game.

What Richter believed was unclear. He wasn't a Christian apologist. Mitchell watched Richter for signs of partiality. But there were none. He dissected each thinker with the same severity. He was grudging in his approval and comprehensive in his complaints.

At semester's end, there was a take-home final exam. Richter handed out a single sheet of paper containing ten questions. You were free to consult your books. There was no way to cheat. The answers to such questions couldn't be found anywhere. No one had formulated them yet.

Mitchell didn't remember any strain in completing the exam. He worked hard but effortlessly. He sat at the oval dining table he used for a desk, surrounded by a scatter of notes and books. Larry was baking banana bread in the kitchen. Occasionally, Mitchell went and had a piece. Then he returned and started up where he'd left off. While he wrote, he felt, for the first time, as though he weren't in school anymore. He wasn't answering questions to get a grade on a test. He was trying to diagnose the predicament he felt himself to be in. And not just *his* predicament, either, but that of everyone he knew. It was an odd feeling. He kept writing the names Heidegger and Tillich but he was thinking about himself and all his friends. Everyone he knew was convinced that religion was a sham and God a fiction. But his friends' replacements for religion didn't look too impressive. No one had an answer for the riddle of existence. It was like that Talking Heads song. "And you may ask yourself, 'How did I get here?' . . . And you may tell yourself, 'This is not my beautiful house. And you may tell yourself, 'This is not my beautiful wife.'" As he responded to the essay questions, Mitchell kept bending his answers toward their practical application. He wanted to know why he was here, and how to live. It was the perfect way to end your college career. Education had finally led Mitchell out into life.

Immediately after handing in the exam, he forgot all about it. Graduation was nearing. He and Larry were busy making plans for their trip. They bought backpacks and subzero sleeping bags. They pored over maps and budget-travel guides, sketching possible itineraries. A week after the exam, Mitchell came into the Faunce House post office and found a letter in his mail slot. It was from Professor Richter, on university stationery. It asked him to come and see Richter in his office.

Mitchell had never been to Richter's office before. Before going, he picked up two iced coffees from the Blue Room—an extravagant gesture, but it was hot out, and he liked his professors to remember him. He carried the tall covered cups through the midday sun to the redbrick building. The departmental secretary told him where to find Richter, and Mitchell started up the stairs to the second floor.

All the other offices were empty. The Buddhists had left for summer vacation. The Islamicists were down in D.C., giving the State Department insight into the "frame of reference" of Abu Nidal, who had just remotely detonated a car bomb inside the French embassy in West Beirut.

Only the door at the end of the hall was open, and inside it, wearing a necktie despite the sultry weather, was Richter.

Richter's office wasn't the bare cell of an absentee professor, inhabited only during office hours. Neither was it the homey den of a department chair, with lithographs and a Shaker rug. Richter's office was formal, almost Viennese. There were glass-fronted bookcases full of leather-bound theology books, an ivory-handled magnifying glass, a brass inkstand. The desk was massive, a bulwark against the creeping ignorance and imprecision of the world. Behind it, Richter was writing notes with a fountain pen.

Mitchell stepped in and said, "If I ever had an office, Professor Richter, this is the kind of office I'd have."

Richter did an amazing thing: he smiled. "You just might get the chance," he said.

"I brought you an iced coffee."

Richter stared across the desk at the offering, mildly surprised, but tolerant. "Thank you," he said. He opened a manila folder and took out a sheaf of papers. Mitchell recognized it as his take-home exam. It appeared to have writing all over it, in an elegant hand.

"Have a seat," Richter said.

Mitchell complied.

"I've taught at this college for twenty-two years," Richter began. "In all of that time, only once have I received a paper that displays the depth of insight and philosophical acumen that yours does." He paused. "The last student of whom I could say this is now the dean of Princeton Theological Seminary."

Richter stopped, as though waiting for his words to sink in. They didn't, particularly. Mitchell was pleased to have done well. He was used to doing well in school, but he still enjoyed it. Beyond that, his mind didn't travel.

"You are a graduating senior this year, is that correct?"

"One week left, Professor."

"Have you ever given serious thought to pursuing a career in scholarship?"

"Not serious thought, no."

"What are you planning to do with your life?" Richter said.

Mitchell smiled. "Is my father hiding under your desk?" he said.

Richter's brow furrowed. He was no longer smiling. He folded his hands, taking a new direction. "I sense from your exam that you are personally engaged with matters of religious belief. Am I right?"

"I guess you could say that," Mitchell said.

"Your surname is Greek. Were you raised in the Orthodox tradition?"

"Baptized. That was about it."

"And now?"

"Now?" Mitchell took a moment. He was accustomed to keeping quiet about his spiritual investigations. It felt odd to talk about them.

But Richter's expression was nonjudgmental. He was bent forward in his chair, hands clasped on the desk. He was looking away, presenting only his ear. Under this encouragement, Mitchell opened up. He explained that he had arrived at college without knowing much about religion, and how, from reading English literature, he'd begun to realize how ignorant he was. The world had been formed by beliefs he knew nothing about. "That was the beginning," he said, "realizing how stupid I was."

"Yes, yes." Richter nodded quickly. The head-bowing suggested personal experience with thought-tormented states. Richter's head remained low, listening. "I don't know, one day I was just sitting there," Mitchell went on, "and it hit me that almost every writer I was reading for my classes had believed in God. Milton, for starters. And George Herbert." Did Professor Richter know George Herbert? Professor Richter did. "And Tolstoy. I realize Tolstoy got a little excessive, near the end. Rejecting *Anna Karenina*. But how many writers turn against their own genius? Maybe it was Tolstoy's obsession with truth that made him so great in the first place. The fact that he was willing to give up his art was what made him a great artist."

Again the sound of assent from the gray eminence above the desk blotter. The weather, the world outside, had ceased to exist for a moment. "So last summer I gave myself a reading list," Mitchell said. "I read a lot of Thomas Merton. Merton got me into Saint John of the Cross and Saint John of the Cross got me into Meister Eckhart and *The Imitation of Christ*. Right now I'm reading *The Cloud of Unknowing*."

Richter waited a moment before asking, "Your search has been purely intellectual?"

"Not only," Mitchell said. He hesitated and then confessed, "I've also been going to church."

"Which one?"

"You name it." Mitchell smiled. "All kinds. But mostly Catholic."

"I can understand the attraction of Catholicism," Richter said. "But putting myself back in the time of Luther, and considering the excesses of the Church at the time, I think I would have sided with the schismatics."

In Richter's face Mitchell now saw the answer to the question he'd been asking all semester. He hesitated and asked, "So you believe in God, Professor Richter?"

In a firm tone, Richter specified, "I am a Christian religious believer."

Mitchell didn't know what that meant, exactly. But he understood why Richter was splitting hairs. The designation allowed him room for reservations and doubts, historical accommodations and dissent.

"I had no idea," Mitchell said. "In class I couldn't tell if you believed anything or not."

"That's the way the game is played."

They sat there together, companionably sipping their iced coffees. And Richter made his offer.

"I want you to know that I think you have the potential to do significant work in contemporary Christian theological studies. If you would be at all inclined, I would see to it that you get a full scholarship to the Princeton Theological Seminary. Or to Harvard or Yale Divinity School, if you so prefer. I do not often exercise myself to this extent on behalf of students, but in this case I feel compelled to do so."

Mitchell had never considered going to divinity school. But the idea of studying theology—of studying *anything*, as opposed to working nine-to-five—appealed to him. And so he'd told Richter that he would seriously think about it. He was taking a trip, a year off. He promised to write Richter when he got back and to tell him what he'd decided.

Given all the difficulties ganging up on Mitchell—the recession, his dubious degree, and, today, this morning's fresh rebuff from Madeleine—the trip was the only thing he had to look forward to. Now, heading back to his apartment to dress for the commencement procession, Mitchell told himself that it didn't matter what Madeleine thought of him. He would soon be gone.

His apartment, on Bowen Street, was only two blocks from Madeleine's much nicer building. He and Larry occupied the second floor of an old clapboard tenement house. In five minutes he was climbing the front stairs.

Mitchell and Larry had decided to go to India one night after watching a Satyajit Ray film. They hadn't been entirely serious at the time. From then on, however, whenever anybody asked what they were doing after graduation, Mitchell and Larry replied, "We're going to India!" Reaction among their friends was universally positive. No one could come up with a reason why they shouldn't go to India. Most people said that they wished they could come along. The result was that, without so much as buying plane tickets or a guidebook—without really knowing anything about India—Mitchell and Larry began to be seen as enviable, brave, free-thinking individuals. And so finally they decided that they had better go.

Little by little, the trip had come into focus. They added a European leg. In March, Larry, who was a theater major, had lined up the job as research assistants with Professor Hughes, which gave the trip a professional gloss and placated their parents. They'd bought a big yellow map of India and hung it on the kitchen wall.

The only thing that had nearly derailed their plans was the "party" they had thrown a few weeks ago, during Reading Period. It was Larry's idea. What Mitchell hadn't known, however, was that the party wasn't a real party but Larry's final project for the studio art course they were taking. Larry, it turned out, had "cast" certain guests as "actors," giving them directions on how to behave at the party. Most of these directions involved insulting, coming on to, or freaking out the unsuspecting guests. For the first hour of the party, this resulted in everyone having a bad time. Friends came up to tell you that they'd always distrusted you, that you'd always had bad breath, et cetera. Around midnight, the downstairs neighbors, a married couple named Ted and Susan (who, Mitchell could see retrospectively, had been ridiculously costumed in terry-cloth bathrobes and fluffy slippers, Susan with curlers in her hair), burst angrily through the door, threatening to call the cops because of the loud music. Mitchell tried to calm them down. Dave Hayek, however, who was six-four,

and in on the hoax, stomped across the kitchen and physically threatened the neighbors. In response, Ted pulled a (fake) gun from the pocket
of his bathrobe, threatening to shoot Hayek, who cowered on the floor,
pleading, while everyone else either froze in fear or rushed for the doors,
spilling beer over everything. At that point, Larry had turned on all the
lights, climbed onto a chair, and informed everyone, ha ha, that none of
this was real. Ted and Susan took off their robes to reveal street clothes
underneath. Ted showed everyone that the gun was a squirt gun. Mitchell couldn't believe that Larry had failed to inform him, the party's co-
host, about the party's secret agenda. He'd had no idea that Carlita
Jones, a thirty-six-year-old graduate student, had been following the
"script" when, earlier in the evening, she had locked Mitchell and herself
in a bedroom, saying, "Come on, Mitchell. Let's do the nasty. Right here
on the floor." He was greatly surprised that sex offered openly in this way
(as it often was in his fantasies) proved in reality to be not only unwel-
come but frightening. Yet despite all this and how enraged he was at
Larry for using the party to fulfill his course requirements (though
Mitchell should have been suspicious when the art professor herself had
shown up), Mitchell knew even later that night, after everyone had left—
even while he screamed at Larry, who was getting sick over the balcony,
"Go on! Puke your guts out! You deserve it!"—that he would forgive Larry
for turning their house and party into bad performance art. Larry was his
best friend, they were going to India together, and Mitchell had no choice.

Now he let himself into his apartment and went straight to Larry's
door, flinging it open.

On a futon mattress, his face half-hidden in a bush of Garfunkel hair,
Larry lay on his side, his thin frame forming a Z. He looked like a figure
at Pompeii, someone who'd curled up in a corner as the lava and ash came
through the window. Thumbtacked to the wall above his head were two
photographs of Antonin Artaud. In the photo on the left, Artaud was
young and unbelievably handsome. In the other, taken a brief decade
later, the playwright looked like a withered maniac. It was the speed and
totality of Artaud's physical and mental disintegration that appealed to
Larry.

"Get up," Mitchell said to him.

When Larry didn't respond, Mitchell picked up a Samuel French
script from the floor and tossed it at his head.

Larry groaned and rolled onto his back. His eyes fluttered open, but he seemed in no rush to regain consciousness. "What time is it?"

"It's late. We've got to get going."

After a long moment, Larry sat up. He was on the small side, with a puckish or faun-like quality to his face, which, depending on the light or how much he'd been partying, could look either as high-cheekboned as Rudolf Nureyev or as hollow-cheeked as the figure in Munch's *The Scream*. Right now, it was somewhere in between.

"You missed a good party last night," he said.

Mitchell was stone-faced. "I'm over parties."

"Now, now, Mitchell, don't be extreme. Is this how you're going to be on our trip? A drag?"

"I just saw Madeleine," Mitchell said with urgency. "She decided to start talking to me again. But then I said something she didn't like, and now she isn't."

"Nice job."

"She broke up with Bankhead, though."

"I know she did," Larry said.

An alarm went off in Mitchell's head. "How do you know?" he asked.

"Because she left the party last night with Thurston Meems. She was on the *prowl*, Mitchell. I told you to come. Too bad you're over parties."

Mitchell stood up straighter to blunt the force of this revelation. Larry knew, of course, of Mitchell's obsession with Madeleine. Larry had heard Mitchell extol her virtues and defend or contextualize her more questionable attributes. Mitchell had revealed to Larry, as you did only to a real friend, the extent of his crazy thinking when it came to Madeleine. Still, Mitchell had his pride, and showed no reaction. "Get your ass up," he said, withdrawing into the hall. "I don't want to be late."

Back in his room, Mitchell closed the door and went to sit in his desk chair, hanging his head. Certain details of the morning, previously illegible, were slowly revealing significance, like skywriting. Madeleine's disheveled hair. Her hangover.

Suddenly, with savage decisiveness, he spun around and ripped off the lid of the cardboard box that was lying on his desk. Inside was his graduation robe. Taking it out, he stood up and pulled the shiny acrylic fabric over his head and shoulders. The tassel, class pin, and mortarboard were shrink-wrapped in separate sheets of plastic. After ripping these off, and screwing the tassel into the mortarboard so thoroughly it made a dent, Mitchell unfolded the cap's bat wings and set it on his head.

He heard Larry pad into the kitchen. "Mitchell," Larry called, "should I bring a joint?"

Without answering, Mitchell went to stand before the mirror on the back of his bedroom door. Mortarboards were medieval in origin. They were as old as "The Cloud of Unknowing." That was why they looked so ridiculous. That was why he looked so ridiculous wearing one.

He remembered a line from Meister Eckhart: "Only the hand that erases can write the true thing."

Mitchell wondered if he was supposed to erase himself, or his past, or other people, or what. He was ready to begin erasing immediately, as soon as he knew what to rub out.

When he came out into the kitchen, Larry was making coffee, wearing his cap and gown, too. They looked at each other with mild amusement.

"Definitely bring a joint," Mitchell said.

•

Madeleine took the long way back to her building.

She was furious at everyone and everything, at her mother for making her invite Mitchell over in the first place, at Leonard for not calling, at the weather for being cold, and at college for ending.

It was impossible to be friends with guys. Every guy she'd ever been friends with had ended up wanting something else, or had wanted something else from the beginning, and had been friends only under false pretenses.

Mitchell wanted revenge. That was all this was. He wanted to hurt her and he knew her weak spots. It was absurd of him to say that he wasn't mentally attracted to her. Hadn't he been after her all these years? Hadn't he told her that he "loved her mind"? Madeleine knew she wasn't as smart as Mitchell. But was Mitchell as smart as Leonard? What about that? That was what she should have told Mitchell. Instead of crying and running away, she should have pointed out that Leonard was perfectly happy with her level of intelligence.

This thought, shiny with triumph, dimmed on the immediate reflection that Leonard and she were no longer going out.

Gazing at Canal Street through the distortion of tears—they refracted a stop sign at a Cubist angle—Madeleine allowed herself once again to wish the forbidden wish of getting back together with Leonard. It seemed to her that if she could just have that one thing, all her other problems would be bearable.

The clock on the Citizens Bank read 8:47. She had an hour to get dressed and up the hill.

Up ahead, the river appeared, green and unmoving. A few years ago, it had caught on fire. For weeks the fire department had tried to put out the conflagration without success. Which invited the question of how, exactly, did you douse a burning river? What could you do, when the retardant was also the accelerant?

The lovelorn English major contemplated the symbolism of this.

In a thin little park she'd never noticed before, Madeleine sat on a bench. Natural opiates were flooding her system and, after a few minutes, she started to feel a bit better. She dried her eyes. From now on, she wouldn't have to see Mitchell ever again, if she didn't want. Or Leonard, either. Though at this moment she felt abused, abandoned, and ashamed of herself, Madeleine knew that she was still young, that she had her whole life ahead of her—a life in which, if she persevered, she might do something special—and that part of persevering meant getting past moments just like this one, when people made you feel small, unlovable, and took away your confidence.

She left the park, climbing a small cobblestone lane back to Benefit Street.

At the Narragansett, she let herself into the lobby and took the elevator up to her floor. She felt tired, dehydrated, and still in need of a shower.

As she was putting her key in the door, Abby opened it from inside. Her hair was stuffed into the graduation cap. "Hi! We thought we were going to have to leave without you."

"Sorry," Madeleine said, "my parents take forever. Can you wait for me? I'll be really fast."

In the living room, Olivia was painting her toenails, her feet up on the coffee table. The telephone began to ring, and Abby went to get it.

"Pookie said you left with Thurston Meems," Olivia said, applying polish. "But I told her that couldn't possibly be true."

"I don't want to talk about it," Madeleine said.

"Fine. I don't even care," Olivia said. "But Pookie and I just want to know one thing."

"I'm going to take a quick shower."

"It's for you," Abby said, holding out the phone.

Madeleine had no desire to talk to anybody. But it was better than fending off more questions.

She took the receiver and said hello.

"Madeleine?" It was a guy's voice, unfamiliar.

"Yes."

"This is Ken. Auerbach." When Madeleine didn't respond, the caller said, "I'm a friend of Leonard's."

"Oh," Madeleine said. "Hi."

"I'm sorry to call on graduation. But I'm leaving today and I thought I should call you before I go." There was a pause during which Madeleine tried to catch up to the reality of the moment, and before she did, Auerbach said, "Leonard's in the hospital."

No sooner had he delivered this news than he added, "Don't worry. He's not hurt. But he's in the hospital and I thought you should know. If you didn't already. Maybe you knew."

"No, I didn't," Madeleine replied in what sounded to her like a calm tone. Keeping it that way, she added, "Can you hold on a minute?" Pressing the receiver against her chest, she picked up the base of the phone, which was on an extralong cord, and carried it out of the living room and back to her bedroom, where it just barely reached. She closed the door and lifted the handset to her ear. She was worried her voice might break when she spoke again.

"What's the matter? Is he O.K.?"

"He's *fine*," Auerbach assured her. "Physically he's fine. I was worried I might freak you out if I called but—yeah, no—he's not injured or anything like that."

"Then what is he?"

"Well, at first he was a little manic. But now he's really depressed. Like, clinically."

For the next several minutes, while rain clouds passed over the capitol dome framed by her window, Auerbach told Madeleine what had happened.

It had started with Leonard not being able to sleep. He came to class complaining of exhaustion. At first, no one paid much attention. Being exhausted was in large measure what being Leonard was all about. Previously, Leonard's exhaustion had had to do with the inherent demands of the day, with getting up, getting dressed, making it to campus. It wasn't that he hadn't slept; it was that being awake was too much to bear. By contrast, Leonard's present exhaustion had to do with the night. He felt too wired to go to bed, he said, and so began staying up until three or four in the morning. When he forced himself to turn off the lights and get into bed, his heart raced, and he broke into a sweat. He tried to read, but his thoughts kept racing, and soon he was pacing his apartment.

After a week of this, Leonard had gone to Health Services, where a doctor, accustomed to seeing stressed-out undergrads near semester's end, prescribed sleeping pills and told Leonard to stop drinking coffee. When the pills didn't work the doctor prescribed a mild tranquilizer, and then a stronger one, but even this brought Leonard no more than two or three hours of shallow, dreamless, nonreplenishing sleep per night.

It was right around then, Auerbach said, that Leonard stopped taking his lithium. It wasn't clear if Leonard had done this on purpose or just forgot. But pretty soon he was calling people on the telephone. He called everybody. He talked for fifteen minutes, or a half hour, or an hour, or two hours. At first, he was entertaining, as always. People were happy to hear from him. He called his friends two or three times a day. Then five or six. Then ten. Then twelve. He called from his apartment. He called from pay phones around campus, the locations of which he had memorized. Leonard knew about a phone in the subbasement of the physics lab, and of a cozy telephone closet in the administration building. He knew about a broken pay phone on Thayer Street that recycled your coin. He knew about unguarded phones in the philosophy department. From each and every one of these phones Leonard called to tell his listeners how exhausted he was, how insomniac, how insomniac, how exhausted. All he could do, apparently, was talk on the phone. As soon as the sun rose, Leonard telephoned his early-rising friends. Having been up all night, he called to speak to people not yet in the mood for conversation. From them, he moved on to other people, people he knew well or had barely met, students, departmental secretaries, his dermatologist, his advisor. When it got too late on the East Coast to call anyone, Leonard went through his phone book, looking up the numbers of friends on the West Coast. And when it got too late to call Portland or San Francisco, Leonard faced the terrifying three or four hours when he was alone in his apartment with his own disintegrating mind.

That was the phrase Auerbach used, telling the story to Madeleine. "Disintegrating mind." Madeleine listened, trying to fit the picture Auerbach was sketching with the Leonard she knew, whose mind was anything but weak.

"What do you mean?" Madeleine said. "Are you saying Leonard's going crazy?"

"That's not what I'm saying," Auerbach said.

"What do you mean his mind is disintegrating?"

"That's what he told me it felt like. To him," Auerbach said.

As his mind began to come apart, Leonard sought to keep it together by talking into a plastic handset, to reach and interact with another person, to outfit that person with a precise description of his despair, his physical symptoms, his hypochondriacal surmises. He called to ask people about their moles. Did they ever have a mole that looked suspicious? That bled or changed shape? Or a red thingy on the shaft of their penises? Could that be herpes? What did herpes look like? What was the difference between a herpes lesion and a chancre? Leonard strained the decorum of masculine friendship, Auerbach said, by calling his male friends and inquiring about the state of their erections. Had they ever failed to get it up? If so, under what conditions? Leonard began referring to his erections as "Gumbies." These were erections that bent, that were as pliable as the old childhood figurine. "I get a total Gumby sometimes," he said. He worried that biking through Oregon one summer had compromised his prostate. He went to the library and found a study of erectile dysfunction in Tour de France athletes. Because Leonard was brilliant and historically hilarious, he'd built up a huge reserve of good feeling in people, memories of great times with him, and, now, in his million phone calls, he began to draw on this reserve, one call at a time, as people waited through his kvetching and tried to coax him out of his depression, and it was a long time before he exhausted his reserve of being liked and admired.

Leonard's dark moods had always been part of his appeal. It was a relief to hear him enumerate his frailties, his misgivings about the American formula for success. So many people at college were jacked up on ambition, possessors of steroidal egos, clever but cutthroat, diligent but insensitive, shiny but dull, that everyone felt compelled to be upbeat, down with the program, all systems firing, when everyone knew, in his or her heart, that this wasn't how they really felt. People doubted themselves and feared the future. They were intimidated, scared, and so talking to Leonard, who was all these things times ten, made people feel less bad about themselves, and less alone. Leonard's calls were like telephone therapy. Plus, he was way worse off than everybody else! He was Dr. Freud and Dr. Doom, father confessor and humble penitent, shrink and shrunk. He put on no show. He wasn't a fake. He spoke honestly and listened with compassion. At their best, Leonard's phone conversations were a kind of art and a form of ministry.

And yet, Auerbach said, there was a change to Leonard's pessimism about this time. It deepened; it purified. It lost its previous comedic habiliments, its air of shtick, and became unadulterated, lethal, pure despair. Whatever Leonard, who'd always been "depressed," had had before, it wasn't depression. *This* was depression. This monotone monologue delivered by an unbathed guy lying on his back in the middle of the floor. This unmodulated recitation of his young life's failures, failures that in Leonard's mind already foredoomed him to a life of ever-diminishing returns. "Where's Leonard?" he kept asking, on the phone. Where was the guy who could write a twenty-page paper on Spinoza with his left hand while playing chess with his right? Where was the professorial Leonard, purveyor of obscure information on the history of type in Flanders versus Wallonia, deliverer of disquisitions on the literary merits of sixteen Ghanaian, Kenyan, and Ivory Coast novelists, all of whom had been published in a sixties-era paperback series called "Out of Africa" that Leonard had once found at the Strand and purchased for fifty cents apiece and read every volume of? "Where's Leonard?" Leonard asked. Leonard didn't know.

Slowly it began to dawn on Leonard's friends that it didn't matter whom Leonard called on the phone. He forgot who was on the other end and, whenever one person managed to hang up, Leonard called somebody else and picked up right where he'd left off. And people were *busy*.

They had other things to do. So gradually his friends began to make up excuses when Leonard called. They said they had a class or a meeting with a professor. They minimized talking time and, after a while, stopped answering the phone altogether. Auerbach himself had done this. He felt guilty about it now, which was why he had called Madeleine. "We knew Leonard was in bad shape," he said, "but we didn't know he was in *that* bad a shape."

All this led up to the day Auerbach's phone rang around five in the afternoon. Suspecting that it was Leonard, he didn't pick up. But the phone kept ringing and ringing and finally Auerbach couldn't stand it anymore and answered.

"Ken?" Leonard said in a quavering tone. "They're giving me an incomplete, Ken. I'm not going to graduate."

"Who says?"

"Prof. Nalbandian just called. He says there's no time for me to make up the work I've missed. So he's giving me an incomplete."

This didn't come as a surprise to Auerbach. But the vulnerability of Leonard's voice, the child-lost-in-the-woods cry of it, made Auerbach want to say something soothing. "That's not so bad. He's not flunking you."

"That's not the *point*, Ken," Leonard said, aggrieved. "The point is that he's one of my professors, who I'm hoping will write recommendations for me. I've fucked everything up, Ken. I'm not going to graduate on time, with everyone else. If I don't graduate, then they're going to cancel my internship at Pilgrim Lake. I don't have any money, Ken. My parents aren't going to help me. I don't know how I'm going to make it. I'm only twenty-two and I've fucked up my life!"

Auerbach tried to reason with Leonard, to talk him down, but no matter what arguments he offered, Leonard remained fixed on the direness of his situation. He kept complaining about having no money, how his parents didn't help him like most kids at Brown, the disadvantage he'd been at his whole life and how this, too, had led to his precarious emotional state. They went around and around for over an hour, Leonard breathing heavily into the mouthpiece, his voice sounding increasingly desperate, while Auerbach ran out of things to say and began offering tactics that sounded silly even to him, for instance that Leonard needed to stop thinking so much about himself, that he should go outside and look at the magnolias blooming on the green—had he seen the magnolias?—that he might try comparing his situation with that of people truly desperate, South American gold miners, or quadriplegics, or patients with advanced MS, that life wasn't as bad as Leonard was making it out to be. And then Leonard did something he'd never done before. He hung up on Auerbach. It was the only time during his telephonic mania that Leonard had been the first to hang up, and it scared Auerbach. He called again and got no answer. Finally, after calling a couple of other people who knew Leonard, Auerbach decided to go to Planet Street, where he found Leonard in a frantic state. After much coaxing, he finally persuaded Leonard to let him take him to Health Services, and the doctor there admitted Leonard for the night. The next day, they sent him to Providence Hospital, where he was now in the psychiatric ward, receiving treatment.

Given more time, Madeleine could have separated and identified the welter of emotions that were now surging through her. There was a foreground of panic. Behind this were embarrassment and anger for being the last to know. But underneath everything, bubbling up, was a strange buoyancy.

"I've known Leonard since he was first diagnosed," Auerbach said. "Freshman year. He's fine if he takes his medicine. He's always been fine. He just needs some support right now. That's basically why I called."

"Thanks," Madeleine said. "I'm glad you did."

"So far, a few of us have been holding down the ship, visiting-hours-wise. But everybody's booking today. And—I don't know—I'm sure Leonard would like to see you."

"Did he say that?"

"He didn't *say* that. But I saw him last night and I'm sure he would."

With that, Auerbach gave her the address of the hospital and the number of the nurses' station, and said goodbye.

Madeleine was now filled with purpose. Putting the receiver down firmly, she strode out her bedroom door and back into the living room.

Olivia still had her legs on the coffee table, letting her toenails dry. Abby was pouring a pink smoothie from a blender into a glass.

"You traitors!" Madeleine shouted.

"What?" Abby said, surprised.

"You knew!" Madeleine cried. "You knew Leonard was in the hospital the whole time! That's why you said he wouldn't be at the party."

Abby and Olivia exchanged a look. Each was waiting for the other to speak.

"You knew and you didn't tell me!"

"We did it for your own good," Abby said, looking full of concern. "We didn't want you to get upset and start obsessing. I mean, you were already barely going to your classes. You were just getting over Leonard and we thought that—"

"How would you like it if Whitney was in the hospital and I didn't tell you?"

"That's different," Abby said. "You and Leonard broke up. You weren't even speaking."

"That doesn't matter," Madeleine said.

"I'm still going *out* with Whitney."

"How could you know and not tell me?"

"O.K.," Abby said. "*Sorry*. We're really sorry."

"You lied to me."

Olivia shook her head, unwilling to accept this. "Leonard's crazy," she said. "Do you realize that? I'm sorry, Maddy, but Leonard—is—crazy. He wouldn't leave his apartment! They had to call security to break down his door."

These details were new. Madeleine absorbed them for later analysis. "Leonard is not crazy," she said. "He's just depressed. It's an illness."

She didn't know if it was an illness. She didn't know anything about it. But the speed with which she plucked this assurance from the air had the added benefit of making her believe what she was saying.

Abby was still looking sympathetic, going cow-eyed, tilting her head to the side. Her upper lip had smoothie on it. "We were just worried about you, Mad," she said. "We were worried you might use this to get back with Leonard."

"Oh, so you were protecting me."

"You don't have to be snide," Olivia said.

"I can't believe I wasted my senior year living with you two."

"Oh, like it's been a real joy living with you!" Olivia said with ferocious cheer. "You and your *Lover's Discourse*. Give me a break! You know that line you're always quoting? About how nobody would fall in love unless they read about it first? Well, all you *do* is read about it."

"I think you have to agree it was pretty nice of us to ask you to live with us," Abby said, licking smoothie off her lip. "I mean, we found this place and put down the security deposit and everything."

"I wish you'd never asked me," Madeleine said. "Then maybe I'd be living with somebody I could trust."

"Let's go," Abby said, turning away from Madeleine with an air of finality. "We've got to get up to the march."

"My nails aren't dry," Olivia said.

"Let's go. We're late."

Madeleine didn't wait to hear more. Turning, she went to her room and closed the door. When she was sure Abby and Olivia were gone, she gathered up her own graduation gear—the cap and gown, the tassel—and made her way down to the lobby. It was 9:32. She had twelve minutes to get to campus.

The quickest way up the hill—and the direction in which she didn't run the risk of overtaking her roommates—was up Bowen Street. Bowen Street had its own perils, however. Mitchell lived there and she was in no mood to run into him again. She proceeded cautiously around the corner and, not seeing him, hurried by his house and began climbing the slope.

The path was slippery from the rain. By the time she reached the top, Madeleine's loafers were caked with mud. Her head began to pound again and, as she hurried along, a gust of her own bodily scent rose out of the collar of her dress. For the first time, she examined the stain. It could have been anything. Nevertheless, she stopped, pulled the graduation robe over her head, and continued climbing.

She pictured Leonard barricaded in his apartment, with security officers breaking down his door, and a fearful tenderness took hold of her.

And yet there was this countervailing buoyancy, a balloon rising in her despite the immediate emergency . . .

Reaching Congdon Street, she picked up speed. In a few blocks she saw the crowds. Policemen had stopped traffic, and people in raincoats were filling Prospect and College Streets, in front of the art building and the library. The wind was whipping up again, the tops of the elms shaking above the dark sky.

Passing by Carrie Tower, Madeleine heard a brass band tuning up. Grad students and medical students were lining up along Waterman Street, while ceremonially dressed officials checked the formation. She wanted to go through Faunce House Arch onto the green, but the line was blocking her. Instead of waiting, she proceeded farther along Faunce House and down the steps of the post office, intending to reach the green through the underground passage. As she was crossing the space, a thought occurred to her. She checked her watch again. It was 9:41. She had four minutes.

Madeleine's mailbox was on the bottom row of the front-facing boxes. To dial the combination, she went down on one knee, which made her feel hopeful and vulnerable at once. The brass door opened on the age-darkened slot. Inside was a single envelope. Calmly (for the successful candidate exhibited neither anxiety nor haste), Madeleine pulled it out.

It was the letter from Yale, torn, and enclosed in a plastic USPS envelope bearing a printed notice: "This article of mail was damaged en route to the recipient. We apologize for the delay."

She opened the heat-sealed plastic and gingerly pulled out the paper envelope, trying not to tear it further. It had been caught in a sorting machine. The postmark read "April 1, 1982."

The Faunce House post office knew all about acceptance letters. Yearly, they poured in, from medical schools, from law schools, from graduate programs. Students had knelt before these boxes just as she was now doing to pull out letters that transformed them instantly into Rhodes Scholars, senatorial aides, fledgling reporters, Wharton matriculants. As Madeleine opened the envelope, it occurred to her that it wasn't very heavy.

Dear Ms. Hanna,

This letter is to inform you that the Yale Graduate Program in English will not be able to offer you admission in the coming academic year, 1982–1983. We receive many qualified applicants each year and regret that we cannot always

She made no sound. She betrayed no sign of disappointment. Gently, she closed her P.O. box, spinning the dials, and, rising to full height, walked with good posture across the post office. Near the door, finishing the work the USPS processing center had started, she tore the letter in two, pitching the pieces into the recycling bin.

Students A, B, C, and D have applied to Yale graduate school. If A is the editor of *The Harvard Crimson*; B a Rhodes scholar who published a monograph on *Paradise Lost* in the *Milton Quarterly*; C a nineteen-year-old prodigy from England who speaks Russian and French and is related to Prime Minister Thatcher; and D an English major whose submission contained a so-so paper on the linking words in *Pearl* plus a score on the logic portion of the GRE of 520, which student doesn't stand an ice cube's chance in hell of getting accepted?

She'd been rejected way back in April, two months ago. Her fate had been sealed before she'd even broken up with Leonard, which meant that the one thing she'd been counting on to lift her spirits these last three weeks had been an illusion. Another crucial bit of information withheld from her.

There were shouts on the green. With resignation, Madeleine set the mortarboard on her head like a dunce cap. She left the post office, climbing up the steps to the green.

In the open verdant space, families were waiting for the procession to begin. Three little girls had climbed into the bronze lap of the Henry Moore sculpture, smiling and giggling, while their father knelt in the grass to take photographs. Squads of alumni were staggering about, celebrating reunions, wearing straw boaters or Brown baseball caps emblazoned with their year.

In front of Sayles Hall people began to cheer. Madeleine looked as a Paleolithic graduate, a bog person of an alumnus enfolded in a striped blazer, was pushed into view by a retinue of blond grandchildren or great-grandchildren. From the arms of his wheelchair a raft of helium balloons rose into the spring air, each red balloon painted with a brown "Class of '09." The old man had his hand up to accept the applause. He was grinning with long, ghoulish teeth, his face lit with satisfaction beneath the Beefeater's hat on his head.

Madeleine watched the happy old man pass by. At that moment, the band launched into the processional music, and the commencement march began. The university's CEO-like president, wearing striped velvet academic robes and a floppy Florentine cap, led the march, holding a medieval lance. Following him were plutocratic trustees, and the red-haired, macrocephalic living members of the Brown family, and assorted provosts and deans. Seniors, walking two abreast, streamed up from

Wayland Arch and across the green. The parade headed past University Hall in the direction of the Van Wickle gates, where parents—including Alton and Phyllida—were expectantly massed.

Madeleine watched the march, waiting for a place to jump in. She scanned the faces for someone she knew, her friend Kelly Traub or even Lollie and Pookie Ames. At the same time, her apprehension at running into Mitchell again, or Olivia and Abby, made her hold back, standing slightly behind a paunchy father toting a video camera.

She couldn't remember which side her tassel was supposed to hang on, left or right.

The graduating class had close to twelve hundred members. They kept coming, two by two, smiling and laughing, giving fist pumps and high fives. But each person who swept by was someone Madeleine had never seen before. After four years at college, nobody was anybody she knew.

Only about a hundred seniors had passed so far, but Madeleine didn't wait for the rest. The face she wanted to see wasn't here, anyway. Turning, she walked back through Faunce House Arch and headed up Waterman in the direction of Thayer Street. Hurrying, breaking almost into a run, holding her cap on with one hand, she reached the corner, where traffic was flowing. A minute later, she flagged down a taxi and told the driver to take her to Providence Hospital.

•

They were just finishing the joint when the line began to move.

For a half hour Mitchell and Larry had been standing in the blustery shade of Wriston Quad, the midpoint in a long black line of graduating seniors that stretched from the main green down the long path to the ivy-covered arch behind them, and out along Thayer Street. The narrow sidewalks tidied up the line ahead and behind, but in the open space of the quad it bulged, becoming an outdoor party. People were milling around, circulating.

Mitchell blocked the wind with his body so that Larry could light the joint. Everyone was complaining about how cold it was and moving back and forth to stay warm.

There were a lot of ways to defy the day's solemnities. Some people were wearing their caps at funny angles. Others had decorated them with stickers or paint. Girls opted for feather boas, or Spring Break sun-glasses, or mirrored earrings like mini disco balls. Mitchell made the observation that such shows of disobedience were commonplace at grad-uation ceremonies and, therefore, as time-honored as the traditions they tried to subvert, before taking the joint from Larry and defying the day's solemnity in his own commonplace way.

"*Gaudeamus igitur*," he said, and took a drag.

Like an egg swallowed by a black snake, the signal to march was work-ing its way, by a nearly invisible peristalsis, along the twists and turns of the assembled marchers. But no one appeared to be moving yet. Mitchell kept squinting ahead to see. Finally the signal reached the people immedi-ately in front of Larry and Mitchell and, all at once, the entire line surged forward.

They passed the joint back and forth, smoking it more quickly now.

Ahead in line Mark Klemke turned, wiggling his eyebrows, and said, "I'm naked under this robe."

A lot of people had brought cameras with them. Commercials had told them to record this moment on film, and so they were going ahead and recording it.

It was possible to feel superior to other people and like a misfit at the same time.

They lined you up in kindergarten, alphabetically. On fourth-grade field trips you took your partner's hand to push past the musk ox or the steam turbine. School was a perpetual lineup, ending in this final one. Mitchell and Larry made their way slowly up from the leafy dimness of Wriston Quad. The ground was still coolish, unsunned. Some prankster had climbed the statue of Marcus Aurelius to place a mortarboard on the stoic's head. His horse had an "82" painted on its steel flank. After ascending the steps alongside Leeds Theatre, they continued up past Sayles Hall and Richardson onto the green. The sky looked like some-thing out of El Greco. Somebody's program blew past.

Larry offered the roach, but Mitchell shook his head. "I'm stoned," he said.

"Me, too."

They were taking small, chain-gang steps, approaching the covered stage set up in front of University Hall before a sea of white folding chairs.

At the top of the path, the line halted. Feeling a wave of fatigue, Mitchell was reminded why he didn't like to get high in the morning. After the initial rush of energy, the day became a boulder you had to push uphill. He would have to stop smoking pot on his trip. He would have to clean up his act.

The line began moving again. Through the elms, in the distance, Mitchell glimpsed the downtown skyline, and then the Van Wickle gates were looming straight ahead, and along with a thousand classmates Mitchell was carried through them.

People were making obligatory hooting noises, throwing up their caps. The crowd outside was dense and child-starved. From the mass of middle-aged faces, those of Mitchell's own, particular parents emerged with arresting clarity. Deanie, in a blue blazer and London Fog raincoat, was beaming at the sight of his youngest son, having forgotten, apparently, that he'd never wanted Mitchell to go to college in the East and be ruined by liberals. Lillian was waving both hands in the attention-getting way of small people. Under the estranging power of the marijuana, not to mention four years at college, Mitchell was depressed by the tacky denim sun visor his mother was wearing and by his parents' general lack of sophistication. But something was happening to him. The gates were doing something to him already, because as he raised his hand to wave back at his parents, Mitchell felt ten years old again, tearing up, choked with feeling for these two human beings who, like figures from myth, had possessed the ability throughout his life to blend into the background, to turn to stone or wood, only to come alive again, at key moments like this, to witness his hero's journey. Lillian had a camera. She was taking pictures. That was why Mitchell didn't have to bother.

Larry and he whirled on past the cheering crowd and down the slope of College Street. Mitchell kept an eye out for the Hannas, but didn't see them. He didn't see Madeleine, either.

At the bottom of the slope, the procession lost momentum, and the graduating class of 1982, drifting to the curbside, became onlookers themselves.

Mitchell took off his cap and wiped his forehead. He didn't feel like celebrating, particularly. College had been easy. The idea that graduating was any kind of accomplishment seemed laughable to him. But he *had* enjoyed himself, thoroughly, and right now he was reverentially buzzed, and so he stood and applauded his classmates, trying to join in the jubilation of the day as best he could.

He wasn't thinking religious thoughts, or reciting the Jesus Prayer, when he noticed Professor Richter marching down the hill toward him. It was the faculty brigade now, professors and assistant professors in full academic regalia, their doctoral hoods hemmed in velvet signifying their disciplines and lined with satin representing *their* alma maters, the crimson of Harvard, the green of Dartmouth, the light blue of Tufts.

It surprised Mitchell that Professor Richter would take part in such silly pageantry. He could have been at home reading Heidegger, but instead he was here, wasting his time to parade down a hill in honor of yet another commencement ceremony, and to parade with what appeared to be absolute exhilaration.

At the genuine endpoint of his college career, Mitchell was left with that startling sight: Herr Doktor Professor Richter prancing by, his face lit with a childlike joy it had never displayed in the seminar room for Religion and Alienation. As if Richter had found the cure for alienation. As if he'd beaten the odds of the age.

•

"Congratulations!" the taxi driver said.

Madeleine glanced up, momentarily confused, before she remembered what she was wearing.

"Thank you," she said.

Since most streets around campus were blocked off, the driver was taking the long way around, going down Hope Street to Wickenden.

"You a med student?"

"Excuse me?"

The driver lifted his hands from the wheel. "We're going to the hospital, right? So I thought maybe you're planning on being a doctor."

"No, not me," Madeleine answered nearly inaudibly, looking out the window. The driver took the message and was silent the rest of the way.

As the cab crossed the river, Madeleine took off her cap and gown. The interior of the car smelled of air freshener, something noninterventionist, like vanilla. Madeleine had always liked air fresheners. She'd never thought anything about it until Leonard had told her that it indicated a willingness, on her part, to avoid unpleasant realities. "It isn't like the room doesn't smell bad," he'd said. "It's just that you can't smell it." She'd thought she'd caught him in a logical inconsistency, and had cried out, "How can a room smell bad if it smells nice?" And Leonard had replied, "Oh, it still smells bad all right. You're mistaking properties with substance."

These were the kinds of conversations she had with Leonard. They were part of why she liked him so much. You could be going anywhere, doing anything, and an air freshener would lead to a little symposium.

She wondered now, though, if his many-branching thoughts had in fact led straight to where he was now.

The taxi pulled up to a hospital that called to mind a badly aging Holiday Inn. Eight stories tall, glass-fronted, the white building looked soiled, as though it had absorbed the filth from the adjoining streets. The concrete urns flanking the entrance contained no flowers, only cigarette butts. A spidery figure suggestive of blue-collar hard luck and work-related illness was propelling himself with a walker through the perfectly functioning automatic doors.

In the atrium-like lobby, Madeleine made two wrong turns before finding the front desk. The receptionist took one look at her before asking, "You here for Bankhead?"

Madeleine was taken aback. Then she glanced around the waiting room and saw that she was the only white person there.

"Yes."

"Can't let you go up yet. Too many people up there already. Soon as someone comes down, I'll let you up."

This was another surprise. Leonard's emotional collapse, indeed his entire self-presentation as a nonperforming adult, wasn't consistent with a surplus of sickroom visitors. Madeleine was jealous of the unknown company.

She signed in and took a seat facing the elevators. The carpet bore a mood-elevating design of blue squares, each framing a child's crayon drawing: a rainbow, a unicorn, a happy family. People had brought in take-out food to eat while they waited, foam containers of jerk chicken and barbecued brisket. In the chair opposite her, a toddler was napping.

Madeleine gazed at the carpet without benefit.

After twenty long minutes, the elevator doors opened and two young white guys got off. Reassuringly, both were male. One guy was tall with B-52 hair, the other short, wearing a T-shirt with the famous photograph of Einstein sticking out his tongue.

"He seemed good to me," the first guy said. "He seemed better."

"That was better? Jesus, I need a cigarette."

They passed by without noticing Madeleine.

As soon as they were gone, she went up to the receptionist.

"Fourth floor," the woman said, handing her a pass.

The large-capacity elevator, built to accommodate stretchers and medical equipment, rose slowly, with Madeleine its single occupant. Up past Obstetrics and Rheumatology, past Osteology and Oncology, beyond all the ills that could happen to the human body, none of which had happened to Leonard, the elevator carried her to the Psychiatric Unit, where what happened to people happened in the head. She'd been prepared, by the movies, for a site of harsh incarceration. But except for a red button that opened the double doors from the outside (a button that had no corresponding release *inside*), there was little sign of confinement. The corridor was pale green, the linoleum highly polished, squeaky underfoot. A food cart stood against a wall. The few patients visible in their rooms— *mental patients*, Madeleine couldn't help thinking—were passing time as all convalescents would, reading, dozing, staring out the window.

At the nursing station she asked for Leonard Bankhead and was directed to the dayroom at the end of the hall.

As soon as Madeleine stepped in, the light made her wince. The brightness of the dayroom seemed itself a therapy against depression. No shadows were allowed. Madeleine squinted, looking around at the Formica tables where robed and slippered patients sat alone or in the company of shoe-wearing visitors. A TV was bolted to an elevated rack in one corner, the volume loud. Evenly spaced windows gave views of city roofs jutting and dropping toward the bay.

Leonard was sitting in a chair fifteen feet away. A guy with glasses was leaning forward, speaking to him.

"So, Leonard," the guy with the glasses was saying. "You manufactured a little mental illness to get in here and get some help. And now you're in and you've *got* some help, and you realize maybe you're not so bad off as you thought."

Leonard appeared to be listening intently to what the guy was saying. He wasn't wearing a hospital robe, as Madeleine expected, but his normal clothes—work shirt, carpenter's pants, blue bandanna on his head. All that was missing were his Timberlands. Leonard had on open-toed hospital slippers, with socks. His stubble was longer than usual.

"You had some issues that weren't being addressed by your therapy," the guy with the glasses said, "and so you had to exaggerate them in order to bring them into a bigger arena and have them dealt with." Whoever the guy was, he seemed tremendously satisfied by his interpretation. He sat back, looking at Leonard as if expecting applause.

Madeleine took this opportunity to come forward.

Seeing her, Leonard rose from his chair.

"Madeleine. Hey," he said softly. "Thanks for coming."

And so it was established: the gravity of Leonard's predicament outweighed the fact that they'd broken up. Nullified it. Which meant that she could hug him, if she wanted.

She didn't, however. She was worried that physical contact might be against the rules.

"Do you know Henry?" Leonard said, keeping up the formalities. "Madeleine, Henry. Henry, Madeleine."

"Welcome to visiting hours," Henry said. He had a deep voice, the voice of authority. He was wearing a Madras jacket that pinched under the arms and a white shirt.

The terrible brightness of the room had the effect of making the floor-to-ceiling windows reflective, even though it was daylight outside. Madeleine saw the ghost image of herself looking at an equally ghostly Leonard. One young woman who had no visitors—and who was in a bathrobe, with wild, uncombed hair—was circling the room, muttering to herself.

"Nice place, huh?" Leonard said.

"It seems O.K."

"It's a state hospital. This is where people go if they don't have the money to go to somewhere like Silverlake."

"Leonard is a little disappointed," Henry explained, "not to be in the company of first-class depressives."

Madeleine didn't know who Henry was or why he was here. His jocularity seemed, at the least, insensitive, if not downright malicious. But Leonard didn't seem bothered. He took in everything Henry said with a disciple-like neediness. This, and the way he occasionally sucked on his upper lip, were the only things that seemed off about him.

"The flip side of self-loathing is grandiosity," Leonard observed.

"Right," Henry said. "So if you're going to crack up, you want to crack up like Robert Lowell."

The choice of the phrase *crack up* struck Madeleine as less than ideal as well. She resented Henry for it. At the same time, the fact that Henry was belittling Leonard's illness suggested that maybe it wasn't so serious.

Maybe Henry was handling this the right way. She was eager for any pointers. But levity was beyond her. She felt painfully awkward and tongue-tied.

Madeleine had never been close to anyone with a verifiable mental illness. She instinctively avoided unstable people. As uncharitable as this attitude was, it was part and parcel of being a Hanna, of being a positive, privileged, sheltered, exemplary person. If there was one thing Madeleine Hanna was not, it was mentally unstable. That had been the script, anyway. But sometime after finding Billy Bainbridge in bed with two women, Madeleine had become aware of the capacity in herself for a helpless sadness not unlike clinical depression; and certainly in these last weeks, sobbing in her room over her breakup with Leonard, getting wasted and having sex with Thurston Meems, pinning her last hope on being accepted to a graduate school she wasn't even sure she wanted to attend, broken by love, by empty promiscuity, by self-doubt, Madeleine recognized that she and a mentally ill person were not necessarily mutually exclusive categories.

A line from Barthes she remembered: *Every lover is mad, we are told. But can we imagine a madman in love?*

"Leonard's concerned they're going to keep him in here indefinitely, which I don't think is the case." Henry was talking again. "You're fine, Leonard. Just tell the doctor what you told me. They're just keeping you in here for observation."

"The doctor's supposed to call in a minute," Leonard informed Madeleine.

"You manufactured a little mental illness to get in here and get some help," Henry repeated once more. "And now you feel better and you're ready to go home."

Leonard leaned forward, all ears. "I just want to get out of here," he said. "I had to take three incompletes. I just want to finish up those classes and graduate."

Madeleine had never seen Leonard on such good behavior. The willing schoolboy, the star patient.

"That's a good thing," Henry said. "That's a healthy thing. You want your life back."

Leonard looked from Henry to Madeleine and robotically repeated, "I want my life back. I want to get out of here and finish my incompletes and graduate."

A nurse stuck her head into the dayroom.

"Leonard? Dr. Shieu's on the phone for you."

As eagerly as someone interviewing for a job, Leonard stood up. "Here goes," he said.

"Tell the doctor what you told me," said Henry.

When Leonard had left, they both remained silent. Finally Henry spoke.

"I'm guessing you're Leonard's girlfriend," he said.

"Unclear at this point," Madeleine replied.

"He's in a fugue state." Henry rotated his index finger in the air. "Just a tape loop, going around and around."

"But you just told him he was fine."

"Well, that's what Leonard needs to hear."

"You're not a doctor, though," she said.

"No," Henry said. "But I *am* a psych major. Which means I've read a lot of Freud." He broke into a big, awkward, flirtatious Cheshire cat grin.

"And here we are," Madeleine tartly replied, "living in post-Freudian times."

Henry bore this dig with something like pleasure. "If you *are* Leonard's girlfriend," he said, "or if you're thinking of *becoming* Leonard's girlfriend, or if you're thinking of getting back together with him, my advice would be not to do that."

"Who are you, anyway?"

"Just someone who knows, from personal experience, how attractive it can be to think you can save somebody else by loving them."

"I could have sworn we just met," Madeleine said. "And that you don't know anything about me."

Henry stood up. With a slightly offended air but undiminished confidence, he said, "People don't save other people. People save themselves."

He left her with that to think about.

The woman with the uncombed hair was staring up at the TV, tying and untying the belt of her robe. A young black woman, college-age herself, was sitting at a table with what looked to be her parents. They seemed used to the surroundings.

After a few more minutes, Leonard returned. The woman with the uncombed hair called out, "Hey, Leonard. Did you see any lunch out there?"

"I didn't," Leonard said. "Not yet."

"I could use some lunch."

"Another half hour, it'll be here," Leonard said helpfully.

He had the air more of a doctor than of a patient. The woman seemed to trust him. She nodded and turned away.

Leonard sat in the chair and leaned forward, jiggling his knee.

Madeleine was trying to think of something to say, but everything she thought of sounded like an attack. *How long have you been in here? Why didn't you tell me? Is it true you were diagnosed three years ago? Why didn't you tell me you were on medication? My roommates knew and I didn't!*

She settled on "What did the doctor say?"

"She doesn't want to discharge me yet," Leonard said equably, bearing up to the news. "She doesn't want to *talk* about discharging me yet."

"Just go along with her. Just stay here and rest. I bet you could finish your incompletes in here."

Leonard looked from side to side, speaking softly so that no one would overhear. "That's about all I can do. Like I said, this is a state hospital."

"Meaning what?"

"Meaning it's mostly just throwing medicine at people."

"Are you taking anything?"

He hesitated before answering. "Lithium, mostly. Which I've been on awhile. They're recalibrating my dose."

"Is it helping?"

"Some side effects, but yeah. Essentially the answer is yes."

It was hard to tell if this was indeed so, or if Leonard wanted it to be.

He seemed to be concentrating intensely on Madeleine's face, as though it would provide him crucial information.

Abruptly he turned and regarded his reflection in the window, rubbing his cheeks.

"They only let us shave once a week," he said. "An orderly has to be there while we do it."

"Why?"

"Razor blades. That's why I look like this."

Madeleine glanced around the room to see if anyone was touching. No one was.

"Why didn't you call me?" she asked.

"We broke up."

"Leonard! If I knew you were depressed, that wouldn't have mattered."

"The breakup was *why* I was depressed," Leonard said.

This was news. This was, in an inappropriate but real way, good news.

"I sabotaged you and me," Leonard said. "I see that now. I'm able to think a little more clearly now. Part of growing up in the kind of family I come from, a family of alcoholics, is that you begin to normalize disease and dysfunctionality. Disease and dysfunctionality are normal for me. What's not normal is feeling . . ." He broke off. He inclined his head, his dark eyes focusing on the linoleum, as he continued: "Remember that day you said you loved me? Remember that? See, you could do that because you're basically a sane person, who grew up in a loving, sane family. You could take a risk like that. But in *my* family we didn't go around saying we loved each other. We went around screaming at each other. So what do I do, when you say you love me? I go and undermine it. I go and reject it by throwing Roland Barthes in your face."

Depression didn't necessarily ruin a person's looks. Only the way Leonard was moving his lips, sucking them and biting them occasionally, indicated that he was on any drugs.

"And so you left," he continued. "You walked out. And you were right to do that, Madeleine." Leonard looked at her now, his face full of sorrow. "I'm damaged goods," he said.

"You are not."

"After you left that day, I lay down on my bed and didn't get up for a week. I just lay there thinking how I'd sabotaged the best chance I ever had to be happy in life. The best chance I ever had to be with someone smart, beautiful, and sane. The kind of person I could be a team with." He leaned forward and gazed with intensity into Madeleine's eyes. "I'm sorry," he said. "I'm sorry for being the kind of person who would do a thing like that."

"Don't worry about that now," Madeleine said. "You have to concentrate on feeling better."

Leonard blinked three times in quick succession. "I'm going to be in here for at least another week," he said. "I'm missing graduation."

"You wouldn't have gone, anyway."

Here, for the first time, Leonard smiled. "You're probably right. How was it?"

"I don't know," Madeleine said. "It's going on right now."

"Right now?" Leonard looked out the window, as if he could check. "You're missing it?"

Madeleine nodded. "I wasn't in the mood."

The woman in the bathrobe who'd been lazily circling the room now zeroed in on them. Under his breath Leonard said, "Watch out for this one. She can turn on you in a second."

The woman shuffled closer and stopped. Bending at the knees, she appraised Madeleine closely.

"What are you?" she said.

"What am I?"

"Where are your people from?"

"England," Madeleine said. "Originally."

"You look like Candice Bergen."

She wheeled around to grin at Leonard. "And you're 007!"

"Sean Connery," Leonard said. "That's me."

"You look like 007 gone all to hell!" the woman said. There was an edge to her tone. Leonard and Madeleine, playing it safe, said nothing until she moved on.

The woman in the bathrobe belonged in here. Leonard, in Madeleine's opinion, didn't. He was here only because of his intensity. Had she known from the outset about his manic depression, his messed-up family, his shrink habit, Madeleine would never have allowed herself to get so passionately involved. But now that she was passionately involved, she found little to regret. To feel so much was its own justification.

"What about Pilgrim Lake Lab?" she said.

"I don't know." Leonard shook his head.

"Do they know?"

"I don't think so."

"That's not until September," Madeleine said. "That's a long time from now."

The TV jabbered on its hooks and chains. Leonard sucked his upper lip in the weird new way.

Madeleine took his hand.

"I'll still go with you, if you want," she said.

"You will?"

"You can finish your incompletes in here. We can stay in Providence for the summer and then move out there in September."

Leonard was quiet, taking this in.

Madeleine asked, "Do you think you can handle it? Or would it be better to just rest awhile?"

"I think I can handle it," Leonard said. "I want to get back to work."

They were silent, looking at each other.

Leonard leaned closer.

"'Once the first avowal has been made,'" he said, quoting Barthes from memory, "'"I love you" has no meaning whatever.'"

Madeleine frowned. "Are you going to start that again?"

"No, but—think about it. That means the first avowal *does* have meaning."

Light came into Madeleine's eyes. "I'm done then, I guess," she said.

"Not me," Leonard said, holding her hand. "Not me."

Pilgrims

Mitchell and Larry reached Paris in late August after a summer of boredom and desperate employment.

At Orly, lifting his backpack from the luggage carousel, Mitchell found that his arms were sore from the inoculations he'd gotten in New York two days earlier: cholera in the right, typhus in the left. He'd felt feverish on the flight over. Their low-priority seats were in the last row, across from the malodorous lavatories. Mitchell had dozed fitfully through the long transatlantic night until the cabin lights blazed on and a flight attendant shoved a half-frozen croissant in front of his face, which he nevertheless nibbled as the huge passenger jet made its descent over the capital.

Among mostly French nationals (tourist season was drawing to a close), they boarded an un-air-conditioned bus and glided noiselessly along smooth highways into the city. Getting off near the Pont de l'Alma, they retrieved their backpacks from the undercarriage and began trudging up the brightening avenue. Larry, who spoke French, walked ahead, looking for Claire's apartment, while Mitchell, who didn't have a girlfriend in France or anywhere else, expended no effort in trying to get them where they were going.

Jet lag added to his slight delirium. It was morning by the clock but deepest nighttime in his body. The rising sun forced him to squint. It seemed unkind somehow. And yet, at street level, everything had been arranged to please the eye. The trees were thick with late-summer leaves. They wore iron grilles around their trunks, like aprons. The broadness of the sidewalk accommodated newspaper kiosks, dog walkers, chic ten-year-old girls on their way to the park. A sharp scent of tobacco arose from the curbside, which was the way Mitchell had thought Europe would smell, earthy, sophisticated, and unhealthy, all at once.

Mitchell hadn't wanted to start their trip in Paris. Mitchell had wanted to go to London, where he could visit the Globe Theatre, drink Bass ale, and understand what people were saying. But Larry had found two extremely cheap tickets on a charter flight to Orly, and since their money had to last the next nine months, Mitchell didn't see how he could refuse. He didn't have anything against Paris, per se. At any other time, he would have jumped at the chance to go to Paris. The problem with Paris, in the present case, was that Larry's girlfriend was doing a year abroad there and they were going to stay in her apartment.

This, too, was the cheapest option. Therefore, inarguable.

As Mitchell fiddled with the belt of his backpack, his fever spiked a half degree.

"I'm not sure if I'm getting the cholera or the typhus," he said to Larry.

"Probably both."

Aside from the romantic opportunities, Paris appealed to Larry because he was a Francophile. He'd spent a summer during high school working at a restaurant in Normandy, learning to speak the language and to chop vegetables. At college, his proficiency in French had won him a room in French House. The plays Larry directed at Production Workshop, the student-run theater, were inevitably by French Modernist playwrights. Since coming east to college, Mitchell had been trying to wash the Midwest off himself. Sitting around in Larry's room, drinking the muddy espresso Larry made and hearing him talk about "the theater of the absurd," seemed like a good way to start. With his black turtleneck and little white Keds, Larry looked like he'd just returned not from a history lecture but from the Actors Studio. He already had full-blown adult addictions to caffeine and foie gras. Unlike Mitchell's parents, whose artistic enthusiasms ran to Ethel Merman and Andrew Wyeth, Larry's parents, Harvey and Moira Pleshette, were devotees of high culture. Moira ran the Wave Hill visual arts program. Harvey served on the boards of the New York City Ballet and the Dance Theatre of Harlem. During the Cold War, Irina Kolnoskova, second ballerina of the Kirov

Ballet, had stayed in hiding at the Pleshettes' house, in Riverdale, after defecting. Larry, only fifteen at the time, had ferried champagne splits and graham crackers to the ballerina's bedside, where Kolnoskova alternately wept, watched game shows, or coaxed him to massage her young, spectacularly deformed feet. For Mitchell, Larry's stories of drunken cast parties held at their house, of stumbling on Leonard Bernstein making out with a male dancer in the upstairs hallway, or of Ben Vereen singing a song from *Pippin* at Larry's older sister's wedding, were as astounding as tales of meeting Joe Montana or Larry Bird would have been for another kind of boy. The Pleshettes' refrigerator was the first place Mitchell had encountered gourmet ice cream. He still remembered the thrill of it: coming down to the kitchen one morning, the majestic Hudson visible in the window, and opening the freezer to see the small round tub of exotically named ice cream. Not a greedy half gallon, as they had at Mitchell's house in Michigan, not cheap ice *milk*, not vanilla, chocolate, or strawberry but a flavor he had never dreamed of before, with a name as lyrical as the Berryman poems he was reading for his American poetry class: rum raisin. Ice cream that was also a drink! In a precious pint-size container. Six of these lined up next to six bags of dark French roast Zabar's coffee. What *was* Zabar's? How did you get there? What was lox? Why was it orange? Did the Pleshettes really eat fish for breakfast? Who was Diaghilev? What was a gouache, a pentimento, a rugelach? *Please tell me*, Mitchell's face silently pleaded throughout his visits. He was in New York, the greatest city in the world. He wanted to learn everything, and Larry was the guy who could teach him.

Moira never paid her parking tickets, just stashed them in the glove box. When Harvey found out, he shouted at the dinner table, "That's fiscal irresponsibility!" The Pleshettes attended family therapy sessions, all six of them going weekly to a shrink in Manhattan to hash out their conflicts. Like Mitchell's father, Harvey had served in World War II. He dressed in khaki suits and bow ties, smoked Dominican cigars, and was in every way a member of that superconfident, supermature generation that went to war. And yet once a week Harvey lay on a mat, on the floor of a shrink's office, and listened without complaint as his children hurled abuse at him. The floor mat subverted hierarchy. Supine, all the Pleshettes achieved equality. Only the therapist reigned above, in his Eames chair.

At the end of the war, Harvey had been stationed in Paris with the U.S. Army. It was a time he liked to talk about, his exuberant recollections of *les femmes parisiennes* often causing Moira's expression to grow pinched. "I was twenty-two and a lieutenant in the American army. We had the run of the place. We'd liberated Paris and it was ours! I had my own driver. We used to motor along the avenues handing out stockings and chocolate bars. That was all it took." Every four or five years, the Pleshettes went back to France to tour the paternal war sites. In a sense, by coming to Paris now at the same age, Larry was reenacting his father's youth, back when the Americans had marched into the city.

That was no longer the case. There was nothing American about the avenue they were trudging along. Up ahead, a billboard advertised a film called *Beau-père*, the poster showing a teenage girl, topless, in her father's lap. Larry walked by without noticing.

It would be years before Mitchell developed an understanding of the layout of Paris, years before he could deploy the word *arrondissement*, much less learn that the numbered districts were laid out in a spiral. He was used to grid cities. That the First Arrondissement might rub up against the Thirteenth, without the Fourth or Fifth getting in between, would have been inconceivable to him.

Claire lived not far from the Eiffel Tower, however, and, later on, Mitchell would calculate that her apartment had been in the fashionable Seventh, and that it must have been expensive.

Her street, when they managed to find it, was a cobblestone relic of medieval Paris. The sidewalk was too narrow to navigate with their packs, so they had to walk in the street, past the toy cars.

The name on the bell was "Thierry." Larry pressed it. After a long delay, the lock buzzed. Mitchell, who'd been resting against the door, tumbled into the lobby as it opened.

"Walk much?" Larry said.

Back on his feet, Mitchell stood aside to let Larry enter, then hip-checked him back down the front steps, and went in first.

"Fuck you, Mitchell," Larry said in a tone almost of affection.

Like snails hauling their shells, they slowly ascended the staircase. It got darker the higher they climbed. On the sixth floor they waited in near-total blackness until a door at one end opened and Claire Schwartz stepped into the frame of light.

She was holding a book, her expression more that of a library patron who'd been momentarily distracted than that of a girl eagerly awaiting her boyfriend's arrival from across the sea. Her long honey-colored hair was hanging down in front of her face, but she ran her hand through it, tucking a portion behind her right ear. This seemed to make her face once again available for emotion. She smiled and cried out, "Hi, hon!"

"Hi, hon," Larry responded, hurrying to her.

Claire was three inches taller than Larry. She bent her knees while they embraced. Mitchell hung back in the shadows until they were finished.

Finally, Claire noticed him and said, "Oh, hi. Come on in."

Claire was two years younger than they were, still a junior in college. Larry had met her at a summer theater workshop at SUNY Purchase—he was doing theater, she was studying French—and this was the first time that Mitchell had met her. She was wearing a peasant blouse, blue jeans, and long multiform earrings that resembled miniature wind chimes. Her rainbow-colored socks had individual toes. The book she was holding was called *New French Feminisms*.

Though auditing a class at the Sorbonne taught by Luce Irigaray and titled The Mother-Daughter Relationship: The Darkest of Dark Continents, Claire had followed maternal example by setting out guest towels. The apartment she was subletting wasn't the usual *chambre de bonne*, with a fold-down bed and a shared WC in the hall, of a visiting student. It was tastefully furnished with framed paintings, a dining table, and a kilim rug. After Mitchell and Larry had taken off their packs, Claire asked them if they wanted coffee.

"I'm dying for coffee," Larry said.

"I make it with a *pression*," Claire said.

"That's fabulous," Larry said.

As soon as Claire put down her book and stepped into the kitchen, Mitchell gave Larry a look. "Hi, *hon*?" he whispered.

Larry looked back at him evenly.

It was painfully clear that, if Mitchell hadn't been there, Claire wouldn't be making coffee. If Larry and Claire were alone, they would already be having reunion sex. Under other circumstances, Mitchell would have made himself scarce. But he didn't know anybody in Paris and had nowhere to go.

He did the next best thing, which was to turn and stare out the window.

Here, momentarily, things improved. The window gave onto a view of dove-gray roofs and balconies, each one containing the same cracked flowerpot and sleeping feline. It was as if the entire city of Paris had agreed to abide by a single understated taste. Each neighbor was doing his or her own to keep up standards, which was difficult because the French ideal wasn't clearly delineated like the neatness and greenness of American lawns, but more of a picturesque disrepair. It took courage to let things fall apart so beautifully.

Turning from the window, Mitchell looked around the apartment again and realized something troubling: there was no place for him to sleep. Come nighttime, Claire and Larry would climb into the only bed together, leaving Mitchell to roll out his sleeping bag on the floor in front of it. They would turn out the lights. As soon as they thought he was asleep, they would begin fooling around, and for the next hour or so, Mitchell would be forced to listen to his friend getting laid five feet away.

He picked up *New French Feminisms* from the nearby dining table.

The austere cover bore a regiment of names. Julia Kristeva. Hélène Cixous. Kate Millett. Mitchell had seen lots of girls at school reading *New French Feminisms*, but he'd never seen a guy reading it. Not even Larry, who was small and sensitive and into all things French, had read it.

Suddenly Claire called out excitedly, "I love that book!"

She came out of the kitchen beaming and took it from his hands. "Have you read it?"

"I was just looking at it."

"I'm reading it for this class I'm taking. I just finished this essay by Kristeva." She opened the book and flipped through it. Her hair fell in front of her face and she impatiently tossed it back. "I've been reading a lot of stuff on the body, and how the body has always been associated with the feminine. So it's interesting that, in Western religion, the body is always seen as sinful. You're supposed to mortify the body and transcend it. But what Kristeva says is that we have to look at the body again, especially the maternal body. She's basically a Lacanian, except she doesn't agree that signification and language come from castration fears. Otherwise we'd all be psychotic."

Like Larry, Claire was blond, blue-eyed, and Jewish. But whereas Larry had secular parents who didn't go to temple even on the High Holidays and who held seders in which the *afikoman* wasn't a matzoh but a Twinkie (the product of childish mischief years ago, which had now perversely become its own tradition), Claire's parents were Orthodox Jews who lived by the letter of the law. Their mammoth house in Scarsdale had not two sets of plates in order to keep kosher but two separate kitchens. There were Saturdays when the maid forgot to leave lights on when the Schwartzes dwelt in darkness. Once, Claire's younger brother had been rushed to the hospital in an ambulance (Talmudic wisdom holding that a medical emergency contravened the prohibition against riding in cars on the Sabbath). Nevertheless, Mr. and Mrs. Schwartz had refused to ride along with their writhing son, setting off instead, nearly mad with worry, for the hospital on foot.

"The whole thing about Judaism and Christianity," Claire said, "and just about every monotheistic religion, is that they're all patriarchal. Men made these religions up. So guess who God is? A man."

"Watch out, Claire," Larry said. "Mitchell was a religious studies major."

Claire grimaced and said, "Oh, my God."

"I'll tell you what I learned in religious studies," Mitchell said with a slight smile. "If you read any of the mystics, or any decent theology—Catholic, Protestant, kabbalistic—the one thing they all agree on is that God is beyond any human concept or category. That's why Moses can't look at Yahweh. That's why, in Judaism, you can't even spell out God's name. The human mind can't conceive what God is. God doesn't have a sex or anything else."

"Then why is he a man with a long white beard on the Sistine Chapel?"

"Because that's what the masses like."

"The masses?"

"Some people need a picture. Any great religion has to be inclusive. And to be inclusive you have to accommodate different levels of sophistication."

"You sound just like my father. Whenever I tell him how sexist Judaism is, he tells me it's tradition. Because it's tradition, that means it's good. You have to live with it."

"I'm not saying that. I'm saying that for some people, tradition is good. For others, it's not so important. Some people think that God reveals Himself through history, others that revelation is progressive, that maybe the rules or interpretation changes over time."

"The whole idea of revelation is teleological and bogus."

Back in Scarsdale, facing down her father in their Chagall-lined living room, Claire had no doubt stood just as she was standing now: feet planted apart, hands on hips, torso leaning slightly forward. Despite being irritated by her, Mitchell was also impressed—as Mr. Schwartz must also have been impressed during their arguments—with the force of Claire's will.

He realized she was waiting for him to respond and so he said, "Bogus how?"

"The whole idea of God's revealing 'Himself' through history is silly. The Jews build the temple. Then the temple gets destroyed. So the Jews have to build it again so that the Messiah shows up? The idea that God is waiting around for stuff to happen—like, if there *was* such a thing as God, he would even care what people are doing—is totally anthropocentric and so totally, totally male! Before the patriarchal religions were created, people worshipped the Goddess. The Babylonians did, the Etruscans did. The religion of the Goddess was organic and environmental—it was about the cycle of nature—as opposed to Judaism and Christianity, which are just about imposing the law and raping the land."

Mitchell glanced at Larry to see that he was nodding in agreement. Mitchell might have nodded, too, if he were going out with Claire, but Larry looked sincerely interested in the Goddess of the Babylonians.

"If you dislike a conception of God as masculine," Mitchell said to Claire, "why replace it with one that's feminine? Why not get rid of the whole idea of a gendered divinity?"

"Because it *is* gendered. It *is*. Already. Do you know what a mikva is?" She turned to Larry. "Does he know what a mikva is?"

"I know what a mikva is," Mitchell said.

"O.K., so my mom goes to a mikva every month after her period, right? To cleanse herself. To cleanse herself from what? From the power to give birth? To create life? They turn the greatest power a woman has into something they should be ashamed about."

"I agree with you, that's absurd."

"But it's not about the mikva. The whole institutionalized form of

Western religion is all about telling women they're inferior, unclean, and subordinate to men. And if you actually believe in any of that stuff, I don't know what to say."

"You're not having your period right now, are you?" Mitchell said.

Claire's expressive face went blank. "I can't believe you just said that," she said.

"I was just kidding," Mitchell said. His face was suddenly hot.

"What a total sexist thing to say."

"I was *kidding*," he repeated, his voice tight.

"You have to get to know Mitchell," Larry said. "He's an acquired taste."

"I'm in agreement with you!" Mitchell tried again with Claire, but the more he protested, the more insincere he sounded, and finally he shut up.

There was one bright side to the day: since it still felt like the middle of the night for Larry and Mitchell, there was no reason not to start drinking immediately. By early afternoon they were in the Luxembourg Gardens, sharing a bottle of *vin de table*. The sky had grown cloudy, casting the flowers and yellow gravel paths in a sharp gray light. Old men were playing *boules* nearby, bending at the knee and releasing silver balls from their fingertips. The balls made pleasant clicks when they struck one another. The sound of satisfactory, social democratic retirement.

Claire had changed into a sundress and a pair of sandals. She didn't shave her legs, and the hair on them was slight and blond, tapering out at her thighs. She seemed to have forgiven Mitchell. He, in turn, was doing his best to be likeable.

Under the influence of the wine Mitchell began to feel happier, his jet lag in temporary remission. They walked down to the Seine, across the Louvre and the Tuileries Gardens. Sanitation workers were sweeping the parks and sweeping the curbs, their uniforms impossibly clean.

Larry said that he wanted to cook dinner, so Claire, who no longer kept kosher, took them to an outdoor market near her building. Larry plunged in among the stalls, ogling produce, sniffing cheeses. He bought carrots, fennel, and potatoes, conversing with the farmers. The poultry stand made him stop and put a hand to his chest. "Oh my God, *poularde de Bresse*! That's what I'm making!"

Back at Claire's apartment, Larry unwrapped the chicken with a flourish. *"Poulet bleu.* See? They've got these blue feet. That's how you know they come from Bresse. We used to roast these at the restaurant. They're fabulous."

He set to work in the tiny kitchen, chopping and salting, melting butter, three pans going at once.

"I'm sleeping with Julia Child," Claire said.

"More like the Galloping Gourmet," Mitchell said.

She laughed. "Honey?" she said, kissing Larry's cheek. "I'm going to go read while you obsess over your little chicken."

Claire settled on the bed with her anthology. Hit by a new surge of fatigue, Mitchell wished he could lie down, too. Instead, he unzipped his backpack, digging under his clothes for the books he'd brought along. Mitchell had tried to travel as light as possible, packing two of everything, shirts, pants, socks, underwear, plus a sweater. But when it came time to winnow the stack of reading material, he'd failed to be stringent, bringing with him a cache that included *The Imitation of Christ*, *The Confessions of St. Augustine*, Saint Teresa's *Interior Castle*, Merton's *Seeds of Contemplation*, Tolstoy's *A Confession and Other Religious Writings*, and a sizeable paperback of Pynchon's *V.*, along with a hardback edition of *God Biology: Toward a Theistic Understanding of Evolution*. Finally, before leaving New York, Mitchell picked up a copy of *A Moveable Feast* at St. Mark's Bookshop. His plan was to send each book back home when he finished it, or to give it away to anyone who was interested.

He took the Hemingway out now, sitting down at the dining table, and read from where he'd left off:

The story was writing itself and I was having a hard time keeping up with it. I ordered another rum St. James and I watched the girl whenever I looked up, or when I sharpened the pencil with a pencil sharpener with the shavings curling into the saucer under my drink.

I've seen you, beauty, and you belong to me now, whoever you are waiting for and if I never see you again, I thought. You belong to me and all Paris belongs to me and I belong to this notebook and this pencil.

He tried to imagine what it had been like to be Hemingway, in Paris, in the 1920s. To write those clear, seemingly unadorned, yet complex sentences that would change forever the way Americans wrote prose. To do all that and then go out to dinner where you knew how to order the perfect seasonal wine to go with your *huîtres*. To be an American in Paris back when it was O.K. to be American.

"Are you actually reading that?"

Mitchell looked up to find Claire staring at him from the bed.

"Hemingway?" she said dubiously.

"I thought it would be good for Paris."

She rolled her eyes and went back to her book. And Mitchell went back to his. Or tried. Except that now all he could do was stare at the page.

He was perfectly aware that certain once-canonical writers (always male, always white) had fallen into disrepute. Hemingway was a misogynist, a homophobe, a repressed homosexual, a murderer of wild animals. Mitchell thought this was an instance of tarring with too wide a brush. If he was to argue this with Claire, however, he ran the risk of being labeled a misogynist himself. More worryingly, Mitchell had to ask himself if he wasn't being just as knee-jerk in resisting the charge of misogyny as college feminists were in leveling it, and if his resistance didn't mean that he was, somewhere deep down, prone to misogyny himself. Why, after all, had he bought *A Moveable Feast* in the first place? Why, knowing what he did about Claire, had he decided to whip it out of his backpack at this particular moment? Why, in fact, had the phrase *whip it out* just occurred to him?

Rereading Hemingway's sentences, Mitchell recognized that they were, indeed, implicitly addressed to the male reader.

He crossed and uncrossed his legs, trying to concentrate on his book. He felt embarrassed to be reading Hemingway and angry about being made to feel embarrassed. It wasn't as if Hemingway was even his favorite writer! He'd hardly read any Hemingway!

Fortunately, a little while later, Larry announced that dinner was served.

At the small table meant to accomodate a Parisian bachelor, Claire and Mitchell sat while Larry served them. He carved the chicken, sequestering the white meat, dark meat, and drumsticks on a platter, and spooned out the dripping vegetables.

"Yum," Claire said.

The chicken was scrawny by American standards, and cosmetically inferior. One leg seemed to have acne.

Mitchell took a bite.

"Huh?" Larry prompted. "Did I tell you or did I tell you?"

"You told us," Mitchell said.

When they were finished eating, Mitchell insisted on doing the dishes. He stacked them next to the sink while Larry and Claire carried what was left of the wine over to the bed. Claire had taken off her sandals and was now barefoot. She stretched her legs across Larry's lap, sipping from her glass.

Mitchell rinsed the dishes under the tap. The European dish soap was either eco-friendly or tariff-protected. Either way it didn't make enough suds. Mitchell got the dishes reasonably clean and quit. He'd been awake, at that point, for thirty-three hours.

He came back into the main room. On the bed, Larry and Claire were a Keith Haring: two loving human figures that fit perfectly together. Mitchell observed them for a long moment. Then, with sudden resolve, he crossed the room and hoisted his backpack onto his shoulders.

"Where's the best place to find a hotel around here?" he asked.

There was a pause before Claire said, "You can stay here."

"That's O.K. I'll find a hotel."

He hooked his waist strap.

Without arguing, Claire jumped right in to giving directions. "If you take a right outside my building, and then a left at the next street, you'll come to Avenue Rapp. There's a lot of hotels on that."

"Mitchell, stay," Larry urged. "It's cool with us if you stay."

In what he hoped was an unaggrieved tone, Mitchell said, "I'll just get a room someplace. See you guys tomorrow."

He didn't realize the hall was dark until he'd shut the door behind him. He couldn't see a thing. He was about to knock on Claire's door again when he noticed an illuminated button on the wall. When he pressed it, the corridor lights came on.

He was descending past the third floor when the lights timed out again. This time, he couldn't find a button, and so had to grope his way down two more flights to the lobby.

When he reached the street, Mitchell saw that it had begun to rain.

He'd foreseen a moment like this, where he would be exiled from the warm, dry sublet so that Larry could peel off Claire's clothes and press his face between her coltish legs. That he had foreseen this moment but hadn't managed to prevent it seemed only, as he turned toward Avenue Rapp, to confirm his basic stupidity. It was the stupidity of an intelligent person, but stupidity nonetheless.

The force of the rain increased as Mitchell wandered the surrounding blocks. The quarter, which had looked so charming from Claire's window, seemed less so now, on the street, in the rain. The shops were shuttered, graffiti-covered, the sodium-vapor streetlamps giving off an evil light.

Hadn't they just gotten *out* of college? Weren't they finished with undergraduate politics? And yet here they were, staying with a women's studies major on a junior-year-abroad program. Under the pretense of becoming a critic of patriarchy, Claire uncritically accepted every fashionable theory that came her way. Mitchell was glad to be out of her apartment. He was happy to be out in the rain! It was worth it to pay for a hotel if it meant not listening to Claire spout her platitudes for one more second! How could Larry stand going out with her? How could Larry have a girlfriend like that? What was the matter with him?

It was possible, of course, that some of the anger Mitchell felt at Claire was misdirected. It was possible that the female he was really mad at was Madeleine. All summer long, while Mitchell had been in Detroit, he'd been under the illusion that Madeleine was available again. The thought that Bankhead had been dumped, and was suffering, had never failed to lift Mitchell's spirits. He'd even rationalized that it had been *a good thing* that Madeleine had gone out with Bankhead. She needed to get guys like him out of her system. She needed to grow up, as Mitchell did, too, before they could be together.

Then, less than forty-eight hours ago, on the night before he left for Paris, Mitchell had run into Madeleine on the Lower East Side. He and Larry had taken the train from Riverdale into the city. They were sitting in Downtown Beirut, around ten p.m., when, out of the blue, Madeleine had come in with Kelly Traub. Larry had directed Kelly in a show once. They immediately started talking shop, leaving Madeleine and Mitchell alone. At first, Mitchell had been worried that Madeleine was still mad at him, but even in the feeble lighting of the bombed-out bar, he could tell that wasn't the case. She seemed genuinely pleased to see him, and, in his elation, Mitchell had started doing tequila shots. The night proceeded from there. They left Downtown Beirut and went somewhere else. Mitchell knew it was hopeless. He was about to leave for Europe. But it was summer, in New York, the streets as hot as Bangkok, and Madeleine was pressing against him as they rode across town in a cab. The last thing Mitchell remembered, he was standing outside a different bar, in Greenwich Village, blurrily watching Madeleine get into another cab, alone. He was wildly happy. But when he went back inside the bar and started talking to Kelly, he discovered that Madeleine was not, in fact, available at all. Madeleine and Bankhead had gotten back together shortly after graduation and were now about to move to Cape Cod.

The only thing that had cheered him up over the summer had been an illusion. Now, in his disappointment, Mitchell tried to forget about Madeleine and to concentrate on the fact that the last three months had at least put money in his pocket. He'd gone back to Detroit to live rent-free. His parents were happy to have him at home, and Mitchell was happy to have his mother cook his meals and do his laundry while he searched the classifieds. It had never occurred to him how few useful skills he'd acquired in college. There were no openings for religious studies tutors. The ad that caught his attention read: "Drivers Wanted—All Shifts." On the basis of his valid driver's license alone, Mitchell was hired the same night. He worked twelve-hour shifts, from six p.m. to six a.m., plying Detroit's East Side. At the wheels of the badly maintained cabs, which he had to rent from the taxi company, Mitchell trolled deserted streets for fares or, to save gas, parked down by the river, waiting for a call to come over the radio. Detroit wasn't a taxi town. There was almost no foot traffic. No one hailed him from the curb, especially at three or four in the morning. The other cabdrivers were a meager bunch. Instead of the plucky immigrants or wise-talking locals he'd expected to find, the crew was made up of serious losers. These were guys who had clearly failed at every other job they'd had. They had failed manning gas pumps, failed selling popcorn at movie concession stands, failed helping brothers-in-law install PVC piping in low-end condominiums, failed in committing petty crime, in collecting trash, in doing yard work, failed in schools and in marriages, and now they were here, failing as cabdrivers in desperate Detroit. The only other educated driver, who had a law degree, was in his sixties and had been let go from his firm for emotional instability. Late at night, when radio traffic reached a standstill, the drivers gathered in a lot by the river, near the old Medusa Cement plant. Mitchell listened to their conversations, saying nothing, remaining aloof lest they realize where he came from. He tried to seem tightly wound, doing his best Travis Bickle, to keep anyone from messing with him. It worked. The other guys left him alone. Then he drove off, parked on a dead-end street, and read *The Aspern Papers* with a flashlight.

He drove a single mother with four kids from one ramshackle house to another at three in the morning. He ferried a surprisingly polite drug dealer to a drop-off. He took a smooth Billy Dee Williams lookalike with crimped hair and gold chains to sweet-talk his way past the police lock of a woman who didn't seem to want to let him in, but did.

What the cabbies talked about in the roundups was always the same thing: a report that one of them, from the thirty or so working, had actually made money. Every night at least one driver pulled in two or three hundred bucks. Most guys didn't seem to be making anything like that much. After a week on the job, Mitchell added up his total fares against what he'd paid for the cab and gas. He divided this by the number of hours worked and came up with an hourly wage of −$0.76. Essentially, he was paying East Side Taxi to drive its cars.

Mitchell spent the rest of the summer busing tables at a brand-new taverna-style restaurant in Greektown. He was partial to the older establishments on Monroe Street, restaurants like the Grecian Gardens or the Hellas Café, where his parents had taken him and his brothers as children for big family occasions, restaurants full, in those days, not of suburbanites coming downtown to drink cheap wine and order flaming appetizers but of formally dressed immigrants with an air of dignity and displacement about them, an abiding melancholy. The men gave their hats to a girl, usually the owner's daughter, who stacked them neatly in the coatroom. Mitchell and his brothers, in clip-on neckties, sat quietly at the table, the way kids didn't anymore, while Mitchell's grandparents, great-aunts, and great-uncles conversed in Greek. To pass the time he examined their humongous earlobes and tunnel-like nostrils. He was the only thing that could make the old people smile: just to pat his cheeks or run their hands through his wavy hair. Bored by the long dinners, Mitchell was allowed, while the adults were having their coffee, to go up to the display case, to spoon out a mint from the dish beside the cash register, and to press his face against the glass and stare in at the varieties of cigars for sale. In the café across the street, men were playing backgammon or reading Greek newspapers exactly as they would have done in Athens or Constantinople. Now his Greek grandparents were dead, Greektown becoming a kitsch tourist destination, and Mitchell just another suburbanite, no more Greek than the artificial grapes hanging from the ceiling.

His busboy uniform consisted of brown polyester bell-bottoms, a brown polyester shirt with monster lapels, and an orange polyester vest that matched the upholstery of the restaurant booths. Every night the vest and shirt got covered with grease and his mother had to wash it overnight so that he could wear it the next day.

One night, Coleman Young, the mayor, came in with a group of mobsters. One of them, vicious with drink, directed his ragged gaze at Mitchell.

"Hey, you. Motherfucker. Come over here."

Mitchell came over.

"Fill my water glass, motherfucker."

Mitchell filled his glass.

The man dropped his napkin on the floor. "I dropped my napkin, motherfucker. Pick it up."

The mayor didn't look happy, sitting with this crew. But dinners like these were part of the job.

At home, Mitchell counted his tips, telling his parents how cheap India was going to be. "You can live on like five dollars a day. Maybe less."

"What's the matter with Europe?" Dean said.

"We're going to Europe."

"London's a nice spot. Or France. You could go to France."

"We're *going* to France."

"I don't know about this India," Lillian said, shaking her head. "You're liable to catch something over there."

"I'm sure you are aware," Dean said, "that India is one of the so-called 'nonaligned' nations. You know what that means? It means they don't want to choose between the U.S. of A. and Russia. They think Russia and America are moral equivalents."

"How will we get in touch with you over there?" Lillian asked.

"You can send letters to American Express. They hold them."

"England's a nice spot," Dean said. "Remember when we went to England that time? How old were you?"

"I was eight," Mitchell said. "So I've been to England. Larry and I want to go someplace different. Somewhere non-Western."

"Non-Western, eh? I've got an idea. Why don't you go to Siberia? Why don't you visit one of those gulags they've got over there in the Evil Empire?"

"Siberia would actually be pretty interesting."

"What happens if you get sick?" Lillian said.

"I won't get sick."

"How do you know you won't get sick?"

"Let me ask you this," Dean said. "How long do you expect the trip to be? Two, three months?"

"More like eight," Mitchell said. "Depends on how long our money holds out."

"*Then* what are you going to do? With your degree in religious studies."

"I'm thinking of applying to divinity school."

"Divinity school?"

"They have two tracks. People go either to become ministers or theologians. I'd go the scholarly route."

"And then what? Be a professor somewhere?"

"Maybe."

"What does a religious studies professor make?"

"I have no idea."

Dean turned to Lillian. "He thinks this is a minor detail. Salary range. Minor."

"I think you'd make a wonderful professor," Lillian said.

"Yeah?" Dean said, contemplating this. "My son the professor. I suppose you could get tenure with a deal like that."

"If I'm lucky."

"That tenure's a good deal. It's un-American. But it's nice work if you can get it."

"I have to go," said Mitchell. "I'm late for work."

What he was late for, actually, was his catechism class. Unbeknown to anyone, as secretly as if he were buying drugs or visiting a massage parlor, Mitchell had been attending weekly meetings with Father Marucci, at St. Mary's, the Catholic church at the end of Monroe Street. When Mitchell had first rung the bell of the rectory, and explained his reasons, the stocky priest had looked at him dubiously. Mitchell explained that he was thinking of converting to Catholicism. He spoke of his interest in Merton, especially Merton's own tale of conversion, *The Seven-Storey Mountain*. He told Father Marucci pretty much what he'd told Professor Richter. But either because Father Marucci wasn't terribly concerned about making converts or because he'd seen Mitchell's type before, he hadn't pressed hard. Giving Mitchell some materials to read, he'd sent him on his way, telling him to come back and talk if he wanted.

Father Marucci was straight out of the old *Boys Town* movie, as gruff as Spencer Tracy. Mitchell sat in his office, overawed by the large crucifix on the wall and the painting of the Sacred Heart of Jesus over the transom of the door. The old-fashioned radiators bore filigree. The furniture was heavy and solid, the pull rings on the window shades like miniature life preservers.

With narrow blue eyes the priest scrutinized him.

"You read the books I gave you?"

"Yes, I did."

"Any questions?"

"I've got more of a concern than a question."

"Shoot."

"Well, I've been thinking that, if I'm going to become a Catholic, then I'd better be able to obey the rules."

"Not a bad idea."

"Most of them I can handle. But I'm not married. I'm only twenty-two. I don't know when I'll *get* married. It might be a while. So the rule I'm worried about, mainly, is premarital sex."

"Unfortunately, you don't get to pick and choose."

"I know that."

"Listen, a girl's not a watermelon you plug a hole in to see if it's sweet."

Mitchell liked that. This was the kind of no-nonsense spiritual advice he needed. At the same time, he didn't see how it made celibacy any easier.

"You think about it," Father Marucci said.

Outside, the neon signs of Greektown were just coming on. Otherwise, downtown Detroit was empty, just this little block-long glow, and, across Woodward, a night game getting under way at Tiger Stadium. On the warm summer evening breeze Mitchell could smell the river. Tucking the catechism pamphlet into the pocket of his vest, he walked to the restaurant and went to work.

He spent the next eight hours busing tables. He assisted people in their feeding. Customers left chewed pieces of meat on their plates, gristle. If Mitchell found a kid's retainer in a pile of pilafi, he returned it in a take-out carton to avoid embarrassment. After clearing tables, he set them again. He could clear a four-top in one shot, carrying the plates stacked in his arms.

Q: What does the term "flesh" mean when referring to the whole man?

A: When referring to the whole man, the term "flesh" means man in his state of weakness and mortality.

Geri, the owner's wife, liked to commandeer a back booth. She was a large, disordered woman, like a child's drawing that didn't stay within the lines. The waiters supplied her with a steady stream of scotch and sodas. Geri started the nights bright with drink, as if expecting a party. Later, she became sullen. To Mitchell one night she said, "I never should have married a Greek. You know what Greeks are like? I'll tell you. They're like sand niggers. No difference. You Greek?"

"Half," Mitchell said.

"I feel sorry for you."

Q: In which shape will the dead rise?

A: The dead will rise in their own bodies.

This was bad news for Geri. In previous jobs, Mitchell had always found ways to goof off. Restaurant work made that impossible. His only downtime was the fifteen minutes when he bolted his dinner. Mitchell rarely ordered the gyros. The meat wasn't lamb but a beef-and-pork composite, like an eighty-pound can of Spam. Three separate spits revolved in the front window, while the chefs poked and prodded them, carving off slices. The wife of one of the cooks, Stavros, had a heart condition. Two years ago she'd slipped into a coma. Every day before coming to work he stopped into the hospital to sit by her bedside. He was under no illusions about the prospects for her recovery.

Q: Who says that prayer is always possible even while cooking?

A: It is Saint John Chrysostom (around 400 AD) who says that prayer is always possible even while cooking.

And so the summer dragged on. Busing tables, scraping uneaten food, bones and fat, and napkins used for nose-blowing into the huge plastic-lined garbage bin, adding greasy plates to the never-diminishing pile dwarfing the Yemeni dishwasher (the only guy with a job worse than his), Mitchell worked seven shifts a week until he'd earned enough money to buy a plane ticket to Paris and $3,280 in American Express Travelers Cheques. Within a week he was gone, first to New York and, three days later, to Paris, where he now found himself with no place to stay, walking in the rain along Avenue Rapp.

The gutters were overflowing. The rain spattered against his skull, working its way down his collar. A late-night work crew was arranging rag bundles in the street to direct the flow of water. Mitchell walked three more blocks until he saw a hotel on the opposite corner. Ducking into the entranceway, he found it already occupied by another luckless back-packer, a guy in a rain poncho, water droplets falling from the tip of his long nose.

"Every hotel in Paris is booked up," the guy said. "I've been to every one."

"Did you ring the doorbell?"

"Three times so far."

They had to ring twice more to summon the concierge. She arrived fully dressed, her hair in order. She looked them over with a cold eye and said something in French.

"She only has one room," the guy said. "She wants to know if we'll share."

"You were here first," Mitchell said generously.

"It'll be cheaper if we split it."

The concierge led them up to the third floor. Unlocking the door, she stood aside to let them inspect the room.

There was only one bed.

"*C'est bien?*" the woman said.

"She wants to know if it's O.K.," the guy told Mitchell.

"We don't have much choice."

"*C'est bien,*" the guy said.

"*Bonne nuit,*" the concierge said, and retired.

They took off their packs and set them down, water puddling on the floor.

"I'm Clyde," the guy said.

"Mitchell."

While Clyde washed up at the minuscule room sink, Mitchell took a guest towel and went down the hall to the WC. After peeing, he pulled the chain on the toilet, feeling like a train engineer. Returning to the room, he was gratified to find that Clyde had already got into bed and was facing the wall. Mitchell undressed down to his underwear.

The problem was what to do with his money pouch.

Not wanting to wear a fanny pack, like a tourist, and yet not wanting to carry valuables in his luggage, either, Mitchell had bought a fly-fishing wallet. It was waterproof, with a leaping trout design and a reinforced zipper. The wallet had elastic loops for wearing on your belt. But because wearing the wallet on his belt would be the same as wearing a fanny pack, Mitchell had tied the pouch to his belt loop with a string, slipping it inside the waistband of his jeans. It was safe there. But now he had to find somewhere to keep it for the night, while sharing the room with a stranger.

In addition to traveler's checks, the pouch contained Mitchell's passport, immunization records, five hundred francs exchanged from seventy dollars the day before, and a recently activated MasterCard. After failing to dissuade Mitchell from setting off for India, Dean and Lillian had insisted on giving him something for emergencies. Mitchell knew, however, that using a credit card would create a running balance of filial obligation, which he would then need to pay off in monthly or weekly telephone calls home. The MasterCard was like a tracking device. Only after resisting Dean's pressure for a solid month had Mitchell given in and accepted the card, but his plan was never to use it.

With his back to the bed, he untied the pouch from his belt loop. He considered hiding it under the dresser or behind the mirror but finally carried it to the bed and put it under his pillow. He climbed in and switched off the light.

Clyde remained turned toward the wall.

For a long time they lay without speaking. Finally Mitchell said, "You ever read *Moby-Dick*?"

"Long time ago."

"Remember where Ishmael gets into bed at the boardinghouse, at the beginning? He lights a match and there's this Indian, all covered with tattoos, sleeping next to him?"

Clyde was quiet a moment, thinking about that. "Which one of us is the Indian?" he asked.

"Call me Ishmael," Mitchell said, in the dark.

Circadian rhythms woke him early. The sun wasn't up but the rain had stopped. Mitchell could hear Clyde's deep nocturnal breathing. He managed to fall back asleep, and when he woke up again it was broad daylight and Clyde was nowhere to be found. When he looked under his pillow, the money pouch was gone.

He leapt out of bed, instantly panicked. While tearing off the blankets and sheets and feeling under the mattress, Mitchell had a thought. Traveler's checks took the worry out of traveling. In the event of loss or theft, you presented the serial numbers of the checks to American Express and the company replaced them. This made the serial numbers just as important as the checks themselves, however. If someone stole your checks and you didn't have the serial numbers, you were in big trouble. Since the checks came with a warning against carrying them in your luggage, it followed that you shouldn't carry the serial numbers in your luggage, either. But where else could you carry them? The only safe place, it had seemed to Mitchell, was in the fly-fishing wallet along with the traveler's checks themselves. And that was where Mitchell had stashed them until he could think of a better idea.

He had been aware of a central flaw in this reasoning, but it had seemed manageable until this moment.

The vision of returning home in humiliation, his round-the-world trip lasting two days, appeared to him in all its ghastliness. But then he looked behind the bed and saw the money pouch on the floor.

He was on his way out of the hotel when the concierge detained him. She spoke quickly, and in French, but he understood the essence of what she was saying: Clyde had paid half of the room rate; Mitchell owed the other half.

The exchange rate was just over seven francs to the dollar. Mitchell's share of the room was 280 francs, or around $40. If he wanted to keep the room another night, he would have to pay $80. He was hoping to live on $10 a day in Europe, so $120 represented nearly two weeks of his budget. Mitchell fought the temptation to cave and pay for the hotel with the MasterCard. But the thought of the statement arriving in his parents' mail, providing the information that on his first night out he was already staying at a hotel, gave him the strength to resist. From his money pouch he took 280 francs and gave it to the concierge. Telling her that he wouldn't be staying another night, he went back up to the room and got his backpack, and went out to search for something cheaper.

He passed two patisseries within the first block. In the windows, the colorful pastries sat in crinkly paper cups, like nobles wearing ruffs. He had 220 francs left, about $30, and was determined not to cash another check until the following day. Crossing Avenue Rapp, he entered a park and found a metal chair where he could sit in the shade and not spend money.

The weather had turned warmer, the rainstorm leaving blue skies in its wake. As he had the day before, Mitchell marveled at the beauty of the surroundings, the park's plantings and pathways. Hearing a foreign language coming from people's mouths allowed Mitchell to imagine that everyone was having an intelligent conversation, even the balding woman who looked like Mussolini. He checked his watch. It was nine-thirty a.m. He wasn't supposed to meet Larry until five that evening.

Mitchell had requested (cannily, he'd thought) that his traveler's checks be issued in a denomination of twenty dollars each. Small valuations would encourage economizing between visits to the AmEx office. One hundred and sixty-four separate twenty-dollar checks made a thick stack, however. Along with his passport and other documentation, the checks packed the fisherman's wallet tightly, creating a noticeable bulge in his pants. If Mitchell shifted the wallet to his hip, it looked less like a codpiece but more like a colostomy bag.

A heavenly smell of warm bread was wafting from a boulangerie across the street. Mitchell put his nose up in the air, like a dog. In his *Let's Go: Europe*, he found the address of a youth hostel in Pigalle, near Sacré Coeur. It was a hike, and by the time he got there he was sweaty and light-headed. The man behind the desk, who had pitted cheeks and tinted aviator glasses, told Mitchell the hostel was fully booked and directed him down the street to a cheap pension. There a room cost 330 francs per night, or almost $50, but Mitchell didn't know what else to do. After changing more money at a bank, he took a room, left his pack, and went out to salvage what he could of his day.

Pigalle was both seedy and touristy. A foursome of Americans with southern accents stood outside the Moulin Rouge, the husbands ogling the photos of the dancers, while one of the wives sassed, "You boys buy us something at Cartier's, we might let you see the show." Beyond the Art Nouveau entrance of the métro station a streetwalker was pelvically beckoning motorists. Wherever Mitchell went along the sloping streets of the neighborhood, the white dome of Sacré Coeur remained in view. Finally, he climbed the hill and entered the church's massive doors. The vault seemed to draw him upward like liquid in a syringe. Imitating the other worshippers, he crossed himself and genuflected as he entered a pew, the gestures making him feel instantly reverent. It was amazing that all this was still going on. Closing his eyes, Mitchell recited the Jesus Prayer for five or six minutes.

On his way out, he stopped in the gift store to examine the paraphernalia. There were gold crosses, silver crosses, scapulars of various colors and shapes, something called a "Veronica," something else called "the Black Scapular of the Seven Dolours of Mary." Rosaries gleamed in the glass case, black-beaded, each a circular invitation, with a crucifix distending from the end.

Beside the cash register, a small book was prominently displayed. It was called *Something Beautiful for God* and showed on its cover a photograph of Mother Teresa, casting her eyes heavenward. Mitchell picked the book up and read the first page:

I should explain, in the first place, that Mother Teresa has requested that nothing in the nature of a biography or biographical study of her should be attempted. "Christ's life," she wrote to me, "was not written during his lifetime, yet he did the greatest work on earth—he redeemed the world and taught mankind to love his Father. The Work is his Work and to remain so, all of us are but his instruments, who do our little bit and pass by." I respect her wishes in this, as in all other matters. What we are expressly concerned with here is the work she and her Missionaries of Charity—an order she founded—do together, and the life they live together, in the service of Christ, in Calcutta and elsewhere. Their special dedication is to the poorest of the poor; a wide field indeed.

A few years ago, Mitchell would have set the book back down, if not ignored it altogether. But in his new state of mind, enhanced by his time in the cathedral, he paged through the illustrations, which were listed as follows: "A board outside the Home for the Dying"; "A frail baby enfolded in the arms of Mother Teresa"; "An ailing woman hugs Mother Teresa"; "A man suffering from leprosy has his nails cut"; "Mother Teresa helps a boy too weak to feed himself."

Exceeding his budget twice in the same morning, Mitchell bought the book, paying twenty-eight francs.

On a quiet street off Rue des Trois-Frères, he took the AmEx serial numbers out of his money pouch and wrote them down in the back of *Something Beautiful for God.*

Throughout the day, Mitchell's hunger came and went. Toward afternoon, it came and stuck around. Passing sidewalk cafés, he eyed the food on people's plates. Just after two-thirty, he broke down and had a café au lait, standing up at the counter to save two francs. He spent the rest of the day at the Musée Jean Moulin because it was free.

When Mitchell got to Claire's sublet that evening, Larry opened the door. Inside, instead of a languorous postcoital atmosphere, Mitchell detected a whiff of strain. Larry had opened a bottle of wine, which he was drinking alone. Claire was on the bed, reading. She smiled perfunctorily at Mitchell but didn't get up to greet him.

Larry asked, "So, did you find a hotel?"

"No, I slept in the streets."

"You did not."

"All the hotels were full! I had to share a room with this guy. The same bed."

Larry visibly enjoyed this news. "Sorry, Mitchell," he said.

"You went to bed with a guy?" Claire spoke up from the bed. "On your first night in Paris?"

"Gay Paree," Larry said, filling a glass for Mitchell.

After a few more minutes, Claire went to the bathroom to wash up for dinner. As soon as she shut the door behind her, Mitchell leaned toward Larry. "O.K., we've seen Paris. Now let's go."

"Very funny, Mitchell."

"You said we'd have a place to stay."

"We do have a place."

"*You* do."

Larry lowered his voice. "I'm not going to see Claire for six months, maybe more. What can I do? Stay here one night and then split?"

"Good idea."

Larry gazed up at Mitchell. "You look really pale," he said.

"That's because I haven't eaten all day. And you know why I haven't eaten? Because I spent forty dollars on a room!"

"I'll make it up to you."

"This was not the plan," Mitchell said.

"The plan was to have no plans."

"Except that you've got a plan. Getting laid."

"And you wouldn't?"

"Of course I would."

"So there you go."

The two friends faced each other, neither giving way.

"Three days and we're out of here," Mitchell said.

Claire came out of the bathroom, holding a hairbrush. She bent over so that her long tresses fell forward, nearly touching the ground. For a full thirty seconds she combed her mane with downward strokes before snapping up and flinging her hair behind her, smooth and puffed out.

She asked where they wanted to eat.

Larry was putting on his unisex tennies. "How about couscous?" Larry said. "Mitchell, have you ever had couscous?"

"No."

"Oh, you have *got* to have couscous."

Claire made a wry face. "Whenever somebody comes to Paris," she said, "they have to go to the Latin Quarter and have couscous. Couscous in the Latin Quarter is so encoded!"

"You want to go somewhere else?" Larry said.

"No," Claire said. "Let's be unoriginal."

When they got down to the street, Larry put his arm around Claire, whispering in her ear. Mitchell followed behind.

They zigzagged across the city, in evening's flattering light. Parisians looked good already; now they looked even better.

The restaurant Claire took them to, in the Latin Quarter's narrow streets, was small and hectic, the walls covered in Moroccan tiles. Mitchell sat facing the window, watching the people streaming past outside. At one point, a girl who looked to be in her early twenties, with a Joan of Arc haircut, passed right in front of the glass. When Mitchell looked at her, the girl did an amazing thing: she looked back. She met his gaze with frank sexual meaning. Not that she *wanted* to have sex with him, necessarily. Only that she was happy to acknowledge, on this late-summer evening, that he was a man and she a woman, and if he found her attractive, that was all right with her. No American girl had ever looked at Mitchell like that.

Deanie was right: Europe was a nice spot.

Mitchell kept his eyes on the woman until she had disappeared. When he turned back to the table, Claire was staring at him, shaking her head.

"Pivot head," she said.

"What?"

"On the way over here you checked out every single woman we passed."

"I did not."

"Yes, you did."

"Foreign country," Mitchell said, trying to make light of it. "I'm taking an anthropological interest."

"So you see women as some tribe you have to study?"

"You're in for it now, Mitchell," Larry said. He was obviously going to be of no help whatsoever.

Claire was looking at Mitchell with undisguised contempt. "Do you always objectify women or just when you're traveling in Europe?"

"Just looking at women doesn't mean I objectify them."

"What are you doing to them, then?"

"*Looking* at them."

"Because you want to fuck them."

This was, more or less, true. Suddenly, in the castigating light of Claire's gaze, Mitchell was ashamed of himself. He wanted women to love him, all women, beginning with his mother and going on from there. Therefore, whenever *any* woman got mad at him, he felt maternal disapproval crashing down upon his shoulders, as if he'd been a naughty boy.

In response to this shame, Mitchell did another guy thing. He went silent. After they ordered, and the wine and food arrived, he concentrated on eating and drinking and said very little. Claire and Larry seemed to forget he was there. They talked and laughed. They fed each other forkfuls of food.

Outside, the crowds were getting even thicker. Mitchell tried his best not to stare out the window but suddenly something caught his eye. It was a woman in a tight dress and black boots.

"Oh, my God!" Claire screamed. "He did it again!"

"I was just looking out the window!"

"You are such a pivot head!"

"What do you want me to do? Wear a blindfold?"

But Claire was happy now. She was ecstatic at her victory over Mitchell, made so obvious by his visible discomfort. Her cheeks flushed with pleasure.

"Your friend hates me," she said, leaning her head against Larry's shoulder.

Larry lifted his eyes to Mitchell's eyes, not unsympathetically. He put his arm around Claire.

Mitchell didn't begrudge him that. He would have done the same in Larry's position.

As soon as dinner was over, Mitchell excused himself, saying he felt like taking a walk.

"Don't be mad at me!" Claire pleaded. "You can look at all the women you want. I promise I won't say a thing."

"That's O.K.," Mitchell said. "I'm just going back to my hotel."

"Come by Claire's tomorrow morning," Larry said, trying to ease things. "We can go to the Louvre."

At first, fury alone propelled Mitchell. Claire wasn't the first college girl to call him out for sexist behavior. It had been happening for years. Mitchell had always assumed that his father's generation were the bad guys. Those old farts who'd never washed a dish or folded socks—they were the real target of feminist rage. But that had been merely the first assault. Now, in the eighties, arguments about the equitable division of household chores, or the inherent sexism of holding a door open for "a lady," were old arguments. The movement had become less pragmatic and more theoretical. Male oppression of women wasn't just a matter of certain deeds but of an entire way of seeing and thinking. College feminists made fun of skyscrapers, saying they were phallic symbols. They said the same thing about space rockets, even though, if you stopped to think about it, rockets were shaped the way they were not because of phallocentrism but because of aerodynamics. Would a vagina-shaped *Apollo 11* have made it to the moon? Evolution had created the penis. It was a useful structure for getting certain things done. And if it worked for the pistils of flowers as well as the inseminatory organs of Homo sapiens, whose fault was that but Biology's? But no—anything large or grand in design, any long novel, big sculpture, or towering building, became, in the opinion of the "women" Mitchell knew at college, manifestations of male insecurity about the size of their penises. Girls were always going on about "male bonding," too. Anytime two or more guys were having a good time, some girl had to make it sound pathological. What was so great about feminine friendships, Mitchell wanted to know? Maybe they could use a little female bonding.

Fulminating like this, talking under his breath, Mitchell found himself at the Seine. He began crossing one of the bridges—the Pont Neuf. The sun had set and the streetlamps come on. Halfway out, in one of the semicircular seating areas, a group of teenagers had gathered. A guy with pouffy, Jean-Luc Ponty hair was strumming an acoustic guitar while his friends listened, smoking and passing a wine bottle around.

Mitchell watched them as he passed by. Even as a teenager he hadn't been a teenager like that.

A little farther on, he leaned against the railing and stared down at the dark river. His anger had subsided, replaced by a general displeasure with himself.

It was probably true that he objectified women. He thought about them all the time, didn't he? He looked at them a lot. And didn't all this thinking and looking involve their breasts and lips and legs? Female human beings were objects of the most intense interest and scrutiny on Mitchell's part. And yet he didn't think that a word like *objectification* covered the way these alluring—but intelligent!—creatures made him feel. What Mitchell felt when he saw a beautiful girl was more like something from a Greek myth, like being transformed, by the sight of beauty, into a tree, rooted on the spot, forever, out of pure desire. You couldn't feel about an object the way Mitchell felt about girls.

Excusez-moi: women.

There was another point in Claire's favor. All the while she'd been accusing Mitchell of objectifying women, he'd been secretly objectifying her. She had such an incredible ass! It was so round and perfect and *alive*. Every time Mitchell stole a glance at her ass he had the weird feeling that it was staring back, that Claire's ass didn't necessarily agree with its owner's feminist politics but was perfectly happy to be admired, that Claire's ass, in other words, had a mind of its own. Plus, Claire was his best friend's girlfriend. She was off-limits. This wildly increased her appeal.

A tour boat ablaze with lights passed under the bridge.

The more Mitchell read about religions, the world religions in general and Christianity in particular, the more he realized that the mystics were all saying the same thing. Enlightenment came from the extinction of desire. Desire didn't bring fulfillment but only temporary satiety until the next temptation came along. And *that* was only if you were lucky enough to get what you wanted. If you didn't, you spent your life in unrequited longing.

How long had he been secretly hoping to marry Madeleine Hanna? And how much of his desire to marry Madeleine came from really and truly liking her as a person, and how much from the wish to possess her and, in so doing, gratify his ego?

It might not even be that great to marry your ideal. Probably, once you attained your ideal, you got bored and wanted another.

The troubadour was playing a Neil Young song, reproducing the lyrics down to their last twang and whine without knowing what they meant. Older, better-dressed people were promenading by toward the floodlit buildings on either bank. Paris was a museum displaying exactly itself.

Wouldn't it be nice to be done with it? To be done with sex and longing? Mitchell could almost imagine pulling it off, sitting on a bridge at night with the Seine flowing by. He looked up at all the lighted windows along the river's arc. He thought of all the people going to sleep or reading or listening to music, all the lives contained by a great city like this, and, floating up in his mind, rising just above the rooftops, he tried to feel, to vibrate among, all those million tremulous souls. He was sick of craving, of wanting, of hoping, of losing.

For a long time the gods had been in close contact with humanity. Then they became disgusted, or discouraged, and they removed themselves. But maybe they would come back again, approach the stray soul who was still curious.

Returning to his hotel, Mitchell hung out in the lobby on the off chance some friendly English-speaking travelers showed up. None did. He went up to his room, got a towel, and took a tepid shower in the communal bathroom. At his present rate of expenditure, Mitchell's money would never hold out long enough for them to get to India. He had to start living differently tomorrow.

Back in his room, he pulled down the mouse-colored bedspread and climbed naked into bed. The bedside lamp was too dim to read by, so he removed the shade.

Part of the work of the Sisters is to pick up the dying from the streets of Calcutta, and bring them into a building given to Mother Teresa for the purpose (a sometimes temple dedicated to the cult of the goddess Kali), there, as she puts it, to die within sight of a loving face. Some do die, others survive and are cared for. This Home for the Dying is dimly lit by small windows high up in the walls, and Ken was adamant that filming was quite impossible there. We had only one small light with us, and to get the place adequately lighted in the time at our disposal was quite impossible. It was decided that, nonetheless, Ken should have a go, but by way of insurance he took, as well, some film in an outside courtyard where some of the inmates were sitting in the sun. In the processed film, the part taken inside was bathed in a particularly beautiful soft light, whereas the part taken outside was rather dim and confused.

How to account for this? Ken has all along insisted that, technically speaking, the result is quite impossible. To prove the point, on his next filming expedition—to the Middle East—he used some of the same stock in a similarly poor light, with completely negative results . . . Mother Teresa's Home for the Dying is overflowing with love, as one senses immediately on entering it. This love is luminous, like the haloes artists have seen and made visible round the heads of the saints . . . I am personally persuaded that Ken recorded the first authentic photographic miracle.

Mitchell put the book down, switching off the light and stretching out in the lumpy bed. He thought about Claire, at first angrily but soon enough erotically. He imagined going to her apartment and finding her alone, and soon she was on her knees in front of him, taking him into her mouth. Mitchell felt guilty for fantasizing about his friend's girlfriend but not guilty enough to stop. He didn't like what this fantasy of Claire on her knees in front of him said about him, so next he imagined himself generously going down on her, making her come like she'd never come before. At this point he came himself. He turned onto his side, dripping onto the hotel carpet.

Almost immediately, the tip of his penis felt cold and he shook it one last time and fell back into bed, desolate.

The next morning, Mitchell shouldered his pack and carried it down the stairs to the lobby, where he paid for the room and left. Breakfast was a coffee and the biscuit that came with it. His plan was to try the youth hostel again or, if need be, to spend a night on Claire's floor. When he got to her building, however, he saw Larry sitting on the steps. His backpack was next to him. He appeared to be smoking a cigarette.

"You don't smoke," Mitchell said, coming up to him.

"I'm starting." Larry puffed on the cigarette a few times, experimentally.

"Why do you have your backpack?"

Larry gave Mitchell full access to his intense blue-eyed gaze. The filterless cigarette adhered to his full lower lip.

"Claire and I broke up," he said.

"What happened?"

"She thinks she might be into women. She's not sure. Anyway, we're going to be apart, so."

"She dumped you?"

Larry winced, nearly imperceptibly. "She says she doesn't want to be 'exclusive.'"

Mitchell looked away to save Larry embarrassment. "Figures," he snorted. "You're just a sacrificial victim."

"Of what?"

"Sexist male and all that shit."

"I think *you* were the one she thought was the sexist male, Mitchell."

Mitchell could have objected, but he didn't. There was no need. He had his friend back.

Now their trip could finally begin.

•

On her fourteenth birthday, in November 1974, Madeleine had received a present from her older sister, Alwyn, who was away at college. The package had arrived in the mail, wrapped in psychedelic-patterned paper and sealed with red wax bearing the impressions of crescent moons and unicorns. Somehow Madeleine had known not to open the thing in front of her parents. Once she got it up to her room and was lying on her bed, she took off the wrapping paper to find a shoebox inside, its lid marked in black ink with the words "Bachelorette's Survival Kit." Inside, in handwriting so infinitesimal that it seemed accomplished by an awl, was the following note:

Dear Little Sis,

Now that you're fourteen and have started HIGH school, I thought I should let you know a few things about S-E-X so you

163

don't get yourself, as the Father Figure would say, "in trouble."
Actually, I'm not worried about you getting in trouble at all. I
just want my little sister to have some F-U-N!!! So here's your
new, handy-dandy "Bachelorette's Survival Kit" containing
everything a modern, sensuous woman needs for total
fulfillment. Boyfriend not included.

    Happy Birthday,
      Love, Ally

Maddy was still in her school clothes. Holding the shoebox with one
hand, she took out the objects with the other. The first, a small foil package, meant nothing to her, not even when she turned it over and saw the
helmeted figure on the front. Pressing her finger against the package,
she could feel something slippery inside.

Then it came to her. "Oh my God!" she said. "Oh-my-God-I-can't-
believe-it!"

She ran to the door and locked it. Then, thinking better, she un-
locked it and ran back to the bed, where she got the foil package and the
box and took them both into her bathroom, where she could lock the
door without arousing suspicion. She lowered the lid of the toilet and sat
down.

Madeleine had never seen a condom package before, much less held
one in her hand. She ran the ball of her thumb over it. The implication
of the shape inside stirred feelings in her she wasn't quite able to describe. The lubricious medium the condom swam in was both repellent
and fascinating. The circumference of the ring frankly startled her. She
hadn't given much detailed thought to the extent of the male erection.
Thus far, boys' erections were something she and her friends giggled
about and mostly didn't mention. She thought she'd felt one once, during
a slow dance at summer camp, but she couldn't be sure: it might have
been the boy's belt buckle. In her experience, erections were occult oc-
currences happening elsewhere, like the bulging of a bullfrog's throat
in a distant swamp, or a puffer fish inflating in a coral reef. The only
erection Madeleine had seen with her own eyes belonged to her grandmother's Labrador, Wylie, which had rawly emerged from its fur sock as
the dog maniacally humped her leg. A thing like that was enough to keep
you from thinking about erections forever. The distasteful nature of that

image, however, didn't blot out the sheer revelatory nature of the condom she now held in her hand. The condom was an artifact of the adult world. Beyond her life, beyond her school, there was an agreed-upon system no one talked about, whereby pharmaceutical companies made prophylactics for men to buy and roll onto their penises, legally, in the United States of America.

The next two items Madeleine took out of the box were part of a novelty set, the sort that issued from vending machines in men's rooms, which was where Alwyn, or more likely Alwyn's boyfriend, had probably gotten it along with the condom. The set included: a red rubber ring studded with wiggly stalks and labeled "French tickler"; a gag made of blue plastic consisting of two moving figures, a man with a hard-on and a woman on all fours, the lever of which, when Maddy moved it back and forth, caused the half-inch stud to prong the woman doggy-style; a small tube of "Pro-long" cream, which she didn't even want to open; and two hollow silver "Ben Wa" balls that came with no instructions and looked, frankly, like pinballs. At the bottom of the box was the strangest thing of all, a thin miniature breadstick with black fuzz stuck to it. The breadstick was taped to a three-by-five card. Madeleine brought it close to her face to read the handwritten label: "Dehydrated Prick. Just add water." She looked at the tiny breadstick again, then at the fuzz, and then she dropped the card and shouted out, "Gross!"

It was a while before she picked it up again, touching the edge of the three-by-five card farthest from the fuzz. Keeping her head back, she reexamined the fuzz to confirm that it was, in fact, pubic hair. Alwyn's, most likely, though possibly her boyfriend's. It wouldn't have been beyond Ally to go to that length of verisimilitude. The hair was black and curly and had been clipped and glued to the base of the breadstick. The idea that it was possibly a guy's pubic hair revolted and excited Madeleine at the same time. But it was probably Ally's, that weirdo. What a funny, crazy sister she had! Alwyn was completely strange and unpredictable, a nonconformist, a vegetarian, a college war protester, and since Madeleine wanted to be some of these things, too, she loved and admired her sister (while continuing to think that she was totally weird). She put the dehydrated prick back into the box and picked up the little plastic couple again. She moved the lever, watching the man's penis enter the bent-over woman.

The memory of the Bachelorette's Survival Kit came back to Madeleine now, in October, as she stood at the small airport in Provincetown, waiting for Phyllida and Alwyn to arrive from Boston. The night before, unexpectedly, Phyllida had telephoned with the news that Alwyn had left her husband, Blake, and that she, Phyllida, had flown up to Boston to try to intervene. She'd found Alwyn staying at the Ritz Hotel, maxing out her joint AmEx card and messengering bottles of mother's milk to the house in Beverly where she'd left her six-month-old, Richard, in the care of his father. Having failed to persuade Alwyn to return home, Phyllida had decided to bring her to Cape Cod in the hope that Madeleine could talk some sense into her. "Ally only agreed to come for the day," Phyllida said. "She doesn't want us ganging up on her. We're coming in the morning and leaving in the afternoon."

"What am I supposed to tell her?" Madeleine had said.

"Tell her what you think. She listens to you."

"Why doesn't Daddy talk to her?"

"He has. It ended in a shouting match. I'm at my wit's end, Maddy. You don't have to do anything. Just be your sensible, reasonable self."

Hearing that, Madeleine almost wanted to laugh. She was desperately in love with a boy who'd been hospitalized, twice, for manic depression. For the last four months, instead of focusing on her "career," she'd been nursing Leonard back to health, cooking his meals and cleaning his clothes, calming his anxieties and cheering him out of his frequent low moods. She'd been putting up with the serious side effects brought on by his new, higher dosage of lithium. No doubt largely due to all this, Madeleine had found herself, one night at the end of August, kissing Mitchell Grammaticus outside Chumley's on Bedford Street, kissing him and enjoying it, before fleeing back to Providence and Leonard's sickbed. The last thing she felt herself to be was sensible or reasonable. She had just started living like a grown-up and she'd never felt more vulnerable, frightened, or confused in her life.

After she moved out of her apartment on Benefit Street, in June, Madeleine had stayed at Leonard's place, alone, until he got out of the hospital. She felt excited to be entrusted with his things. She played his Arvo Pärt records on the stereo, lying on the couch and listening with closed eyes exactly the way Leonard did. She flipped through his books, reading his marginalia. Next to dense passages by Nietzsche or Hegel,

Leonard drew faces, either smiling or frowning, or just put an "!" At night she slept in one of Leonard's shirts. Everything in the apartment had been left exactly as it was when Leonard was taken to the hospital. There was an open notebook on the floor, in which it appeared that Leonard had been trying to figure out how long his money would hold out. The bathtub was full of newspapers. Sometimes, the emptiness of the apartment made Madeleine want to cry for all it suggested about Leonard's aloneness in the world. Not a picture of his parents or sister anywhere. Then one morning, moving a book, she found a photograph lying underneath. It was one he'd taken of her on their first trip to the Cape, showing her lying on a motel bed, reading and eating a Klondike bar.

After three days, unable to bear the filth a minute longer, she broke down and began cleaning. At Star Market, she bought a mop, a mop bucket, a pair of rubber gloves, and an assortment of cleansers. She knew she was setting a bad precedent even while she was doing it. She mopped the floor, dumping buckets of black water down the toilet. She went through seven rolls of paper towels, wiping crud off the bathroom floor. She threw out the mildewed shower curtain and bought a new one, bright pink for revenge. She tossed everything from the refrigerator and scrubbed the shelves. After stripping Leonard's mattress, she balled up the sheets, intending to drop them off at the corner laundry, but instead threw them in a trash can behind the building, replacing them with her own. She hung curtains in the windows and bought a paper shade for the bare bulb hanging from the ceiling.

A few leaves on the ficus tree were beginning to turn brown. Feeling the soil, Madeleine found it dry. She mentioned this to Leonard during visiting hours one day.

"You can water my tree," he said.

"No way. The last time you gave me so much grief."

"You have permission to water my tree."

"That doesn't sound like a request, though."

"Will you please water my ficus tree for me?"

She watered the tree. In the afternoons, when the sun came through the front window, she pulled it into the light and misted the leaves.

Every afternoon, she went down to the hospital to see Leonard.

The doctor had adjusted Leonard's medication, eliminating his facial tic, and this alone made him seem much improved. He talked mainly about all the drugs he was on, their uses and contraindications. Saying their names seemed to calm him, as though he were uttering incantations: lorazepam, diazepam, chlorpromazine, chlordiazepoxide, haloperidol. Madeleine couldn't keep them straight. She wasn't sure if Leonard was taking these drugs or other people in the unit were. By this time he was well versed in the clinical histories of most of his fellow patients. They treated him like an intern, discussing their cases with him, asking for information about the drugs they were taking. Leonard operated in the hospital the same way he did at school. He was a font of information: the answer man. Every now and then, he had a bad day. Madeleine would enter the dayroom to find him sullen, full of despair about not having graduated and concerned about his ability to handle his duties at Pilgrim Lake: the usual list of complaints. He repeated them over and over.

Leonard hoped to stay in the hospital only a couple of weeks. But in the end he was there for twenty-two days. On the day of his release, in late June, Madeleine drove downtown to pick him up in her new car, a Saab convertible with twelve thousand miles on it. The car was a graduation present from her parents. "Even though we didn't get to see you graduate," Alton joked, discussing Madeleine's disappearance that day. Among the throng of parents outside the Van Wickle gates, Alton and Phyllida had waited for Madeleine to march by; when she hadn't, they thought they'd somehow missed her. After having searched for her on College Street, they'd tried calling her apartment, but got no answer. Finally, they stopped by and left a note for her, saying that they were worried and had decided not to go back to Prettybrook "as planned." Instead, they were going to wait for her in the lobby of the Biltmore, which was where Madeleine found them that afternoon. She told them that she'd missed the march because Kelly Traub, with whom she'd been walking, had fallen and sprained her ankle, and she'd had to help her get to Health Services. Madeleine wasn't sure if her parents believed her, but, relieved that she was all right, they hadn't pressed her about it. Instead, Alton had called a few days later to instruct Madeleine to go out and buy herself a car. "Used," he stipulated. "One or two years old. That way you escape a lot of the depreciation." Madeleine had done as instructed, finding the convertible in the *Pro-Jo* classifieds. It was white, with fawn-colored bucket seats, and as she waited outside the hospital entrance, Madeleine put the top down so that Leonard could see her as the nurse brought him down in a wheelchair.

"Nice ride," he said, getting in.

They hugged for a long time, Madeleine sniffling, until Leonard pulled away.

"Let's get out of here. I've had enough of this place."

For the rest of the summer Leonard was touchingly fragile. He spoke in the softest of tones. He watched baseball on TV, holding Madeleine's hand.

"You know what *paradise* means?" he asked.

"It doesn't mean 'paradise'?"

"It means 'walled garden.' From the Persian. That's what a baseball stadium is. Especially Fenway. A walled garden. Look how green it is! It's so soothing to just sit here and look at the field."

"Maybe you should watch golf," Madeleine said.

"Even greener."

The lithium made him thirsty all the time, and sporadically nauseated. He developed a mild tremor in his right hand. During his weeks in the hospital, Leonard had gained almost fifteen pounds, and he continued putting on weight all through July and August. His face and body looked puffy and there was a roll of fat, like a buffalo's hump, on the back of his neck. Along with his thirst, Leonard had to pee constantly. He had stomachaches and suffered bouts of diarrhea. Worst of all, the lithium made his mind feel sluggish. Leonard claimed that there was an "upper register" that he couldn't reach anymore, intellectually. To counteract this, he chewed even more tobacco, and started smoking cigarettes as well as smelly little cigars for which he'd developed a fondness in the hospital. His clothes reeked of smoke. His mouth tasted like an ashtray and of something else, too, a metallic chemical taste. Madeleine didn't like it.

As a result of all this, a side effect of the side effects, Leonard's libido decreased. After making love twice or three times a day from the excitement of being reunited, they slowed down, and then nearly ceased having sex altogether. Madeleine wasn't sure what to do. Should she pay more attention to Leonard's problem, or less? She'd never been particularly hands-on, in bed. Life hadn't required it. Guys hadn't seemed to care, or to notice, being so hands-on themselves. One night, she at-tacked the problem as she might a drop shot on the tennis court: she ran full out, getting there seemingly in time, then bent low and flicked her return—which hit the tape and fell back, dead, on her side of the court.

She didn't try again after that. She stayed back, playing her usual baseline game.

All of this might have bothered Madeleine more if Leonard's needi-ness hadn't appealed to her so much. There was something pleasing about having her big Saint Bernard all to herself. He didn't want to go out even to a movie anymore. Now he was interested only in his doggy bed, his doggy bowl, and his mistress. He laid his head on her lap, wanted to be petted. He wagged his tail whenever she came in. Always so demon-strably *there*, her big fuzz buddy, her big old slobbery fuzzeroo.

Neither of them had a job. The long summer days passed slowly. With the student population gone, College Hill was somnolent and green. Leonard kept his medications in his Dopp kit under the bathroom sink. He always closed the door when taking them. Twice a week, he went to see his shrink, Bryce Ellis, and returned from these appointments emotionally abraded and exhausted. He flopped onto the mattress for another hour or two, and finally got up to put on a record.

"You know how old Einstein was when he proposed the special the-ory of relativity?" he asked Madeleine one day.

"How old?"

"Twenty-six."

"So?"

"Most scientists do their best work in their early twenties. I'm twenty-two, almost twenty-three. I'm in my intellectual prime right now. Except that I have to take a drug every morning and every night that makes me stupid."

"It doesn't make you stupid, Leonard."

"Yes, it does."

"It doesn't seem very scientific to me," she said, "to decide you'll never be a great scientist just because you haven't discovered anything by the time you're twenty-two."

"Those are the facts," Leonard said. "Forget the drug. Even normal, I'm not remotely on a trajectory to make a scientific breakthrough."

"Say you don't make a breakthrough," Madeleine said. "How do you know you won't come up with some tiny breakthrough that ends up benefiting people? I mean, maybe you won't figure out that space is curved. Maybe you'll find a way to make cars run on water so there won't be any pollution."

"Inventing a hydrogen engine would constitute a major breakthrough," Leonard said gloomily, lighting a cigarette.

"O.K., but not every scientist was young. What about Galileo? How old was he? What about Edison?"

"Can we not talk about this anymore?" Leonard said. "I'm getting depressed."

This made Madeleine quiet.

Leonard took a long drag on his cigarette and exhaled loudly. "Not *depressed* depressed," he said, after a moment.

As dedicated as Madeleine was to nursing Leonard, as satisfying as it was to see him getting better, she sometimes needed to get out of the stifling studio. To escape the humidity, she went to the air-conditioned library. She played tennis with two guys from the Brown tennis team. Some days, not wanting to go back to the apartment, Madeleine walked around the empty campus, trying her best to think about herself for a few minutes. She stopped in to see Professor Saunders, only to be troubled at the sight of the elderly scholar wearing shorts and sandals. She browsed the stacks at College Hill Bookstore, virtuously selecting used copies of *Little Dorrit* and *The Vicar of Bullhampton*, which she fully intended to read. Now and then she treated herself to an ice cream cone and sat on the steps of Hospital Trust, watching other young couples going by, holding hands or kissing. She finished her ice cream and started back to the apartment, where Leonard was waiting.

All through July his condition remained delicate. By August, however, Leonard appeared to be turning the corner. Every now and then, he sounded like his old self. One morning, making toast, Leonard held up a package of Land O'Lakes butter. "I've got a question," he said. "Who was the first person who noticed that the knees of the Land O'Lakes squaw look like breasts? Some guy in Terre Haute is having breakfast, and he looks at the butter package and thinks, 'Check out those knees.' But that's only part of the story. After this insight, some other guy had to decide to cut out *another* pair of knees, from the back of the package, and to paste these behind the butter package the squaw's holding in front of her chest, and then to cut around the edges of the butter package so that it flips up like she's flashing her breasts. All this happened with no documentation whatsoever. The principals have been lost to history."

They started leaving the apartment. One day they drove to Federal Hill to have pizza. Afterward, Leonard insisted that they go into a cheese shop. It was dark inside, the shades drawn. The smell was a presence in the room. Behind the counter, an old white-haired man was busy doing something they couldn't see. "It's eighty degrees out," Leonard whispered, "and this guy won't open the windows. That's because he's got a perfect bacterial mix in here and he doesn't want to let it out. I read a paper where these chemists from Cornell identified two hundred different strains of bacteria in a tub of rennet. It's an aerobic reaction, so whatever's in the air affects the flavor. Italians know all that instinctively. This guy doesn't even *know* what he knows."

Leonard stepped up to the counter. "Vittorio, how are you?"

The old man turned and squinted. "Hello, my friend! Where you been? I haven't seen you long time."

"I was under the weather, Vittorio."

"Nothing serious, I hope. Don't tell me! I don't want to know. I got problems of my own."

"What do you recommend today?"

"What do you mean 'recommend.' Cheese! Same as always. The best. Who's your girlfriend?"

"This is Madeleine."

"You like cheese, young lady? Here, taste. Take some home with you. And get rid of this guy. He's no good."

Yet another revelation about Leonard: he was friends with the old Italian cheese maker on Federal Hill. Maybe that was where he'd been going when Madeleine used to see him waiting for the bus in the rain. To visit his friend Vittorio.

At the end of August, they packed up their things, putting boxes in storage and cramming the rest into the trunk and backseat of the Saab, and lit out for the Cape. It was hot, in the nineties, and they drove with the top down all the way out of Rhode Island. The wind made it difficult to talk or listen to the stereo, however, so they put the top up as they crossed into Massachusetts. Madeleine had a Pure Prairie League tape that Leonard tolerated until they stopped at a gas station with a minimart, when he bought a cassette of *Led Zeppelin's Greatest Hits* and played it the rest of the way over the Sagamore Bridge and onto the peninsula. At a roadside place in Orleans, they stopped for lobster rolls. Leonard seemed in good spirits. But, as they started driving again, scrub pines passing on either side, he began to nervously smoke his little cigars and to fidget in the passenger seat. It was a Sunday. Most traffic was headed in the opposite direction, weekenders or summer renters making their way back to the mainland, sports equipment roped to the roofs of their vehicles. In Truro, Highway 6 split into 6A, and they followed this carefully, slowing down when blue Pilgrim Lake appeared on their right. Near the lake's end they saw the sign for Pilgrim Lake Laboratory and turned down a gravel drive that ran between dunes in the direction of Cape Cod Bay.

"Who took my saliva?" Leonard said, as the buildings, where they were to live for the next nine months, appeared. "Do you have my saliva? Because I can't find mine right now."

During their quick visit the previous spring, Madeleine had been too preoccupied with her new relationship to notice much more about Pilgrim Lake Laboratory than its beautiful beachfront location. It was amazing to think that legends like Watson and Crick had worked or stayed in the former whaling settlement, but most names of the biologists at Pilgrim Lake now—including the lab's present director, David Malkiel—were new to her. The one actual laboratory they'd toured during that visit hadn't looked much different from the chemistry labs at Lawrenceville.

Once they'd moved up to Pilgrim Lake, however, and started living there, Madeleine realized how wrong her first impressions of the place had been. She hadn't expected that there would be six indoor tennis courts, or a gym full of Nautilus equipment, or a screening room that showed first-run films on weekends. She hadn't expected that the bar would be open twenty-four hours, or that it would be full of scientists at three in the morning, awaiting test results. She hadn't expected the limousines ferrying pharmaceutical executives and celebrities in from Logan to eat with Dr. Malkiel in his private dining room. She hadn't expected the *food*, the expensive French wines and breads and olive oils hand-selected by Dr. Malkiel himself. Malkiel raised huge sums of money for the lab, lavishing it on the resident scientists and luring others to visit. It was Malkiel who had bought the Cy Twombly painting that hung in the dining hall and who had commissioned the Richard Serra that stood behind the Animal House.

Madeleine and Leonard arrived at Pilgrim Lake during the Summer Genetics Seminar. Leonard had to take the famous "Yeast Class," taught by Bob Kilimnik, the biologist to whose team he'd been assigned. He went off every morning like a frightened schoolboy. He complained that his brain wasn't working and that the other two research fellows on his team, Vikram Jaitly and Carl Beller, both of whom had gone to MIT, were smarter than he was. But it was just a two-hour class. The rest of the day was free. A relaxed atmosphere prevailed at the lab. A lot of undergraduates were around (called Urts, for undergraduate research technicians), including a lot of women close to Madeleine's age. Almost every night there was a party where people did slightly queer, science-nerd things, such as serving daiquiris in Erlenmeyer flasks or evaporating dishes, or autoclaving clams instead of steaming them. Still, it was fun.

After Labor Day, things grew more serious. The Urts left, radically decreasing the female population, bringing an end to the summer parties and the whiff of romance in the air. In late September, *The Sunday Telegraph* began publishing the odds from Ladbrokes on the upcoming Nobel Prizes. As the days passed and the other prizes in science were awarded—to Kenneth Wilson in Physics and to Aaron Klug in Chemistry—people began to speculate, at dinner, on who would win for Physiology or Medicine. The leading candidates were Rudyard Hill, of Cambridge, and Michael Zolodnek. Zolodnek was a resident at Pilgrim Lake, living in one of the saltboxes on the Truro side of the property. Then, in the early morning of October 8, a whooshing sound awoke Madeleine and Leonard from a sound sleep. Going to the window, they saw a helicopter landing on the beach in front of their building. Three satellite news vans were parked in the lot. They threw on clothes and raced to the conference center, where they learned, to their delight, that the Nobel had been awarded not to Michael Zolodnek but to Diane MacGregor. The seats in the amphitheater were already filled with press reporters and Pilgrim Lake staff. Standing in the back of the room, Madeleine and Leonard watched Dr. Malkiel escort MacGregor to a podium bedecked with a bouquet of microphones. MacGregor was dressed in an old rain-coat and Wellies, exactly as she had been the few times Madeleine had caught sight of her on the beach, walking her black standard poodle. She'd made an attempt to arrange her white hair for the press conference. This detail, along with her diminutive size, gave her the quality of a small child, despite her age.

At the podium MacGregor smiled, twinkled, and looked besieged all at once.

The questions began:

"Dr. MacGregor, where were you when you heard the news?"

"I was asleep. Just like I am right now."

"Could you tell us what your scientific work is about?"

"I could. But then *you'd* be asleep."

"What do you plan to do with the money?"

"Spend it."

These answers would have given Madeleine a crush on Diane Mac-Gregor if she hadn't had one already. Though she'd never talked to Mac-Gregor, everything she'd learned about the seventy-three-year-old recluse had turned MacGregor into Madeleine's favorite biologist. Unlike the other scientists at the lab, MacGregor employed no assistants. She worked entirely alone, without sophisticated equipment, analyzing the mysterious patterns of coloration in the corn she grew in a plot of land behind her house. From talking to Leonard and other people, Madeleine understood the basics of MacGregor's work—it had to do with gene transmission, and the way traits are copied, transposed, or deleted—but what she really admired was the solitary and determined way MacGregor carried it out. (If Madeleine ever became a biologist, Diane MacGregor would be the kind of biologist she would want to be.) Other scientists at the lab ridiculed MacGregor for not having a phone or for her general eccentricity. If MacGregor was so out of it, though, why did everyone have to talk about her all the time? Madeleine guessed that MacGregor made people uneasy because of the purity of her renunciation and the simplicity of her scientific method. They didn't want her to succeed, because that would invalidate the rationale for their research staffs and bloated budgets. MacGregor could also be opinionated and blunt. People didn't like that in anyone, but they liked it less in a woman. She'd been languishing in the biology department at the University of Florida, in Gainesville, when Dr. Malkiel's predecessor, recognizing her genius, had raised the money to bring her to Pilgrim Lake and set her up with a lifetime position. That was the other thing that amazed Madeleine about MacGregor. She'd been at Pilgrim Lake since 1947! For thirty-five years she'd been inspecting her corn with Mendelian patience, receiving no encouragement or feedback on her work, just showing up every day, involved in her own process of discovery, forgotten by the world and not caring. And now, finally, *this*, the Nobel, the vindication of her life's work, and though she seemed pleased enough, you could see that it hadn't been the Prize she was after at all. MacGregor's reward had been the work itself, the daily doing of it, the achievement made of a million unremarkable days.

In her own small way, Madeleine understood what Diane Mac-Gregor was up against at the male-dominated lab. At every dinner party she and Leonard went to, Madeleine inevitably ended up in the kitchen, helping with the other wives and girlfriends. She could have refused to do this, of course, but then she'd only look as if she was trying to prove a point. Also, it was annoying to sit and listen to the men's competitive discussions. And so she washed dishes and ended up resenting it. Her only other social interactions were playing tennis with Malkiel's young wife, Greta—who treated Madeleine like a hitting coach—or hanging out with the other bedfellows. That was the term used for the partners of the research fellows: bedfellows. Nearly every single research fellow was a guy. Most of the senior biologists were male as well, and so there was only Diane MacGregor, if you didn't count the lab techs, for Madeleine to root for and to try, in her own fashion, to imitate.

Considering that Leonard's fellowship covered their food and lodging, there was no reason Madeleine couldn't spend all her time reading, sleeping, and eating. But she had no intention of doing that. Despite her lack of focus over the summer, her future in academia had received a boost. Along with an A on her honors thesis, Madeleine had received a personal note from Professor Saunders encouraging her to turn her thesis into a shorter paper and to forward it to one M. Myerson at *The Janeite Review*. "It just may be publishable!" Saunders had written. Though the fact that M. Myerson was, in fact, Professor Saunders's wife, Mary, lent an air of nepotism to this recommendation, an in was still an in. In Saunders's office, when Madeleine had stopped by to see him, he had also loudly decried Yale's rejection of her, saying that she'd been a victim of intellectual fashion.

Then, on a mid-September weekend, Madeleine attended a conference on Victorian literature at Boston College that pointed her in a new direction. At the conference, which was held at a Hyatt with a greenery-filled lobby and tubular glass elevators, she met two people as crazy about nineteenth-century books as she was. Meg Jones was a fit college softball pitcher with pixieish hair and a strong jaw. Anne Wong was a ponytailed Stanford grad with an Elsa Peretti heart necklace, a Seiko watch, and a faint accent of her native Taiwan. Anne was currently in the poetry M.F.A. program at the University of Houston but was planning to get a Ph.D., in English, in order to make a living and satisfy her parents. Meg was already in the Ph.D. program at Vanderbilt. She called Austen "the divine Jane," and spouted facts and figures about her like a sports bettor. There had been eight children in Austen's family, Jane the youngest girl. She had suffered from Addison's disease, like John F. Kennedy. She came down with typhus in 1783. *Sense and Sensibility* was originally published as *Elinore and Marianne*. Austen once accepted a proposal of marriage from a man named Bigg-Wither, but after sleeping on it, she changed her mind. She was buried in Winchester Cathedral.

"Are you thinking of going into Austen studies?" Anne Wong asked Madeleine.

"I don't know. I had a chapter on her in my thesis. But you know who I'm also into? It's a little embarrassing."

"Who?"

"Mrs. Gaskell."

"I love Mrs. Gaskell!" Anne Wong cried.

"Mrs. Gaskell?" Meg Jones said. "I'm trying to think of something to reply to that."

What Madeleine sensed at the conference was the emergence of a new class of academics. They were talking about all the old books she loved, but in new ways. The topics included: "Women of Property in the Victorian Novel," "Victorian Women Writers and the Woman Question," "Masturbation in Victorian Literature," and "The Prison of Womanhood." Madeleine and Anne Wong heard Terry Castle give a paper on "the invisible lesbian" in Victorian literature, and they glimpsed, from a distance, Sandra Gilbert and Susan Gubar coming out of a *"Madwoman in the Attic"* talk where there were no seats left.

The thing about the Victorians, Madeleine was learning, was that they were a lot less Victorian than you thought. Frances Power Cobbe had lived openly with another woman, referring to her as her "wife." In 1868, Cobbe had published an article in *Fraser's Magazine* entitled "Criminals, Idiots, Women, and Minors. Is the Classification Sound?" Women were restricted from owning and inheriting property in early Victorian Britain. They were restricted from participating in politics. And it was under these conditions, while they were classified literally among idiots, that Madeleine's favorite women writers had written their books.

Seen this way, eighteenth- and nineteenth-century literature, especially that written by women, was anything but old hat. Against tremendous odds, without anyone giving them the right to take up the pen or a proper education, women such as Anne Finch, Jane Austen, George Eliot, the Brontës, and Emily Dickinson had taken up the pen anyway, not only joining in the grand literary project but, if you could believe Gilbert and Gubar, creating a new literature at the same time, playing a man's game while subverting it. Two sentences from *The Madwoman in the Attic* particularly struck Madeleine. "In recent years, for instance, while male writers seem increasingly to have felt exhausted by the need for revisionism which Bloom's theory of the 'anxiety of influence' accurately describes, women writers have seen themselves as pioneers in a creativity so intense that their male counterparts have probably not experienced its analog since the Renaissance, or at least since the Romantic era. The son of many fathers, today's male writer feels hopelessly belated; the daughter of too few mothers, today's female writer feels that she is helping to create a viable tradition which is at last definitely emerging."

Over two and a half days Madeleine and her new friends attended sixteen seminars. They snuck into a cocktail party for an insurance underwriters' convention and ate free food. Anne kept ordering sex on the beach at the Hyatt bar, and giggling each time. Unlike Meg, who dressed like a longshoreman, Anne wore floral dresses from Filene's Basement, and heels. On their last night, back in her room, Anne laid her head on

Madeleine's shoulder and confessed that she was still a virgin. "Not only Taiwanese!" she cried. "But a Taiwanese virgin! I'm hopeless!"

As little as she had in common with Meg and Anne, Madeleine couldn't remember having a better time. The entire weekend, they didn't once ask if she had a boyfriend. They just wanted to talk about literature. The last morning of the conference, the three exchanged addresses and phone numbers and had a three-way hug, promising to stay in touch.

"Maybe we'll all end up in the same department!" Anne cheerily said.

"I doubt anybody'd hire three Victorianists," Meg said matter-of-factly.

On the way back to Cape Cod, and for days afterward, Madeleine felt a rush of happiness every time she remembered Meg Jones calling them all "Victorianists." The word made her fuzzy aspirations suddenly real. She'd never had a word for the thing she wanted to be. At a rest stop she put four quarters into a pay phone to call her parents in Prettybrook.

"Daddy, I know what I want to be."

"What?"

"A Victorianist! I just went to the most incredible conference."

"Do you have to specialize already? You haven't even started grad school."

"No, Daddy, this is it. I know it! The field is so wide open."

"Get in somewhere first," Alton said, laughing. "Then we'll talk about it."

Back at Pilgrim Lake, at her desk, she tried to get down to work. She'd brought most, if not all, of her favorite books with her. Her Austen, Eliot, Wharton, and James. From Alton, who still had connections at the Baxter library, she'd managed to score a huge stack of Victorian criticism on long-term loan. After doing the requisite reading and making additional notes, Madeleine began trying to condense her thesis into a publishable size. Her Royal typewriter was the same one on which she'd typed her honors thesis. It was the same typewriter on which Alton had typed *his* college papers. Madeleine loved the black steel machine, but the keys were beginning to stick. Sometimes when she was typing quickly two or three keys would glom together and she'd have to separate them with her fingers, gaining a new understanding of the term *manual typewriter*.

Unsticking the keys or changing the ribbon left her fingers ink-stained. The inside of the typewriter was repulsive: there were dust balls, eraser filings, bits of paper, cookie crumbs, and hair. Madeleine was amazed the thing still worked. Once she became aware of how dirty her typewriter was, she couldn't stop thinking about it. It was like trying to sleep in the grass after someone mentioned worms. Trying to clean the Royal wasn't easy. It weighed a ton. No matter how many times she managed to lug it to the sink and turn it over, it never stopped leaking detritus. Bringing it back to her desk, she put a sheet of paper in the roller and set to work again, but the nagging thought that gunk remained in the typewriter, as well as the constant sticking of the keys, made her forget what she'd been writing. And so she took the typewriter back to the sink and got the rest of the gunk out with an old toothbrush.

In this manner, Madeleine tried to become a Victorianist.

She hoped to get her abridged essay rewritten by December, in time to include it as a writing sample in her grad school applications. To have the article accepted by *The Janeite Review* by then and list it as "forthcoming" on her résumé would be an additional boon. Yale's rejection, like that of a boyfriend she wasn't sure she liked that much, had predictably increased its allure. Nevertheless, she wasn't going to stay home waiting for the call. She was going to play the field this time, and therefore had been flirting with rich old Harvard, urbane Columbia, cerebral Chicago, and trustworthy Michigan, as well as giving face time even to lowly Baxter College. (If Baxter didn't accept her into its mediocre program in English, despite her being the daughter of the former president, Madeleine would take this as a sign to give up the idea of becoming an academic altogether.) But she didn't expect to go to Baxter. She prayed that she wouldn't have to go to Baxter. To that end, she began studying for the GRE again, hoping to raise her scores on the math and logic sections. To prepare for the English literature test, she filled in her gaps by reading through *The Oxford Book of English Verse*.

With none of this, however—with neither the writing nor the reading—did she make much headway, for the simple irrefutable reason that her duty to Leonard came first. Now that they were on Cape Cod, Leonard didn't have a local therapist to talk to. He had to make do with telephone therapy, once a week, with Bryce Ellis in Providence. Additionally, he'd started seeing a new psychiatrist, Dr. Perlmann, at Mass General, with whom he had no rapport. Under pressure to perform at the lab, Leonard came back to the apartment every night and began telling Madeleine his troubles. He treated Madeleine like the next best thing to therapy. "I was shaking like a madman today. I can barely make media anymore because of my tremor. I keep dropping stuff. I dropped a flask today. Agar broth all over the place. I know what Kilimnik's thinking. He's thinking, 'Why did they give this guy a fellowship?'"

Leonard kept his diagnosis a secret at Pilgrim Lake. He knew from experience that when people found out he'd been hospitalized and, especially, that he was taking a drug twice a day to stabilize his mood, they treated him differently. Sometimes people wrote him off, or avoided him. Madeleine had promised not to tell anyone, but in August, in New York, she'd confessed to Kelly Traub. She'd sworn Kelly to secrecy, but Kelly would inevitably tell one person, swearing her to secrecy, and that person would tell one person, and so on and so on until Leonard's condition became general knowledge.

Madeleine couldn't worry about that now. The important thing, on this October day, as she waited for the puddle-jumper carrying Phyllida and Alwyn from Boston, was to keep them from finding out. Hopefully, Alwyn's marital crisis would deflect attention away from Madeleine's own relationship, but just to be sure, Madeleine was planning to keep her family's face time with Leonard as brief as possible.

The tiny airport consisted of a single runway and Quonset-hut-like terminal. Outside, in the fall sunshine, a small crowd of people was waiting, either chatting or staring into the sky for the arriving airplane.

To meet her mother, Madeleine put on a pair of khaki linen shorts, a white blouse, and a navy sweater with a white striped V-neck. One good thing about being out of college—and living on Cape Cod, not far from Hyannisport—was that nothing now prevented Madeleine from dressing in the Kennedy-esque style in which she felt most comfortable. She'd always been a failed bohemian, anyway. Sophomore year, she'd bought an electric-blue satin bowling shirt with the name "Mel" stitched on the pocket and began wearing it when she went to parties at Mitchell's apartment. But she must have worn it once too often, because one night he made a face and said, "What? Is that your arty shirt?"

"What do you mean?"

"You wear that bowling shirt whenever you hang out with me and my friends."

"Larry has one just like it," Madeleine defended herself.

"Yeah, but his is all pitted out. Yours is in perfect condition. It's like Louis the Fourteenth's bowling shirt. It shouldn't say 'Mel' on the pocket. It should say 'The Sun King.'"

Madeleine smiled to herself, remembering that. By now, Mitchell was in France, or Spain, or wherever. The night she'd run into him, in New York, had begun with Kelly's taking her to an off-off-Broadway production of *The Cherry Orchard*. The ingenuity of the production—baskets of cherry petals had been piled up between the seats, so that the audience could smell the fragrance of the orchard the Ranevskys were selling along with their estate—and the interesting-looking faces in the crowd put Madeleine on notice that she was in a great city. After the play, Kelly had taken Madeleine to a bar popular with recent Brown grads. No sooner had they walked in than they ran into Mitchell and Larry. The boys were on their way to Paris the next day, and in a celebratory farewell mood. Madeleine had two vodka tonics, while Mitchell drank tequila, and then Kelly wanted to go to Chumley's in the Village. The four of them piled into a cab, Madeleine sitting on Mitchell's lap. It was well after midnight, the windows open onto tropically warm streets, and she didn't seem to be minimizing physical contact with Mitchell but leaning back against him. The fact that they ignored the sexual component of her sitting on his lap increased its excitement. Madeleine looked out the window, while Mitchell talked to Larry. Every bump conveyed secret information. All the way crosstown on East Ninth Street. If Madeleine felt guilty, she rationalized that she deserved one night to cut loose after her virtuous summer. Besides, no one in the cab was playing cop. Certainly not Mitchell, who, as the cab ride continued, did a brazen thing. Reaching under her shirt, he began stroking her skin, running a finger along her rib cage. No one could see what he was doing. Madeleine let him continue, both of them pretending to be absorbed in talking to Kelly and Larry, respectively. After a number of blocks, Mitchell's hand moved higher. His finger tried to slip under the right cup of her bra, at which point she clamped her arm down, and his hand retreated.

In Chumley's, Mitchell entertained everyone by telling the story of his own stint as a taxi driver over the summer. Madeleine talked to Kelly for a while, but it wasn't long before she ended up in the corner next to Mitchell. Despite her vodka haze she was aware that she was purposefully neglecting to mention the name Leonard. Mitchell showed her the marks on his upper arms where he'd been inoculated that afternoon. Then he bounded away to buy more drinks. She'd forgotten how much fun Mitchell could be. In comparison with Leonard, Mitchell was so low-maintenance. An hour or so later, when Madeleine went outside to hail a cab, Mitchell followed her, and the next thing she knew he was kissing her and she was kissing him back. It didn't go on long, but much longer than it should have. Finally, she broke away and cried, "I thought you wanted to be a monk!"

"The flesh is weak," Mitchell said, grinning at her.

"Go!" Madeleine said, punching him in the chest. "Go to India!"

He was looking at her with his big eyes. He reached out to take her hands. "I love you!" he said. And Madeleine had surprised herself by replying, "I love you, too." She meant that she loved him but didn't *love* love him. That, at least, was one possible interpretation, and, on Bedford Street, at three a.m., Madeleine decided not to clear up the matter further. Kissing Mitchell once more, briefly and dryly, she hailed a cab and made her escape.

The next morning, when Kelly asked her what had happened with Mitchell, Madeleine had lied.

"Nothing."

"I think he's cute," Kelly said. "He's better-looking than I remember."

"You think?"

"He's sort of my type."

Hearing this, Madeleine received another surprise: she felt jealous. Apparently, she wanted to keep Mitchell for herself, even while denying him. There was no end to her selfishness.

"He's probably on the plane by now," she said, and left it at that.

On the train back to Rhode Island, Madeleine began to suffer pangs of remorse. She decided that she had to tell Leonard what had happened, but by the time the train reached Providence, she realized that this would only make things worse. Leonard would think that he was losing her because of his illness. He would feel sexually inadequate, and he wouldn't be wrong, exactly. Mitchell was gone, out of the country, and soon

Madeleine and Leonard would be moving to Pilgrim Lake. With that in mind, Madeleine refrained from confessing. She threw herself back into the task of loving and caring for Leonard, and after a while the experience of kissing Mitchell that night began to seem as though it had taken place in an alternate reality, dreamlike and ephemeral.

Now, over the bay from Boston, picking its way among small cottony clouds, the ten-seater commuter plane appeared in the Cape Cod sky, descending toward the peninsula. Among the other greeters Madeleine watched the plane land and taxi along the runway, the force of its propellers flattening the dune grass on either side.

Ground personnel rolled a metal stairway up to the plane's front door, which opened from inside, and passengers began disembarking.

Madeleine knew that her sister's marriage was in trouble. She knew that her job today was to be helpful and understanding. But as Phyllida and Alwyn emerged from the plane Madeleine couldn't help wishing that she was waving not hello but goodbye. She had hoped to delay any parental visit until Leonard's side effects had subsided, which all his doctors insisted would be the case soon. It wasn't so much that Madeleine was ashamed of Leonard, but that she was disappointed at having Phyllida see him in his present state. Leonard wasn't himself. Phyllida was bound to get the wrong impression. Madeleine wanted her mother to meet the real Leonard, the boy she'd fallen in love with, who would be showing up any day now.

On top of this, seeing Alwyn was likely to be unpleasant. In the days when her big sister had sent her the Bachelorette's Survival Kit, back when Alwyn had been in step with the sixties and the birthright that came with them to denounce whatever she didn't like and to respond to whatever whim she pleased—dropping out of college, for instance, after her first year to drive around the country on the back of her boyfriend Grimm's motorcycle, or having a surprisingly cute pet white rat named Hendrix, or apprenticing to a candlemaker who insisted on following ancient Celtic methods—Alwyn had seemed to be blazing a trail of antimaterialistic, morally engaged creativity. But by the time Madeleine reached the age that Alwyn had been then, she realized that her sister's iconoclasm and liberationist commitments had just been part of a trend. Alwyn had done the things she had done and voiced the political opinions she'd voiced because all her friends were acting and talking the same way. You were supposed to feel bad about missing the sixties, but Madeleine didn't. She felt as if she'd been spared a lot of nonsense, that her generation, while inheriting much that was good from that decade, had a healthy distance from it as well, saving them from the whiplash that resulted from being a Maoist one minute and a suburban mother, in Beverly, Massachusetts, the next. When it turned out that Alwyn wasn't going to spend her life riding on the back of Grimm's motorcycle, when Grimm left her in a campground in Montana without even saying goodbye, Alwyn called home to ask Phyllida to wire money for a plane ticket to Newark, and, a day and a half later, she moved back into her old bedroom in Prettybrook. She spent the next two years (while Madeleine was finishing high school) working a series of service jobs and going to community college, studying graphic design. Over that time, the allure Alwyn had had in her younger sister's eyes dimmed considerably, if it didn't disappear altogether. Once again, Alwyn adapted to her surroundings. She hung out at the local pub, the Apothecary, with friends of hers who hadn't managed to get out of Prettybrook, either, all of them reverting to the scruffy, preppy clothes they'd worn in high school, cords, crew necks, L.L.Bean moccasins. One night at the Apothecary she'd met Blake Higgins, a reasonably nice-looking, medium-dumb guy who'd gone to Babson and lived in Boston, and soon Alwyn started visiting him up there, and dressing the way Blake, or Blake's family, liked her to, fancier, more expensively, wearing blouses or dresses from Gucci or Oscar de la Renta, preparing herself to be somebody's wife. Alwyn had been married for four years, in her most recent incarnation, and now this attempt to form a cohesive self was coming apart, too, apparently, and Madeleine was being called in, as the more together sister, to help shore it up.

She could see her mother and sister descending the staircase from the plane, Phyllida holding the banister, Alwyn's Janis Joplin mane, the one vestige of her former hippie self, whipping in the breeze. As they advanced over the tarmac Phyllida called out brightly, "We're from the Swedish Academy! Here to see Diane MacGregor."

"Isn't it amazing that she won?" Madeleine said.

"It must have been thrilling to be here."

They hugged, and Phyllida said, "We had dinner the other night with the Snyders. Professor Snyder is retired from Baxter, in biology, and I had him explain Dr. MacGregor's work to me. So I'm fully up to date! 'Jumping genes.' I'm looking forward to talking to Leonard all about it."

"He's pretty busy today," Madeleine said, trying to sound casual. "We didn't know you were coming until last night and he has to work."

"Of course, we don't want to take up his time. We'll just say hello for a minute."

Alwyn was carrying two little bags, one over each shoulder. She'd put on weight and her face looked more freckled than ever. She allowed herself to be hugged for a moment before pulling away.

"What did Mummy tell you?" she asked. "Did she tell you I *left* Blake?"

"She said you guys were having trouble."

"No. I left him. I've had it. The marriage is over."

"Don't be dramatic, dear," Phyllida said.

"I'm not being dramatic, Mummy," Alwyn said. She glared at Phyllida but, perhaps scared to confront her directly, turned to deliver her argument to Madeleine. "Blake works all week long. Then on weekends he plays golf. He's like a fifties dad. And we have hardly any babysitting. I wanted a live-in nanny but Blake said he didn't want someone in the house all the time. So I told him, 'You're never in the house! You try taking care of Richard full-time. I'm out of here.'" Alwyn grimaced. "The problem now is my boobs are going to burst."

Out in the open, within view of other people, she took hold of her engorged breasts with both hands.

"Ally, please," Phyllida said.

"Please, what? You wouldn't let me express any milk on the plane. What do you expect?"

"It was hardly private. And the flight was so short."

"Mummy was worried the men in the next row would get their rocks off," Alwyn said.

"It's bad enough the way you insist on nursing Richard in public. But to use that contraption—"

"It's a breast pump, Mummy. Everybody has them. You didn't because your generation put all the babies on formula."

"You two seem to have turned out all right."

When Alwyn had become pregnant, a little over a year ago, Phyllida had been thrilled. She'd gone up to Beverly to help decorate the nursery. She and Alwyn had gone shopping together for baby clothes, and Phyllida had shipped Alwyn and Maddy's old candlestick crib up from Prettybrook. Their mother-daughter solidarity lasted until the birth. Once Richard arrived in the world, Alwyn suddenly became an expert on infant care and didn't like anything their mother did. When Phyllida brought home a pacifier one day, Alwyn acted as if she'd suggested feeding the baby ground glass. She said that the brand of baby wipes Phyllida bought were "toxic." And she jumped down Phyllida's throat when Phyllida had referred to breast-feeding as a "fad." Why Alwyn insisted on breast-feeding Richard as long as she had was a mystery to Phyllida. When she'd been a young mother, the only person she knew who insisted on breast-feeding her children was Katja Fridliefsdottir, their neighbor from Iceland. The entire process of having a baby had become incredibly complicated, in Phyllida's opinion. Why did Alwyn have to read so many baby books? Why did she need a breast-feeding "coach"? If breast-feeding was so "natural," as Alwyn was always claiming it was, why was a coach necessary? Did Ally need a breathing coach, or a sleeping coach?

"This must be your graduation present," Phyllida said as they came to the car.

"This is it. I love it. Thank you so much, Mummy."

Alwyn climbed into the backseat with her bags. "I never got a car from you and Daddy," she said.

"You didn't graduate," Phyllida said. "But we helped you with the down payment on your house."

As Madeleine started the engine, Phyllida continued, "I wish I could persuade your father to buy a new car. He's still driving that awful Thunderbird of his. Can you imagine? I was reading in the newspaper about an artist who had himself *buried* in his car. I tore it out for Alton."

"Daddy probably liked that idea," Madeleine said.

"No, he didn't. He's gotten very solemn on the subject of death. Ever since he turned sixty. He's been doing all kinds of calisthenics in the basement."

Alwyn unzipped one of her bags and took out the breast pump and an empty bottle. She began unbuttoning her shirt. "How far is it to your place?" she asked Madeleine.

"About five minutes."

Phyllida glanced back to see what Alwyn was doing. "Can you put up the roof, please, Madeleine?" she said.

"Don't worry, Mummy," Alwyn said. "We're in P-town. All the men are gay. No one's interested."

Following orders, Madeleine put the top up. When the roof had finished moving and clicked in place, she drove out of the airport parking lot onto Race Point Road. The road led through protected dunes, white against the blue sky. Around the next curve, a few isolated contemporary houses popped up, with sundecks and sliding doors, and then they were entering the hedged lanes of Provincetown.

"Since you're feeling so overwhelmed, Ally," Phyllida said, "maybe now would be a good time to wean Richard the Lionhearted."

"They say it takes at least six months for a baby to develop the full antibodies," Alwyn said, pumping.

"I wonder if that's scientific."

"All the studies say at least six months. I'm going to do a year."

"Well," Phyllida said, with a sly look at Madeleine, "then you'd better get back home to your child."

"I don't want to talk about it anymore," Alwyn said.

"All right. Let's talk about something else. Madeleine, how are you liking it up here?"

"I love it. Except that I feel stupid sometimes. Everybody here got an eight hundred on their math SAT. But it's beautiful, and the food's amazing."

"And is Leonard enjoying it?"

"He likes it," Madeleine lied.

"And do you have enough to do?"

"Me? *Tons.* I'm rewriting my thesis to submit it to *The Janeite Review.*"

"You're going to be published? Marvelous! How can I subscribe?"

"The article's not accepted yet," Madeleine said, "but the editor wants to see it, so I'm hoping."

"If you want to have a career," Alwyn said, "my advice is don't get married. You think things have changed and there's some kind of gender equality now, that men are different, but I've got news for you. They're not. They're just as shitty and selfish as Daddy was. Is."

"Ally, I don't like to hear you talk that way about your father."

"*Jawohl,*" Alwyn said, and went quiet.

The quaint village, with its weathered houses, small, sandy yards, and feisty rosebushes, had been steadily emptying since Labor Day, the vacationing crowds along Commercial Street thinning to a population of townies and year-round transplants. As they passed the Pilgrim Monument, Madeleine idled the car so that Phyllida and Alwyn could see it. The only tourists around were a family of four who were staring up at the stone pillar.

"You can't climb it?" one of the kids said.

"It's just to look at," the mother said.

Madeleine started driving again. Soon they reached the other end of town.

"Doesn't Norman Mailer live here?" Phyllida inquired.

"He has a house on the water," Madeleine said.

"Your father and I met him once. He was *very* drunk."

In another few minutes, Madeleine made the turn into the Pilgrim Lake Laboratory gate and came down the long drive to the parking lot near the dining hall. She and Phyllida got out, but Alwyn remained seated with the pump. "Just let me finish this side," she said. "I'll do the other side later."

They waited in the bright autumn sunshine. It was midday, in the middle of the week. The only person visible outside was a guy with a baseball cap making a delivery of seafood to the kitchen. Dr. Malkiel's vintage Jaguar was parked a few spaces away.

Alwyn finished and began screwing the lid onto the baby bottle. Her mother's milk looked weirdly green. Unzipping the other bag, which turned out to be insulated and to contain a freezer pack, she placed the bottle inside and got out of the car.

Madeleine gave her mother and sister a quick tour of the compound. She showed them the Richard Serra, the beachfront, and the dining hall before taking them along the boardwalk back toward her building.

As they passed the genetics lab, Madeleine pointed it out. "That's where Leonard works."

"Let's go in and say hello," Phyllida suggested.

"I need to go to Maddy's apartment first," Alwyn said.

"That can wait. We're here already."

Madeleine wondered if Phyllida was trying to punish Alwyn by this, to make her suffer for her sins. Since she didn't want to stay in the lab long, anyway, this suited her fine, and she took them inside. She had some difficulty finding her way. She'd only been in the lab a few times and the corridors all looked the same. Finally, she saw the handwritten sign that read "Kilimnik Lab."

The lab was a brightly lit space of organized disorder. Cardboard boxes were stacked on shelves and in the corners of the room. Test tubes and beakers filled the wall cabinets and stood in formations on the lab tables. A spray bottle of disinfectant had been left next to a nearby sink, along with a box of something called KimWipes.

Vikram Jaitly, wearing a fat Cosby sweater, was sitting at his desk. He looked up, in case it was Kilimnik coming in, but, seeing Madeleine, he relaxed. She asked him where Leonard was.

"He's in the thirty-degrees room," Vikram said, pointing across the lab. "Go on in."

A refrigerator with a padlock stood next to the door. Madeleine peered in the window to see Leonard, his back turned, standing in front of a machine that was vibrating. He was wearing a bandanna, shorts, and a T-shirt, which wasn't exactly what she'd been hoping for. But there was no time to get him to change now, so she opened the door and they all went in.

Vikram had meant centigrade. The room was warm. It smelled like a bakery.

"Hi," Madeleine said, "we're here."

Leonard turned. He hadn't shaved, and his face was expressionless. The machine behind him was making a rattling noise.

"Leonard!" Phyllida said. "So nice to meet you at last."

This snapped Leonard out of his daze. "Hi there," he said. He came forward and held out his hand. Phyllida looked momentarily startled, but then shook Leonard's hand and said, "I hope we're not interrupting you."

"No, I was just doing some grunt work. I apologize for the smell in here. Some people don't like it."

"All in the name of science," Phyllida said. She introduced Alwyn.

If Phyllida was surprised by Leonard's appearance, she didn't show it. She immediately started talking about Dr. MacGregor's jumping genes, recounting everything she'd learned from her dinner conversation. Then she asked Leonard to explain his work.

"Well," Leonard said, "we're working with yeast, and this is where we grow the yeast. This contraption here is called a shaker table. We put the yeast in there to aerate it." He opened the lid and removed a flask filled with yellow liquid. "Let me show you."

He led them outside to the main room and set the flask on the table. "The experiment we're running has to do with the mating of yeast."

Phyllida raised her eyebrows. "I didn't know yeast were so interesting. Dare I ask the details?"

As Leonard began to explain the research he was involved in, Madeleine relaxed. This was the kind of thing Phyllida liked: to be informed by experts in the field, any field.

Leonard had taken a glass straw from a drawer and inserted it into the flask. "What I'm doing now is I'm pipetting some yeast onto a slide, so we can take a look at it."

"God, *pipette!*" Alwyn said. "I haven't heard that word since high school."

"There are two kinds of yeast cells, haploid cells and diploid cells. Haploid cells are the only type that mate. They come in two types: a cells and alpha cells. In mating, the a cells go for the alpha cells and the alpha cells go for the a cells." He put the slide into the microscope. "Take a look."

Phyllida stepped forward and bent her face to the lens.

"I don't see anything," she said.

"You have to focus it here." When Leonard raised his hand to show her, it shook slightly, and he took hold of the edge of the table.

"Oh, there they are," Phyllida said, focusing by herself.

"See them? Those are yeast cells. If you look close, you'll notice that some are bigger than the others."

"Yes!"

"The big ones are the diploid cells. The haploids are smaller. Focus on the smaller ones, the haploids. Some should be elongating. That's what they do prior to mating."

"I see one that has a . . . protuberance on one end."

"That's called a shmoo. That's a haploid getting ready to mate."

"A shmoo?" Alwyn said.

"It's from *Li'l Abner*," Leonard explained. "The comic strip."

"How old do I look to you?" Alwyn said.

"I remember Li'l Abner," Phyllida said, still gazing into the microscope. "He was the country bumpkin. *Not* very amusing, as I recall."

"Tell them about the pheromones," Madeleine said.

Leonard nodded. "Yeast cells send out pheromones, which are sort of like a chemical perfume. A cells send out an a pheromone and alpha cells send out an alpha pheromone. That's how they attract each other."

Phyllida stared into the microscope for another minute, giving little reports on what she was seeing. Finally she lifted her head. "Well, I'll never think of yeast in quite the same way. Do you want to take a look, Ally?"

"No thanks. I'm finished with mating," Alwyn said sourly.

Ignoring this, Phyllida said, "Leonard, I understand about the haploids and the diploids. But tell me what you're trying to learn about them."

"We're trying to figure out why the progeny of a given cell division can acquire different developmental fates."

"Oh, dear. Maybe I shouldn't have asked."

"It's not that complicated. Remember the two types of haploid cells, a type and alpha type?"

"Yes."

"Well, of each of those haploids, there are two types as well. We call them mother cells and daughter cells. Mother cells can bud and create new cells. Daughter cells can't. Mother cells can also switch their sex—go from being an a to an alpha—in order to mate. We're trying to figure out why the mother cells can do that but their children can't."

"I know why," Phyllida said. "Because Mother knows best."

"There are a million possible reasons for this asymmetry," Leonard went on. "We're testing one possibility, which has to do with the HO gene. It's complicated, but basically what we're doing is cutting out the HO gene and putting it in backward so that it can be read from the other DNA strand in the other direction. If this affects the daughter cell's ability to switch, then that means the HO is what's controlling the asymmetry."

"I'm afraid you lost me."

This was the first time Madeleine had heard Leonard open up about his work. Up until now, all he'd done was complain. He didn't like Bob Kilimnik, who treated him like hired help. He said that the actual lab work was about as interesting as combing out head lice. But now Leonard seemed genuinely interested in what he was doing. His face was animated as he spoke. Madeleine's happiness at seeing him coming alive again made her forget the fact that he was overweight, and wearing a bandanna, in front of her mother, and made her listen to what he was saying.

"The reason we study yeast cells is because they're fundamentally like human cells, only a lot simpler. Haploids resemble gametes, our sex cells. The hope is, what we figure out about yeast cells might apply to human cells. So if we can figure out how and why they bud, we might learn something about arresting that process. There's some evidence that budding yeast is analogous to the budding of cancer cells."

"So you're finding a cure for cancer?" Phyllida said with excitement.

"Not in this study," Leonard said. "I was just talking in general. What we're doing here is testing one hypothesis. If Bob is right, this will have big implications. If not, at least we've ruled out one possibility. And we can move on from there." He lowered his voice. "In my opinion, the hypothesis for this study is sort of way out there. But nobody asked my opinion."

"Leonard, when did you know you wanted to be a scientist?" Phyllida asked.

"In high school. I had this great biology teacher."

"Do you come from a long line of scientists?"

"Not at all."

"What do your parents do?"

"My father used to have an antiques store."

"Really. Where?"

"In Portland. Oregon."

"And do your parents still live there?"

"My mom does. My father lives in Europe now. They're divorced."

"Oh, I see."

Here Madeleine said, "Mummy, we should go."

"What?"

"Leonard needs to get back to work."

"Oh, of course. Well. It's been so nice meeting you. I'm sorry we have so little time today. We just flew in on a mad whim."

"Stay longer next time."

"I'd love to. Maybe I can come back for a visit with Madeleine's father."

"That would be great. I'm sorry I'm so busy today."

"No need to apologize. The march of progress!"

"More like creep," Leonard said.

As soon as they were outside, Alwyn demanded to be taken to Madeleine's apartment. "I'm going to start leaking all over the front of my dress."

"Does that happen?" Madeleine said, wincing.

"Yes. It's like being a cow."

Madeleine laughed. She was so relieved the meeting was over that she almost didn't mind dealing with the family emergency now. She led Alwyn and Phyllida across the parking lot to her building. Alwyn began unbuttoning her blouse before she was even in the door. Once inside, she plopped down on the sofa and took her breast pump out of its bag again. She unfastened the left side of her nursing bra and attached the suction cup to her breast.

"Very low ceilings," Phyllida said, determinedly looking away.

"I know," Madeleine said. "Leonard has to hunch."

"But the view's lovely."

"Oh my God," Alwyn said, sighing with pleasure. "This is such a relief. Supposedly some women have orgasms from breast-feeding."

"I do love an ocean view."

"See what you missed from not breast-feeding us, Mummy?"

Closing her eyes, Phyllida said in a commanding tone, "Will you please do that somewhere else?"

"We're family," Alwyn said.

"You are in front of a *large picture window,*" Phyllida said. "Anyone walking by can see right in."

"Okay. God. I'll use the bathroom. I've got to pee, anyway." She got up, holding the pump and the rapidly filling baby bottle, and went into the bathroom. She closed the door.

Phyllida smoothed the skirt of her suit and sat down. She lifted her eyes to Madeleine's, smiling with forbearance. "It's never easy on a marriage when a baby comes along. It's a wonderful event. But it puts a strain on the relationship. That's why it's so important to find the right kind of person to raise a family with."

Madeleine was determined to ignore any subtext. She was going to be all text. "Blake's great," she said.

"He's wonderful," Phyllida agreed. "And Ally's wonderful. And Richard the Lionhearted is divine! But the situation at home is dreadful."

"Are you talking about me?" Alwyn said from the bathroom. "Stop talking about me."

"When you're finished in there," Phyllida called back, "I want us all to have a talk."

The toilet flushed. A few seconds later, Alwyn emerged, still pumping milk. "I don't care what you say, I'm not going back," she said.

"Ally," Phyllida said, employing her most sympathetic tone, "I understand that you're having difficulties in your marriage. I can imagine that Blake, like every member of the male species, has certain lapses when it comes to taking care of children. But the one who's being most hurt by your leaving—"

"Certain lapses!"

"—is Richard!"

"There's no other way to convince Blake that I'm serious."

"But to leave your child!"

"With his *father*. I left my baby with his father."

"But he needs his mother at his age."

"You're just worried Blake can't take care of him. Which is exactly my point."

"Blake has to work," Phyllida said. "He can't stay home."

"Well, he's going to have to now."

Exasperated, Phyllida stood up again and went to the window. "Madeleine," she said, "talk to your sister."

As the younger sibling, Madeleine hadn't been in this position before. She didn't want to humiliate Alwyn. And yet there was something intoxicating about being asked to sit in judgment of her.

Having detached the suction cup from her breast, Alwyn was now dabbing her nipple with a handful of toilet paper, her lowered head giving her a double chin.

"Tell me what's been going on with you guys," Madeleine said softly.

Alwyn looked up with an aggrieved expression, brushing her leonine hair out of her face with her free hand. "I'm not me anymore!" she cried. "I'm Mommy. *Blake* calls me Mommy. First it was just if I was holding Richard, but now we're alone and he says it. Like because I'm a mother he thinks I'm *his* mother. It's so *weird*. Before we got married we used to

195

divide all the chores. But the minute we had a kid Blake started acting like it makes total sense that I do all the laundry and shop for groceries. All he does is work, *all the time*. He's constantly worrying about money. He doesn't do anything around the house. I mean *anything*. Including have sex with me." She glanced at Phyllida. "Sorry, Mummy, but Maddy asked me how it's going." She looked back at Madeleine. "That's how it's going. It's not going."

Madeleine listened to her sister sympathetically. She understood that Alwyn's complaints about her marriage were complaints about marriage and men in general. But, like anyone in love, Madeleine believed that her own relationship was different from every other relationship, immune from typical problems. For this reason, the chief effect of Alwyn's words was to make Madeleine secretly and intensely happy.

"What are you going to do with that?" Madeleine asked, indicating the baby bottle.

"I'm going to take it back to Boston and send it to Blake."

"That's crazy, Ally."

"Thanks for the support."

"Sorry. I mean, Blake sounds like he's being a total shit. But I agree with Mummy. You have to think about Richard."

"Why is it *my* responsibility?"

"Isn't that obvious?"

"Why? Because I had a baby? Because I'm a 'wife' now? You don't know anything about it. You're barely out of college."

"Oh, and that means I can't have an opinion?"

"It means you need to grow up."

"I think you're the one who's refusing to grow up," Madeleine said.

Alwyn's eyes grew slitty. "Why, when I do something, is it always crazy Ally? Crazy Ally moving into a hotel. Crazy Ally abandoning her children. I'm always the crazy one and Maddy's always the sensible one. Yeah, right."

"Well, I'm not the one messengering my mother's milk!"

Alwyn gave her a strange, fierce smile. "There's nothing wrong with your life, I bet."

"I didn't say that."

"There's nothing crazy about your life."

"If I ever have a baby and take off, you have my permission to tell me I'm acting crazy."

Alwyn said, "What about if you start dating somebody crazy?"

"What are you talking about?" Madeleine said.

"You know what I'm talking about."

"Ally," Phyllida said, turning around, "I don't appreciate the tone you're taking with your sister. She's just trying to help."

"Maybe you should ask Maddy about the prescription bottle in the bathroom."

"What bottle?"

"You know what I'm talking about."

"Did you snoop in my medicine cabinet?" Madeleine said, her voice rising.

"It was right out on the counter!"

"You snooped!"

"Stop it," Phyllida said. "Ally, wherever it was, it's none of your concern. And I don't want to hear one word about it."

"That makes total sense!" Alwyn cried. "You come out here to see if Leonard's husband material, and when you find a serious problem—like that he's maybe on *lithium*—you don't want to hear about it. Whereas *my* marriage—"

"It was wrong of you to read the prescription."

"*You* were the one who sent me into the bathroom!"

"Not to invade Maddy's privacy. Now, both of you—*enough*."

They spent the rest of the afternoon in Provincetown. They had lunch at a restaurant near Whaler's Wharf, with fishing nets hung on the walls. A sign in the window informed customers that the establishment would be closing in another week. After lunch, the three of them walked silently down Commercial Street, looking at the buildings and stopping into the souvenir shops and stationery shops that were still open, and going out onto the pier to see the fishing boats. They went through the motions of having a proper visit (even though Madeleine and Alwyn would barely look at each other) because they were Hannas and this was how Hannas behaved. Phyllida even insisted on having ice cream sundaes, unusual for her. At four o'clock, they got back into the car. Driving to the airport, Madeleine stomped the gas pedal as if squashing a bug, and Phyllida had to tell her to slow down.

The plane to Boston was on the runway when they arrived, its propellers already spinning. Happier clans, seeing people off, were hugging or waving. Alwyn joined the waiting passengers without saying goodbye to Madeleine, quickly striking up a conversation with a fellow passenger to show how friendly and agreeable other people found her to be.

Phyllida said nothing until she was about to pass through the gate.

"I hope the winds have calmed down. It was a little bumpy coming in."

"It seems calmer," Madeleine said, looking at the sky.

"Please thank Leonard for us again. That was awfully nice of him to take time out of his day."

"I will."

"Goodbye, dear," Phyllida said, and then walked out across the landing strip and up the stairway of the commuter plane.

Clouds were gathering in the west as Madeleine drove back to Pilgrim Lake. The sun was already beginning its descent, the angle of its light turning the dunes the color of butterscotch. Cape Cod was one of the few places on the East Coast where you could watch the sun set. Gulls were plunging straight down into the water, as if trying to bash in their tiny brains.

Back at her apartment, Madeleine lay on the bed for a while, staring up at the ceiling. Going to the kitchen, she heated water for tea but didn't make it, and ate half a chocolate bar instead. Finally, she took a long shower. She'd just gotten out when she heard Leonard come in.

She wrapped a towel around herself and went out to him, putting her arms around his neck. "Thank you," she said.

"For what?"

"For putting up with my family. For being so nice."

She couldn't tell whether Leonard's T-shirt was damp or she was. She turned her face up to his, begging for a kiss. He didn't seem to want to, so she went up on her toes and started it herself. She tasted the faint metallic tang and pushed past it, slipping one hand under his T-shirt. She let her towel fall to the ground.

"Well, O.K. then," Leonard said. "Is this my reward for being good?"

"This is your reward for being good," Madeleine said.

He walked her, somewhat awkwardly, backwards into the bedroom, lowered her onto the bed, and began taking off his clothes. Madeleine lay on her back, waiting, silent. When Leonard climbed on top of her she responded, kissing him and stroking his back. She reached down and placed her hand against his penis. Its surprising hardness, after months of not being so, made it feel twice as big as Madeleine remembered. She hadn't realized how much she'd missed it. Leonard rose on his knees, his dark eyes hoovering up every aspect of her body. Propping himself up on one arm, he took hold of his cock, moving it in a circular fashion, almost putting it in, but not quite. For one mad instant Madeleine considered letting him. She didn't want to break the mood. She wanted to abandon herself to risk in order to show him how much she loved him. She arched her back, guiding him in. But as Leonard pushed farther in, Madeleine thought better and said, "Hold on."

She tried to be as quick as possible. Throwing her legs over the side of the bed, she opened the bedside table drawer and took out her diaphragm case. She removed the disk, with its rubbery smell. The spermicide tube was all crumpled up. In her haste Madeleine squeezed out too much jelly and it dripped onto her thigh. She spread her knees apart, squeezing the device into a figure eight, and inserted it deep inside her until she felt it pop open. After wiping her hand on the sheet, she rolled back to Leonard.

When he began kissing her she noticed the sour, metallic taste again, stronger than ever. She realized, with a sinking feeling, that she was no longer aroused. But that didn't matter. What mattered was that they complete the act. With this in mind, she reached down to help things along, but Leonard was no longer hard. As if she hadn't noticed, Madeleine resumed kissing him. With desperation she began to feed on Leonard's sour mouth, trying to appear excited and to excite him in turn. But after half a minute, Leonard pulled away. He rolled heavily onto his side, facing away from her, and was silent.

A long cold moment ensued. For the first time ever, Madeleine regretted meeting Leonard. He was defective, and she wasn't, and there was nothing she could do about it. The cruelty of this thought felt rich and sweet and Madeleine indulged in it for another minute.

But then this, too, faded away, and she felt sorry for Leonard and guilty for being so selfish. She reached over and stroked Leonard's back. He was crying now and she tried to comfort him, saying the required things, kissing his face, telling him that she loved him, she loved him, everything was going to be fine, she loved him so much.

She curled up against him, and they both were quiet.

And then they must have fallen asleep, because when she woke again the room was dark. She got up and dressed. Putting on her peacoat, she went out of the building to the beach.

It was just after ten o'clock. The lights of the dining hall and bar were still blazing. Directly ahead of her, the quarter moon lit up shreds of clouds moving quickly over the dark bay. The wind was strong. Blowing in Madeleine's face, it seemed personally interested in her. It had come all this way, across the continent, to deliver a message to her.

She concentrated on what the doctor at Providence Hospital had said, the one time they spoke. It often took a while to get the appropriate dosage right, she said. Side effects were typically worse at first. Given that Leonard had functioned well on lithium in the past, there was no reason he wouldn't do so in the future. It was only a question of recalibrating the dosage. Many patients with manic depression lived long and productive lives.

She hoped all this was true. Being with Leonard made Madeleine feel exceptional. It was as if, before she'd met him, her blood had circulated grayly around her body, and now it was all oxygenated and red.

She was petrified of becoming the half-alive person she'd been before.

As she stood staring out at the black waves, a sound reached her ears. A soft thudding quickly approaching over the sand. Madeleine turned as a dark shape shot out, moving low to the ground. In another second she recognized Diane MacGregor's standard poodle, galloping past. The dog's mouth was open, tongue unfurled, her body as elongated and directed as an arrow.

A few moments later, MacGregor herself appeared.

"Your dog scared me," Madeleine said. "It sounded like a horse."

"I know just what you mean," MacGregor said.

She was dressed in the same raincoat as at the press conference two weeks ago. Her gray hair was hanging limply on either side of her creased intelligent face.

"Which way did she go?" MacGregor asked.

Madeleine pointed. "She went thataway."

MacGregor squinted into the darkness.

They stood together on the beach, feeling no need to speak further. Finally Madeleine broke the silence. "When do you go to Sweden?"

"What? Oh, in December." MacGregor seemed to be uninterested.

"I don't understand why the Swedes would bring anyone to Sweden in December, do you?"

"Summer would be nicer."

"There will be hardly any daylight at all! I suppose that's why they came up with the prizes. To give the Swedes something to do during the winter."

Suddenly the dog sped past again, ripping up sand.

"I don't know why it makes me so happy to watch my dog run," Mac-Gregor said. "It's like a piece of me gets to hitch a ride." She shook her head. "This is what it's come to. Living vicariously through my poodle."

"There are worse things."

After a few more passes, the poodle returned, prancing in front of her owner. Noticing Madeleine, the animal went up to sniff her, and began rubbing her head against Madeleine's legs.

"She's not very attached to me," MacGregor said, looking on objectively. "She'll go to anyone. If I died, she'd forget me in a second. Wouldn't you?" she said, calling the poodle over and scratching her vigorously under the chin. "Yes, you would. You would, you would."

•

After they left Paris, going from France to Ireland, then back south, all the way through Andalusia and to Morocco, Mitchell began sneaking off to churches any chance he could. This was Europe and there were churches everywhere, spectacular cathedrals as well as quiet little chapels, all of them still functioning (though usually empty), each one open to a wandering pilgrim, even one like Mitchell who wasn't sure he qualified. He went into these dark, superstitious spaces to stare at faded frescoes or crude, bloody paintings of Christ. He peered into dusty reliquary jars containing the bones of Saint Whoever. Moved, solemn, he lit votive candles, always with the same inappropriate wish: that someday, somehow, Madeleine would be his. Mitchell didn't believe the candles worked. He was opposed to petitional prayer. But it made him feel a little better to light a candle for Madeleine and to think about her for a minute, in the peacefulness of an old Spanish church, while, outside, the sea of faith retreated "down the vast edges drear and naked shingles of the world."

Mitchell was perfectly aware of how strangely he was behaving. But it didn't matter because no one was around to notice. In stiff-backed pews, smelling candle wax, he closed his eyes and sat as still as possible, opening himself up to whatever was there that might be interested in him. Maybe there was nothing. But how would you ever know if you didn't send out a signal? That's what Mitchell was doing: he was sending out a signal to the home office.

On the trains, buses, and boats that took them to all these places, Mitchell read the books in his backpack one by one. The mind of Thomas à Kempis, the author of *The Imitation of Christ*, was difficult to connect with. Parts of Saint Augustine's *Confessions*, especially the information about his self-pleasuring youth and his African wife, were eye-opening. *Interior Castle*, however, by Saint Teresa of Avila, proved to be a gripping read. Mitchell devoured it on the overnight ferry ride from Le Havre to Rosslare. From the Gare St. Lazare, they'd gone to Normandy to visit the restaurant Larry had worked at during high school. After a huge lunch with the family owners, followed by a night in their house, they proceeded to Le Havre for the crossing. The seas were rough. Passengers stayed awake at the bar, or tried to sleep on the floor of the open cabin. Exploring belowdecks, Mitchell and Larry gained entry to a vacant officers' lounge, with a Jacuzzi and beds, and amid this unwarranted luxury, Mitchell read about the soul's progress toward mystical union with God. *Interior Castle* described a vision that Saint Teresa had had involving the soul. "I thought of the soul as resembling a castle, formed of a single diamond or a very transparent crystal, and containing many rooms, just as in heaven there are many mansions." At first, the soul lay in darkness outside the castle walls, plagued by the venomous snakes and stinging insects of its sins. By the power of grace, however, some souls crawled out of this swamp and knocked at the castle door. "At length they enter the first rooms of the basement of the castle, accompanied by numerous reptiles which disturb their peace, and prevent their seeing the beauty of the building; still, it is a great gain that these persons should have found their way in at all." All night long, while the ferry pitched and rolled, and Larry slept, Mitchell read how the soul progressed through the other six mansions, edifying itself with sermons, mortifying itself by penance and fasting, performing charity, meditating, praying, going on retreats, shedding its old habits and growing more perfect, until it became betrothed to the Spouse. "When our Lord is pleased to take pity on the sufferings, both past and present, endured through her longing for Him by this soul . . . He, before consummating the celestial marriage, brings her into His mansion or presence chamber. This is the seventh Mansion, for as He has a dwelling-place in heaven, so has He in the soul, where none but He may abide and which may be termed a second heaven." What struck Mitchell about the book wasn't so much imagery like that, which seemed borrowed from the Song of Songs, but its practicality. The book was a guide for the spiritual life, told with great specificity. For instance, describing mystical union, Saint Teresa wrote: "You may fancy that such a person is beside herself and that her mind is too inebriated to care for anything else. On the contrary, she is far more active than before in all that concerns God's service." Or, later: "This presence is not always so entirely realized, that is, so distinctly manifest, as at first, or as it is at times when God renews his favour; otherwise the recipient could not possibly attend to anything else nor live in society." That sounded authentic. It sounded like something that Saint Teresa, writing five hundred years ago, had experienced, as real as the garden outside her convent window in Avila. You could tell the difference between someone making things up and someone using metaphorical language to describe an ineffable, but real, experience. Just after dawn, Mitchell went up on deck. He was light-headed from sleeplessness and giddy from the book. As he stared at the gray ocean and the misty coast of Ireland, he wondered what room his soul was in.

They spent two days in Dublin. Mitchell made Larry visit the Joyce shrines, Eccles Street and the Martello tower. Larry took Mitchell to see Jerzy Grotowski's "poor theater" group. The next day, they hitchhiked to the west. Mitchell tried to pay attention to Ireland, and especially to County Cork, where his mother's side of the family came from. But it rained all the time, fog covered the fields, and by then he was reading Tolstoy. There were some books that reached through the noise of life to grab you by the collar and speak only of the truest things. *A Confession* was a book like that. In it, Tolstoy related a Russian fable about a man who, being chased by a monster, jumps into a well. As the man is falling down the well, however, he sees there's a dragon at the bottom, waiting to eat him. Right then, the man notices a branch sticking out of the wall, and he grabs on to it, and hangs. This keeps the man from falling into the dragon's jaws, or being eaten by the monster above, but it turns out there's another little problem. Two mice, one black and one white, are scurrying around and around the branch, nibbling it. It's only a matter of time before they will chew through the branch, causing the man to fall. As the man contemplates his inescapable fate, he notices something else: from the end of the branch he's holding, a few drops of honey are dripping. The man sticks out his tongue to lick them. This, Tolstoy says, is our human predicament: we're the man clutching the branch. Death awaits us. There is no escape. And so we distract ourselves by licking whatever drops of honey come within our reach.

Most of what Mitchell read in college hadn't conveyed Wisdom with a capital W. But this Russian fable did. It was true about people in general and it was true about Mitchell in particular. What were he and his friends doing, really, other than hanging from a branch, sticking their tongues out to catch the sweetness? He thought about the people he knew, with their excellent young bodies, their summerhouses, their cool clothes, their potent drugs, their liberalism, their orgasms, their haircuts. Everything they did was either pleasurable in itself or engineered to bring pleasure down the line. Even the people he knew who were "political" and who protested the war in El Salvador did so largely in order to bathe themselves in an attractively crusading light. And the artists were the worst, the painters and the writers, because they believed they were living for art when they were really feeding their narcissism. Mitchell had always prided himself on his discipline. He studied harder than anyone he knew. But that was just his way of tightening his grip on the branch.

What Larry thought about Mitchell's reading list was unclear. Most of the time he limited his reaction to the raising of one tawny Riverdale eyebrow. Having been members of the college art scene, Larry and Mitchell were used to people undergoing radical self-transformations. Moss Runk (this was a girl) had arrived at Brown as an apple-cheeked member of the cross-country team. By junior year, she had repudiated the wearing of gender-specific clothing. Instead, she covered herself in shapeless garments that she made herself out of hot-looking thick gray felt. What you did with a person like Moss Runk, if you were Mitchell and Larry, was you pretended not to notice. When Moss came up to them in the Blue Room, moving in her hovercraft way owing to the long hem of her robe, you slid over so she could sit down. If someone asked what she was, exactly, you said, "That's Moss!" Despite her odd clothes, Moss

Runk was still the same cheerful Idahoan she'd always been. Other people thought she was weird, but not Mitchell and Larry. Whatever had led to her drastic sartorial decision was something that Mitchell and Larry didn't inquire about. Their silence registered solidarity with Moss against all the conventional people in their down vests and Adidas sneakers who were majoring in economics or engineering, spending the last period of total freedom in their lives doing nothing the least bit unordinary. Mitchell and Larry knew that Moss Runk wasn't going to be able to wear her androgynous outfits forever. (Another nice thing about Moss was that she wanted to be a high school principal.) There would come a day when, in order to get a job, Moss would have to hang up her gray felt and put on a skirt, or a business suit. Mitchell and Larry didn't want to be around to see it.

Larry treated Mitchell's interest in Christian mysticism the same way. He noticed. He made it clear he noticed. But he made no comment, for the time being.

Besides, Larry was undergoing his own transformations on the road. He bought a purple silk scarf. His smoking, which Mitchell had thought a temporary affectation, became habitual. At first Larry bought cigarettes singly, which apparently you could do, but soon he was buying whole packs of Gauloises Bleues. Strangers began bumming cigarettes off him, skinny, Gypsy-looking dudes who put their arms around Larry's shoulder, Euro-style. Mitchell felt like Larry's chaperone, waiting for these confabs to end.

In addition, Larry didn't appear to be sufficiently heartbroken. There was a moment, on the ferry to Rosslare, when he'd gone on deck to smoke a moody cigarette. It was understood that he was thinking about Claire. But he tossed the cigarette overboard, the smoke drifted away, and that was that.

From Ireland they returned to Paris, and took an overnight sleeper to Barcelona. The weather felt almost balmy. Along the Ramblas, jungle wildlife was for sale, wise-looking macaques, Technicolor parrots. Heading farther south, they stayed a night each in Jerez and Ronda, before moving on for three days in Sevilla. Then, realizing how close they were to North Africa, they decided to continue south to Algeciras and ride the ferry across the Strait of Gibraltar to Tangier. They spent their first days in Morocco failing to buy hash. Their guidebook listed the location of a bar in Tétouan where hash could be easily scored but included a warning, at the bottom of the same page, comparing Moroccan prisons to the Turkish jail in *Midnight Express*. Finally, in the small mountain village of Chaouen, they came into their hotel to find two Danes sitting in the lobby, with a softball-size chunk of hash on the table in front of them. Mitchell and Larry spent the next days gloriously stoned. They wandered the narrow beehive streets, listening to the muezzins' emotional cries, and drank bright green glasses of mint tea in the town square. Chaouen was painted light blue to blend in with the sky. Even the flies couldn't find it.

It was in Morocco that they realized their backpacks were a mistake. The coolest guys they met weren't the expeditionists with their camping gear. The coolest guys were the travelers who'd just returned from Ladakh carrying nothing more than a tote. Backpacks were unwieldy. They marked you as a tourist. Even if you weren't an overweight waddling American, with a backpack on you were. Mitchell got stuck entering train compartments and had to wave his arms frantically to wriggle free. Getting rid of their backpacks was impossible, however, because, as they returned to Europe in October, the weather was already turning cooler. Leaving the warmth of southern France, they headed up into autumnal Lausanne, breezy Lucerne. They took out their sweaters.

In Switzerland Mitchell hit on the idea of using his MasterCard to buy things that would alarm his parents when they received the statements. Over three weeks he made charges of: 65 Swiss francs ($29.57) for a Tyrolean pipe and tobacco from Totentanz: Zigarren und Pfeifen; 72 Swiss francs ($32.75) for a meal in a Zurich restaurant called Das Bordell; 234 Austrian schillings ($13) for an English edition of Charles Colson's memoir *Born Again*; and 62,500 lire ($43.54) for a subscription to a Communist magazine, published in Bologna, to be shipped once a month to the Grammaticus home address in Detroit.

They reached Venice on a cloud-cushioned afternoon in late October. Unable to afford a gondola, they spent their first hours in the city traversing bridges and flights of stairs that all seemed to lead, as in an Escher drawing, back to the same piazza, with the same burbling fountain and duo of old men. After finding a cheap pensione, they went out to visit the Piazza San Marco. In the dimly lit museum in the Doge's Palace, Mitchell found himself staring at a mysterious object in a vitrine. Made of badly corroded metal links, the object consisted of a circular belt from which another belt hung down. The label read: *cintura di castita*.

"That chastity belt was the most horrifying thing I've ever seen in my life," Mitchell said later, over dinner at a budget restaurant.

"That's why they call them the Dark Ages," Larry said.

"That was beyond dark." He leaned forward, lowering his voice. "There were two openings. One in front for the vagina, and one in back for the asshole. With serrated metal teeth. If you took a shit with one of those things on, your shit would be extruded like cake frosting."

"Thanks for the image," Larry said.

"Imagine having one of those things on for months and months. For years! How would you keep it clean?"

"You'd be the queen," Larry said. "You'd have someone to clean it for you."

"A lady-in-waiting."

"Just one of the perks."

They refilled their wineglasses. Larry was in a good mood. The speed with which he'd gotten over Claire was stunning. Maybe he hadn't really liked Claire all that much. Maybe he disliked Claire as much as Mitchell did. The fact that Larry could get over Claire in a matter of weeks, whereas Mitchell remained heartbroken over Madeleine—even though he hadn't gone out with Madeleine—meant one of two things: either Mitchell's love for Madeleine was pure and true and earthshakingly significant; or he was addicted to feeling forlorn, he *liked* being heartbroken, and the "emotion" he felt for Madeleine—somewhat increased by the flowing chianti—was only a perverted form of self-love. Not love at all, in other words.

"Don't you miss Claire?" Mitchell asked.

"I do."

"You don't seem like you do."

Larry took this in, staring back into Mitchell's eyes, but saying nothing.

"What was she like in bed?"

"Now, now, Mitchell," Larry lightly scolded.

"Come on. What was she like?"

"She was *wild*, Mitchell. Unbelievably wild."

"Tell me."

Larry took a sip of wine, considering. "She was dutiful. She was the kind of girl who says, 'O.K. Lie on your back.'"

"And then she'd blow you?"

"Um, yeah."

"'Lie on your back.' Like at the doctor's."

Larry nodded.

"That sounds pretty decent."

"It wasn't that great."

This was more than Mitchell could bear. "What do you mean!" he cried. "What are you complaining about?"

"I wasn't that into it."

Mitchell leaned away from the table, as if to distance himself from such heresy. He drained off his glass of wine and ordered another.

"That's over our budget," Larry cautioned.

"I don't care."

Larry ordered more wine too.

They drank wine until the proprietor of the restaurant told them he was closing. Staggering back to their hotel, they fell into the big double bed. At one point, in his sleep, Larry rolled on top of Mitchell, or Mitchell dreamed this. He had an erection. He thought he might throw up. Somebody in his dream was sucking his cock, or Larry was, and then he woke up to hear Larry say, "Ugh, you stink," without pushing him away, however. And then Mitchell passed out again, and in the morning they both acted as if nothing had happened. Maybe nothing had.

By late November, they reached Greece. From Brindisi they had taken a ferry smelling of diesel fuel to Piraeus, and found a room in a hotel not far from Syntagma Square. Gazing from the balcony of this hotel, Mitchell had a revelation. Greece wasn't part of Europe. It was the Middle East. Flat-roofed gray high-rises like the one he was in extended all the way to the hazy horizon. Steel girders protruded from the roofs and exteriors, making the buildings look barbed, bristling against the acrid atmosphere. He might have been in Beirut. The thick smog was mixed with tear gas on a daily basis as police battled protesters down in the streets. Protest marches occurred constantly, against the government, against CIA interference, against capitalism, against NATO, and in support of the return of the Elgin marbles. Greece, the birthplace of democracy, stymied by free speech. In coffeehouses everyone had an informed opinion, and no one could get anything done.

A few old widows, clad head to toe in black, reminded Mitchell of his grandmother. He recognized the sweets and the pastries, the sound of the language. But most of the people looked foreign to him. The men, on the whole, were a head shorter than he was. Mitchell felt like a Swede, looming over them. Here and there he saw a facial resemblance, but that was as far as it went. Among the anarchists and yellow-toothed poets in the bar across from his hotel, or the gorilla-necked cabdrivers who drove him around, or the entitled Orthodox priests he saw on the streets and in the smoky chapels, Mitchell had never felt more American in his life.

Everywhere they ate, the food was lukewarm. Moussaka and pastitsio, lamb and rice, fried potatoes, okra in tomato sauce—all were kept a few degrees above room temperature in trays in open kitchens. Larry began ordering grilled fish, but Mitchell, loyal to memory, continued to eat the dishes his grandmother had made for him as a boy. He kept expecting to get a nice hot plate of moussaka, but after his fourth slice in three days he realized that Greeks *liked* their food lukewarm. Simultaneous with this realization, as if his previous ignorance had protected him, came his first stomach troubles. He fled back to his hotel room and spent the next three hours on an oddly low toilet, staring at that day's edition of *I Kathimerini*. The photographs showed Prime Minister Papandreou, a riot at Athens University, police firing tear gas, and an unbelievably wrinkled woman whom the photo caption identified, impossibly, as Melina Mercouri.

The Greek alphabet was the final defeat to him. At twelve he used to sit at his yia yia's feet, her golden boy, learning the Greek alphabet. But he'd never gotten past sigma and now he'd forgotten everything except A and Ω.

After three days in Athens, they decided to set out for the Peloponnese by bus. Before leaving, they stopped at the American Express office to cash traveler's checks. First, however, Mitchell inquired at the General Services window for any mail being held for them. The woman handed Mitchell two envelopes. He recognized the flowery cursive on the first envelope as his mother's. But it was the second envelope that made his heart jump. On the front, his name and the "c/o American Express" address had been typed on a manual typewriter in need of a new ribbon. The *as* and *s* in his surname were nearly inkless. Turning it over, he read the return address: M. Hanna, Pilgrim Lake Laboratory, Starbuck #12, Provincetown, MA 02657.

Quickly, as though the envelope contained profanity, Mitchell stuffed the letter into the back pocket of his jeans. In the line for the tellers' windows, he opened the letter from Lillian instead.

Dear Mitchell,

Ever since we got the condo in Vero Beach, your father and I have been "snowbirds," but this year we can really claim the title. On Tuesday we flew "Herbie" all the way from Detroit down to Fort Myers. It was pretty fancy, flying in your own private plane, and the whole trip only took six hours. (I remember when it used to take us twenty-four hours by car!) I enjoyed watching the country pass by far, far below. You don't fly as high as in a real airliner, so you can really see the terrain, all the rivers meandering this way and that and, of course, the farmland, which reminded me of one of Grammy's old patchwork quilts. I can't say the trip was very conducive to conversation, though. You can hardly hear a thing over the engine and your father had his headphones on most of the time, in order to listen to the "traffic," so I had no one to talk to except Kerbi, who was in my lap. (I just now noticed that "Herbie" and "Kerbi" rhyme.)

Your father pointed out the sights to me along the way. We flew right over Atlanta, and over some big swamps, which made me a little anxious. If you had to land there, there would be nothing for miles and miles but snakes and alligators.

As you can tell from all this, your mother wasn't exactly a model "co-pilot." Dean kept telling me to stop worrying and that he had everything "under control." But the plane ride was so bumpy it was impossible for me to read my book. All I could do was stare out the window, and after a while even the good ol' USA didn't look all that interesting. But we got here in one piece, at least, and now we're in Vero, where the weather is, as usual, too hot. Winston is coming up from Miami on Christmas Day (he's got some kind of recording session on Christmas Eve, he says, and can't make it until then). Nick and Sally are flying in with little Nick tomorrow night. Dean and I are planning to pick them up at the Ft. Lauderdale Airport and take them to a real nice place we found in Fort Pierce, just off A1A, on the water.

It's going to feel strange not to have our "baby" with us at Christmas this year. Your father and I are thrilled that you and Larry have this chance to "see the world." After all the hard work you did at college, you deserve it. I think of you every day and try to imagine where you might be and what you might be doing. Usually I know where you're living and sleeping. Even at college we usually knew what your apartment looked like, so it wasn't so hard for me to picture you in my mind's eye. But now I don't know where you are most of the time, and so am grateful for any postcard you send. We got your postcard from Venice with the arrow pointing to "our hotel." I couldn't quite make out the hotel itself, but I'm glad it's "dirt cheap," as you said in your note. Venice looks like a magical place, a perfect locale for a young "literary man" to get inspiration.

Kerbi has a spot on his backside where the fur's nearly gone. He's been licking it something fierce. The way he twists himself into a pretzel to get at the itch always makes me laugh. (I wish I could do that when I get an itch on <u>my</u> back!) If it doesn't get better in a few days, I'll have to take Kerbi to the vet.

I'm writing this from our patio, under the umbrella, trying to stay out of the sun. Even in wintertime, the sun down here dries out my skin, no matter how much moisturizer I slather on. Right now, "the ol' dad" is sitting in the living room, arguing with some politician on TV (I'll spare you the salty language, but the gist is "Bull- - - -!") I don't understand how anyone can watch so much news in one day. Dean told me to tell you, when you get to Greece, to be sure to tell "all those socialists over there, 'Thank God for Ronald Reagan.'"

Speaking of "God," a package for you from "The Paulist Fathers" arrived at the lake house in Michigan before we left.

I know you're thinking of applying to divinity school and that it may have something to do with that, but it got me wondering a little. Your last letter—not the postcard from Venice but the one on the blue paper that folds into a letter (I think they're called aerograms?)—didn't sound like you. What did you mean about the "Kingdom of God" not being a place but a state of mind and that you thought you saw "glimmers" of it? You know I tried for years to find a church to take you boys to, and that I've never been quite able to believe in anything, as much as I'd like to. So I think I do understand your interest in religion. But all this "mysticism" you write about in your letters, and "the Dark Night of the Soul," can sound a little "far out," as your brother Winston would say. You've been gone for four months now, Mitchell. We haven't seen you, and it's hard for us to get a good picture of how you're doing. I'm glad Larry is traveling with you, because I think I would worry even more if you were traveling all by yourself. Your father and I are still not too thrilled that you're going to India, but you're an adult now and can do what you like. But we are very concerned that there is no way to contact you, or for you to contact us in case of an emergency.

Okay, that's enough advice from Mom for now. As much as we miss you, and will miss you especially at Christmas, your father and I are happy that you have been able to undertake this big adventure. From the day you were born, Mitchell, you have been the most precious gift to us, and though I'm not sure I believe in "God," I do thank "someone up there" every single day for giving us a son as wonderful, loving, and talented as you. Ever since you were little I've always known that you were going to grow up and make something of yourself. As Grammy always told you, "Hit 'em high, boy, hit 'em high."

I found a really nice little writing desk at an antique store in Vero and am having them put it in the guest bedroom here, so it will be ready for you when you visit. With all the experiences you've been having on your trip, you might want to

That was as far as Mitchell got before the person behind him tapped him on the shoulder. It was a woman, older than he was, in her thirties.

"There's a teller free," she said.

Mitchell thanked her. Putting Lillian's letter back into its envelope, he proceeded to the open window. As he was countersigning his traveler's checks, the next window became free and the woman who'd been in line behind him went up to it. She smiled at Mitchell, and he smiled back. When the teller had counted out his drachmas, Mitchell returned to look for Larry.

Not seeing him, he sat down in a lobby chair and pulled out Madeleine's letter again. He wasn't sure that he wanted to read it. For the past week, ever since the night in Venice, when he'd got so incredibly drunk, Mitchell had been recovering his emotional equilibrium. That was to say, he now thought about Madeleine two or three times a day rather than ten or fifteen. Time and distance were doing their work. The letter, however, threatened to undo this in a few moments. In a world of IBM Selectrics and sleek Olivettis, Madeleine had insisted on typing her papers on a vintage machine, so that her typescripts came out looking like something in an archive. That Madeleine was in love with old-fashioned things like her typewriter had given Mitchell hope that she might love him. Coupled with Madeleine's fidelity to the old machine was her ineptitude with all things mechanical, which explained why she hadn't changed the ribbon, leaving the *a* and *s* inkless (because those keys were worn down from overuse). Obviously, for all his scientific brilliance, Bankhead wasn't up to the job of replacing Madeleine's typewriter ribbon. Obviously, Bankhead was too self-involved, or lazy, or possibly even *opposed* to her using a manual typewriter. Madeleine's letter made it clear that Bankhead was wrong for her and that Mitchell was right, and he hadn't even opened it yet.

Mitchell knew what he should do. If he was serious about maintaining his equilibrium, about detaching himself from earthly things, then he should take the letter across the lobby to the trash can and pitch it in. That was what he should do.

Instead, he put the letter in his knapsack, way down in the inside pocket, where he wouldn't have to think about it.

When he looked up again he saw the woman from the line approaching. She had long, lank blond hair, high cheekbones, and narrow eyes. She wore no makeup and her clothes were odd. Under a baggy T-shirt she wore a long skirt that came down to her ankles. She was wearing running shoes.

"First time in Greece?" she asked, smiling excessively, like a salesperson.

"Yes."

"How long have you been here?"

"Just three days."

"I've been here three months. Most people come here to see the Acropolis. And that's beautiful. It is. The antiquities are really something. But what gets me is all the history. I don't mean the ancient history. I mean the Christian history. So much happened here! Where do you think the Thessalonians were? Or the Corinthians? The apostle John wrote Revelation on the island of Patmos. It just goes on and on. The gospel was revealed in the Holy Land, but Greece is where evangelism began. What brings *you* here?"

"I'm Greek," Mitchell said. "This is where I began."

The woman laughed. "Are you saving that seat for someone?"

"I'm waiting for my friend," Mitchell said.

"I'll just sit a minute," the woman said. "If your friend comes, I'll go."

"That's O.K.," Mitchell said. "We're leaving in a minute."

He thought that had ended it. The woman sat down and began going through her shoulder bag, looking for something. Mitchell scanned the office for Larry again.

"I came here to study," the woman started up again. "At the New Bible Institute. I'm learning Koine. You know what Koine is?"

"That's the language the New Testament was written in. Ancient demotic form of Greek."

"Wow. Most people don't know that. I'm impressed." She leaned toward him and said in a quiet voice, "Are you a Christian?"

Mitchell hesitated to answer. The worst thing about religion was religious people.

"I'm Greek Orthodox," he said finally.

"Well, that's Christian."

"The Patriarch will be pleased to know that."

"You've got a good sense of humor, don't you?" the woman said, not smiling for the first time. "You probably use that to skate over a lot of problems in your life."

This provocation worked. Mitchell turned his head to look at her directly.

"The Orthodox Church is like the Catholic Church," the woman said. "They're Christian but they're not always Bible-believing. They've got so much ritual going on, it sometimes distracts from the message."

Mitchell decided it was time to make his move. He stood up. "Nice meeting you," he said. "Good luck with the Koine."

"Nice meeting you!" the woman said. "Can I ask you one question before you go?"

Mitchell waited. The fixity of her gaze was unnerving.

"Are you saved?"

Just say yes, Mitchell thought. Say yes and get going.

"That's difficult to say," he said.

Right away he realized his mistake. The woman stood up, her blue eyes lasering in on his. "No, it isn't," she said. "It's not difficult, at all. You just ask Jesus Christ to come into your heart and He will. That's what I did. And it changed my life. I wasn't always a Christian. I spent most of my life apart from God. Didn't know Him. Didn't care about Him. I wasn't doing drugs or anything. I wasn't running around all night. But there was this emptiness inside me. Because I was living for myself."

To his surprise, Mitchell found himself listening to her. Not to her fundamentalist script about being saved or accepting the Lord. But to what she was saying about her own life.

"It's a funny thing. You're born in America. You grow up and what do they tell you? They tell you that you have a right to the pursuit of happiness. And that the way to be happy is to get a lot of nice stuff, right? I did all that. Had a house, a job, a boyfriend. But I wasn't happy. I wasn't happy because all I did every day was think about myself. I thought that the world revolved around me. But guess what? It doesn't."

This seemed sound enough, and genuine. Mitchell thought he might be able to agree here and be on his way.

But before he could do that, the woman said, "When we were standing in line, you were reading a letter. It was from your mother."

Mitchell raised his chin. "How did you know that?"

"I just felt that right now."

"You looked over my shoulder."

"I did not!" she said, playfully slapping him. "Go on now. God just put it on my heart right now that you were reading a letter from your mother. But I want to tell you something. The Lord sent you a letter at

American Express too. You know what it is? It's me. *I'm* that letter. The Lord sent me without my even knowing it, so that I could end up behind you in line and tell you how the Lord loves you, how He died for you."

Just then, near the elevators, Larry appeared.

"There's my friend," Mitchell said. "Nice talking with you."

"Nice talking to *you*. Have a nice time in Greece and God Bless."

He was halfway across the lobby when she tapped him on the shoulder again.

"I just wanted to give you this."

In her hand was a pocket-size New Testament. Green, like a leaf.

"You take this and read the Gospels. Read about the good news of Jesus. And remember, it's not complicated. It's simple. The only thing that matters is that you accept Jesus Christ as your Lord and Savior and then you'll have eternal life."

To get away from her, to shut her up, Mitchell took the book and continued on out of the lobby.

"Where were you?" he said to Larry when he reached him. "I've been waiting for like an hour."

Twenty minutes later, they were on their way the Peloponnese. The bus traveled for miles through the overbuilt basin of the city before climbing to a coastal road. The other passengers carried bundles on their laps: booty from the big city. Every few miles a shrine marked the site of a traffic fatality. The bus driver stopped to leave a coin in one offertory box. Later, he pulled the bus over to a roadside café and, without explanation, went inside to have lunch, while the passengers waited patiently in their seats. Larry got off to have a smoke and a coffee. Mitchell pulled Madeleine's letter out of his knapsack, looked at it again, and put it back.

They reached Corinth in mid-afternoon. After trudging around the Temple of Apollo in a mild drizzle, they repaired to a restaurant to get out of the rain, and Mitchell took out his New Testament to reacquaint himself with what Saint Paul had written to the Corinthians back around AD 55.

He read:

For it is written, I will destroy the wisdom of the wise, and will bring to nothing the understanding of the prudent:

And:

> For ye are yet carnal
> It is reported commonly that there is fornication among you

> It is good for a man not to touch a woman. Nevertheless, to avoid
> fornication, let every man have his own wife, and let every woman
> have her own husband. I say therefore to the unmarried and
> widows, It is good if they abide even as I. But if they cannot con-
> tain, let them marry: for it is better to marry than to burn.

The woman who'd given him the pocket New Testament had left her card
inside, along with an Athens phone number. Her name was Janice P.

She must have been reading over my shoulder, Mitchell decided.

Winter was coming on. From Corinth they took a minibus south-
ward toward the Mani, stopping for the night in the small mountain village of Andritsena. The temperature was crisp, the air pine-scented, the
local retsina a shocking pink. The only room they could find was above
a taverna. It was unheated. As thunderclouds moved in from the north,
Larry got into one of the beds, complaining about the cold. Mitchell kept
his sweater on. When he was sure Larry was asleep, he took out Madeleine's letter and began reading it by the faint red light on the bedside
table.

To his surprise, the letter itself wasn't typed but handwritten in
Madeleine's tiny script. (She may have looked normal on the outside, but
once you'd seen her handwriting you knew she was deliciously complicated inside.)

Aug. 31, 1982

Dear Mitchell,

    I'm writing this from the train, the same Amtrak you and
I took when you came to Prettybrook for Thanksgiving
sophomore year. It was colder then, the trees were bare, and my
hair was "feathered" (it was still the seventies, if you'll
remember). But you didn't seem to mind.

    I've never told you this before, but the entire way down on
the train for Thanksgiving, I was thinking about sleeping with

you. For one thing, I could tell that you wanted to very badly. I knew it would make you happy and I wanted to make you happy. Aside from that, I had the idea that it would be good for me. I'd only slept with one boy at that point. I was worried that virginity was like getting your ears pierced. If you didn't keep an earring in, the hole might close up. Anyway, I went off to college prepared to be as unemotional and dastardly as a guy. And you appeared in that little window of opportunity.

Then of course you were devastatingly charming all weekend. My parents loved you, my sister started flirting with you—and I got possessive. You were <u>my</u> guest, after all. So I went up to the attic one night and sat on your bed. And you did exactly <u>Nothing</u>. After about a half hour, I went back downstairs. At first I just felt insulted. But after a while I felt mad. I decided you weren't man enough for me, etc. I vowed never to sleep with you, ever, even if you wanted to. Then, the next day, we took the train back to Providence, and we laughed the whole way. I realized that it was much better this way. For once in my life I wanted to have a friend who wasn't a girlfriend and wasn't a boyfriend. Aside from our recent slip-up, that's what you've been to me. I know it hasn't made you happy. But to me it's been incredible, and I always thought that, deep down, you felt this too.

Sophomore year is a long time ago now. It's the eighties. The trees along the Hudson are green and leafy and I feel about a hundred years older. You aren't the boy I rode this train with, Mitchell. I don't have to feel sorry for you anymore, or go to bed with you out of affection and pity. You're going to do all right for yourself. In fact, I need to be wary of you now. You were rather aggressive last night. Jane Austen might say "importunate." I told you not to kiss me, but you went right on doing it. And even though, once it got going, I didn't exactly complain (I was drunk!), I woke up this morning, at Kelly's, feeling so guilty and confused that I decided I had to write you right away.

(The train is shaking. I hope you can read this.)

I have a <u>boyfriend</u>, Mitchell. I'm serious about him. I didn't want to talk about my boyfriend last night because you always get mad when I do, and because, to be honest, I came down to the city to forget about my boyfriend for a few days. Leonard and I have been having problems lately. I can't go into why. But it's been hard on him, hard on me, and hard on our relationship. Anyway, if I wasn't going out of my mind, I wouldn't have drunk so much last night and I wouldn't have ended up kissing you. I'm not saying I wouldn't have wanted to. Just that I wouldn't have done it.

It's strange, though, because right now, part of me wants to get off at the next station and go back to New York and find you. But it's too late for that. Your plane has probably taken off. You're on your way to India.

Which is a good thing. <u>Because it didn't work out!</u> You didn't become the friend who wasn't a girlfriend or a boyfriend. You became just another importunate male. So what I'm doing in this letter is proactively breaking up with you. Our relationship has always defied categorization, so I guess it makes sense if this letter does too.

Dear Mitchell,

I don't want to see you anymore (even though we haven't been seeing each other).

I want to start seeing other people (even though I'm already seeing someone).

I need some time for myself (even though you haven't been taking up my time).

Okay? Do you get it now? I'm desperate. I'm taking desperate measures.

I expect to be heartbroken, not having you in my life. But I'm already confused enough about my life and my relationship without you confusing me more. I want to break up with you, as hard as that may be—and as stupid as it may sound. I've always been a sane person. Right now, I feel like I'm falling apart.

Have a great amazing incredible time on your trip. See all the places and sights you wanted to, have all the experiences you're seeking. Maybe someday, at our 50th college reunion, you'll see a wrinkled old lady come up to you with a smile, and that will be me. Maybe then you can tell me about all the things you saw in India.

Take care,
Maddy

P.S. Sept. 27
I've been carrying this letter around for almost a month, contemplating whether to send it or not. And I keep not sending it. I'm on Cape Cod now, up to my ears in biologists, and I may not survive.

P.P.S. Oct. 6
I just got off the phone with your mother. I realized I didn't have an address for you. Your mother said you were "on the road" and couldn't be reached but that you would be picking up your mail sometime at AmEx in Athens. She gave me the address. By the way, you should maybe call your parents. Your mother sounds worried.

Okay. I'm sending this.
M.

Somewhere above the taverna's roof, in the black Greek sky, two thunderheads collided, loosing torrents of rain on the village and turning the sloping streets into waterfalls. Five minutes later, while Mitchell was reading the letter for the second time, the electricity went out.

In the darkness, he lay awake, evaluating the situation. He understood that Madeleine's letter was a devastating document. And he was suitably devastated. On the other hand, Madeleine had been putting Mitchell off so long that her refusals were like boilerplate that his eyes skimmed over, looking for possible loopholes or buried clauses of real significance. In this regard he found a lot to like. There was the mood-elevating revelation that Madeleine had wanted to sleep with him on that long-ago Thanksgiving break. There was a hotness to the missive that seemed unlike Madeleine but promised a whole new side to her. She was worried that the hole might close up? *Madeleine* had written this? He'd heard that women were just as filthy-minded as guys were, but he'd never believed it. If Madeleine had been thinking about sex on that train ride, however, while turning the pages of her *Vogue*, if she had come up to the attic intent on fucking, then it was obvious that he'd never been able to read her at all. This thought sustained him for a good while, as the storm churned overhead. Of all the other things Madeleine might have chosen to do, she had sat down and written Mitchell a letter. She'd said that she enjoyed kissing him and that she had an urge to get off the train and come back to New York. She had typed Mitchell's name and licked the envelope and typed her return address, so that he could write her back, so that he knew where to find her, if he wanted to look.

Every letter was a love letter.

Of course, as love letters went, this one could have been better. It was not very promising, for instance, that Madeleine claimed not to want to see him for the next half-century. It was dispiriting that she had insisted that she was "serious" about her "boyfriend" (though cheering that they were having "problems"). Mostly, what Mitchell took from the letter was the painful fact that he had missed his chance. His chance with Madeleine had come early, sophomore year, and he'd failed to seize it. This further depressed him because it suggested that he was destined to be a voyeur in life, an also-ran, a loser. It was just as Madeleine said: he wasn't man enough for her.

The following days were a tribulation to the spirit. In Kalamata, a seaside city that smelled not of olives, as Mitchell expected, but of gasoline, he kept meeting his doppelgangers. The waiter at the restaurant, the boat repairman, the hotel owner's son, the female bank teller: they all looked exactly like him. Mitchell even resembled a few icons in the crumbling local church. Instead of providing a sense of homecoming, the experience sapped Mitchell, as if he'd been photocopied over and over again, a faint reproduction of some clearer, darker original.

The weather turned colder. At night the temperature dropped into the low 40s. Wherever they went, half-built structures rose from the rocky hillsides. To encourage new construction, the Greek parliament had passed a law that exempted people from paying taxes on unfinished homes. The Greeks had responded, craftily, by leaving the top floors of their houses perpetually uncompleted, while dwelling snugly beneath. For two cold nights, in the village of Itylo, Mitchell and Larry slept for one dollar apiece on the unfinished third story of a house belonging to the Lamborghos family. The oldest son, Iannis, had chatted them up as they got off the bus in the town square. Soon he was showing them the roof, littered with rebar and cinder block, where they could sleep beneath the stars, using their sleeping bags and Ensolite pads for the first and only time on their trip.

Despite the language barrier, Larry began spending time with Iannis. While Mitchell drank coffee in the village's one café, still secretly smarting from Madeleine's letter, Iannis and Larry went on walks into the surrounding, goat-filled hillsides. Iannis had the jet-black mane and chest-revealing shirt of a Greek singing idol. His teeth were bad, and he was something of a hanger-on, but he seemed friendly enough, if you felt like being friendly, which Mitchell didn't. When Iannis offered to drive them back to Athens, however, saying he had business there, Mitchell didn't see how he could refuse, and the next morning they set off in Iannis's tiny, Yugoslavian-made automobile, Larry sitting in front, Mitchell in the rumble seat behind.

Christmas was approaching. The streets around their hotel, a nondescript gray building to which Iannis referred them, were decorated with lights. The temperature alone reminded them that it was time to leave for Asia. After Iannis left to take care of his business, Larry and Mitchell went to a travel agent to buy their airplane tickets. Athens was famous for its cheap airfares, and so it proved: for less than five hundred dollars, they each got an open-ended ticket, Athens–Calcutta–Paris, on Air India, leaving the following night.

Iannis took them to a seafood restaurant that evening, and to three different bars, before dropping them back at the hotel. The next morning Mitchell and Larry went to the Plaka and bought new, smaller bags. Larry chose a gaily striped shoulder bag made from hemp; Mitchell a dark duffel bag. Back at their hotel, they transferred essential belongings into the new packs, trying to keep them as light as possible. They got rid of their sweaters, their pairs of long pants, their tennis shoes, their sleeping bags and pads, their books, even their shampoo. Mitchell culled his Saint Teresa, his Saint Augustine, his Thomas Merton, his Pynchon, relieving himself of everything but the thin paperback of *Something Beautiful for God*. Whatever they didn't need, they put in their backpacks and carried to the post office, shipping it back to the States by slow boat. Coming onto the street again, they high-fived each other, feeling like real travelers for the first time, footloose and unencumbered.

Mitchell's bright mood didn't last long. Among the items he'd kept was Madeleine's letter, and when they got back to their hotel, he locked himself in the bathroom to read it once again. This time through, it seemed more dire, more final, than before. Coming out of the bathroom, he lay down on his bed and closed his eyes.

Larry was smoking on the balcony. "We haven't seen the Acropolis yet," he said. "We have to see it."

"I've seen it," Mitchell muttered.

"We haven't climbed it."

"I don't feel like it right now."

"You come all the way to Athens and you're not going to see the Acropolis?"

"I'll meet you," Mitchell said.

He waited until Larry was gone before allowing himself to cry. It was a combination of things, Madeleine's letter, first and foremost, but also the aspects of his personality that had made her feel such a letter necessary, his awkwardness, his charm, his aggressiveness, his shyness, everything that made him almost but not quite the guy for her. The letter felt like a verdict on his entire life so far, sentencing him to end up here, lying on a bed, alone, in an Athenian hotel room, too weighed down by self-pity to go out and climb the goddamn Acropolis. The idea that he was on some kind of pilgrimage seemed ludicrous. The whole thing was such a joke! If only he wasn't himself! If only he was somebody else, somebody different!

Mitchell sat up, wiping his eyes. Leaning sideways, he pulled the New Testament out of his back pocket. He opened it and took out the card the woman had given him. It said "Athens Bible Institute" at the top and showed the Greek flag with the cross in gold. Her number was written beneath this.

Mitchell dialed it from his room phone. The call didn't go through the first two times (he had the prefix wrong), but on his third try it began ringing. To his amazement, the woman from the AmEx line, Janice P., her voice sounding very close, answered.

"Hello?"

223

"Hi. This is Mitchell. We met the other day at American Express."

"Praise God!" Janice said. "I've been praying for you. And here you are calling. Praise the Lord!"

"I found your card, so."

"Are you ready to accept the Lord into your heart?"

This was rather sudden. Mitchell looked up at the ceiling. There was a crack running its length.

"Yes," he said.

"Praise the Lord!" Janice said again. She sounded truly happy, enthused. She began talking about Jesus and the Holy Spirit, while Mitchell listened, experimentally. He was playing along and not playing along. He wanted to see what it felt like. "I told you we were meant to meet!" Janice said. "God put it on my heart to talk to you and now you're ready to be saved! Praise Jesus." Next she was talking about the book of Acts, and Pentecost, about Jesus ascending to heaven but giving Christians the gift of the Holy Spirit, the Comforter, the wind that surpasseth all understanding. She explained the gifts of the Spirit, speaking in tongues, healing the sick. She sounded thrilled for Mitchell but also as though she could have been talking to anyone at all. "The Spirit listeth where it wills. It's as real as the wind. Will you pray with me now, Mitchell? Will you get down on your knees and accept Jesus as your Lord and Savior?"

"I can't right now."

"Where are you?"

"In my hotel. In the lobby."

"Then wait until you're alone. Go into a room alone and get down on your knees and ask the Lord to come into your heart."

"Have you ever spoken in tongues?" Mitchell asked.

"I was given the gift of tongues once, yes."

"How does that happen?"

"I asked for it. Sometimes you have to ask. One day I was praying and I just started praying to receive my tongues. All of a sudden, the room got really warm. It was like Indiana in the summertime. *Humid.* There was a presence there. I could feel it. And then I opened my mouth and God gave me the gift of tongues."

"What did you say?"

"I don't know. But there was a man there, a Christian, who recognized the language I was speaking. It was Aramaic."

"The language of Jesus."

"That's what he said."

"Can I speak in tongues, too?"

"You can ask. Sure you can. Once you've accepted Jesus as your Lord and Savior, you just ask the Father to give you the gift of tongues, in Jesus' name."

"And then what?"

"Open your mouth!"

"And it'll just happen?"

"I'll pray for you. Praise God!"

After hanging up, Mitchell went out to see the Acropolis. He wore both of his remaining shirts in order to stay warm. Reaching the Plaka, he passed by the souvenir stands selling imitation Grecian urns and plates, sandals, worry beads. A T-shirt on a hanger proclaimed "Kiss Me I'm Greek." Mitchell began climbing up the dusty switchbacks to the ancient plateau.

When he reached the top, he turned and gazed back down at Athens, a giant bathtub filled with dirty suds. Clouds were swirling dramatically overhead, pierced by sunbeams that fell like spotlights on the distant sea. The majestic altitude, the clean scent of pine trees, and the golden light lent the atmosphere a true sense of Attic clarity. Scaffolding covered the Parthenon, as well as a smaller temple nearby. Aside from that, and a lone guard station at the far end of the summit, there were no signs of officialdom anywhere, and Mitchell felt free to roam wherever he wanted.

The wind bloweth where it listeth.

Unlike every other famous tourist sight Mitchell had seen in his life, the Acropolis was more impressive in reality; no postcard or photograph could do it justice. The Parthenon was both bigger and more beautiful, more heroically conceived and constructed, than he'd imagined.

Larry was nowhere in sight. Mitchell walked over the rocks, behind the small temple. When he was certain no one could see him, he got down on his knees.

Maybe listening to a woman going on about "living for Christ" represented the exact sort of humbling that Mitchell needed in order to die to his old conceited self. What if the meek really *would* inherit the earth? What if the truth was simple, so that everyone could grasp it, and not complex, so that you needed a master's degree? Mightn't the truth be perceived through an organ other than the brain, and wasn't that what faith was all about? Mitchell didn't know the answers to these questions, but as he stood gazing down from the ancient mountain, sacred to Athena, he entertained a revolutionary thought: that he and all his enlightened friends knew nothing about life, and that maybe this (crazy?) lady knew something big.

Mitchell closed his eyes, kneeling on the Acropolis.

He was aware inside himself of an infinite sadness.

Kiss me I'm dying.

He opened his mouth. He waited.

The wind whipped up, blowing litter between the rocks. Mitchell could taste dust on his tongue. But that was about it.

Nothing. Not even a syllable of Aramaic. After another minute, he got up and brushed himself off.

He descended the Acropolis quickly, as if fleeing a disaster. He felt ridiculous for having tried to speak in tongues and, at the same time, disappointed for not having been able to. The sun was going down, the temperature dropping. In the Plaka, souvenir vendors were closing up their stands, neon signs blinking on in the windows of neighboring restaurants and coffee shops.

He passed his hotel three times without recognizing it. While he was out, the elevator had broken down. Mitchell climbed the stairwell to the second floor and came down the soulless hallway, putting his key in the lock.

As soon as he pushed open the door, there was movement in the dark room, furtive and quick. Mitchell felt for the switch on the wall and, finding it, revealed Larry and Iannis in the center of the room. Larry was lying on the bed, his jeans around his ankles, while Iannis knelt beside it. Mustering a fair amount of composure under the circumstances, Larry said, "Surprise, surprise, Mitchell." Iannis crouched down, disappearing from sight.

"Hi," Mitchell said, and switched off the light. Stepping out of the room, he shut the door behind him.

At a restaurant across the street Mitchell ordered a carafe of retsina and a plate of feta cheese and olives, not even trying to speak a few words of Greek, just pointing. It all made sense now. Why Larry had gotten over Claire so quickly. Why he'd disappeared so often to smoke cigarettes with sketchy Europeans. Why he'd been wearing that purple silk scarf around his neck. Larry had been one person in New York and now he was a different person. This made Mitchell feel very close to his friend, even though he now suspected that this was where their trip together ended. Larry wouldn't be flying to India with Mitchell tonight. Larry was going to stay awhile longer in Athens with Iannis.

After an hour, Mitchell went back to the hotel, where all this was confirmed. Larry promised to meet him in India, in time to work for Professor Hughes. The two of them hugged, and Mitchell carried his light duffel bag down to the lobby to get a cab to the airport.

By nine o'clock that night he was buckled into his economy seat aboard an Air India 747, leaving Christian airspace at a velocity of 522 miles per hour. The flight attendants wore saris. Dinner was a delicious vegetarian medley. He'd never really expected to speak in tongues. He didn't know what good it would have done him, even if he had.

Later, as the cabin lights went out and the other passengers tried to sleep, Mitchell switched on his reading light. He read *Something Beautiful for God* for the second time, paying close attention to the photographs.

Brilliant Move

Shortly after learning that Madeleine's mother not only didn't like him but was actively trying to break them up, at a time of year on the Cape when the brevity of daylight mimicked the diminishing wattage of his own brain, Leonard found the courage to take his destiny, in the form of his mental disorder, into his own hands.

It was a brilliant move. The reason Leonard hadn't thought of it earlier was just another side effect of the drug. Lithium was very good at inducing a mental state in which taking lithium seemed like a good idea. It tended to make you just sit there. Sitting there, at any rate, was pretty much what Leonard had been doing for the last six months since getting out of the hospital. He'd asked his psychiatrists—both Dr. Shieu at Providence Hospital and his new shrink, Perlmann, at Mass General—to explain the biochemistry involved in lithium carbonate (Li_2CO_3). Humoring him as a "fellow scientist," they'd talked about neurotransmitters and receptors, decreases in norepinephrine releases, increases in serotonin synthesis. They'd listed, but hadn't elaborated on, the possible downsides of taking lithium, and then mainly to discuss yet more drugs that would be helpful in minimizing the side effects. All in all, it was a lot of pharmacology and pharmaceutical brand names for Leonard to digest, especially in his compromised mental condition.

Four years ago, when Leonard had been officially diagnosed with manic depression in the spring semester of his freshman year, he hadn't thought much about what the lithium was doing to him. He'd just wanted to get back to feeling normal. The diagnosis had seemed like one more thing—like lack of money, and his messed-up family—that had threatened to keep Leonard from getting ahead, just when he was beginning to feel that his luck had finally changed. He took his meds twice daily, like an A student. He started therapy, first seeing a mental health counselor at Health Services before finding Bryce Ellis, who took pity on Leonard's student poverty and charged him on a sliding scale. For the next three years, Leonard treated his manic depression like a concentration requirement in something he wasn't much interested in, doing the bare minimum to pass.

Leonard had grown up in an Arts & Crafts house whose previous owner had been murdered in the front hall. The grisly history of 133 Linden Street had kept the house on the market for four years until Leonard's father, Frank, bought it for half the original asking price. Frank Bankhead owned an antique-print shop on Nob Hill specializing in British lithographs. It was a terrible business, even back then, the shop a place where Frank could go during the days to smoke his pipe and wait for cocktail hour. Growing up, Leonard was made to understand by Frank that the Bankheads were "old Portland," by which he meant the families who'd come to Oregon when it was still part of the Northwest Territory. There wasn't much sign of this, no Bankhead Street downtown, not so much as an old signboard or a plaque saying "Bankhead" anywhere, or a bust of a Bankhead in the Oregon Historical Society. But there were Frank's three-piece tweed suits, and his old-fashioned manners. There was his shop, full of things that no one wanted to buy: lithographs not of the city's early days or anything that might interest a local, but of places like Bath or Cornwall or Glasgow. There were hunt prints, scenes of revelry in London taverns, sketches of pickpockets, two prize Hogarths that Frank could never part with, and a lot of junk.

The print shop barely broke even. The Bankheads survived on dwindling income from stocks that Frank had inherited from his grandfather. Every so often, at an estate sale, he got his hands on a valuable print that he would then resell for a profit (sometimes flying to New York to do so). But the trajectory of the business was downward, in contrast to his social pretensions, and that was why Frank had got interested in the house.

He first heard about it from a client who lived in the neighborhood. The previous owner, a bachelor named Joseph Wierznicki, had been knifed to death, just inside his front door, with such violence that the police had said the crime was "personal." No one had been apprehended. The story had made the papers, complete with photos of the blood-spattered walls and flooring. And that might have been the end of it. In due course, the house was put on the market. Workers cleaned and re-furbished the front hall. But a statute on the books requiring real estate agents to reveal any information that might affect resale obligated them to mention the house's criminal history. When prospective buyers heard about the murder, they looked into it (if still interested), and, as soon as they saw the photographs, they declined to make offers.

Leonard's mother refused to even consider the idea. She didn't think she could bear the strain of moving, especially into a haunted house. Rita spent most days in her bedroom, leafing through magazines or watch-ing *The Mike Douglas Show*, her "water" glass on the bedside table. Every so often she became a whirlwind of domestic activity, decorating every inch of the house at Christmastime or cooking elaborate six-course din-ners. For as long as Leonard could remember, his mother was either in retreat from other people or forcefully trying to impress them. The only other person he knew who was as unpredictable as Rita was Frank.

That was a fun parlor game to play: from which side of the family had his mental instability descended. There were so many possible sources, so much spoiled fruit on the family trees of the Bankhead and Richard-son clans. Alcoholics populated both sides. Rita's sister, Ruth, had led a wild life, sexually and financially. She'd been arrested a few times and had attempted suicide at least once that he knew. Then there were Leonard's grandparents, whose rectitude had something desperate about it, as though it was holding back a tide of riotous impulse. Despite his father's buttoned-up appearance, Leonard knew him to be depressive as well as misanthropic, prone, when drunk, to ranting about "the vulgus" and to fits of grandiosity, where he talked about moving to Europe and living in high style.

The house appealed to Frank's conception of himself. It was a much nicer, bigger house than he could otherwise afford, with detailed wood-work in the parlor, a tiled fireplace, and four bedrooms. One afternoon, coming home from the shop early, he took Rita and Leonard to see it. When they arrived at the house, Rita refused to get out of the car. So Frank took Leonard, only seven at the time, in alone. They toured the house with the real estate agent, Frank pointing out where Leonard's new bed-room would be on the first floor, and the backyard where, if he wanted, he could build a tree house.

He brought Leonard back to the car, where Rita was sitting.

"Leonard has something to tell you," Frank said.

"What?" Leonard said.

"Don't be smart. You know perfectly well what."

"There aren't any bloodstains, Mom," Leonard said.

"And?" Frank coaxed.

"The whole floor's brand-new. In the front. It's new tiles."

Rita remained straight-backed in the front seat. She was wearing sun-glasses, as she always did when she went out, even in winter. Finally, she took a long sip from her "water" glass—it went everywhere with her, ice cubes jingling—and got out of the car.

"Hold my hand," she said to Leonard. Together, without Frank, they went up the front steps and across the porch into the house. They looked at all the rooms together.

"What do you think?" Rita asked when they were finished.

"It's a nice house, I guess."

"It wouldn't bother you living here?"

"I don't know."

"What about your sister?"

"She *wants* to move here. Dad told her what it's like. He said she could pick out her own carpet."

Before giving her answer, Rita demanded that Frank take her to Bryant's for dinner. Leonard wanted to go home and play baseball but they made him come along. At Bryant's, Frank and Rita ordered marti-nis, quite a few of them. Before long they were laughing and kissing, and pooh-poohing Leonard's reluctance to eat the oysters they ordered. Rita had suddenly decided that the murder was an attraction. It gave the house a "history." In Europe, people were used to living in houses where other people had been murdered or poisoned.

"I don't know why you're so scared to live there," she chided Leonard.

"I'm not scared," he said.

"I've never seen such a fuss, have you?" she asked Frank.

"No, never," Frank said.

"I didn't make a fuss," Leonard said, growing frustrated. "*You* did. I don't care where we live."

"Oh, well, maybe we won't bring you with us, if you keep up that attitude!"

They kept laughing and drinking, while Leonard stormed away from the table and stared into the jukebox, flipping the selections again and again.

A month later, the family moved into 133 Linden, acquiring, along with the new house, one more thing for Frank and Rita to fight about.

All of this, as Leonard later learned from his therapists, amounted to emotional abuse. Not to be made to live in a house where a murder had taken place but to be the go-between in his parents' affairs, to be constantly asked his opinion before he was mature enough to give one, to be made to feel that he was somehow responsible for his parents' happiness and, later, their unhappiness. Depending on the year or the therapist he was seeing, he'd learned to ascribe just about every facet of his character as a psychological reaction to his parents' fighting: his laziness, his overachieving, his tendency to isolate, his tendency to seduce, his hypochondria, his sense of invulnerability, his self-loathing, his narcissism.

The next seven years were chaotic. There were constant parties at the house. Some antiques dealer from Cincinnati or Charleston was always in town and needed to be entertained. Frank presided over these soggy get-togethers, refilling everyone's drinks, the adults carousing, shrieking, women falling out of their chairs, their dresses flying up. Middle-aged men wandered into Janet's bedroom. Leonard and Janet had to serve drinks or hors d'oeuvres at these parties. On many nights, after the guests had left and sometimes while they were still there, arguments broke out, Frank and Rita shouting at each other. In their bedrooms on separate floors, Leonard and Janet turned up their stereos to drown out the noise. The fights were about money, Frank's failure in business, Rita's spending. By the time Leonard turned fifteen, his parents' marriage was over. Frank left Rita for a Belgian woman named Sara Coorevits, an antiquities dealer from Brussels whom he'd met at a show in Manhattan and, it turned out, had been having an affair with for five years. A few months later, Frank sold the shop and moved to Europe, just as he always said he would. Rita retreated to her bedroom, leaving Janet and Leonard to get themselves through high school. Six months later, with creditors circling, Rita rather heroically bestirred herself to get a job at the local YMCA, becoming in time, somewhat miraculously, a director whom all the kids loved and called "Mrs. Rita." She often worked late. Janet and Leonard made their own dinners and then went to their rooms. And it seemed like the thing that had been murdered in the house was their family.

But this was the thought of a depressive. An *aspiring* depressive, at the time. That was the odd thing about Leonard's disease, the almost pleasurable way it began. At first his dark moods were closer to melancholy than to despair. There was something enjoyable about wandering around the city alone, feeling forlorn. There was even a sense of superiority, of being *right*, in not liking the things other kids liked: football, cheerleaders, James Taylor, red meat. A friend of his, Godfrey, was into bands like Lucifer's Friend and Pentagram, and for a while Leonard spent a lot of time at Godfrey's house listening to them. Since Godfrey's parents couldn't abide the infernal racket, Godfrey and Leonard listened with headphones. First Godfrey donned the set, lowered the needle on the record, and began to writhe in silence, indicating with his blown-away facial expressions the depth of the depravity he was being treated to. Then it was Leonard's turn. They played songs backwards to hear the hidden satanic messages. They studied the dead-baby lyrics and putrescent cover art. In order to actually hear music at the same time, Leonard and Godfrey stole money from their parents and bought tickets to concerts at the Paramount. Waiting in line, in Portland's constant drizzle, with a few hundred other maladjusted teens was the closest Leonard ever came to feeling part of something. They saw Nazareth, Black Sabbath, Judas Priest, and Motordeath, a band that frankly sucked but whose shows featured naked women performing animal sacrifices. You could be a fan of darkness, a connoisseur of despair.

For a while, the Disease—which was still nameless at the time—cooed to him. It said, Come closer. It flattered Leonard that he felt *more* than most people; he was more sensitive, *deeper*. Seeing an "intense" film like *Mean Streets* would leave Leonard stricken, unable to speak, and it would take three girls putting their arms around him for an hour to bring him back. Unconsciously, he began to milk his sensitivity. He was "really depressed" in study hall or "really depressed" at some party, and before long a group would form around him, looking concerned.

He was a desultory student. Teachers labeled him "bright but un-motivated." He blew off homework, preferring to lie on the couch and watch television. He watched *The Tonight Show*, the late movie, and the late-late movie. In the mornings he was exhausted. He fell asleep in class, reviving after school to screw around with his friends. Then he went back home, stayed up late again, watching TV, and the cycle repeated.

And *still* this wasn't the Disease. Being depressed about the state of the world—air pollution, mass starvation, the invasion of East Timor—wasn't the Disease. Going into the bathroom and staring at his face, no-ticing the ghoulish veins beneath his skin, checking out his nose pores until he was convinced that he was a hideous creature whom no girl could ever love—even this wasn't the Disease. This was a character-ological prelude, but it wasn't chemical or somatic. It was the anatomy of melancholy, not the anatomy of his brain.

Leonard suffered his first real bout of depression in the fall of his sophomore year of high school. One Thursday night, Godfrey, who'd just gotten his license, came by in his parents' Honda and picked Leonard up. They drove around with the stereo cranked. Godfrey had gone soft on him. He insisted on listening to Steely Dan.

"This is bullshit," Leonard said.

"No, man, you've got to give it a chance."

"Let's listen to some Sabbath."

"I'm not into that stuff anymore."

Leonard regarded his friend. "What's your deal?" he said, though he knew the answer already. Godfrey's parents were religious (not Methodist, like Leonard's family, but people who actually read the Bible). They'd sent Godfrey to a church camp over the summer and there, amid the trees and the woodpeckers, the ministers had done their work on him. He would still drink and smoke pot but he'd given up his Judas Priest and his Motordeath. Leonard didn't mind that, so much. He was getting sick of that stuff himself. But that didn't mean he was going to let God-frey off the hook.

He gestured toward the eight-track player. "This stuff is fey."

"The musicianship's really good on this album," Godfrey insisted. "Donald Fagen was classically trained."

"Let me tell you something, God-frey, if we're going to drive around,

237

listening to this pussy shit, I might as well drop trou and let you blow me now."

With that, Leonard searched the glove box for something more appealing, coming up with a Big Star album of which he was quite fond.

A little before midnight, Godfrey dropped him at his house and Leonard went inside and straight to bed. When he woke up the next morning, something was the matter with him. His body ached. His limbs felt encased in cement. He didn't want to get up, but Rita came in, barking that he was going to be late. Somehow Leonard managed to climb out of bed and get dressed. Skipping breakfast, he left the house, forgetting his backpack, and walked to Cleveland High. A storm was moving in, the light crepuscular over the dingy shop fronts and overpasses. All day, as Leonard carted his body from class to class, ominous, bruise-colored clouds massed outside the windows. Teachers kept bitching at him for not having his books. He had to borrow paper and pens from other students. Twice, he shut himself into a bathroom stall and, for no discernible reason, began to weep. Godfrey, who'd had as much to drink as Leonard had, seemed just fine. They went to lunch together but Leonard had no appetite.

"What's the matter with you, man? Are you stoned?"

"No. I think I'm getting sick."

At three-thirty, instead of showing up for J.V. football practice, Leonard went straight home. A sense of impending doom, of universal malevolence, pursued him the entire way. Tree limbs gesticulated menacingly in his peripheral vision. Telephone lines sagged like pythons between the poles. When he looked up at the sky, however, he was surprised to find that it was cloudless. No storm. Clear weather, the sun pouring down. He decided that there was something wrong with his eyes.

In his bedroom, he got down his medical books, trying to figure out what was wrong with him. He'd bought an entire set at a garage sale, six huge color-illustrated textbooks with deliciously gruesome titles: *Atlas of Diseases of the Kidney*, *Atlas of Diseases of the Brain*, *Atlas of Diseases of the Skin*, and so on. The medical books were what first got Leonard interested in biology. The photographs of anonymous sufferers exerted a morbid attraction for him. He liked to show particularly gross pictures to Janet to make her scream. *Atlas of Diseases of the Skin* was best for that.

Even with the lights on in his bedroom, Leonard couldn't see that well. He had the feeling that there was something physically behind his eyes, blocking the light. In *Atlas of Diseases of the Endocrine System* he came across something called a pituitary adenoma. This was a tumor, typically small, that formed in the pituitary gland, often pressing on the optic nerve. It caused blindness and altered pituitary function. This led, in turn, to "low blood pressure, fatigue, and the inability to handle difficult or stressful situations." Too much pituitary function and you became a giant, too little and you were a nervous wreck. As impossible as it sounded, Leonard seemed to be suffering both states at once.

He closed the book and collapsed on his bed. He felt as if he were being violently emptied out, as if a big magnet were pulling his blood and fluids down into the earth. He was weeping again, unstoppably, his head like the chandelier in his grandparents' house in Buffalo, the one that was too high for them to reach and that every time he visited had one fewer bulb alight. His head was an old chandelier, going dark.

When Rita returned home that evening to find Leonard, fully dressed, in bed, she told him to get ready for dinner. When he said he wasn't hungry she set one less place at the table. She didn't go into his room again that night.

From his first-floor bedroom, Leonard could hear his mother and sister discussing him as they ate. Janet, not usually his supporter, asked what was wrong with him. Rita said, "Nothing. He's just lazy." He heard them doing the dishes, Janet going into her room after dinner and talking on the telephone.

The next morning, Rita sent Janet in to check on him. She came to the edge of his bed.

"What's the matter with you?"

Even this little show of sympathy made Leonard want to burst into tears again. He had to struggle not to, covering his face with one arm.

"Are you faking?" Janet whispered.

"No," he managed to get out.

"It smells in here."

"Then leave," Leonard said, even though he wanted her to stay, wanted more than anything for his sister to crawl in beside him like she used to do when they were little.

He heard Janet's footsteps cross the room and go down the hall. He heard her say, "Mom, I think he's really sick."

"Probably he has a test he didn't study for," Rita said, cackling mirthlessly.

Soon they left and the house was quiet.

Leonard lay under blankets, entombed. The bad smell Janet had detected was his body rotting. His back and face were covered with zits. He needed to get up and wash himself with pHisoderm but he didn't have the energy.

In the corner of his room was his old table hockey set, the Bruins against the Blackhawks. As a twelve-year-old Leonard had mastered the skills required to beat his older sister and all his friends. He insisted on always being the Bruins. He'd made up names for each player, one Italian, one Irish, one American Indian, and one French Canadian. He'd kept stats on each player in a notebook reserved for that purpose, with a drawing of a hockey stick and a flaming puck on the front. As he played the game, sliding the metal rods to move the players around the ice and flicking the knobs to shoot, Leonard gave a running commentary. "DiMaglio takes the puck off the glass. He passes it to McCormick. McCormick gives it to Sleeping Bear, who passes it to Lecour, who shoots AND SCORES!" On and on, in his piercing, prepubescent voice, Leonard narrated his lopsided victories, jotting down Lecour's goals and Sleeping Bear's assists before he forgot. He obsessed over the stats, eager to run up Lecour's goal tally even by playing Janet, who could barely operate the controls. How Janet hated playing table hockey with Leonard! And how justified she had been, he saw now. All Leonard cared about was winning. Winning made him feel good, or at least better, about himself. It didn't matter if the other person could play or not.

The Disease, which otherwise distorted his perception, brought such personality defects into painful clarity.

But it wasn't just himself Leonard despised. He hated the jocks at school, he hated the Portland "pigs" in their cruisers, the 7-Eleven clerk who told Leonard that if he wanted to read *Rolling Stone* he had to buy it; he hated any and all politicians, businessmen, gun owners, Bible-thumpers, hippies, fat people, the reintroduction of the death penalty in the execution by firing squad of Gary Gilmore in Utah, the entire state of Utah, the Philadelphia 76ers for beating the Portland Trailblazers, and Anita Bryant most of all.

He missed the next week of school. But by the end of the following weekend he was up and around again. This had largely to do with the appearance of Godfrey outside Leonard's bedroom window on Friday afternoon. Around three-thirty that day, Janet came home from school, dropping her books on the kitchen table. A few minutes later, Leonard smelled her heating up a mini frozen pizza in the toaster oven. Soon she was on the phone to her boyfriend. Leonard was listening to his sister, thinking how fake she sounded and how Jimmy, her boyfriend, didn't know what she was really like, when someone tapped on his bedroom window. It was Godfrey. When he saw Godfrey out there, Leonard wondered if maybe he wasn't as depressed as he thought. He was happy to see his friend. He forgot about everything in the world that he hated, and got up to open the window.

"You could use the front door," Leonard said.

"Not me," Godfrey said, climbing in the window. "I'm strictly a back-door man."

"You should try the old lady next door. She's waiting for you right now."

"How about your sister?"

"O.K., you can leave now."

"I've got weed," Godfrey said.

He held up the baggie. Leonard stuck his nose into the bag and his depression lifted another notch. It smelled like the Amazonian rain forest, like putting your head between the legs of a native girl who had never heard of Christianity. They went out behind the garage to smoke some of it up, standing under the roof overhang to stay out of the rain. And that was where, figuratively, Leonard pretty much stayed for the remainder of high school, under an overhang, smoking pot in the drizzle. It was always raining in Portland and there was always an overhang nearby, behind the school, under the Steel Bridge in Waterfront Park, or beneath the leaky branches of a wind-desolated white pine in somebody's backyard. Leonard wasn't sure how he managed it, but somehow he dragged himself back to school the following Monday. He got used to crying secretly in the bathroom at least twice a day and to pretending to be all right when he came out. Without knowing what he was doing he began self-medicating, getting stoned most every day, drinking tall-boys at his or Godfrey's house in the afternoons, going to parties on the weekends and getting totally baked. The house was party central every weekday afternoon. Kids came by with six-packs and weed. They always wanted to hear about the murder. Leonard embellished on the tale, saying that there were still bloodstains when they moved in. "Hey, they might still be there if you look close." Janet fled these parties as if from raw sewage. She always threatened to tell but never did. By five o'clock Leonard and his friends were out in the alleys, riding their skateboards and crashing into things, laughing hysterically at spectacular wipeouts.

None of this represented mental health, but it got him through. The Disease wasn't yet well established in him. It was possible to anesthetize himself during his days or weeks of depression.

And then an amazing thing happened. In his junior year, Leonard started getting his act together. There were a couple of reasons for this. The first was that Janet had left for Whitman College, in Walla Walla, Washington, at the end of August, a four-and-a-half-hour drive from Portland. Though they'd mostly ignored each other growing up, Leonard found the house lonely without her. Janet's departure made living at home that much more unbearable. And it showed him a way out.

It was a chicken-egg deal. Leonard could never tell which came first, his desire to become a better student or the energy and focus that allowed him to do so. From that September on, he threw himself into his studies. He began to finish his reading assignments and to turn in essays on time. He paid the bare minimum attention it took for him to get A's on math exams. He did well in chemistry, though he preferred biology, which seemed to him more tangible, more "human," somehow. As Leonard's grades improved, he was put in advanced classes, which he found even more to his liking. It was fun to be one of the smart kids. In English, they were reading *Henry IV, Part 2*. Leonard couldn't help but secretly identify with Henry's speech of farewell to his former life of laxity. Though seriously behind in math at the start of the year, by the time he took the SATs, in the spring, he was more than caught up, and aced both the math and verbal sections. He discovered in himself a capacity for unbroken concentration, studying for ten hours at a time, taking breaks only to wolf down a sandwich. He started finishing papers *early*. He read Stephen Jay Gould's *Ontogeny and Phylogeny* and *Ever Since Darwin* just because he was interested. He wrote Gould a fan letter and received a postcard back from the great biologist. "Dear Leonard, Thank you for your letter. Keep sluggin'. S. J. Gould." On the front was a portrait of Darwin in the National Portrait Gallery. Leonard hung it over his desk.

Two years later, when Leonard could look back with the benefit of a medical finding, he came to suspect that he'd spent his last two years in high school in a condition of borderline mania. Every time he reached for a word, it was there. Whenever he needed to make an argument, entire paragraphs formed in his head. He could just open up in class and keep going, while also making people laugh. Even better, his new confidence and achievement allowed him to be generous. He excelled at school without showing off, his unbearable table-hockey persona nowhere in evidence. With schoolwork coming so easily to him, Leonard had time to help his friends with *their* work, never making them feel bad about their difficulties, explaining math patiently to kids who had no clue about math. Leonard felt better than he'd ever felt in his life. His grade point average went from 2.9 to 3.7 in a single semester. Senior year, he took four A.P.s, getting 5s in biology, English, and history, and a 4 in Spanish. Was it a bad thing that his blood contained an antidote to the depression he'd suffered the previous spring? Well, if so, nobody was complaining, not his teachers, not his mother, and certainly not the college counselor at Cleveland High School. In fact, it was the memory of his last two years in high school, when the Disease hadn't yet grown fangs and was more of a blessing than a curse, that had given Leonard the idea for his brilliant move.

Leonard applied to three schools, all in the East because the East was far away. The school he got into that gave him the most financial aid was Brown, a place he didn't know much about but which had been recommended by his counselor. After a lot of long-distance wrangling on the phone with Frank, who was now complaining about European tax rates and pleading poverty, Leonard succeeded in getting his father to agree to pay for his room and board. At that point he sent in his letter of acceptance to Brown.

Once it was clear that Leonard was going far away, Rita tried to make up for lost time. She took a week off work to go on a road trip with Leonard. They drove to Walla Walla to see Janet, who'd stayed at Whitman for the summer, working in the college library. Rita surprised Leonard by tearing up at the wheel, telling him how proud she was of him. As though he was already a mature adult, Leonard suddenly understood the dynamic between himself and Rita. He understood that she had been naturally fonder of Janet, felt guilty about this, and found fault with him to justify her prejudice. He understood that, as a male, Leonard reminded Rita of Frank, and that she either consciously or unconsciously held him at a slight distance as a result. He understood that he had unwittingly assumed Frank's attitudes, belittling Rita in his private thoughts the way Frank had done out loud. In short, Leonard understood that his entire relationship with his mother had been determined by a person who was no longer around.

On the day he left for Providence, Rita drove him to the airport. They waited in the lounge together before his flight. Rita, in sunglasses, big and round in the latest style, and with a chiffon scarf tied over her hair, sat with sphinx-like immobility.

"That college you picked sure is a long way away," she said. "Should I take it personally?"

"It's a good school," Leonard said.

"It's not Harvard," Rita said. "Nobody's heard of it."

"It's Ivy League!" Leonard protested.

"Your father cares about things like that. Not me."

Leonard wanted to get mad at her. But he understood, with that new grown-up brain of his, that Rita was denigrating his new college only because it was something that he wanted that wasn't her. For a moment, he saw things from her perspective. First Frank had left her, then Janet, and now him. Rita was all alone.

He stopped thinking about this because it was making him sad. As soon as he could, he got up, hugged his mother, and headed down the concourse.

Leonard didn't shed a tear until he'd taken his seat on the airplane. He turned to the window, hiding his face. The takeoff thrilled him—the sheer force of it. He stared out at the jet engine, marveling at the thrust required to rip him from the earth at such great speed. Sitting back, closing his eyes, he urged the engines on, as though they were doing a necessary violence. He didn't look out the window again until Portland was long gone.

At first, everyone Leonard met at college seemed to be from the East Coast. His roommate, Luke Miller, was from D.C. The girls across the hall, Jennifer Talbot and Stephanie Friedman, were from New York City and Philly, respectively. The rest of the people on his hall were from Teaneck, Stamford, Amherst, Portland (Maine), and Cold Spring. His third week on campus, Leonard met Lola Lopez, a Bambi-faced girl with a caramel complexion and a tidy afro, who was from Spanish Harlem. She was sitting in the quad, reading Zora Neale Hurston, when Leonard pretended to need directions to the Ratty. He asked her where she was from and what her name was, and when she told him, he asked her what the difference was between Spanish Harlem and regular Harlem. "I have to finish this for class," Lola said, and went back to her book.

The only West Coasters Leonard met were from California, which was another planet. "Keep California Dis-Oregonized," read many a bumper sticker on cars with Golden State plates, to which their neighbors replied with a motto of their own: "Welcome to Oregon. Enjoy Your Visit. Now Go Home." But at least the Californians Leonard met at school knew where he was from. Everyone else, from the South, Northeast, or Midwest, just asked about the rain. "Doesn't it rain a lot there?" "I hear it rains all the time." "How do you like the rain out there?"

"It's not as bad as Seattle," Leonard told them.

It didn't bother him much. He'd turned eighteen in August and the Disease, as though waiting for him to reach legal drinking age, began to flood him with intoxicants. Two things mania did were to keep you up all night and to enable nonstop sex: pretty much the definition of college. Leonard studied at the Rockefeller Library every night until midnight, like a yeshiva student davening over the Torah. At the stroke of twelve he headed back to West Quad, where there was always a party going on, usually in his room. Miller, a Milton grad who'd already had four years away from home to refine his Dionysian methods, bolted two huge Burmester speakers to the ceiling. He kept an industrial-size canister of nitrous oxide like a silver torpedo in the corner by his bed. Any girl who sucked on the rubber hose inevitably fainted into your arms like a damsel in distress. Leonard found he didn't need such stratagems. Without really trying, he had grown into the thing girls wanted. By December, he began hearing reports of a list in the girls' bathroom in Airport Lounge, a list of the cutest guys on campus that included his name. One night Miller delivered a note from a punked-out English girl named Gwyneth, with dyed red hair and witchy black fingernails. The note said, "I want your bod."

She got it. So did everybody else. A representative image of Leonard's freshman year would be of a guy lifting his head from an act of cunnilingus long enough to take a bong hit and give a correct answer in class. Not sleeping made it easier to two-time somebody. You could leave one girl's bed at five a.m., cross campus, and slide into bed with somebody else. Everything went fine, Leonard's grades were good, he was absorbed intellectually and erotically—until he went without sleep for a week during Reading Period. After his last exam, he threw a party in his room, passed out in bed with a girl he couldn't recognize the next morning, not because he didn't know her (the girl was, in fact, Lola Lopez) but because the ensuing depression had blinded him to everything but his agony. It colonized every cell of his body, a concentrate of anguish seemingly secreted, drip by drip, into his veins like a toxic by-product of the previous days of mania.

True mania, this time. So many magnitudes beyond the exhilarated spirits of his high school days that it bore little resemblance. Mania was a mental state every bit as dangerous as depression. At first, however, it felt like a rush of euphoria. You were completely captivating, completely charming; everybody loved you. You took ridiculous physical risks, jumping out of a third-floor dorm room into a snowbank, for instance. It made you spend your year's fellowship money in five days. It was like having a wild party in your head, a party at which you were the drunken host who refused to let anyone leave, who grabbed people by the collar and said, "Come on. One more!" When those people inevitably did vanish, you went out and found others, anyone and anything to keep the party going. You couldn't stop talking. Everything you said was brilliant. You just had the best idea. Let's drive down to New York! Tonight! Let's climb on top of List and watch the sunrise! Leonard got people to do these things. He led them on incredible escapades. But at some point things began to turn. His mind felt as if it was fizzing over. Words became other words inside his head, like patterns in a kaleidoscope. He kept making puns. No one understood what he was talking about. He became angry, irritable. Now, when he looked at people, who'd been laughing at his jokes an hour earlier, he saw that they were worried, concerned for him. And so he ran off into the night, or day, or night, and found other people to be with, so that the mad party might continue . . .

Like a drunk on a bender, Leonard had a blackout afterward. He woke up next to Lola Lopez in a state of utter collapse. Lola managed to get him up, however. She led him by the arm to Health Services, telling him not to worry, to hold on to her and that he'd be all right.

It seemed especially cruel, then, three days later, in the hospital, when the doctor came into the room to tell Leonard that he suffered from something that would never go away, something that could only be "managed," as if managing, for an eighteen-year-old looking out on life, could be any life at all.

In September, when Madeleine and Leonard were newly arrived at Pilgrim Lake, the dune grass was a lovely shade of light green. It waved and bent as if the landscape were a painted Japanese screen. Saltwater rivulets trickled through the marshes, and scrub pines clustered together in discreet groves. The world reduced itself, here, to basic constituents—sand, sea, sky—keeping trees and flower species to a minimum.

As the summer people left and the weather turned colder, the purity of the landscape only increased. The dunes turned a shade of gray that matched the sky. The days grew noticeably shorter. It was the perfect environment for depression. It was dark when Leonard got up in the morning and dark when he returned from the lab. His neck was so fat he couldn't button his shirt collars. The proof that lithium stabilized one's mood was confirmed every time Leonard saw himself naked in the mirror and didn't kill himself. He wanted to. He thought he had every right. But he couldn't work up the requisite self-loathing.

This should have made him feel good, but feeling "good" was also out of reach. Both his highs and his lows were evened out, leaving him feeling as though he lived in two dimensions. He was on an increased daily dose of lithium, 1,800 milligrams, with correspondingly severe complications. When he complained to Dr. Perlmann at his weekly appointment at Mass General, an hour and a half away, the natty, shiny-headed psychiatrist always said the same thing: "Be patient." Perlmann seemed more interested in Leonard's life at Pilgrim Lake Lab than in the fact that his signature now looked like that of a ninety-year-old. Perlmann wanted to know what Dr. Malkiel was like. He wanted to hear gossip. If Leonard had stayed in Providence, under the care of Dr. Shieu, he would have already been on a lower dose, but now he was back to square one.

In the library at Pilgrim Lake, Leonard tried to learn more about the drug he was on. Reading at the pace of a second-grader, effectively moving his lips, Leonard learned that lithium salts had been used for mood disorders as far back as the nineteenth century. Then, largely because people couldn't patent it to make money, the therapy had fallen out of favor. Lithium had been used to treat gout, hypertension, and heart disease. It had been the key ingredient in 7 Up (originally named Bib-Label Lithiated Lemon-Lime Soda) until the 1950s. At the moment, clinical trials were under way to test lithium's efficacy in treating Huntington's chorea, Tourette's syndrome, migraine and cluster headache, Ménière's disease, and hypokalemic periodic paralysis. The drug companies had it the wrong way around. Instead of starting with an illness and developing a drug to treat it, they developed drugs and then tried to figure out what they were good for.

What Leonard knew about lithium without reading was that it made him torpid and fuzzy-brained. His mouth was always dry, no matter how much he drank, and tasted as if he were sucking on a steel screw. One of the reasons he chewed tobacco was to cover the metallic taste. Due to the tremors in his hands, he had no coordination (he couldn't play Ping-Pong anymore, or even catch a ball). And, though all his doctors insisted that the lithium wasn't at fault, Leonard's sex drive was much reduced. He wasn't impotent or unable to perform; he just didn't have a lot of interest. Probably this had to do with how unattractive and prematurely old the drug made him feel. At the Provincetown pharmacy, Leonard went shopping not only for razor blades but also for Mylanta and Preparation H. He was always coming out of the drugstore clutching a little plastic bag, scared the bag's transparency would reveal the embarrassing product inside, and so holding it even tighter against his little titties in the Cape Cod wind. Leonard patronized the P-town pharmacy in order to avoid the convenience store at the lab, where he ran the risk of running into someone he knew. To keep Madeleine from going with him, he had to come up with an excuse, the most unassailable of which, of course, was his manic depression. He didn't invoke it outright. He just mumbled that he *wanted to be alone*, and Madeleine backed off.

As a consequence of his physical and mental malfunctioning, there was another problem he was dealing with: the power had shifted in his relationship with Madeleine. Early on, *Madeleine* had been the needy one. She got jealous when Leonard talked to other girls at parties. She flashed warning signs of insecurity. Finally, she'd thrown in the towel completely and told him, "I love you." In response, Leonard had acted cool and cerebral, figuring that by keeping Madeleine in doubt he could bind her to him more closely. But Madeleine surprised him. She broke up with him on the spot. Once Madeleine was gone, Leonard regretted the Roland Barthes incident. He castigated himself for being such a douche. He spent multiple sessions with Bryce examining his motivations. And though Bryce's analysis of the situation—that Leonard was frightened of intimacy and so had self-protectively made fun of Madeleine's avowal—was pretty much on the mark, that didn't bring Madeleine back. Leonard missed her. He got depressed. Stupidly, he stopped taking his lithium, hoping to feel better. But all he felt was anxious. Anxious and depressed. He wore out the ear of every friend he had, talking incessantly about how much he missed Madeleine, how he wanted her back, and how he'd messed up the best relationship he'd ever had. Knowing that his friends were getting tired of hearing this, Leonard modulated his monologues, partly out of a storyteller's instinct to vary a narrative and partly because, by then, his anxieties were multiplying. So he told his friends about his money worries and his health worries until he finally lost track of what he was saying and to whom he was saying it. Around this time Ken Auerbach had shown up, with two guys from security, and taken him to Health Services. And the really crazy thing was that, when he was transferred to the hospital the next day, Leonard was *pissed*. He was pissed at being admitted to the psych ward without enjoying the prior benefit of a total manic blowout. He should have been up for three nights running. He should have fucked eight chicks and snorted blow and done jelly shots off the stomach of a stripper named Moonstar. Instead, all Leonard had done was sit in his apartment, abusing his Rolodex, wearing out his telephonic welcome, and spiraling down until he ended in medical lockup with the other head cases.

By the time he got out, three weeks later, the power dynamics had completely reversed. Now *he* was the needy one. True, he had Madeleine back, which was a wonderful thing. But Leonard's happiness was compromised by the constant fear of losing her again. His unsightliness threw Madeleine's beauty into relief. Next to her in bed, he felt like a pudgy eunuch. Every hair on his thighs sprouted from an inflamed follicle. Sometimes, when Madeleine was asleep, Leonard would gently pull the covers off her to stare at her glowing, rosy skin. What was interesting about being the needy one was how much in love you felt. It was almost worth it. This dependency was what Leonard had guarded himself against feeling all his life, but he couldn't do it anymore. He'd lost the ability to be an asshole. Now he was smitten, and it felt both tremendous and scary.

Madeleine had tried to brighten up his studio while he was in the hospital. She'd put new sheets on the bed and had hung curtains in the windows and a pink shower curtain. She'd scrubbed the floors and counters. She professed to be glad to be living with him and to be rid of Olivia and Abby. But during the long, hot summer, Leonard began to see why Madeleine might eventually tire of slumming it with her nearly penniless boyfriend. Whenever a roach scurried out of the toaster, she looked as though she was going to be sick. She wore sandals in the shower to protect herself from the mildew. The first week after Leonard was back, Madeleine stayed with him every day. But the week after that she began going out to the library or to see her old thesis advisor. Leonard didn't like Madeleine to leave the apartment. He suspected the reason she went out wasn't because she loved Jane Austen or Professor Saunders, but to get away from him. In addition to going to the library, Madeleine played tennis two or three times a week. One day, trying to convince her not to go, Leonard said that it was too hot out to play tennis. He suggested she go to an air-conditioned movie with him instead.

"I need some exercise," Madeleine said.

"I'll give you some exercise," he boasted emptily.

"Not that kind."

"How come you always play with guys?"

"Because guys can beat me. I need some competition."

"If I said that, you'd call me sexist."

"Look, if Chrissie Evert lived in Providence, I'd play *her*. But all the girls I know here stink."

Leonard knew what he sounded like. He sounded like every drag of a girlfriend he'd ever had. In order to stop sounding that way, he pouted, and, in the following silence, Madeleine gathered her racquet and can of balls and left.

As soon as Madeleine was gone he leapt up and ran to the window. He watched her leave the building in her tennis whites, her hair tied back, a sweatband around the wrist of her serving arm.

There was something about tennis—its aristocratic rituals, the prim silence it enforced on its spectators, the pretentious insistence on saying "love" for zero and "deuce" for tied, the exclusivity of the court itself, where only two people were allowed to move freely, the palace-guard rigidity of the linesmen, and the slavish scurrying of the ball boys—that made it clearly a reproachable pastime. That Leonard couldn't say this to Madeleine without making her angry suggested the depth of the social chasm between them. There was a public tennis court near his house in Portland, old and cracked, half-flooded most of the time. He and Godfrey used to go out there to smoke weed. That was as close as Leonard got to playing tennis. By contrast, for two solid weeks in June and July, Madeleine got up every morning to watch *Breakfast at Wimbledon* on her portable Trinitron, which she'd installed in Leonard's apartment. From the mattress, Leonard groggily watched her nibble English muffins while she watched the matches. That was where Madeleine belonged: at Wimbledon, on Centre Court, curtseying for the queen.

He watched her watching Wimbledon. It made him happy to see her there. He didn't want her to leave. If Madeleine left, he would be alone again, as he'd been growing up in a house with his family, as he was in his head and often in his dreams, and as he'd been in his room at the psych ward.

He barely remembered his first days at the hospital. They put him on Thorazine, an antipsychotic that knocked him out. He slept for fourteen hours. Before he was admitted, the head nurse had taken Leonard's sharps from his overnight bag (his razor, his toenail clippers). She took away his belt. She asked him if he had any valuables, and Leonard handed over his wallet, containing six dollars.

He awoke in a small room, a single, without a phone or a TV. At first, it looked like a normal hospital room, but then he began to notice little differences. The bed frame and the hinges of the bedside tray were welded together, without screws or bolts that a patient might take apart and cut himself with. The hook on the door wasn't fixed in place but attached to a bungee cord that stretched under excess weight, to prevent someone hanging himself on it. Leonard wasn't allowed to close the door. There was no lock on the door, or on any doors in the unit, including the bathroom stalls. Surveillance was a central feature of the psych ward: he was constantly aware of being watched. Oddly, this was reassuring. The nurses weren't surprised by the state he was in. They didn't think he was to blame. They treated Leonard as if he'd injured himself in a fall or a car accident. Their half-bored ministrations probably did more than anything—even the drugs—to get Leonard through those first dark days.

Leonard was a "self-admit," meaning that he could leave anytime he wanted. He'd signed a consent form, however, agreeing to give the hospital twenty-four-hour notice before doing so. He consented to be given medications, to abide by the rules of the unit, to uphold standards of cleanliness and hygiene. He signed whatever they put in front of him. Once a week, he was allowed to shave. A nurse's aid brought him a disposable razor, standing by while he used it, and then took it back. They kept him on a strict schedule, getting him up at six a.m. for breakfast and ushering him through a series of daily activities, therapy, group therapy, crafts class, more group therapy, gym, before visiting hours in the afternoon. Lights were out at nine p.m.

Every day, Dr. Shieu stopped by to talk. Shieu was a small woman with papery skin and an alert demeanor. She seemed interested mainly in one thing: whether Leonard was suicidal or not.

"Good morning, Leonard, how are you feeling today?"

"Exhausted. Depressed."

"Are you feeling suicidal?"

"Not actively."

"Is that a joke?"

"No."

"Any plans?"

"Excuse me?"

"Are you planning to harm yourself? Fantasizing about it? Going over scenarios in your head?"

"No."

Manic-depressives, it turned out, were at a higher risk for suicide than depressives. Dr. Shieu's number one priority was to keep her patients alive. Her second priority was to get them well enough to leave the hospital before their insurance benefits ran out in thirty days. Her pursuit of these objectives (which ironically mimicked the tunnel vision of mania itself) led to a strong reliance on drug therapy. She automatically placed schizophrenic patients on Thorazine, a drug people likened to a "chemical lobotomy." Everyone else received sedatives and mood stabilizers. Leonard spent his morning therapy sessions with the psychiatric resident discussing all the stuff he, Leonard, was on. How was he "tolerating" the valium? Was it making him nauseated? Constipated? Yes. Thorazine could cause tardive dyskinesia (repetitive motions, often involving the mouth and lips), but this was often temporary. The resident prescribed additional medications to counteract Leonard's side effects and, without asking him how he was *feeling*, sent him on his way.

The clinical psychologist, Wendy Neuman, was at least interested in Leonard's emotional history, but he saw her only for group therapy. Gathered in the folding chairs of the meeting room, they made a diverse group with the drug-addicted, a perfect democracy of collapse. There were older white guys with M.I.A. tattoos and black dudes who played chess all day, a middle-aged female accounts clerk who drank as much as an English rugby team, and one small young woman, an aspiring singer, whose mental illness took the form of a desire to have her right leg amputated. To stimulate discussion, they passed a book around, a battered hardback with a split spine. The book was called *Out of Darkness, Light* and contained personal testimonies of people who had recovered from mental illnesses or had learned to cope with a chronic diagnosis. It was borderline religious while professing not to be. They sat in the unkind fluorescence of the meeting room, each reading a paragraph aloud before handing it to the next person. Some people treated the book as if it were a mysterious object. They mispronounced *deity*. They didn't know what *cur* meant. The book was badly out of date. Some contributors referred to depression as "the blues" or "the black dog." When the book came to him, Leonard read off his paragraph with a cadence and diction that made it clear he'd come to the hospital straight from College Hill. He was under the impression, those first days, that mental illness admitted of hierarchy, that he was a superior form of manic-depressive. If dealing with a mental illness consisted of two parts, one part medication and the other therapy, and if therapy proceeded faster the smarter you were, then many people in the group were at a disadvantage. They could barely remember what had happened in their lives, much less draw connections between events. One guy had a facial tic so pronounced that it seemed to literally shake coherent thoughts from his head. He would twitch and forget what he'd been saying. His problems were physiological, the basic wiring of his brain faulty. Listening to him was like listening to a radio tuned between channels: every so often a non sequitur came barking in. Leonard paid sympathetic attention as people spoke about their lives. He tried to take comfort in what they said. But his main thought was of how much worse off they were than he. This belief made him feel better about himself, and so he clung to it. But then it was Leonard's turn to tell *his* story, and he opened his mouth and out came the most nicely modulated, well-articulated bullshit imaginable. He talked about the events that led up to his breakdown. He recited swaths of the *DSM III* that he'd apparently committed to memory without trying. He showed off how smart he was because that was what he was used to doing. He couldn't stop himself.

That was when Leonard realized something crucial about depression. The smarter you were, the *worse* it was. The sharper your brain, the more it cut you up. As he was speaking, for instance, Leonard noticed Wendy Neuman cross her arms over her chest, as if to defend herself against the blatant insincerity of what he was saying. To win her back, Leonard admitted to this insincerity, saying, "No, I take that back. I'm lying. Lying is what I do. It's part of my disease." He eyed Wendy to see if she was buying this, or if she regarded it as further insincerity. The closer Leonard monitored her reactions, the further he got from telling the truth about himself, until he trailed off, feeling embarrassed and hot-faced, an eyesore of denial.

The same thing happened in his sessions with Dr. Shieu, but in a different way. Sitting in the scratchy armchair in Shieu's office, Leonard wasn't self-conscious about his educated manner of speech. But his mind kept up its play-by-play analysis of the contest under way. In order to be released from the hospital, Leonard had to make it clear that he wasn't suicidal. He knew, however, that Dr. Shieu was on the lookout for any attempt to disguise suicidal ideation (suicidal people being brilliant tacticians when it came to obtaining the opportunity to kill themselves). Therefore, Leonard didn't want to seem *too* upbeat. At the same time, he

254

didn't want to appear to be not getting better at all. As he answered the doctor's questions, Leonard felt as though he were being interrogated for a crime. He tried, when he could, to tell the truth, but when the truth didn't serve his cause he embellished it, or outright lied. He noted every change in Dr. Shieu's facial expression, interpreting it as either favorable or unfavorable, and shifting his next response accordingly. Often he had the impression that the person answering questions from the scratchy armchair was a dummy he was controlling, that this had been true throughout his life, and that his life had become so involved with operating the dummy that he, the ventriloquist, had ceased to have a personality, becoming just an arm stuffed up the puppet's back.

Visiting hours provided no relief. The friends who showed up divided into two groups. There were the emoters, mostly girls, who treated Leonard gingerly, as if he might break, and there were the jokesters, mostly guys, who thought the way to help him was to make fun of hospital visits in general. Jerry Heidmann brought him a saccharine get-well card, Ron Lutz a smiley-faced helium balloon. From the things that came out of his friends' mouths during visiting hours Leonard gradually understood that they thought depression was like being "depressed." They thought it was like being in a bad mood, only worse. Therefore, they tried to get him to snap out of it. People brought him chocolate bars. They urged him to consider all the good things in his life.

True to form, neither of his parents flew out to see him. Frank called once, having been given his number by Janet. In the course of the short conversation (other patients were waiting to use the community phone), Frank told Leonard three separate times to "hang in there." He invited Leonard to come to Antwerp when he was feeling better. Frank was thinking of moving to Amsterdam now and living on a houseboat. "Come on over and we can make a little boat trip on the canals," he said, before hanging up. Rita cited her herniated disk (the first he'd ever heard of it) for her inability to travel. She did speak with Dr. Shieu, however, and one night called Leonard on a phone at the nurses' station. It was late, about ten p.m., but the night nurse let him take it.

"Hello?"

"What am I going to do with you, Leonard? What? Just tell me."

"I'm in this hospital, Mom. I'm in the psych unit."

"I know that, Leonard. That's why I'm calling, for God's sake. The doctor said you stopped taking your medicine."

Leonard admitted this by remaining silent.

"What's the matter with you, Leonard?" Rita asked.

Anger flared in him. For a moment, it felt like old times. "Well, let's see. First of all, my parents are alcoholics. One of them is probably manic-depressive herself, only undiagnosed. I inherited my condition from her. We both suffer from the same form of the illness. We're not rapid cyclers. We don't go from high to low in a few hours. We ride these long waves of mania or depression. My brain's chemically starved for the neurotransmitters it needs to regulate my moods and then sometimes it's oversupplied with them. I'm messed up biologically because of my genetics and psychologically because of my parents, is what's the matter with me, *Mom*."

"And you still act like a big baby whenever you get sick," Rita said. "I remember how you used to go on and on whenever you had a cold."

"This isn't a cold."

"I know it isn't," Rita said, sounding chastened for the first time, and concerned. "It's serious. I talked with the doctor. I'm worried about you."

"You don't sound like it."

"I am. I am. But Leonard, sweetheart, listen to me. You're a grown person now. When this happened before, and they told me you were in the hospital, I rushed right out there. Didn't I? But I can't be rushing out there the rest of my life every time you forget to take your medicine. That's all this is, you know. It's you being forgetful."

"I was already sick," Leonard said. "That's why I stopped taking my lithium."

"That doesn't make sense. If you'd been taking your medicine, you wouldn't have gotten sick. Now, Leonard, sweetheart, listen to me. You're not on my insurance anymore. Do you realize that? They took you off my policy when you turned twenty-one. Don't worry. I'm going to pay for the hospital. I'll do it, this time, even though I'm not swimming in money. Do you think your father's going to help? No. I'll do it. But when you get out, you have to get your own insurance."

As Leonard heard this, he felt his anxiety spike. He clutched the phone, his vision growing dark. "How am I supposed to get insurance, Mom?"

"What do you mean, how? You graduate from college and go find a job like everybody else."

"I'm not going to graduate!" Leonard cried. "I'm taking three incompletes!"

"Then complete your incompletes. You have to start taking care of yourself, Leonard. You hear me? You're grown-up now and I can't do it. Take your medicine so this doesn't happen again."

Instead of coming to Providence herself, she dispatched his sister. Janet arrived for a weekend, flying out from San Francisco, where she'd taken a marketing job at Gump's. She was living with some older, divorced guy who had a house in Sausalito, and she mentioned a birthday party she was missing and her demanding boss to impress on Leonard the extent of the sacrifice she was making in order to come and hold his hand. Janet seemed genuinely to believe that her problems were more significant than whatever Leonard had to deal with. "I could get depressed if I let myself," she said. "But I don't let myself." She got visibly freaked out by some of the other patients in the dayroom and kept checking her watch. It was a relief when she finally left on Sunday.

By now final exams had begun. Leonard's stream of visitors tapered to one or two a day. He began to live for smoking breaks. In the afternoon and evening, the head nurse handed out cigarettes and other tobacco products. Chewing tobacco wasn't allowed, so Leonard took what the other guys his age, James and Maurice, were into, these thin little moist cigars called Backwoods that came in a foil pouch. They descended in a group, accompanied by either Wendy Neuman or a security guard, to the ground floor of the hospital. On a blacktopped area surrounded by a high fence, they passed a single lighter around and torched up their smokes. The Backwoods were sweet-tasting and delivered a nice kick. Leonard puffed away, pacing back and forth and staring up at the sky. He felt like the Birdman of Alcatraz, only without any birds. As the days passed, he began to feel measurably better. Dr. Shieu attributed this improvement to the lithium kicking in. But Leonard thought it had a lot to do with good old nicotine, with going outside and watching a single cloud sail across the sky. Sometimes he heard cars honking, or kids shouting, or, once, what sounded like a fastball being cleanly clobbered on a nearby baseball diamond, a sound that soothed him instantly, the solid *plonk* of wood against rawhide. Leonard remembered what it felt like to be a Little Leaguer and hit a perfect pitch. That was the beginning of his recovery. Just to be able to remember that, once upon a time, happiness had been as simple as that.

And then Madeleine appeared in the dayroom, missing graduation, and all Leonard had to do was look at her to know that he wanted to be alive again.

There was only one problem. They wouldn't let him out. Dr. Shieu kept playing it safe, putting off the day of Leonard's departure. And so Leonard continued to go to group, and to draw pictures during the craft periods, and to play badminton or basketball during gym.

In the group sessions, there was one patient who impressed Leonard deeply. Her name was Darlene Withers. She was a fireplug of a person and sat with her feet up on the folding chair, hugging her knees, always the first patient to speak up. "Hi, I'm Darlene. I'm an addict and an alcoholic and I suffer from depression. This is my third time being hospitalized for depression. Been here three weeks now, and Ms. Neuman?—I'm ready to leave anytime you say."

She smiled broadly. When she did, her upper lip curled back, pushing out a glistening band of its pink underside. Her family's nickname for her was "Triple-lip." Leonard spent a fair amount of time in group waiting to see Darlene smile.

"I can relate to this story because the writer she say her depression come from low self-esteem," Darlene began. "And that something I'm dealing with on a daily basis. Like lately I been feeling bad about myself because of my present relationship. I was in a committed relationship when I come into the hospital. But since I been in here? I ain't heard from my boyfriend once. He didn't come to visiting hours or nothing. I woke up this morning feeling real sorry for myself. 'You too fat, Darlene. You not good-looking enough. That why he don't come.' But then I start thinking about my boyfriend—and you know what? His bref stink. It do! Every time that man come near me I have to smell his stanky old bref. Why I be in a relationship with someone like that, never brushes his teeth, bad oral hygiene? And the answer come back to me was: That how you feeling about yourself, Darlene. Like you worth so little you got to be with anybody take you."

Darlene was an inspiration in the ward. Often she sat in a corner of the dayroom singing to herself.

"Why you singing, Triple-lip?"

"Singing to keep from crying. You should try it too, instead of moping like you do."

"Who says I'm moping?"

"Moping doesn't cover your sorry ass! They need to come up with a whole new diagnosis for you. Prune-face disorder. That what you got."

According to the stories she told in group, Darlene had dropped out of high school after the tenth grade. She'd been abused by her stepfather and had left home when she was seventeen. She'd worked, briefly, as a prostitute in East Providence, a subject she was surprisingly candid about at one meeting and then never mentioned again. By the time she was twenty she was addicted to heroin and alcohol. To get off the heroin and alcohol, she'd gotten religion. "I was drugging just to dull the pain, you know? Got so doped up I didn't know where I was. Pretty soon I lost my job, my apartment. Lost everything. My life had got to where it was unmanageable. Finally, I moved in with my sister. Now, my sister, she have this dog named Grover. Grover a pit bull mix. Some nights, when I had came back to my sister's apartment, I used to take Grover for a walk. Didn't matter how late it was. When you walking a pit bull don't nobody bother you. You come down the street and everybody like, Ho, shit! Me and Grover we had this cemetery we used to go to, because they had grass over there. And so this one night we back behind the church, and I'm drunk, as usual, and I look at Grover, and Grover look back at me, and all of a sudden he say, 'Why you killing yourself, Darlene?' I swear to God! I know it was just in my mind. But still, it the *truth*. Out of the mouth of a dog! Next day, I went to the doctor, and the doctor sent me over to Sunbeam House, and next thing I know they're admitting me. Didn't even let me go home first. Put me right into a room to detox. *Then*, when I had got myself clean, the depression hit me. Like it was just waiting for me to get off the smack and the alcohol so it could fuck me up good. Excuse my language, Ms. Neuman. I was in Sunbeam House for three months. That was two years ago. And here I am again. Things have been a little hard lately, financial problems, emotional problems. My life getting *better*, but it ain't getting any easier. I just need to keep working my program in terms of my addictions and keep taking my medications in terms of my illness. One thing I learned, between addiction and depression? Depression a lot worse. Depression ain't something you just get *off* of. You can't get *clean* from depression. Depression be like a bruise that never goes away. A bruise in your *mind*. You just got to be careful not to touch where it hurts. It always be there, though. That's all I have. Thanks for listening. Peace."

It didn't surprise Leonard that Darlene was religious. People without hope often were. But Darlene didn't seem weak, credulous, or stupid. Though she often referred to her "Higher Power," and sometimes to "my Higher Power that I choose to call God," she seemed remarkably rational, intelligent, and nonjudgmental. When Leonard was speaking to the group, unfurling the long, tangled loop of his bullshit, he often glanced up to see Darlene listening encouragingly, as though what he was saying wasn't bullshit, or as though, even if it was, Darlene understood his need to say it, to get it out of his system so that he could discover something true and meaningful about himself. Most of the patients with substance abuse problems had picked up the religious inclination of 12-step programs. Wendy Neuman looked like a secular humanist if Leonard ever saw one, but she never tipped her hand one way or another, as was surely right. It was clear that everybody on the unit was barely hanging on. No one wanted to say or do anything that might hinder someone's recovery. In this way the unit was very unlike the world outside, and morally superior to it.

To believe in God wasn't in Leonard's power, however. The irrationality of religious faith had been obvious to him long before reading Nietzsche had confirmed his suppositions. The only religious studies he'd taken was an oversubscribed survey course called Introduction to Eastern Religion. Leonard couldn't remember why he'd signed up. It was the fall semester following his diagnosis the previous spring and he was taking things slow. He sat in the back of the packed lecture hall, did at least half of the reading, and showed up for section but never said anything. What he mainly remembered about the class was this guy who used to show up wearing baggy secondhand suits and beat-up shoes, sort of a drunken preacher or Tom Waits look. He carried a black briefcase with metal edges, the kind of thing that might have contained fifty thousand in cold cash instead of a paperback volume of the Upanishads edited by Mircea Eliade and a half-eaten blondie wrapped in a paper napkin. What Leonard liked about this guy was his manner of gently correcting the untutored opinions offered around the seminar table. The entire class was full of co-op types, vegetarians in overalls and tie-dyed T-shirts. The bias of these kids was that Western religion was responsible for everything bad in the world, the rape of the earth, slaughterhouses, animal testing, whereas Eastern religion was ecological and pacific. Leonard had neither the desire nor the energy to argue these points, but he liked it when Young Tom Waits did. For instance, when they were discussing the concept of ahimsa, Young Waits offered the observation that the Sermon on the Mount made roughly the same point. He impressed Leonard by mentioning that Schopenhauer had tried to interest the European world in Vedantic thought back in 1814, and that the two cultures had been mixing for a long time. His point, again and again, was that truth wasn't the property of any one faith and that, if you looked closely, you found a ground where they all converged.

On another day, they'd gotten off topic. Somebody brought up Gandhi and how his belief in nonviolence had inspired Martin Luther King, which had led to the Civil Rights Act. The speaker's point was that it had actually been a Hindu who had made America, a so-called Christian nation, a more just and democratic place.

At which point Young Waits spoke up. "Gandhi was influenced by Tolstoy," he said.

"What?"

"Gandhi got his philosophy of nonviolence from Tolstoy. They corresponded."

"Um, didn't Tolstoy live in like the nineteenth century?"

"He died in 1912. Gandhi used to write him fan letters. He called Tolstoy his 'great teacher.' So you're right. Martin Luther King got nonviolence from Gandhi. But Gandhi got it from Tolstoy, who got it from Christianity. So Gandhian philosophy really isn't any different from Christian pacifism."

"Are you saying Gandhi was a Christian?"

"Essentially, yes."

"Well, that's wrong. Christian missionaries were always trying to convert Gandhi. But it never worked. He couldn't accept stuff like the resurrection and the Immaculate Conception."

"That's not Christianity."

"Yes, it is!"

"Those are just myths that grew up around the core ideas."

"But Christianity is *full* of myths. That's what's so much better about Buddhism. It doesn't force you to believe anything. You don't even have to believe in a god."

Young Waits tapped his fingers on his briefcase before replying. "When the Dalai Lama dies, Tibetan Buddhists believe his spirit gets reincarnated into another baby. The monks go all over the countryside, examining all the newborns to see which one it is. They bring personal effects of the deceased Dalai Lama to dangle over the babies' faces. Depending on how the babies react, by a secret process—which they can't explain to anyone—they choose the new Dalai Lama. And isn't it amazing that the right baby's always born in Tibet, where the monks can find him, instead of, say, in San Jose? And that it's always a boy baby?"

At the time, infatuated with Nietzsche (and half asleep), Leonard didn't want to get into this argument, the truth of which wasn't that all religions were equally valid but that they were equally nonsensical. When the semester ended he forgot about Young Waits. He didn't think about him again until two years later, after he started going out with Madeleine, when, looking through a packet of snapshots Madeleine kept in her desk, Leonard came across quite a few where Young Waits appeared. A disturbing number, in fact.

"Who *is* this guy?" Leonard asked.

"That's Mitchell," she said.

"Mitchell what?"

"Grammaticus."

"Yeah, Grammaticus. I was in a religious studies class with him."

"That figures."

"Did you used to go out with him?"

"No!" Madeleine objected.

"You look awfully cozy." He held up a photograph where Grammaticus was lying with his curly head in her lap.

Madeleine took the photograph, frowning, and put it back in the desk. She explained that she'd known Grammaticus since freshman year but that they'd had a fight. When Leonard asked her what the fight had been about, she looked evasive and said that it was complicated. When Leonard asked her what was complicated about it, Madeleine admitted that she and Grammaticus had always had a Platonic friendship, at least Platonic on her end, but that more recently he'd been "sort of in love" with her and that his feelings had been hurt because she hadn't returned them.

This information hadn't bothered Leonard at the time. He had sized Grammaticus up according to an animal scale—antler size to antler size—and given himself the clear advantage. In the hospital, however, with plenty of time on his hands, Leonard began to wonder if there was more to the story. He pictured Grammaticus's satyr-like form clambering on top of Madeleine from behind. The image of Grammaticus screwing Madeleine, or of Madeleine going down on him, contained the right mix of pain and arousal to stir Leonard from his deadened sexual state. For reasons Leonard couldn't fathom—but that probably had to do with a need for self-abasement—the idea of Madeleine wantonly betraying him with Grammaticus turned Leonard on. To break the tedium of the hospital, he tortured himself with this twisted fantasy, jerking off in the bathroom stall while holding the lockless door closed with his free hand.

Even after he and Madeleine got back together, Leonard kept tormenting himself in this way. On the day he was discharged, a nurse brought him outside and he got into Madeleine's new car. Belted into the front passenger seat, he felt like a newborn that Madeleine was bringing home for the first time. The city had greened up considerably while Leonard was inside. It looked lovely and lazy. The students were gone and College Hill was deserted and peaceful. They drove back to Leonard's apartment. They began living together. And because Leonard wasn't a baby, because he was a full-grown sick fuck, he spent Madeleine's every absence imagining her blowing her tennis partner in the locker room, or being bent over in the stacks of the library. One day, a week after Leonard's return, Madeleine mentioned that she'd run into Grammaticus on the morning of graduation and that they'd made up. Grammaticus had gone back home to live with his parents but Madeleine had been talking on the phone a lot while Leonard had been in the hospital. She said she would pay for all her long-distance calls and now Leonard found himself checking the New England Bell bills for any calls made to midwestern area codes. Recently, alarmingly, she'd taken the phone into the bathroom and talked with the door closed, explaining afterward that she hadn't wanted to disturb him. (Disturb him from what? From lying in bed, putting on weight like a calf in a veal crate?

From reading the same paragraph of *The Anti-Christ* he'd already read three times?)

At the end of August, Madeleine drove down to Prettybrook to see her parents and get some things from home. A few days after returning, she mentioned offhandedly that she'd seen Grammaticus, in New York, on his way to Paris.

"You just ran into him?" Leonard asked from the mattress.

"Yeah, with Kelly. In some bar she took me to."

"Did you fuck him?"

"What?!"

"Maybe you fucked him. Maybe you want a guy who's not taking massive amounts of lithium."

"Oh, God, Leonard, I told you already. I don't care about that. The doctor says that's not even because of the lithium, right?"

"The doctor says a lot of things."

"Well, do me a favor. Don't talk that way to me. I don't like it. O.K.? And it sounds really awful."

"Sorry."

"Are you getting depressed? You sound depressed."

"I'm not. I'm nothing."

Madeleine lay down on the bed, wrapping herself around him. "You're nothing? You don't feel this?" She put her hand on the fly of his pants. "How does this feel?"

"Nice."

For a little while, it worked, but not long. If, instead of being touched by Madeleine, Leonard had been imagining Madeleine touching Grammaticus, he might have gotten off. But reality wasn't enough for him anymore. And this was a problem larger and deeper than even his illness, a problem he couldn't begin to deal with. And so he closed his eyes and hugged Madeleine tightly.

"Sorry," he said again. "Sorry, sorry."

Leonard felt better around people who were struggling as much as he was. Over the summer he kept in touch with a few patients he'd met in the hospital. Darlene had moved into a friend's apartment in East Providence, and Leonard had gone out to see her a couple of times. She seemed hyperactive. She couldn't sit still and talked nonstop without making much sense. She kept asking, "So, Leonard, you good?" without waiting for an answer. A few weeks later, at the end of July, Darlene's sister, Kimberly, called Leonard, saying that Darlene hadn't been answering her phone. They went out to Darlene's apartment together, where they found Darlene in the midst of a psychotic break. She was under the impression that her neighbors were conspiring to get her kicked out of the building. They were spreading rumors about her to the landlord. She was frightened to go outside, even to take out the trash. The apartment smelled of spoiled food, and Darlene had started drinking again. Leonard had to call Dr. Shieu and explain the situation, while Kimberly persuaded Darlene to take a shower and change her clothes. Somehow they coaxed Darlene, wide-eyed with panic, into the car, and took her to the hospital, where Dr. Shieu was readying her readmission papers. Every day for the next week Leonard went to visiting hours. Darlene was out of it most of the time, but he found it comforting to visit her. He forgot about himself while he was there.

The only thing that got Leonard through the rest of the summer was the prospect of leaving for Pilgrim Lake. At the beginning of August, an envelope from the laboratory arrived. Inside, on beautifully printed pages, each embossed with a letterhead so prominent as to be virtually topographical, were orientation materials. There was a letter addressed to "Mr. Leonard Bankhead, Research Fellow" and personally signed by David Malkiel. The packet put to rest Leonard's fears that the authorities might learn about his hospitalization and rescind his fellowship. He read the list of research fellows and the colleges they'd gone to, and found his name right where it was supposed to be. Along with information about the housing units and other facilities, the envelope contained a form for Leonard to list his "field-of-research preferences." The four research areas at Pilgrim Lake were: Cancer, Plant Biology, Quantitative Biology, and Genomics and Bioinformatics. Leonard put a "1" by Cancer, a "2" by Plant Biology, a "3" by Quantitative Biology, and a "4" by Genomics and Bioinformatics. It wasn't much, but filling out the form and returning it to the lab signified Leonard's first accomplishment that summer, the only tangible sign that he had a postgraduate future.

Once they arrived at Pilgrim Lake the last weekend in August, the signs proliferated. They were given a key to an ample-size apartment. The kitchen cabinets were stocked with brand-new dishes and almost-new pots and pans. The living room had a sofa, two chairs, a dining table, and a desk. The bed was queen-size and all the lights and plumbing functioned. Sharing Leonard's underfurnished studio all summer had felt more like squatting than living together. But there was a newlywed excitement to crossing the threshold of their new waterfront abode. Leonard immediately stopped feeling like an invalid Madeleine was taking care of and began feeling more like himself.

His renewed confidence lasted until the welcoming dinner on Sunday night. At Madeleine's urging, Leonard had worn a tie and jacket. He expected to be overdressed, but when they arrived in the bar adjacent to the dining hall, nearly all the men were wearing coats and ties, and Leonard was left admiring Madeleine's ability to intuit such things. They picked up their name tags and seating assignment and joined the stiff cocktail reception. They'd mingled for no more than ten minutes before the other two guys assigned to Leonard's team came up to introduce themselves. Carl Beller and Vikram Jaitly already knew each other from MIT. Though they hadn't been at Pilgrim Lake any longer than Leonard (that is, two days), they radiated a sense of all-knowingness about the lab and its operations.

"So," Beller asked, "what did you mark for research preference? First choice."

"Cancer," Leonard said.

Beller and Jaitly seemed amused by this.

"That's what everyone marked," Jaitly said. "Like ninety percent."

"So what happened was," Beller explained, "Cancer was so oversubscribed they ended up giving a lot of people their second or third choice."

"What are we?"

"We're Genomics and Bioinformatics," Beller said.

"I put that last," Leonard said.

"Really?" Jaitly said, sounding surprised. "Most people put Quantitative last."

"How do you feel about yeast labs?" Beller asked.

"Sort of partial to *Drosophila*, myself," Leonard said.

"Too bad. Yeast are going to be our world for the next nine months."

"I'm just happy I'm here," Leonard said, with genuine sincerity.

"Sure, it'll look great on our résumés," Jaitly said, snatching an appetizer from a passing tray. "And the creature comforts are seriously large. But even at a place like this you can get stuck in a research backwater."

Like all of the other RFs, Leonard had been hoping to get assigned to the team of a well-known biologist, maybe even Dr. Malkiel himself. A few minutes later, however, when their team leader appeared, Leonard squinted at his nametag without recognition. Bob Kilimnik was a man in his forties with a loud voice and a disinterest in maintaining eye contact. The tweed coat he was wearing looked too hot for the weather.

"So, the gang's all here," Kilimnik said. "Welcome to Pilgrim Lake Lab." He waved one arm, indicating the lavish dining hall, the white-coated waiters, and the rows of tables set with bunches of wildflowers. "Don't get used to it. This isn't what research is usually like. Usually it's take-out pizza and instant coffee."

Administrative assistants began herding everyone in to dinner. After they sat down, the waiter informed them that it was lobster night. In addition to Madeleine, Beller's wife, Christine, and Jaitly's girlfriend, Alicia, were at the table. Leonard was gratified to see that Madeleine was better-looking than both of them. Alicia lived in New York, and complained that she had to drive back right after dinner. Christine wanted to know if anybody else had a bidet in their unit, and what was the deal with that. While the appetizers were served and a bottle of Pouilly-Fuissé made the rounds, Kilimnik asked Beller and Jaitly about various biology professors at MIT, all of whom he seemed to know personally. When the main course arrived, he started explaining the details of his yeast research.

There were a lot of possible reasons for Leonard's inability to follow a good bit of what Kilimnik said. For one thing, Leonard was a little starstruck by the presence of Dr. Malkiel, who, as Kilimnik was talking, appeared at the end of the room. Elegant, his gray hair swept back from his high forehead, Malkiel escorted his wife to the private dining room already full of senior scientists and biomedical executives. In addition, Leonard was distracted by the elaborate table settings, and by the difficulty of eating lobster with his tremor. With his plastic bib tied around his neck, he tried to crack the claws, but they kept slipping onto his plate. He was scared to use the tiny fork to pull out the lobster tail, and finally asked Madeleine to do it for him, making the excuse that, as a West Coaster, he was used to eating crab. Despite all this, at first Leonard kept up with the conversation. The benefits of working with yeast were obvious. Yeasts were simple eukaryotic organisms. They had a short generation time (from one and a half to two hours). Yeast cells could be easily transformed, either by inserting new genes into them or through homologous recombination. Yeasts were genetically uncomplicated organisms, especially compared with plants or animals, and marred by relatively few junk sequences. All this he understood. But as Leonard put a piece of lobster in his mouth, only to feel sick to his stomach, Kilimnik started talking about the "developmental asymmetry between daughter cells." He mentioned "homothallic" and "heterothallic" strains of yeast, and discussed two apparently well-known studies, the first by "Oshima and Takano" and the second by "Hicks and Herskowitz," as though these names should have meant something to Leonard. Beller and Jaitly were nodding.

"Cleaved DNA molecules introduced into yeast promote efficient homologous recombination at the cleaved ends," Kilimnik said. "Going by that, we should be able to put our constructs near CDC36 in the chromosome."

Leonard had stopped eating by this point, and just sipped his water. His brain felt as if it was turning to mush, seeping out of his ears like the green lobster guts on his plate. When Kilimnik went on to say, "In a nutshell, what we're going to do is put an inverted HO gene into daughter cells to see if this affects their ability to switch sex and mate," the only words Leonard understood were *sex* and *mate*. He didn't know what an HO gene was. He was having trouble remembering the difference between *Saccharomyces cerevisiae* and *Schizosaccharomyces pombe*. Fortunately, Kilimnik didn't ask any questions. He told them that anything they didn't know they would learn in the Yeast Class, which he himself would be teaching.

After that dinner Leonard did his best to get up to speed. He read the relevant articles, the Oshima, the Hicks. The material wasn't that difficult, at least not in outline. But Leonard could barely finish a sentence without drifting off. The same thing happened in the Yeast Class. Despite the stimulating effects of a plug of chaw in his cheek, Leonard felt his mind glaze over for ten minutes at a time while Kilimnik lectured at the blackboard. His armpits grew fiery from the fear that he might be called on at any minute and make a fool of himself.

When the Yeast Class ended, Leonard's anxiety quickly turned to boredom. His job was to prepare DNA, cut it with restriction enzymes, and ligate the pieces together. This was time-consuming, but not all that hard. He might have enjoyed the work more if Kilimnik had said an encouraging word or asked his input on anything. But the team leader barely came into the lab. He spent most of the day in his office, analyzing the samples, barely looking up when Leonard came into the room. Leonard felt like a secretary dropping off correspondence to be signed. When he passed Kilimnik on the lab grounds or in the dining hall, Kilimnik often failed to acknowledge him.

Beller and Jaitly got somewhat better treatment, but not much. They began muttering about transferring to another team. The guys next door were working with genetically altered fruit flies, trying to find the cause of Lou Gehrig's disease. As for Leonard, he used Kilimnik's absence to take frequent breaks, going out behind the lab for a smoke in the cool sea breeze.

His main goal in the lab was to conceal his disease. Once he'd prepared the DNA, Leonard had to put it through electrophoresis, which meant dealing with the gel casting trays. He always had to wait until Jaitly and Beller had their backs turned before he tried to pull the well combs out of the agarose, because he never knew, from moment to moment, how bad his tremor might be. After he managed to load the gels and to run them for an hour or so, he then had to stain the samples with ethidium bromide and visualize the DNA under ultraviolet. And when he was done with all that, he had to start over with the next sample.

That was the hardest task of all: keeping the samples straight. Preparing strand after strand of DNA, and sorting, labeling, and storing each one, despite his flickering attention and mental brownouts.

He counted the minutes until he could leave each day. The first thing he did, on returning home every night, was to jump into the shower and brush his teeth. After that, momentarily feeling clean, with no bad taste in his mouth, he hazarded to lie down next to Madeleine on the bed or the sofa and to put his big sodden head in her lap. It was Leonard's favorite time of the day. Sometimes Madeleine read aloud from the novel she was reading. If she had a skirt on he rested his cheek on her super-smooth thighs. Every night, when it came time for dinner, Leonard said, "Let's just stay here." But every night Madeleine made him get dressed, and they went to the dining hall, where Leonard tried not to betray his nausea or to knock over his water glass.

In late September, when Madeleine went off to her Victorian conference in Boston, Leonard nearly fell apart. For the entire three days she was gone he missed her acutely. He kept calling her room at the Hyatt, getting no answer. When Madeleine called she was usually in a rush to get to a dinner or a lecture. Sometimes he could hear other people in the room, happy, functioning people. Leonard tried to keep Madeleine on the phone as long as he could, and as soon as she hung up he counted the hours until it was allowable for him to call her again. When dinnertime rolled around, he showered, put on clean clothes, and set off along the boardwalk to the dining hall, but the prospect of sparring with Beller and Jaitly on some technical subject persuaded him to buy a frozen pizza at the twenty-four-hour mini-mart in the dining hall's basement instead. He heated it up in his apartment and watched *Hill Street Blues*. On Sunday, with his anxiety increasing, he called Dr. Perlmann to explain how he was feeling. Perlmann phoned in a prescription for Ativan to the pharmacy in P-town, and Leonard borrowed Jaitly's Honda to pick it up, saying he was getting allergy medicine.

And so there he was, three and a half weeks into his fellowship, taking his lithium and Ativan, spreading a dollop of Preparation H between his buttocks every morning and night, drinking a glass of Metamucil with his morning O.J., swallowing, as needed, an antinausea pill he forgot the name of. All alone in his splendid apartment, among the geniuses and would-be geniuses, at the end of the spiraling land.

On Monday afternoon Madeleine came back from the conference shining with enthusiasm. She told him about the new friends she'd made, Anne and Meg. She said she wanted to specialize in the Victorians, even though Austen was Regency, technically, and wouldn't qualify. She gushed about meeting Terry Castle, and how brilliant Terry Castle was, and Leonard was relieved to discover that Terry Castle was a woman (and then less relieved to discover that she liked girls). Madeleine's excitement about the future seemed all the more vibrant against Leonard's sudden lack of it. He was more or less sane now, more or less healthy, but he felt none of his usual energy or curiosity, none of his old animal spirits. They went walking on the beach, at sunset. Being manic-depressive didn't make Leonard any less tall. Madeleine still fit perfectly in his arm. But even nature was messed up for him now.

"Does it smell out here to you?" he asked.

"It smells like the ocean."

"I don't smell anything."

Sometimes they drove into Provincetown for lunch or dinner. Leonard tried, as best he could, to take things one day at a time. He did his work at the lab and soldiered through the evenings. He tried to keep his stress levels to a minimum. But a week after MacGregor's Nobel was announced, Madeleine told Leonard, during their evening walk, that her sister, Alwyn, was having "a marriage crisis" and that her mother was bringing her to the Cape to talk things over.

Leonard always dreaded meeting the parents of a girl he was dating. If there had been a blessing to Madeleine's breaking up with him last spring and his ensuing breakdown, it had been the removal of the obligation to meet Mr. and Mrs. Hanna on graduation day. Over the summer, none too eager to be seen in his bloated, shaky state, Leonard had managed to put off the meeting by hiding out in Providence. But he couldn't put it off any longer.

The day started off memorably, if a little too early, with the sound of Jaitly and Alicia going at it in the upstairs apartment. The building they lived in, Starbuck, was a refurbished barn and had absolutely no sound-proofing. It didn't just sound as if Jaitly and Alicia were in the same room with them. It sounded as if they were in the same bed, scrumping right between Madeleine and Leonard, showing them how it was done.

When things quieted down, Leonard got up to take a piss. He swallowed three lithium tablets with his morning coffee, watching dawn spread across the bay. He felt pretty decent, actually. He thought it was going to be one of his good days. He dressed a little better than usual, in khakis and a white button-down shirt. At the lab, he fired up some Violent Femmes on the boom box and started preparing some samples. When Jaitly came in, Leonard kept smiling at him.

"How did you sleep, Vikram?"

"Fine."

"Any mattress burns?"

"What, were you like—you asshole!"

"Don't blame me. I was just lying in bed, minding my own business."

"Yeah, well, Alicia only comes up on the weekends. You've got Madeleine here all the time."

"That I do, Vikram. That I do."

"Could you really hear us?"

"Nah. I'm just giving you shit."

"Don't say anything to Alicia. She'd be so embarrassed! Promise?"

"Your operatic secret is safe with me," Leonard said.

By ten o'clock, however, the mental fog began to move in. Leonard got a headache. His ankles were so swollen from water retention that he felt like Godzilla stomping back and forth from the 30-degrees room. Later, taking a well comb out of a tray, Leonard's hand trembled, creating bubbles in the gel, and he had to throw the tray out and start all over.

He was having GI troubles, too. Taking his pills with coffee on an empty stomach had been a bad idea. Not wanting to stink up the lab bathroom, Leonard went back to his apartment at lunchtime, relieved to find that Madeleine had already left to pick up her mother and sister. He shut himself in the john with *The Atrocity Exhibition*, hoping to be quick, but the propulsive session made him feel so befouled that he stripped down and took a shower. Afterward, instead of re-donning his nice clothes, he put on shorts and a T-shirt and tied a bandanna around his head. He was facing more time in the 30-degrees room and he wanted to be comfortable. He stuck a can of Skoal into one tube sock and heavy-footed it back to the lab.

Madeleine brought her mom and sister by in the afternoon. Phyllida was both more formal and less intimidating than he expected. Her Brahmin accent, the likes of which Leonard hadn't heard outside a 1930s newsreel, was truly astonishing. For the first ten minutes, as he was showing her around the lab, he kept thinking that she was putting it on. The entire experience was like receiving a visit from Her Majesty. Phyllida was all hairdo and handbag, full of high-pitched interrogatives, and eager to put her eye to a microscope and be informed of her subject's latest scientific work. Leonard was pleased to discover that Phyllida was smart, and even had a sense of humor. He went into geek mode, explaining the particularities of yeast, and, for a moment, he felt like a real biologist.

The difficult part of the meeting was with the sister. Despite Madeleine's insistence that her family was "normal" and "happy," the vibe Leonard got from Alwyn suggested otherwise. The hostility coming off her was as easy to see as bromophenol blue dye. Her puffy freckled face had the same ingredients as Madeleine's, only mixed in the wrong proportions. She'd clearly suffered from being the less pretty sister all her life.

She looked bored by everything he said, and in physical discomfort. Leonard was relieved when Madeleine took Alwyn and Phyllida away.

Overall, he thought that the visit had gone reasonably well. He hadn't shaken too visibly; he'd managed to keep up his end of the conversation and to look at Phyllida with polite interest. That evening, when he came back to the apartment, Madeleine greeted him wearing only a bath towel. Then that was gone, too. He took her over to the bed, trying not to think too much. Taking off his pants, he was reassured to see that he had a perfectly adequate erection. He tried to move through this window of opportunity, but the practicalities of birth control shut the window as quickly as it had opened. And then, embarrassingly, he had begun to cry. To press his face into the mattress and weep. Who knew if this was a real emotion? Maybe it was just the drug doing something to him. The calculating presence who inhabited the back of his mind figured that crying would soften Madeleine toward him, would bring her near. And it worked. She cradled him, rubbing his back, whispering that she loved him.

At that point, he must have fallen asleep. When he awoke he was alone. The pillowcase was damp, as was the sheet beneath him. The bedside clock said 10:17. He lay in the dark, his heart beating wildly, seized with the fear that Madeleine had left for good. After a half hour, Leonard got out of bed and took an Ativan; soon, he fell asleep again.

The following Friday, in Perlmann's office at Mass Gen, Leonard stated his case.

"I've been taking eighteen hundred milligrams since June. Now it's October. That's four months."

"And you seem to be tolerating the lithium pretty well."

"Well? Look at my hand." Leonard held it out. It was as steady as a rock. "Just wait. It'll start shaking in a minute."

"Your serum levels look good. Kidney function, thyroid function— both fine. Your kidneys clear the stuff really fast. That's the reason you need this high a dose to keep your lithium level therapeutic."

Leonard had driven to Boston with Madeleine, in the Saab. The night before, a little after ten, Kilimnik had called Leonard at his apartment, saying that he needed a batch of new samples the next morning and that Leonard should prepare them that night. Leonard had gone over to the lab in the dark and had run the gel trays, visualized the

DNA, and left the fragment images on Kilimnik's desk. As he was leaving, he noticed that Beller or Jaitly had left one of the microscopes on. He was about to switch off the illuminator when he noticed that there was a slide on the stage. So he bent over to have a look.

Gazing into a microscope still brought Leonard the same amazement as it had the first time he'd done it, on a used Toys "R" Us model he'd gotten for Christmas when he was ten. It always felt kinetic, as if he wasn't looking through an objective lens so much as diving headfirst into the microscopic world. From being left on, the eyepiece was uncomfortably hot. Leonard turned the coarse focus and then the fine focus and there they were: a herd of haploid yeast cells undulating like children in the surf at Race Point Beach. Leonard could see the cells so clearly he was surprised they didn't react to his presence; but they remained oblivious, as always, swimming in their circle of light. Even in the emotion-free medium of the agar broth, the haploid cells seemed to take their solitary condition as undesirable. One haploid, in the lower left quadrant, was orienting itself toward the haploid cell next to it. There was something beautiful and dance-like about this. Leonard felt like watching the whole performance, but it would take hours and he was tired. Switching off the illuminator, he walked back through the darkness to his building. By that time it was after two.

The next day, Madeleine drove him into Boston. She chauffeured him every week, happy to spend an hour browsing the bookstores in Harvard Square. As they made their way along Route 6, under a low-hanging sky same dull gray color as the saltboxes scattered across the landscape, Leonard examined Madeleine out of the corner of his eye. Under the leveling process of college, it had been possible to ignore the differences in their upbringing. But Phyllida's visit had changed that. Leonard now understood where Madeleine's peculiarities came from: why she said "rum" for "room"; why she liked Worcestershire sauce; why she believed that sleeping with the windows open, even on freezing nights, was healthy. The Bankheads weren't open-window types. They preferred the windows closed and the shades drawn. Madeleine was pro-sunlight and anti-dust; she was for spring cleaning, for beating rugs over porch railings, for keeping your house or apartment as free of cobwebs and grime as you kept your mind free of indecision or gloomy rumination. The confident way Madeleine drove (she often insisted that athletes made better drivers) bespoke a simple faith in herself that Leonard, for all his intelligence and originality of mind, didn't have. You went out with a girl at first because the sheer sight of her made you weak in the knees. You fell in love and were desperate not to let her get away. And yet the more you thought about her, the less you knew who she was. The hope was that love transcended all differences. That was the hope. Leonard wasn't giving up on it. Not yet.

Leaning forward, he opened the glove compartment and searched through the tapes, taking out a Joan Armatrading cassette. He put it in.

"This in no way signals approval on my part," he said.

"I love this tape!" Madeleine said, predictably, endearingly. "Turn it up!"

The late-autumn trees were bare as they came into Boston. Along the Charles, joggers were wearing sweatpants and hoodies, exhaling vapor.

Leonard was forty-five minutes early for his appointment. Instead of going inside the hospital, he walked into a nearby park. The park was in about the same shape he was. The bench he sat on looked as though beavers had gnawed on it. Ten yards away, a statue of a Minuteman, spray-painted with graffiti, rose from the weedy grass. With their flint-lock rifles, the Minutemen had fought for liberty and won. If they'd been on lithium, though, they wouldn't have been Minutemen. They would have been Fifteen-minutemen, or Half-hour-men. They would have been slow to get their rifles loaded and arrive on the battlefield, and by then the British would have won.

At two o'clock, Leonard had gone into the hospital to make his case to Perlmann.

"O.K., you stopped taking your lithium on purpose. But the question is, why did you do that?"

"Because I was sick of it. I was sick of how it made me feel."

"Which was how?"

"Dumb. Slow. Half-alive."

"Depressed?"

"Yes," Leonard allowed.

Perlmann paused to smile. He put a hand on top of his bald head as though to contain a brilliant insight. "You felt horrible *before* you stopped taking your lithium. And that's the dose you want me to put you back on."

"Dr. Perlmann, I've been on this new higher dose for over four months now. And I've been suffering side effects way worse than anything I've ever experienced. What I'm saying is that I feel like I'm being slowly poisoned."

"And I'm saying, as your psychiatrist, that if that were the case we would see evidence of it in your blood work. Nothing that you've described about your side effects sounds out of the ordinary. I would have liked to see them lessening more than they have, but sometimes it takes longer. For your size and weight, eighteen hundred milligrams is not that high. Now, I'm willing to consider lowering your dose at some point. I'm open to it. But the reality is that you're a relatively new patient of mine. I have to evaluate your case in light of that."

"So by coming to see you I put myself in the back of the line again."

"Wrong metaphor. There isn't a line."

"Just a closed door then. Just Joseph K. trying to get into the castle."

"Leonard, I'm not a literary critic. I'm a psychiatrist. I'll leave the comparisons to you."

By the time Leonard rode the elevator down to the hospital lobby he felt exhausted from arguing and pleading. Despite the danger of encountering sick children and getting even more depressed, he ducked into the cafeteria for a coffee and a bear claw. He bought a newspaper and read it cover to cover, killing more than an hour. By the time he went outside to meet Madeleine, at five, the streetlights had come on, the dreary November daylight dying away. A few minutes later the Saab appeared out of the twilight, gliding to the curb.

"How did it go?" Madeleine asked, leaning in for a kiss.

Leonard buckled his seat belt, pretending not to notice. "I was at *therapy*, Madeleine," he answered coldly. "Therapy doesn't 'go.'"

"I was just asking."

"No, you weren't. You want a progress report. 'Are you getting any better, Leonard? Will you stop being a zombie now, Leonard?'"

A moment passed while Madeleine absorbed this. "I can see how you might take it that way, but that's not how I meant it. Really."

"Just get me out of here," Leonard said. "I hate Boston. I've always hated Boston. Every time I've ever been in Boston something bad has happened to me."

Neither of them spoke for a while. After leaving the hospital, Madeleine got onto Storrow Drive, passing along the Charles. It was the long way around, but Leonard didn't feel like telling her.

"Am I not supposed to care how you're doing?" she said.

"You can care how I'm doing," Leonard replied in a quieter voice.

"So?"

"So Perlmann's not lowering my dosage. We're still waiting for my system to acclimate."

"Well, I learned something interesting today," Madeleine said brightly. "I was in a bookstore and I found this article on manic depression and possible cures they're working on." She turned to smile at him. "So I bought it. It's in the backseat."

Leonard made no move to get it. "Cures," he said.

"Cures and new treatments. I didn't read the whole thing yet."

Leonard lay his head back, sighing. "They don't even understand the *mechanism* of manic depression yet. Our knowledge about the brain is vanishingly tiny."

"They say that in the article," Madeleine said. "But they're starting to understand a lot more. The article's about the latest research."

"Are you listening to me? There's no way, without knowing the cause of an illness, that you can come up with a cure."

Madeleine was fighting her way across two crowded lanes of traffic, trying to reach the expressway entrance. In a determinedly cheerful voice, she said, "I'm sorry, sweetie, but part of being manic-depressive means you're, you know, a little depressive. Sometimes you get down on things before you know anything about them."

"Whereas you're an optimist who never heard of a cure you didn't believe in."

"Just read the article," Madeleine said.

After the intersection with Route 3, they stopped for gas. On the hunch that Madeleine, not wanting to cause more friction, would be lenient with him for smoking in the car, Leonard bought a pack of Backwoods. When they were cruising again, he lit one up, cracking the window. It was the one good thing that had happened all day.

By the time they reached the Cape, his mood had improved somewhat. Trying to be nicer, he reached into the backseat and got the magazine, squinting at it in the light from the dashboard. But then he cried out:

"*Scientific American*! Are you kidding me?"

"What's wrong with that?"

"This isn't science. It's journalism. It's not even peer-reviewed!"

"I don't see how that matters."

"You wouldn't. Because you don't know anything about science."

"I was just trying to help."

"You know how you can help? Drive," Leonard said angrily. He opened the window and tossed the magazine out.

"Leonard!"

"Drive!"

They didn't speak the rest of the way back to Pilgrim Lake. When they got out of the car, in front of their building, Leonard tried to put his arm around Madeleine, but she shook it off and went up to the apartment alone.

He didn't follow her. After his absence, he was due back at the laboratory, and it was best if they were apart for a while.

He mounted the boardwalk that led through the dunes, past the sculpture garden, to the genetics lab. It was dark out now, the compound's conglomeration of buildings silvered under a half-moon. There was a chill in the air. The wind brought with it the mouse-cage smell of the Animal House off to his right. He felt almost glad to be going to work. He needed to occupy his mind with nonemotional things.

The lab was empty when he arrived. Jaitly had left him a Post-it that said, cryptically, "Beware the dragon." Leonard turned on the boom box, got a Pepsi from the fridge, for the caffeine, and got down to business.

He'd been working for about an hour when, to his surprise, the door opened and Kilimnik entered. He bore down on Leonard, glowering.

"What did I ask you to do last night?" Kilimnik said in a sharp voice.

"You asked me to run some gel trays."

"A pretty simple task, right?"

Leonard wanted to say that it would have been easier if Kilimnik hadn't called so late, but he thought it wise to say nothing.

"Look at the numbers on these," Kilimnik said.

He thrust out the images. Leonard obediently took them from him.

"These are the same numbers as the series you gave me *two days ago*," Kilimnik said. "You mixed up the samples! What are you, brain-dead?"

"I'm sorry," Leonard said. "I came over last night right after you called me."

"And did a sloppy job," Kilimnik shouted. "How am I supposed to run a study if my lab techs can't follow the simplest protocols?"

Calling Leonard a "lab tech" was intended as an insult. Leonard noted it.

"I'm sorry," he said again, futilely.

"Go," Kilimnik said, dismissing him with a wave. "Get some beauty rest. I don't want you screwing up anything more tonight."

Leonard had no choice but to obey. As soon as he came out of the lab, however, he was so furious that he nearly went back in to tell Kilimnik off. Kilimnik was on his case about mixing up the samples, but the truth was that it didn't matter much. It was abundantly clear—to Leonard, at least—that moving the HO gene to the other DNA strand wasn't going to change the asymmetry between mother and daughter cells. There were a thousand other possible causes for that asymmetry. At the end of this experiment, two to six months from now, Kilimnik would be able to prove, definitively, that the position of the HO gene had no effect on the asymmetry of budding yeast cells and, therefore, that they were now one stalk closer to finding the needle in the haystack.

Leonard imagined saying these things to Kilimnik's face. But he knew he would never do it. He had nowhere to go if he lost his fellowship. And he was failing, failing at the easiest tasks.

Back behind his building he smoked up the rest of his Backwoods until the foil pack was empty.

Madeleine was sitting on the couch when he came in. She had the telephone in her lap, but wasn't talking on it. She didn't look up at him.

"Hi," Leonard said. He wanted to apologize, but doing so proved more difficult than going to the refrigerator to get a Rolling Rock. He stood in the kitchen, swigging from the green bottle.

Madeleine remained on the couch.

Leonard was hoping that if he ignored their earlier fight it might seem as though it hadn't happened. Unfortunately, the phone in Madeleine's lap suggested that she'd been speaking to someone, probably one of her girlfriends, to discuss his bad behavior. A few moments later, in fact, she broke the silence.

"Can we talk?" she said.

"Yes."

"You have to do something about your anger. You lost control in the car today. It was scary."

"I was upset," Leonard said.

"You were violent."

"Oh, come on."

"You were," Madeleine insisted. "You scared me. I thought you were going to hit me."

"All I did was throw the magazine."

"You were in a rage."

She continued speaking. Her speech sounded rehearsed or, if not rehearsed, supplied with phrases that weren't her own, phrases supplied by whomever she'd been speaking with on the phone. Madeleine was saying things about "verbal abuse" and being "hostage to another person's moods" and having "autonomy in a relationship."

"I understand that you're frustrated that Dr. Perlmann keeps giving you the runaround," she said. "But I'm not responsible for that and you can't keep taking it out on me. My mother thinks we have different styles of arguing. It's important for people in a relationship to have rules about the way they argue. What's acceptable and what's not. But when you get out of control like that—"

"You discussed this with your mother?" Leonard said. He gestured toward the phone. "Is that what you were just talking about?"

Madeleine lifted the phone off her lap and set it back on the coffee table. "I talk to my mother about a lot of things."

"But lately mostly about me."

"Sometimes."

"And what does your mother say?"

Madeleine lowered her head. As if giving herself no time for second thoughts, she said quickly, "My mother doesn't like you."

The words hit Leonard like a physical blow. It wasn't just the content of the statement, which was bad enough. It was Madeleine's decision to utter it. A thing like that, once said, was not easily unsaid. It would be there from now on, whenever Leonard and Phyllida were in the same room. It brought up the possibility that Madeleine didn't expect that to happen in the future.

"What do you mean your mother doesn't like me?"

"She just doesn't."

"What *about* me?"

"I don't want to talk about it. That's not what we're discussing."

"We're discussing it now. Your mother doesn't like me? She only met me once."

"And it didn't go very well."

"When she was here? What happened?"

"Well, for one thing, you shook hands with her."

"So?"

"So, my mother's old-fashioned. She doesn't usually shake hands with men. If she does, she's the one to initiate it."

"Sorry. I'm a little behind on my Emily Post."

"And the way you were dressed. The shorts and the bandanna."

"It gets hot in the lab," Leonard protested.

"I'm not justifying how my mother feels," Madeleine said. "I'm just explaining it. You didn't make a good first impression. That's all."

Leonard could see how this might be true. At the same time, he didn't believe that his breach of etiquette could have resulted in Phyllida's turning so definitively against him. But there was another possibility.

"Did you tell her I'm manic-depressive?" he asked.

Madeleine looked at the floor. "She knows," she said.

"You told her!"

"No, I didn't. Alwyn did. She found your pills in the bathroom."

"Your sister went through my stuff? And I'm the one who has bad manners?"

"I got into a huge fight with her about it," Madeleine said.

Leonard went to the sofa and sat next to Madeleine, taking her hands. He felt, suddenly, embarrassingly close to tears.

"Is that why your mother doesn't like me?" he said in a pitiful voice. "Because of my manic depression?"

"It's not just that. She just doesn't think we're right for each other."

"We're great for each other!" he said, trying to smile, and looking into her eyes for confirmation.

But Madeleine didn't give it. Instead, she stared at their clasped hands, furrowing her brow.

"I don't know anymore," she said.

She pulled her hands away, tucking them under her arms.

"What is it, then?" Leonard said, desperate to know. "Is it because of my family? Is it because I'm poor? Is it because I was on financial aid?"

"It has nothing to do with that."

"Is your mother worried I'll pass on my disease to our kids?"

"Leonard, stop."

"Why should I stop? I want to know. You say your mother doesn't like me but you won't say why."

"She just doesn't, that's all."

She got up and took her coat off the chair. "I'm going out for a little while," she said.

"Now I see why you got that magazine," Leonard said, unable to keep from sounding bitter. "You're hoping to find a cure."

"What's wrong with that? You wouldn't like to get better?"

"I'm sorry that I suffer from a mental disease, Madeleine. I know it's terribly uncouth. If my parents had only brought me up better, maybe I wouldn't be this way."

"That's not fair!" Madeleine cried, flaring with real anger for the first time. She turned away, as if disgusted with him, and left the apartment.

Leonard stood rooted to the floor. His eyes were filling, but if he kept blinking fast enough, no tears fell. As much as he hated his lithium, here it was his friend. Leonard could feel the huge tide of sadness waiting to rush over him. But there was an invisible barrier keeping the full reality of it from touching him. It was like squeezing a baggie full of water and feeling all the properties of the liquid without getting wet. So there was at least that to be grateful for. The life that was ruined wasn't entirely his.

He sat on the couch. Through the window he could see the night surf, the crests of waves catching the moonlight. The black water was telling him things. It was telling him that he had come from nothing and would return to nothing. He wasn't as smart as he'd thought. He was going to fail at Pilgrim Lake. Even if he managed to hold on to his fellowship until May, he wasn't going to be asked back. He didn't have money for grad school, or even to rent an apartment. He didn't know what else to do with his life. The fear he'd grown up with, the fear of not having enough money, which no amount of winning scholarships and fellowships had taken away, returned with undiminished force. Madeleine's immunity from want, he realized now, had always been part of her attraction for him. He'd thought he didn't care about her money until this moment, when he realized that, if she left, her money would leave with her. Leonard didn't believe for a minute that Madeleine's mother's objection to him had only to do with his manic depression. The manic depression was just the more allowable of her prejudices. She couldn't have been thrilled that, instead of being Old Money, he was just Old Portland, or that he looked to her like someone in a motorcycle gang, or that he smelled of cheap gas station cigars.

He didn't go after Madeleine. He had acted sufficiently weak and desperate already. It was time now, to the extent possible, to show some backbone and power up. This he achieved by collapsing slowly sideways until he was curled fetally across the sofa.

Leonard wasn't thinking about Madeleine, or Phyllida, or Kilimnik. As he lay on the couch, he thought of his parents, those two planet-size beings who orbited his entire existence. And then he was off, back into the eternally recurring past. If you grew up in a house where you weren't loved, you didn't know there was an alternative. If you grew up with emotionally stunted parents, who were unhappy in their marriage and prone to visit that unhappiness on their children, you didn't know they were doing this. It was just your life. If you had an accident, at the age of four, when you were supposed to be a big boy, and were later served a plate of feces at the dinner table—if you were told to eat it because you liked it, didn't you, you must like it or you wouldn't have so many accidents—you didn't know that this wasn't happening in the other houses in your neighborhood. If your father left your family, and disappeared, never to return, and your mother seemed to resent you, as you grew older, for being the same sex as your father, you had no one to turn to. In all these cases, the damage was done before you knew you were damaged. The worst part was that, as the years passed, these memories became, in the way you kept them in a secret box in your head, taking them out every so often to turn them over and over, something like dear possessions. They were the key to your unhappiness. They were the evidence that life wasn't fair. If you weren't a lucky child, you didn't know you weren't lucky until you got older. And then it was all you ever thought about.

Hard to say how much time passed as Leonard sat on the couch. But after a long while, a light came into his eyes, and he suddenly sat up. Apparently his brain was not completely useless, because he'd just had a brilliant idea. An idea of how to keep Madeleine, defeat Phyllida, and outwit Kilimnik all at once. He jumped up from the sofa. As he made his way to the bathroom he already felt five pounds lighter. It was late. It was time to take his lithium. He opened the bottle and shook out four 300-milligram pills. He was supposed to take three of them. But he took only two. He took 600 milligrams instead of his usual 900, and then he put the rest of the pills back into the bottle and replaced the lid . . .

It had taken a while for anything to happen. The drug dallied coming and going. For the first ten days Leonard felt just as fat, slow, and stupid as ever. But sometime during the second week he experienced periods of mental alertness and rising spirits that felt very much like his old, best self. Using these wisely, Leonard began to jog and to work out at the gym. He lost weight. The bison hump disappeared.

Leonard understood why psychiatrists did what they did. Their imperative, when confronted with a manic-depressive patient, was to nuke the symptoms out of existence. Given the high suicidality of manic-depressives, that was the prudent course of action. Leonard agreed with it. Where he differed was in managing the illness. Doctors counseled patience. They insisted that the body would adjust. And, to an extent, it did. After a while, you'd been on the drugs so long that you couldn't remember what it felt like to be normal. *That* was how you adjusted.

A better way to treat manic depression, it seemed to Leonard, was to find the sweet spot in the lower reaches of mania where side effects were nil and energy went through the roof. You wanted to enjoy the fruits of mania without flipping out. It was like keeping an engine operating at maximum efficiency, all pistons firing, perfect combustion generating maximum speed, without overheating or breaking down.

What had ever happened to Dr. Feelgood? Where had he gone? Now all you got was Dr. Feel-O.K. Dr. Feel-So-So. Doctors didn't want to push the envelope, because it was too dangerous and difficult. What was required was somebody daring, desperate, and intelligent enough to experiment with dosages outside clinical recommendations, someone, that is, like Leonard himself.

At first, he just took fewer pills. But then, needing to reduce in smaller increments than 300 milligrams, he began cutting his pills with an X-acto blade. This worked well enough, but sometimes sent pills shooting onto the floor, where he couldn't find them. Finally, Leonard bought a pill cutter at the P-town pharmacy. The oblong 300-milligram lithium tablets were easily halved, but less easily quartered. Leonard had to place the pill between spongy prongs inside the cutter, closing the lid to bring down the blade. When dividing a pill into fifths or sixths, Leonard had to guesstimate. He took things slowly, dropping his daily dose to 1,600 milligrams for a week and then to 1,400. Since this was what Perlmann promised to do in another six months, Leonard told himself he was just speeding things along a bit. But then he took his dose down to 1,200 milligrams. And then down to 1,000. And finally all the way down to 500.

In a Moleskine notebook, Leonard kept a precise record of his daily dosages, along with notes on his physical and mental state throughout the day.

Nov. 30: Morning: 600 mg. Evening: 600 mg.
Cotton-mouth. Cotton-head. Tremor worse, if anything. Strong
metal taste to saliva.

Dec. 3: Morning: 400 mg. Evening: 600 mg.
Good period this morning. Like a window opened in my Tower of
London head and I could see out for a few minutes. Pretty out
there. Although the gallows are possibly under construction.
Tremor possibly less, too.

Dec. 6: Morning: 300 mg. Evening: 600 mg.
Down four pounds. Good mental energy most of day. Tremor
about the same. Not as thirsty.

Dec. 8: Morning: 300 mg. Evening: 500 mg.
Made it through the night without having to use the bathroom.
Alert all day. Read 150 pp. of Ballard without coming up for air.
No dry mouth.

Dec. 10: Morning: 200 mg. Evening: 300 mg.
Little bit overexuberant at dinner. M. moved my wineglass out of
reach, thinking I was drinking too much. Will increase doses for
next two days up to 300 mg to stabilize.
Hypothesis: Possible that kidney function not as good as Dr. P.
thinks? Or that there are fluctuations? If lithium not flushed from
body, can it be assumed that excess lithium remains in system,
doing its evil business? If so, might this be cause of dead brain,
GI trouble, torpor, etc.? Daily dose may therefore be higher,
effectively, than docs think. Something to think about . . .

Dec. 14: Morning: 300 mg. Evening: 600 mg.
Back to earth, moodwise. Also, no noticeable return of side
effects. Stay on this dose a few days, then lower again.

The notion that he was carrying on significant scientific work entered Leonard's head so smoothly that he didn't recognize its arrival. It
was just suddenly *there*. He was following in the daring tradition of scientists like J.B.S. Haldane, who'd put himself into a decompression
chamber to study the effects of deep-sea diving (and perforated his ear-
drum), or Stubbins Ffirth, who'd poured vomit from a yellow fever patient onto his own cuts to try to prove that the disease wasn't infectious.
Leonard's high school hero, Stephen Jay Gould, had been diagnosed
with peritoneal mesothelioma just the year before, given eight months to
live. Rumors around were that Gould had devised his own experimental
treatment and was doing well.

Leonard planned to confess to Dr. Perlmann what he'd been doing
as soon as he'd compiled enough data to prove his point. Meanwhile, he
had to pretend he was following orders. This involved feigning side effects
that had already disappeared. He also had to calculate when his medications would run out naturally, in order to refill them often enough to
avoid suspicion. All of this was easy to do now that he could think clearly
again.

The problem with being Superman was that everybody else was so
slow. Even at a place like Pilgrim Lake, where everyone had high IQs,
the pauses in people's speech were long enough for Leonard to drop off
his laundry and return before they finished their sentences. So he fin-

ished their sentences for them. To save everyone time. If you paid attention, it was amazingly easy to predict the predicate of a sentence from its subject. Only a few conversational gambits seemed to occur to most people. They didn't like it when you finished their sentences, however. Or: they liked it at first. At first, they thought it indicated a mutual understanding between the two of you. But if you did it repeatedly, they became annoyed. Which was fine, since it meant you didn't have to waste time talking to them anymore.

This was harder on the person you lived with. Madeleine had been complaining about how "impatient" Leonard was. His tremor may have been gone but he was always tapping his foot. Finally, just that afternoon, while helping Madeleine study for the GRE, Leonard, unhappy with the pace at which Madeleine was diagramming a logic problem, had grabbed the pen out of her hand. "This isn't art class," he said. "You'll run out of time if you do it so slow. Come *on*." He drew the diagram in about five seconds, before sitting back and folding his hands over his chest with a satisfied air.

"Give me my pen," Madeleine said, snatching it back.

"I'm just showing you how to do it."

"Will you please get out of here?" Madeleine cried. "You're being so annoying!"

And so it was that Leonard found himself, a few minutes later, vacating the unit in order to let Madeleine study. He decided to walk into Provincetown and lose more weight. Despite the cold, he wore only a sweater, gloves, and his new winter hat, a fur hunting cap with earflaps that tied together. The winter sky was blue as he made his way out of the laboratory grounds and along Shore Road. Pilgrim Lake, not yet frozen, was full of freshwater reeds. The surrounding dunes looked comparatively tall, speckled with clumps of dune grass except for stretches of white sand near the top where the wind kept anything from growing.

Being alone increased the volume of information bombarding him. There was no one around to distract him from it. As Leonard strode along, thoughts stacked up in his head like air traffic over Logan Airport to the northwest. There were one or two jumbo jets full of Big Ideas, a fleet of 707s laden with the cargo of sensual impressions (the color of the sky, the smell of the sea), as well as Learjets carrying rich solitary impulses that wished to travel incognito. All these planes requested permission to land simultaneously. From the control tower in his head Leonard radioed the aircraft, telling some to keep circling while ordering others to divert to another location entirely. The stream of traffic was never-ending; the task of coordinating their arrivals constant from the minute Leonard woke up to the minute he went to sleep. But he was an old pro by now, after two weeks at Sweet Spot International. Tracking developments on his radar screen, Leonard could bring each plane in on schedule while trading a salty remark with the controller in the next seat and eating a sandwich, making everything look easy. All part of the job.

The colder you were, the more calories you burned.

His ebullient mood, the steady pumping of his heart, and the big soft fur hat were enough to keep Leonard warm as he walked along, passing the big houses on the water and the shingled cottages cramming the little lanes. But when he finally arrived in the center of town, he was surprised to see how deserted it was, even on a weekend. Stores and restaurants had started closing up after Labor Day. Now, two weeks before Christmas, only a few were still operating. The Lobster Pot had closed. Napi's was open. Front Street was open. The Crown & Anchor had closed.

He was gratified, therefore, to find a small midday crowd gathered in the Governor Bradford. Climbing on a stool, he looked up at the television, trying to seem like a person with one thought in his head instead of fifty. When the bartender came over, Leonard said, "Are you Governor Bradford?"

"Not me."

"I'd like a pint of Guinness, please," Leonard said, swiveling on his stool and glancing at the other customers. His head was getting hot but he didn't want to take off his hat.

Of the four females in the bar, three were engaged in self-grooming, running their hands through their hair to indicate their readiness for copulation. The males responded by lowering their voices and sometimes pawing the females. If you ignored human qualities like speech and clothing, the primate behaviors became more apparent.

When his Guinness arrived, Leonard swiveled back around to drink it.

"You need to refine your shamrock technique," he said, gazing down into the glass.

"Excuse me?"

Leonard pointed at the foamy head. "This doesn't look like a shamrock. It looks like a figure eight."

"You a bartender?"

"No."

"Then it's not your business, I guess."

Leonard grinned. He said "Cheers," and began sucking down the creamy stout. Part of him wanted to stay in the bar the rest of the afternoon. He wanted to watch football and drink beer. He wanted to watch the human females groom themselves and see what other primate behaviors they exhibited. He, too, was a primate, of course, in the present context, a rogue male. Rogue males stirred up all kinds of trouble. It might be fun to see what he could get going. But he was getting a bad vibe from the bartender, and he felt like walking some more, and so when he finished his drink he pulled a ten-dollar bill out of his jeans and left it on the bar. Without waiting for change he vaulted off the stool and plunged out into the bone-chilling air.

The sky had already begun to grow dark. It was only a little after two and already the day was dying. Staring up, Leonard felt his spirits sink with it. His earlier mental liveliness was beginning to fade. It had been a mistake to drink the Guinness. Thrusting his hands into the pockets of his jeans, Leonard rocked back and forth on his heels. And that was all it took. In further confirmation of his brilliant move, no sooner did his energy sag than he felt it being replenished, as though tiny valves in his arteries were spritzing out the elixir of life.

Buoyed by his brain chemistry, he sauntered farther along Commercial Street. Up ahead, a guy in a leather cap and jacket was going down the steps to the Vault. The throbbing music inside escaped into the street until he closed the door after him.

Homosexuality was an interesting topic, from a Darwinian standpoint. A trait predisposing a population toward sterile sexual relations should have resulted in the disappearance of that trait. But the boys in the Vault were evidence otherwise. It must be an autosomal transmission of some kind, the associated genes hitching rides on sisterly chromosomes.

Leonard proceeded on. He looked at the driftwood sculptures in the shuttered art galleries and the homoerotic postcards in the windows of a stationery store, still open. Right then he noticed a surprising thing.

Across the street, a saltwater taffy shop appeared to be open. The neon sign was lit in the window and he could see a figure moving around inside. Something mysterious but insistent, something that called to his own primate nature, prompted him to draw nearer. He entered the shop, activating a bell on the door. The thing of interest that his cells had been telling him about turned out to be a teenage girl working behind the counter. She had red hair, high cheekbones, and a tight yellow sweater.

"Can I help you?"

"Yes. I have a question. Is it still whale-watching season?"

"Um, I don't know."

"But they have whale-watching boats out here, don't they?"

"I think that's more like in the summer."

"Aha!" Leonard said, not knowing what to say next. He was acutely aware of how small and perfect the girl's body was. At the same time, the sugary smell of the shop reminded him of a candy store he used to go into as a kid with no money to buy anything. Now, he pretended to be interested in the taffy on the shelves, crossing his arms behind his back and browsing.

"I like your hat," the girl said.

Leonard turned and smiled broadly. "You do? Thanks. I just got it."

"Aren't you cold without a coat, though?"

"Not in here with you," Leonard said.

His sensors registered an uptick in wariness on her part, so he quickly added, "How come you're open in winter?"

This proved to be a good move. It gave the girl a chance to vent. "Because my father wants to ruin my whole weekend," she said.

"Your dad owns this place?"

"Yes."

"So you're like the taffy heiress."

"I guess," said the girl.

"You know what you should tell your dad? You should tell him it's December. Nobody wants saltwater taffy in December."

"That's what I *do* tell him. He says people still drive up for the weekend, so we should stay open."

"How many customers have come in today?"

"Like three. And now you."

"Do you consider me a customer?"

She shifted her weight to one hip, growing skeptical. "Well, you're in here."

"I am definitely in here," Leonard said. "What's your name?"

She hesitated. "Heidi."

"Hi, Heidi."

Maybe it was her blush, or the tight fit of her sweater, or it was just part of being a Superman within reach of a super girl, but for whatever reason, Leonard felt himself getting hard at five paces. This was a piece of significant clinical data. He wished he had his Moleskine notebook with him to write it down.

"Heidi," Leonard said. "Hi, Heidi."

"Hello," she said.

"Hi, Heidi," Leonard repeated. "Hi-de-ho. The Hi De Ho Man. Have you ever heard of the Hi De Ho Man, Heidi?"

"Uh-uh."

"Cab Calloway. Famous jazz musician. The Hi De Ho Man. I'm not sure why they called him that. Hi-ho, Silver. Hawaii Five-O."

Her brow wrinkled. Leonard saw he was losing her and so said, "I'm pleased to make your acquaintance, Heidi. Tell me one thing, though. Do you make the saltwater taffy right here?"

"In summer we do. Not now."

"And do you use salt water from the ocean?"

"Huh?"

He approached the counter, close enough to press his boner against the glass front.

"I just always wondered why they call it *saltwater* taffy. Like, do you use salt *and* water, or do you have to use *salt water*?"

Heidi took a step back from the counter. "I've got to do some stuff in the back," she said. "So if you want anything."

For some reason Leonard bowed. "Go to it," he said. "I don't mean to keep you from your labors. It's been nice meeting you, Heidi-Ho. How old are you?"

"Sixteen."

"Do you have a boyfriend?"

She didn't seem to want to say. "Yes."

"He's a lucky guy. He should be in here right now, keeping you company."

"My dad'll be here in a minute."

"I'm sorry I won't be able to meet him," Leonard said, pressing against the counter. "I could tell him to stop ruining your weekends. Before I go, though, I think I'll buy some taffy."

Again he perused the racks. When he bent forward, his hat fell off and he caught it. Perfect reflexes. Like Fred Astaire. He could flip it in the air, end over end, right onto his head if he wanted to.

"Saltwater taffy is always pastel," he commented. "Why is that?"

This time Heidi didn't respond at all.

"You know what I think it is, Heidi? I think pastels are the palette of the seashore. I'll take these pastel green ones, which are the color of dune grass, and I'll take some pink ones, which are like the sun setting on the water. And I'll take these white ones, which are like sea foam, and these yellow ones, which are like the sun on the sand."

He brought all four bags to the counter, then decided to take a few other flavors. Buttercream. Chocolate. Strawberry. Seven bags in all.

"You want all these?" Heidi said, incredulous.

"Why not?"

"I don't know. It's just a lot."

"I like a lot a lot," Leonard said.

She rang up his purchase. Leonard reached into his pocket and took out his cash.

"Keep the change," Leonard said. "But I need a bag to carry all this in."

"I don't have a bag big enough for all this. Unless you want a trash bag."

"A trash bag is perfect," Leonard said.

Heidi disappeared into the back of the shop. She came out with a dark green twenty-five-gallon heavy-duty trash bag and began putting the bags of taffy in it. She had to bend forward to do so.

Leonard stared at her little tits in the tight sweater. He knew exactly what to do. He waited until she lifted the trash bag over the counter. Then, taking it from her, he said, "You know what? Since your dad's not here?" And holding her wrists, he leaned forward and kissed her. Not long. Not deeply. Just a peck on her lips, surprising her totally. Her eyes grew wide.

"Merry Christmas, Heidi," he said, "Merry Christmas," and he whirled out the door into the street.

He was grinning madly now. Slinging the trash bag over his back like a sailor, he strode down the street. His erection hadn't subsided. He was trying to remember what his dose had been that morning and wondering if he might need a touch more.

The logic of his brilliant move rested on one premise: that manic depression, far from being a liability, was an advantage. It was a selected trait. If it wasn't selected for, then the "disorder" would have disappeared long ago, bred out of the population like anything else that didn't increase the odds of survival. The advantage was obvious. The advantage was the energy, the creativity, the feeling of genius, almost, that Leonard felt right now. There was no telling how many great historical figures had been manic-depressives, how many scientific and artistic breakthroughs had occurred to people during manic episodes.

He picked up speed, hurrying home. Came out of the town and passed the lake again, the dunes.

Madeleine was on the couch, her beautiful face stuck into the GRE booklet, when he came in.

Leonard tossed the trash bag on the floor. Without a word he lifted Madeleine off the couch and carried her into the bedroom, laying her on the bed.

He undid his belt and took off his pants and stood before her, grinning.

Without the usual preliminaries, he pulled off Madeleine's tights and underwear and plunged into her as far as he could go. His cock felt wondrously hard. He was giving Madeleine what Phyllida could never give her, and thereby exercising his advantage. He felt the most exquisite sensations at the end of his dick. Nearly weeping with the pleasure of it, he cried out, "I love you, I love you," and he meant what he said.

Afterward, they lay curled up, catching their breath.

Madeleine said slyly, happily, "I guess you *are* better."

At which Leonard sat up. His head wasn't crowded with thoughts. There was only one. Rolling off the bed onto his knees, Leonard took Madeleine's hands in his much bigger hands. He'd just figured out the solution to all his problems, romantic, financial, and strategic. One brilliant move deserved another.

"Marry me," he said.

Asleep in the Lord

Mitchell had never so much as changed a baby's diaper before. He'd never nursed a sick person, or seen anyone die, and now here he was, surrounded by a mass of dying people, and it was his job to help them die at peace, knowing they were loved.

For the past three weeks, Mitchell had been volunteering at the Home for Dying Destitutes. He'd been going five days a week, from nine in the morning until a little after one, and doing whatever needed doing. This included giving the men medicine, feeding them, administering head massages, sitting on their beds and providing company, looking into their faces and holding their hands. It wasn't something you had to learn how to do, and yet, in his twenty-two years on the planet, Mitchell had done few of these things before and some of them not at all.

He'd been traveling for four months, visiting three different continents and nine different countries, but Calcutta felt like the first real place he'd been. This had partly to do with the fact that he was alone. He missed having Larry around. Before Mitchell left Athens, when they'd made their plans to reunite in the spring, the discussion had skirted around the reason Larry was staying on in Greece. That Larry was now sleeping with men wasn't a big deal in the larger scheme of things. But it cast a complicating light on their friendship—and especially the drunken night in Venice—and made them both feel awkward.

If Mitchell had been able to return Larry's affection, his life might have been a lot different right now. As it was, the whole thing was beginning to look fairly comical and Shakespearean: Larry loved Mitchell, who loved Madeleine, who loved Leonard Bankhead. Being alone, in the poorest city on earth, where he didn't know anyone, pay phones were nonexistent, and mail service slow, didn't end this romantic farce, but it got Mitchell offstage.

The other reason Calcutta felt real was that he was here for a purpose. Until now he'd been merely sightseeing. The best he could say about his travels so far was that they described the route of a pilgrimage that had led him to his present location.

He'd spent his first week in the city exploring. He'd attended mass at an Anglican church with a gaping hole in the roof and a congregation of six octogenarians. At a Communist playhouse, he'd sat through a three-hour production of *Mother Courage* in Bengali. He'd walked up and down Chowringhee Road, past astrologers reading faded Tarot cards and barbers cutting hair while squatting at the curb. A street vendor had summoned Mitchell over to look at his wares: a pair of prescription eyeglasses and a used toothbrush. The uninstalled sewer pipe in the road was big enough for a family to camp inside. At the Bank of India, the businessman in front of Mitchell in line was wearing a solar-powered wristwatch. The policemen directing traffic were as expressive as Toscanini. The cows were skinny and wore eye makeup, like fashion models. Everything Mitchell saw, tasted, or smelled was different from what he was used to.

From the minute his plane touched down at Calcutta International Airport at two a.m., Mitchell had found India to be the perfect place to disappear. The trip into the city had proceeded through near-total darkness. Through the curtained rear window of the Ambassador cab, Mitchell discerned stands of eucalyptus trees lining the lightless highway. The apartment buildings, when they reached them, were hulking and dark. The only light came from bonfires burning in the middle of intersections.

The taxi had taken him to the Salvation Army Guest House, on Sudder Street, and it was there that he'd been staying ever since. His roommates were a thirty-seven-year-old German named Rüdiger and a Floridian named Mike, an ex–appliance salesman. The three of them shared a small guest lodge across from the crowded main building. The neighborhood around Sudder Street constituted the city's minimal tourist district. Across the street stood a palmy hotel that catered to old India hands, mainly Brits. A few blocks away, up Jawaharlal Nehru Road, was the Oberoi Grand with its turbaned doormen. The restaurant on the corner, catering to backpacker tastes, served banana pancakes and hamburgers made from water buffalo. Mike claimed you could get bhang lassi on the next street over.

Most people didn't come to India to volunteer for a Catholic order of nuns. Most people came to visit ashrams, smoke ganja, and live on next to nothing. At breakfast one morning, Mitchell had walked into the dining room to find Mike sharing a table with a Californian in his sixties, dressed all in red.

"Anybody sitting here?" Mitchell asked, pointing to an empty chair.

The Californian, whose name was Herb, lifted his eyes to Mitchell's. Herb considered himself a spiritual person. The way he held your gaze let this be known. "Our table is your table," he said.

Mike was munching a piece of toast. After Mitchell sat down, Mike swallowed and said to Herb, "So go on."

Herb sipped his tea. He was balding, with a shaggy gray beard. Around his neck hung a locket bearing a photograph of Bhagwan Shree Rajneesh.

"There's an amazing energy in Poona," Herb said. "It's something you can feel when you're there."

"I've heard about the energy," Mike said, winking at Mitchell. "I'd like to maybe visit. Where is Poona, exactly?"

"Southeast of Bombay," Herb said.

Originally the Rajneeshees—who referred to themselves as "devotees"—had worn saffron clothing. But recently the Bhagwan had decided that there was too much saffron in circulation. So he'd put out the order for his disciples to start wearing red.

"What do you guys do out there?" Mike pursued. "I hear you guys have orgies."

There was toleration in Herb's mild smile. "Let me try to put it in terms you'll understand," he said. "It's not acts in themselves that are good or evil. It's the intention of the acts. For a lot of people, it's best to keep things simple. Sex is bad. Sex is a no-no. But for other people, who have, let's say, attained a higher level of enlightenment, the categories of good and evil pass away."

"So are you saying you have orgies out there?" Mike persisted.

Herb looked at Mitchell. "Our friend here has a one-track mind."

"O.K.," Mike said. "What about levitating? I hear people levitate."

Herb gathered his gray beard in both hands. Finally he allowed, "People levitate."

Throughout this discussion Mitchell busied himself with buttering toast and dropping cubes of raw sugar into his teacup. It was important to scarf down as much toast as possible before the waiters stopped serving.

"If I went to Poona would they let me in?" Mike asked.

"No," Herb said.

"If I wore all red would they?"

"To stay at the ashram you'd have to be a sincere devotee. The Bhagwan would see that you're not sincere, no matter what you're wearing."

"I'm interested, though," Mike said. "I'm just kidding about the sex. The whole philosophy and everything, it's interesting."

"You're full of shit, Mike," Herb said. "I know bullshit when I see it."

"Do you?" Mitchell suddenly said.

The challenge in this was clear, but Herb retained his equanimity, sipping tea. He glanced at Mitchell's cross. "How's your friend Mother Teresa?" he asked.

"She's fine."

"I read somewhere that she was just in Chile. Apparently, she's good friends with Pinochet."

"She travels a lot to raise money," Mitchell said.

"Man," Mike lamented, "I'm starting to feel sorry for myself. You've got the Bhagwan, Herbie. Mitchell's got Mother Teresa. Who do I have? Nobody."

Like the dining room itself, the toast was trying to be British, and failing. The bread slices were the right shape. They *looked* like bread. But instead of being toasted they'd been grilled over a charcoal fire and tasted of ash. Even the unburnt slices had a funny, unbreadlike taste.

People were still coming in to breakfast, filing up from the dormitories on the first floor. A group of sunburned Kiwis entered, each carrying a jar of Marmite, followed by two women with kohl-rimmed eyes and toe rings.

"You know why I came here?" Mike was saying. "I came because I lost my job. The economy's in the toilet, so I thought, what the hell, I'll go to India. You can't beat the exchange rate."

He began to recite a comprehensive list of all the places he'd stayed and things he'd bought for next to nothing. Railway tickets, plates of vegetable curry, huts on the beach at Goa, massages in Bangkok.

"I was in Chiang Mai with the hill tribes—you ever visit the hill tribes? They're wild. We had this guide who took us into the jungle. We were staying in this hut and one of the guys from the tribe, the medicine man or whatever, he comes over with some opium. It was like five bucks! For a chunk this big. Man, did we ever get stoned." He turned to Mitchell. "Have you ever had opium?"

"Once," Mitchell said.

At this Herb's eyes widened. "That surprises me," he said. "That really does. I would have thought Christianity would frown on that kind of thing."

"It depends on the intention of the opium smoker," Mitchell said.

Herb narrowed his eyes. "Somebody's feeling a little hostile this morning," he said.

"No," said Mitchell.

"Yes. Somebody is."

If Mitchell was ever going to become a good Christian, he would have to stop disliking people so intensely. But it was maybe asking too much to begin with Herb.

Fortunately, it wasn't long before Herb got up from the table.

Mike waited for him to get out of earshot. Then he said, "Poona. Sounds like poontang. Having orgies is part of their whole deal. The Bhagwan makes guys wear rubbers. You know what they say to each other? They say, 'I glove you.'"

"Maybe you should join," Mitchell said.

"'I glove you,'" Mike scoffed. "Man. And the chicks buy it. Suck my cock for inner peace. What a racket."

He snorted again and got up from the table. "I gotta go take a shit," he said. "One thing I can't get used to over here? These Asian toilets. Just holes in the floor, all splattery. It's fucking gross."

"Different technology," Mitchell said.

"It's uncivilized," Mike opined, and with a wave he exited the dining room.

Left alone, Mitchell drank more tea and looked around the room, at its faded elegance, the tiled veranda full of potted plants, the white columns marred with electrical wires powering the wicker-bladed fans on the ceiling. Two Indian waiters in dirty white jackets scurried among the tables, serving travelers lounging in silk scarves and cotton drawstring pants. The long-haired, ginger-bearded guy directly across from Mitchell was dressed all in white, like John Lennon on the cover of *Abbey Road*.

Mitchell had always thought he'd been born too late to be a hippie. But he was wrong. Here it was 1983, and India was full of them. As far as Mitchell was concerned, the sixties were an Anglo-American phenomenon. It didn't seem right that continental Europeans, who had produced no decent rock music of their own, should be allowed to fall under its sway, to frug, to form communes, to sing Pink Floyd lyrics in heavily accented voices. That the Swedes and Germans he met in India were still wearing love beads in the eighties only confirmed Mitchell's prejudice that their participation in the sixties had been imitative at best. They liked the nudism, the ecology, the sunshine-and-health bits. As far as Mitchell was concerned, Europeans' relationship to the sixties, as to more and more things nowadays, was essentially spectatorial. They'd looked on from the sidelines and, after a while, tried to join in.

The hippies weren't the only long-haired figures in the dining room, however. Gazing out from the rear wall was none other than Jesus Christ himself. The mural, which for all Mitchell knew existed in every Salvation Army headquarters around the globe, depicted the Son of Man illuminated by a heavenly beam of light, his piercing blue eyes staring straight out at the diners.

A caption proclaimed:

> Christ is the Head of the House.
> The Unseen Guest at Every Meal.
> The Silent Listener to Every Conversation.

At a long table directly beneath the mural, a large group was gathered. The men in this group kept their hair short. The women favored long skirts, bib-collared blouses, and sandals with socks. They were sitting up straight, their napkins in their laps, conversing in low, serious tones.

These were the other volunteers for Mother Teresa.

What if you had faith and performed good works, what if you died and went to heaven, and what if all the people you met there were people you didn't like? Mitchell had eaten breakfast at the volunteers' table before. The Belgians, Austrians, Swiss, and others had welcomed him warmly. They'd been quick to pass the marmalade. They had asked Mitchell polite questions about himself and had politely supplied information about themselves in return. But they told no jokes and seemed slightly pained by those he made. Mitchell had seen these people in action at Kalighat. He'd watched them perform difficult, messy tasks. He considered them impressive human beings, especially in comparison with someone like Herb. But he didn't feel as if he fit in with them.

This wasn't for lack of trying. On his third day in Calcutta, Mitchell had indulged in the luxury of a barbershop shave. In the tumbledown shop, the barber applied hot towels to Mitchell's face, lathered his cheeks and shaved them, and finished by running a battery-powered hand-massaging unit over Mitchell's shoulders and neck. Finally, the barber wheeled Mitchell around to face the mirror. Mitchell looked at himself closely. He saw his pale face, his large eyes, his nose, lips, and chin, and something the matter with it all. The defect wasn't even physical, not a vote of nature so much as people, or not people so much as girls, or not girls so much as Madeleine Hanna. Why didn't she like him enough? Mitchell studied his reflection, searching for a clue. A few seconds later, responding to an urge that was almost violent, he told the barber that he wanted a haircut.

The barber held up a pair of scissors. Mitchell shook his head. The barber held up the electric shaver, and Mitchell nodded.

They had to negotiate the setting, agreeing, after a couple of swipes, on one-sixth of an inch. In five minutes it was done. Mitchell was sheared of his brown curls, which fell in heaps to the floor. A boy in ragged shorts swept them outside into the gutter.

After leaving the barbershop, Mitchell kept checking out his dramatic reflection in the windows along the avenue. He looked like a ghost of himself.

One window Mitchell stopped to look at himself in was that of a jewelry store. He went in and found the case of religious medallions. There were crosses, Islamic crescents, Stars of David, yin-and-yang symbols, and other emblems he didn't recognize. After deliberating among crosses of various styles and sizes, Mitchell chose one. The jeweler weighed the items and elaborately wrapped them, putting them into a satin pouch, placing the pouch into a carved wooden box, and wrapping it with ornate paper before sealing the entire package with wax. As soon as Mitchell was back on the street, he ripped the exquisite package open and took the cross out. It was silver, with a blue inlay. It was not small. At first, he wore the cross inside his T-shirt, but a week later, after he'd become an official volunteer, he began wearing it outside, where everyone, including the sick and dying, could see it.

Mitchell had worried that he might run screaming from the place after ten minutes. But things had gone better than expected. On his first day, he'd been taken around by a friendly, broad-shouldered guy who ran a honeybee farm in New Mexico.

"You'll see there's not much organization around here," the beekeeper said, leading Mitchell down the aisle between the tiers of beds. "People come and go all the time, so you just have to jump in where you can." The enterprise was a lot smaller than *Something Beautiful for God* had led Mitchell to imagine. The men's ward contained fewer than a hundred beds, maybe closer to seventy-five. The women's side was even smaller. The beekeeper showed Mitchell the supply room, where the medications and bandages were kept. He led him past the soot-blackened kitchen and the equally primitive laundry. A nun stood before a vat of boiling water, poking the laundry with a long stick, while another carried wet sheets up to the roof to hang out to dry.

"How long have you been here?" Mitchell asked the beekeeper.

"Couple of weeks. Brought the whole family. This is our Christmas vacation. And New Year's. My wife and kids are working in one of the orphanages. I figured this place might be a little tough on the kids. But taking care of cute little babies? Yeah, sure." With his suntanned skin and blond curls, the beekeeper looked like a surfing legend or an aging quarterback. His gaze was level and serene. "Two things brought me here," he said, before leaving Mitchell on his own. "Mother Teresa and Albert Schweitzer. Couple years ago I went on a real Schweitzer kick. Read everything he wrote. Next thing I know I'm taking premed classes. At *night*. Biology. Organic chemistry. I was twenty years older than anybody else in the class. But I kept going. Finished my premed requirements last year, applied to sixteen medical schools, and got into one. I start next fall."

"What are you going to do with your bees?"

"I'm selling the farm. Turning over a new leaf. Starting a new chapter. Pick your cliché."

Mitchell took it easy that day, settling in. He helped serve lunch, ladling daal into bowls. He brought the patients glasses of water. On the whole, the men were cleaner and healthier than he'd anticipated. A dozen or so were superannuated, with skeletal faces, lying immobile in their beds, but quite a few were middle-aged, and a few even young. It was often hard to tell what they were suffering from. No charts hung from their beds. What was plain was that the men had nowhere else to go.

The nun in charge, Sister Louise, was a martinet with black horn-rimmed eyeglasses. All day long, she stood at the front of the Home, barking orders. She treated volunteers like a nuisance. The rest of the nuns were uniformly gentle and kind. Mitchell wondered how they had the strength, small and delicate-boned as they were, to lift the destitute off the streets into the old ambulance, and how they carried out the bodies when people died.

The other volunteers were a miscellaneous bunch. There was a group of Irish women who believed in papal infallibility. There was an Anglican minister who spoke of the resurrection as "a nice idea." There was a sixty-year-old (gay) New Orleanian who, before coming to Calcutta, had walked the pilgrimage route in Spain, stopping off to run with the bulls in Pamplona. Sven and Ellen, the Lutheran couple from Minnesota, wore matching safari vests, the pockets full of candy bars that the nuns forbade them to give out. The two surly French medical students listened to their Walkmans while they worked and didn't speak to anyone. There were married couples who came to volunteer for a week and college students who stayed a half year or a year. No matter who they were or where they came from, they all tried their best to follow the guiding philosophy.

Whenever Mitchell had seen Mother Teresa on television, meeting presidents or accepting humanitarian awards, looking, every time, like a crone in a fairy tale barging into a grand ball, whenever she stepped up to the microphone that was inevitably too high for her, so that she had to hieratically lift her face to speak into it—a face both girlish and grand-motherly and as indefinable as the oddly accented Eastern European voice that issued from the lipless mouth—whenever Mother Teresa spoke, it was to quote Matthew 25:40: "Whatsoever you do for the least of My brothers, that you do unto Me." This was the scripture she founded her work on, at once an expression of mystical belief and a practical guide for performing charity work. The bodies at the Home for Dying Desti-tutes, broken, diseased, were the bodies of Christ, divinity immanent in each one. What you were supposed to do here was to take this scripture literally. To believe it strongly and earnestly enough that, by some al-chemy of the soul, it happened: you looked into a dying person's eyes and saw Christ looking back.

This hadn't happened to Mitchell. He didn't expect it to, but by the end of his second week he had become uncomfortably aware that he was performing only the simplest, least demanding tasks at the Home. He hadn't given anyone a bath, for instance. Bathing the patients was the main service that the foreign volunteers provided. Every morning, Sven and Ellen, who had a landscaping business back in Minnesota, worked their way down the line of beds, assisting men to the lavatory on the other side of the building. If the men were too weak or sick to walk, Sven got the beekeeper or the Anglican minister to help carry the stretcher. While Mitchell sat administering head massages, he watched people who looked in no way extraordinary perform the extraordinary task of cleaning and wiping the sick and dying men who populated the Home, bringing them back to their beds with their hair wet, their spindly bodies wrapped in fresh bedclothes. Day after day, Mitchell managed not to help with this. He was afraid to bathe the men. He was scared of what their naked bodies might look like, of the diseases or wounds that might lie under their robes, and he was afraid of their bodily effluvia, of his hands touching their urine and excrement.

As for Mother Teresa, Mitchell had seen her only once. She didn't work at the home on a daily basis anymore. She had hospices and or-phanages all over India, as well as in other countries, and spent most of her time overseeing the entire organization. Mitchell had heard that the best way to see Mother Teresa was to attend mass at the Mother House, and so one morning before sunrise, he left the Salvation Army and walked through the dark silent streets to the convent on A.J.C. Bose Road. Entering the candlelit chapel, Mitchell tried not to show how excited he was—he felt like a fan with a backstage pass. He joined a small group of foreigners who had already assembled. On the floor in front of them, other nuns were already praying, not only kneeling but prostrating themselves before the altar.

A flurry of head turnings on the part of the volunteers made him aware that Mother Teresa had entered the chapel. She looked impossibly tiny, no bigger than a twelve-year-old. Proceeding to the center of the chapel, she knelt and touched her forehead to the ground. All Mitchell could see were the soles of Mother Teresa's bare feet. They were cracked and yellow—an old woman's feet—but they seemed invested with the utmost significance.

One Friday morning, his third week in the city, Mitchell rose from bed, brushed his teeth with iodine-treated water, swallowed a chloroquine tablet (against malaria), and, after splashing tap water on his face and nearly hairless head, went off to eat breakfast. Mike joined him, but ate nothing (his stomach was bothering him). Rüdiger came to the table with a book. Finishing quickly, Mitchell went back downstairs to the courtyard and stepped onto Sudder Street.

It was early January, and colder than Mitchell had expected India would be. As he passed the rickshaws outside the front gate, the drivers called to him, but Mitchell waved them off, horrified at the thought of employing a human being as a beast of burden. Reaching Jawaharlal Nehru Road, he waded into traffic. By the time his bus came, ten minutes later, listing perilously from the passengers hanging out the doors, the winter sun had burned off the haze, and the day was heating up.

The neighborhood of Kalighat, in the south, derived its name from the Kali temple at its heart. The temple wasn't much to look at, a kind of local branch building, with headquarters elsewhere, but the streets around it were hectic and colorful. Vendors hawked worship paraphernalia— flower garlands, pots of ghee, lurid posters of the goddess Kali sticking her tongue out—to pilgrims swarming in and out of the temple entrance. Directly behind the temple, sharing a wall with it, in fact—and the reason why the volunteers referred to the place as "Kalighat"—was the home.

Making his way through the throng outside, Mitchell went through the inconspicuous door and down the steps into the semisubterranean space. The tunnel-like room was dim, the only light issuing from street-level windows high in the exterior wall, through which the legs of passing pedestrians could be seen. Mitchell waited for his eyes to adjust. Slowly, as if being rolled in on their beds from a netherworld, the stricken bodies appeared in three shadowy tiers. Able to see now, Mitchell walked down the length of the ward to the supply room in back. There he found the Irish doctor, consulting a sheet of handwritten notes. Her glasses had slid down her nose and she had to tilt her head back to see who had entered.

"Ah, there you are," she said. "I'll have this ready in a moment."

She meant the medicine cart. She was standing in front of it, placing pills into numbered slots in the tray top. Behind her, boxed medical supplies rose to the ceiling. Even Mitchell, who knew nothing about pharmaceuticals, could tell that there was a redundancy problem: there was way too much of a few things (like gauze bandages and, for some reason, mouthwash) and scant wide-spectrum antibiotics like tetracycline. Some organizations shipped medicines days before their expiration dates, claiming deductions on their tax returns. Many of the drugs treated conditions prevalent in affluent countries, such as hypertension or diabetes, while offering no help against common Indian maladies like tuberculosis, malaria, or trachoma. There was little in the way of painkillers—no morphine, no opiate derivatives. Just paracetamol from Germany, aspirin from the Netherlands, and cough suppressant from Liechtenstein.

"Here's something," the doctor said, squinting at a green bottle. "Vitamin E. Good for the skin and libido. Just what these gents need."

She tossed the bottle in the trash, gesturing toward the cart. "It's all yours," she said.

Mitchell maneuvered the cart out of the supply room and started down the line of beds. Dispensing medications was one of the jobs he liked. It was relatively easy work, intimate yet perfunctory. He didn't know what the pills were for. He just had to make sure they went to the right people. Some men were well enough to sit up and take the pills themselves. With others he had to support their heads and help them drink. Men who chewed *paan* had mouths like bloody, gaping wounds. The oldest often had no teeth at all. One after another the men opened their mouths, letting Mitchell place pills on their tongues.

There was no pill for the man in bed 24. Mitchell quickly saw why. A discolored bandage covered half his face. The cotton gauze was deeply recessed into the flesh, as if adhering directly to the skull beneath. The man's eyes were closed, but his lips were parted in a grimace. As Mitchell was taking all this in, a deep voice spoke up behind him.

"Welcome to India."

It was the beekeeper, holding fresh gauze, tape, and a pair of scissors.

"Staph infection," he said, gesturing toward the bandaged man. "Guy probably cut himself shaving. Something simple like that. Then he goes to wash in the river, or perform *puja*, and it's all over. The bacteria get in the cut and start eating away his face. We just changed his bandage three hours ago and now it needs changing again."

The beekeeper was full of information like this, all part of his interest in medicine. Taking advantage of the lack of trained medical staff, he operated in the ward almost as an intern, taking orders from the doctors and performing actual procedures, cleaning wounds, or picking maggots from necrotic flesh with a pair of tweezers.

Now he knelt down, squeezing his body into the narrow space between the beds. When he laid the gauze and tape gently on the bed, the man opened his one good eye, looking frightened.

"It's O.K., fella," the beekeeper said. "I'm your friend. I'm here to help."

The beekeeper was a deeply sincere, deeply good person. If Mitchell was a sick soul, according to William James's categories, then the beekeeper was definitely healthy-minded. ("I mean those who, when unhappiness is offered or proposed to them, positively refuse to feel it, as if it were something mean and wrong.") It was inspiring to think about the beekeeper, tending his bees in the high desert, raising his children and staying passionately in love with his wife (he often spoke of this), producing honey in every direction you looked. And out of this perfect life had come the need to break out of it, to bring it into real difficulty, even hardship, in order to relieve the suffering of others. It was to be around people like the beekeeper that Mitchell had come to Calcutta, to see what they were like and to have their goodness rub off on him.

The beekeeper turned his sunny face up to Mitchell's.

"How you holding up today?" he asked.

"Fine. I'm just giving out the medicine."

"It's good to see you here. How long you been coming now?"

"This is my third week."

"Good man! Some people poop out after a couple days. Keep on keeping on. We need all the help we can get."

"I will," Mitchell said, and he pushed the cart forward.

He finished the beds in the first and second tiers and turned back to get those on the other side of the aisle, against the inner wall. The man in bed 57 was propped up on one elbow, watching Mitchell in a lofty fashion. He had a fine-boned, patrician face, short hair, and a sallow complexion.

As Mitchell offered him his pills the man said, "What is the point of these medications?"

Momentarily startled by his English, Mitchell said, "I'm not sure what they're for, exactly. I could ask the doctor."

The man flared his nostrils. "They are palliatives at best." He made no move to take them. "Where do you come from?" he asked Mitchell.

"I'm American."

"An American would never languish in an institution of this nature. Isn't that correct?"

"Probably not," Mitchell admitted.

"I should also not be here," the man stated. "Years ago, before my illness, it was my fortune to serve in the Department of Agriculture. Perhaps you remember the famines we had in India. George Harrison made his famous concert for Bangladesh. *That* is what everyone remembers. But the situation in India was equally calamitous. Today, as a result of the changes we made in those times, Mother India is again feeding her children. In the last fifteen years agricultural output per capita has risen five percent. We are no longer importing grain. We are growing grain in sufficient quantities to feed a population of seven hundred million souls."

"That's good to know," Mitchell said.

The man went on as though Mitchell hadn't spoken. "I lost my position due to nepotism. There is great corruption in this country. Great corruption! Then, a few years later, I acquired an infection which devastated my kidneys. I have only twenty percent kidney function left. As I am speaking to you, the impurities are building up in my blood. Building up to intolerable levels." He stared at Mitchell with fierce, bloodshot eyes. "My condition requires weekly dialysis. I have been trying to tell the sisters this, but they don't understand. Stupid village girls!"

The agronomist glared for a moment longer. Then, surprisingly, he opened his mouth like a child. Mitchell put the pills in the man's mouth and waited for him to swallow.

When Mitchell finished, he went to find the doctor, but she was busy in the female ward. It wasn't until he'd served lunch and was about to leave that he had a chance to talk with her.

"There's a man here who says he needs dialysis," he told the doctor.

"I'm sure he does," she said, smiling sadly, and, nodding, walked off.

The weekend arrived, and Mitchell was free to do what he liked. At breakfast he found Mike hunched over the table, staring at a photograph.

"You ever been to Thailand?" he said as Mitchell sat down.

"Not yet."

"Place is stupendous." Mike handed the snapshot to Mitchell. "Check out this girl."

The photograph showed a slender Thai girl, not pretty but very young, standing on the porch of a bamboo hut. "Her name's Meha," Mike said. "She wanted to marry me." He snorted. "I know, I know. She's a bar girl. But when we met she'd only been working for like a week. We didn't even do anything at first. Just talked. She said she wanted to learn English, for her job, so we sat at the bar and I taught her some words. She's like *seventeen*. O.K., so then a few days later, I went back to the bar and she was there again and I took her back to my hotel. And then we went to Phuket together for a week. She was like my girlfriend. Anyway, we get back to Bangkok, and she tells me she wants to marry me. Can you believe it? She said she wanted to come back to the States with me. I actually thought about it for a minute, I'm not kidding you. You tell me I could get a girl like that back in the States? Who would cook and clean for me? And who's a piece of ass? No way, man. Those days are over.

American women are all looking after themselves now. They're basically all *men*. So, yeah, I thought about it. But then I'm taking a piss one day and I get this burning in my johnson. I thought she'd given me something! So I went to the bar and ragged her out. Turned out it was nothing. Just some spermicide or whatever getting up my shaft. I went back to apologize but Meha wouldn't talk to me. Had some other guy sitting with her. Some fat Dutch guy."

Mitchell handed the photograph back.

"What do you think?" Mike said. "She's pretty, right?"

"Probably a good idea that you didn't marry her."

"I know. I'm an idiot. But I'm telling you, she was *sexy*, man. *Jesus*." He shook his head, putting the snapshot back into his wallet.

Having nowhere to go on a Saturday, Mitchell lingered at breakfast for another half hour. After the waiters stopped serving and took his plate away, he wandered into the little lending library on the second floor, browsing the shelves of inspirational or religious titles. The only other person there was Rüdiger. He was sitting cross-legged on the floor, barefoot as usual. He had a large head, wide-set gray eyes, and a slight Habsburg jaw, and he was dressed in clothes he made himself, tight-fitting maroon pants that ended at his calves and a sleeveless tunic the color of fresh ground turmeric. The snugness of his clothes, along with his lithe frame and bare feet, gave him a resemblance to a circus acrobat. Rüdiger was a mercurial presence. He had been traveling for seventeen straight years, visiting, by his own claim, every country in the world except North Korea and South Yemen. He'd arrived in Calcutta *by bicycle*, riding the two thousand kilometers from Bombay on an Italian ten-speed and sleeping out in the open beside the road. As soon as he'd got to the city, he'd sold the bike, making enough money to live for the next three months.

Right now he was sitting still, and reading. He didn't look up when Mitchell entered.

Mitchell took a book from the shelves, Francis Schaeffer's *The God Who Is There*. Before he could open it, however, Rüdiger suddenly spoke up.

"I also cut my hair," he said. He ran his hand over his bristly scalp. "I used to have so beautiful curls. But the vanity, it was so *heavy*."

"I'm not sure it was vanity in my case," Mitchell said.

"Then what was it?"

"Sort of a cleansing process."

"But that is the same thing! I know the person you are," Rüdiger said, examining Mitchell closely and nodding. "You think you are not a vain person. You are maybe not so much into your body. But you are probably more vain about how *intelligent* you are. Or how *good* you are. So maybe, in your case, cutting off your hair only made your vanity heavier!"

"It's possible," Mitchell said, waiting for more.

But Rüdiger quickly changed subjects. "I am reading a book what is fantastic," he said. "I am reading this book since yesterday and I am thinking every minute, Wow."

"What is it?"

Rüdiger held up a frayed green hardback. *"The Answers of Jesus to Job.* In the Old Testament, Job is always asking God questions. 'Why do you do so terrible things to me? I am your faithful servant.' He goes on asking and asking. But does God answer? No. God doesn't say nothing. But *Jesus* is a different story. The man who is writing this book has a theory that the New Testament is a direct response to the Book of Job. He does a whole textual analysis, line by line, and let me tell you, it is *thorough*. I come into the library here and I find this book and it is a doozy, as you Americans say."

"We do not say 'doozy,'" Mitchell said.

Rüdiger raised his eyebrows skeptically. "When I was in America they always said 'doozy.'"

"When was that, 1940?"

"1973!" Rüdiger objected. "Benton Harbor, Michigan. I work for a fine printer for three months. Lloyd G. Holloway. Lloyd G. Holloway and his wife, Kitty Holloway. Children: Buddy, Julie, Karen Holloway. I have this idea to become a master printer. And Lloyd G. Holloway, who was my master, always said 'doozy.'"

"O.K.," Mitchell allowed. "Maybe in Benton Harbor. I'm from Michigan, too."

"Please," Rüdiger said dismissively. "Let's not try to understand each other by autobiography."

And with that he went back to his book.

After reading ten pages of *The God Who Is There* (Francis Schaeffer ran a foundation in Switzerland where Mitchell had heard you could stay for free), he put the book back on the shelf and left the library. He spent the rest of the day walking around the city. Mitchell's concern that he wasn't coming up to the mark at Kalighat coexisted, oddly enough, with a surge of real religious feeling on his part. Much of the time in Calcutta he was filled with an ecstatic tranquillity, like a low-grade fever. His meditation practice had deepened. He experienced plunging sensations, as if moving at great speed. For whole minutes he forgot who he was. Outside in the streets, he tried, and often succeeded, in disappearing to himself in order to be, paradoxically, more present.

There was no good way to describe any of this. Even Thomas Merton could only say things like "I have got into the habit of walking up and down under the trees or along the wall of the cemetery in the presence of God." The thing was, Mitchell now knew what Merton meant, or thought he did. As he took in the marvelous sights, the dusty Polo Grounds, the holy cows with their painted horns, he had got in the habit of walking around Calcutta in the presence of God. Furthermore, it seemed to Mitchell that this didn't have to be a difficult thing. It was something every child knew how to do, maintain a direct and full connection with the world. Somehow you forgot about it as you grew up, and had to learn it again.

Some cities have fallen into ruin and some are built upon ruins but others contain their own ruins while still growing. Calcutta was a city like that. Mitchell walked along Chowringhee Road, gazing up at the buildings, repeating a phrase he remembered from Gaddis, *the accumulation of time in walls*, and thinking to himself that the British had left behind a bureaucracy that the Indians had made only more complex, investing the financial and governmental systems with the myriad hierarchies of the Hindu pantheon, with the levels upon levels of the caste system, so that to cash a traveler's check was like passing before a series of demigods, one man to check your passport, another to stamp your check, another to make a carbon of your transaction while still another wrote out the amount, before you could receive money from the teller. Everything documented, checked over, scrupulously filed away, and then forgotten forever. Calcutta was a shell, the shell of empire, and from inside this shell nine million Indians spilled out. Beneath the city's colonial surface lay the real India, the ancient country of the Rajputs, nawabs, and Mughals, and this country erupted too from the baghs and alleyways, and, at some moments, especially in the evening when the music vendors played their instruments in the streets, it was as though the British had never been here at all.

There were graveyards filled with the British dead, forests of eroded obelisks in which Mitchell could make out only a few words. *Lt. James Barton, husband of. 1857–18–. Rosalind Blake, wife of Col. Michael Peters. Asleep in the Lord, 1887.* Tropical vines infiltrated the cemetery, and palm trees grew near family mausoleums. Broken coconut shells lay scattered over the gravel. *Rebecca Winthrop, age eight months. Mary Holmes. Died in childbirth.* The statuary was Victorian and extravagant. Angels kept vigil over graves, their faces worn away. Apollonian temples housed the remains of East India Company officials, the pillars fallen, the pediments askew. *Of malaria. Of typhus.* A groundskeeper came out to see what Mitchell was doing. There was no place in Calcutta to be alone. Even a deserted cemetery had its custodian. *Asleep in the Lord. Asleep in. Asleep.*

On Sunday, he went into the streets even earlier, and stayed out most of the day, getting back to the Guest House in time for afternoon tea. On the veranda, beside a potted plant, he took a fresh blue aerogram out of his backpack and began writing a letter home. Partly because he used his aerograms as an extension of his own journal, and was therefore writing more to himself than to his family, and partly because of the influence of Merton's Gethsemani journals, Mitchell's letters from India were documents of utter strangeness. Mitchell wrote down all kinds of things to see if they might be true. Once written down, he forgot about them. He took the letters to the post office and mailed them without any thought of what impression they would make on his mystified parents back in Detroit. He opened this one with a detailed description of the man with the staph infection that was eating away his cheek. This led to an anecdote about a leper Mitchell had seen begging in the street the day before. From there Mitchell moved into a discussion of misunderstandings people had about leprosy, and how it wasn't really "that contagious." Next, he scribbled a postcard to Larry, in Athens, giving the return address of the Salvation Army. He took Madeleine's letter out of his backpack, thought about what to reply, and put it back again.

While Mitchell was finishing up, Rüdiger appeared on the veranda. He sat down and ordered a pot of tea for himself.

After it arrived, he said, "So tell me something. Why do you come to India?"

"I wanted to go somewhere different from America," Mitchell answered. "And I wanted to volunteer for Mother Teresa."

"So you come here to do good works."

"To try, at least."

"It's interesting about good works. I am German so of course I know all about Martin Luther. The problem is, no matter how much we try to be good, we cannot be good enough. So Luther says you must be justified by faith. But, hey, read some Nietzsche if you want to know about this idea. Nietzsche thought Martin Luther was just making it easy on everybody. Don't worry if you can't do good works, people. Just believe. Have faith. Faith will justify you! Right? Maybe, maybe not. Nietzsche wasn't against Christianity, as everybody thinks. Nietzsche just thought there was only one Christian and that was Christ. After him, it was finished."

He'd worked himself up into a reverie. He was staring up at the ceiling, smiling, his face shining. "It would be nice to be a Christian like that. The first Christian. Before the whole thing went kaput."

"Is that what you want to be?"

"I am just a traveler. I travel, I carry everything I need with me, and I don't have problems. I don't have a job unless I need it. I don't have a wife. I don't have children."

"You don't have shoes," Mitchell pointed out.

"I used to have shoes. But then I realize it is much better without them. I go all over without shoes. Even in New York."

"You went barefoot in New York?"

"It is wonderful barefoot in New York. It is like walking on one big giant tomb!"

The next day was Monday. Mitchell wanted to post his letter first thing, and so he was late getting to Kalighat. A volunteer he'd never seen before already had the medicine cart out. The Irish doctor had returned to Dublin and in her place was a new doctor who spoke only Italian.

Deprived of his usual morning activity, Mitchell spent the next hour floating around the ward, seeing what he could do. In a bed on the top row was a young boy of eight or nine, holding a jack-in-the-box. Mitchell had never seen a child at Kalighat before, and he climbed up to sit with him. The boy, whose head was shaved and who had dark circles under his eyes, handed the jack-in-the-box to Mitchell. Mitchell saw at once that the toy was broken. The lid wouldn't snap shut, keeping the puppet inside. Holding it down with his finger, Mitchell motioned for the boy to turn the crank, and at the appropriate moment, Mitchell released the lid, letting Jack jump out. The boy loved this. He made Mitchell do it over and over again.

By this time it was after ten o'clock. Too early to serve lunch. Too early to leave. Most of the other volunteers were bathing the patients, or stripping the dirty linens off their beds, or wiping down the rubber mats protecting the mattresses—doing, that is, the dirty, smelly jobs that Mitchell should have been doing also. For a moment, he resolved to start right now, *right this minute*. But then he saw the beekeeper coming his way, his arms full of soiled linens, and with an involuntary reflex Mitchell backed through the arch and climbed the stairs straight to the roof.

He told himself he was just going up to the roof for a minute or two, to get away from the disinfectant smell of the ward. He had come back today for a reason, and that reason was to get over his squeamishness, but before doing that, he needed a little air.

On the roof, two female volunteers were hanging wet laundry on the line. One of them, who sounded American, was saying, "I told Mother I was thinking of taking a vacation. Maybe go to Thailand and lie on the beach for a week or two. I've been here almost six months."

"What did she say?"

"She said the only thing important in life is charity."

"That's why she's a saint," the other woman said.

"Can't I become a saint and go to the beach, too?" the American woman said, and they both started laughing.

While they were talking, Mitchell went to the far end of the roof. Peering over the edge, he was surprised to find himself looking down into the inner courtyard of the Kali temple next door. On a stone altar, six goats' heads, freshly slaughtered, were neatly lined up, their shaggy necks bright with blood. Mitchell tried his best to be ecumenical, but when it came to animal sacrifice he had to draw the line. He stared down at the goats' heads awhile longer, and then, with sudden resolve, he went back down the stairs and found the beekeeper.

"I'm back," he said.

"Good man," the beekeeper said. "Just in time. I need a hand."

He led Mitchell to a bed in the middle of the room. Lying on it was a man who, even among the other old men at Kalighat, was especially emaciated. Wrapped in his sheet he looked as ancient and brown-skinned as an Egyptian mummy, a resemblance that his sunken cheeks and curving, blade-like nose emphasized. Unlike a mummy, however, the man had his eyes wide open. They were blue and terrified and seemed to be staring up at something only he could see. The incessant quaking of his limbs added to the impression of extreme terror on his face.

"This gentleman needs a bath," the beekeeper said in his deep voice. "Somebody's got the stretcher, so we'll have to carry him."

It was unclear how they were going to manage this. Mitchell went down to the foot of the bed, waiting while the beekeeper pulled off the old man's sheet. Thus exposed, the man looked even more skeletal. The beekeeper grabbed him under his arms, Mitchell took hold of his ankles, and in this indelicate fashion, they lifted him off the mattress and into the aisle.

They soon realized they should have waited for the stretcher. The old man was heavier than they'd expected, and unwieldy. He sagged between them like an animal carcass. They tried to be as careful as possible, but once they were moving down the aisle there was nowhere to set the old man down. The best thing seemed to be to get him to the lavatory as soon as possible, and in their haste, they began to treat the old man less like a person they were carrying and more like an object. That he didn't seem aware of what was happening only encouraged this. Twice, they bumped him against other beds, fairly hard. Mitchell changed his grip on the old man's ankles, nearly dropping him, and they staggered through the women's ward and into the bathroom in back.

A yellow stone room, with a slab at one end, on which they set the old man down, the bathroom was lit by misty light filtering through a single stone lattice window. Brass spigots protruded from the walls, and a big, abattoir-like drain was sunk in the middle of the floor.

Neither Mitchell nor the beekeeper acknowledged what a lousy job they'd done carrying the old man. He was lying on his back now, his limbs still shaking violently and his eyes wide open, as if screening an endless horror. Slowly they pulled his hospital gown over his head. Underneath, a soggy bandage covered the old man's groin.

Mitchell wasn't frightened anymore. He was ready for whatever he had to do. This was it. This was what he'd come for.

With safety scissors the beekeeper snipped the adhesive tape. The pus-stained swaddling came apart in two pieces, revealing the source of the old man's agony.

A tumor the size of a grapefruit had invaded his scrotum. At first, the sheer size of the growth made it difficult to identify as a tumor; it looked more like a pink balloon. The tumor was so big that it had stretched the normally wrinkled skin of the scrotum as taut as a drum. At the top of the bulge, like the tied-off neck of the balloon, the man's shriveled penis hung to one side.

As the bandage fell away, the old man moved his palsied hands to cover himself. It was the first sign that he knew they were there.

The beekeeper turned on the spigot, testing the water's temperature. He filled a bucket. Holding it aloft, he began pouring it slowly, ceremonially, over the old man.

"This is the body of Christ," the beekeeper said.

He filled another bucket and repeated the process, intoning:

"This is the body of Christ."

"This is the body of Christ."

"This is the body of Christ."

Mitchell filled a bucket himself and began pouring it over the old man. He wondered if the falling water increased the old man's pain. There was no way to tell.

They lathered the old man with antiseptic soap, using their bare hands. They washed his feet, his legs, his backside, his chest, his arms, his neck. Not for a moment did Mitchell believe that the cancerous body on the slab was the body of Christ. He bathed the man as gently as possible, scrubbing around the base of the tumor, which was venomously reddened and seeping blood. He was trying to make the man feel less ashamed, to let him know, in his last days, that he wasn't alone, not entirely, and that the two strange figures bathing him, however clumsy and inexpert, were nevertheless trying to do their best for him.

Once they'd rinsed the man and dried him off, the beekeeper

fashioned a new bandage. They dressed him in clean bedclothes and carried him back to the men's ward. When they deposited him in his bed, the old man was still staring up blindly, shuddering with pain, as though they'd never been there at all.

"O.K., thanks a lot," the beekeeper said. "Hey, take these towels to the laundry, will you?"

Mitchell took the towels, worrying only a little about what was on them. All in all, he felt proud about what had just happened. As he bent over the laundry basket, his cross swung away from his chest, casting a shadow on the wall.

He was on his way to check on the little boy again when he saw the agronomist. The small, intense man was sitting up in bed, his complexion considerably more jaundiced than on the previous Friday, the yellow leaking even into the whites of his eyes, which were a disturbing orange color.

"Hello," Mitchell said.

The agronomist looked at him sharply but said nothing.

Since he had no good news to impart about the prospect of dialysis, Mitchell sat on the bed and, without asking, began massaging the agronomist's back. He rubbed his shoulders, his neck, and his head. After fifteen minutes, when he was finished, Mitchell asked, "Is there anything I can get for you?"

The agronomist seemed to think this over. "I want to shit," he said.

Mitchell was taken aback. Before he could do or say anything, however, a smiling young Indian man appeared before them. It was the barber. He held up a shaving mug, brush, and straight razor.

"Going to shave!" he announced in a jovial tone.

Without further preliminaries he began lathering the agronomist's cheeks.

The agronomist didn't have the energy to resist. "I have to shit," he said again, a little more urgent.

"Shave, shave," the barber repeated, using his only English.

Mitchell didn't know where the bedpans were kept. He was afraid of what would happen if he didn't find one soon, and he was afraid of what would happen if he did. He turned away, looking for help.

All the other volunteers were busy. There were no nuns nearby.

By the time Mitchell turned back, the agronomist had forgotten all about him. Both his cheeks were lathered now. He shut his eyes, grimacing, as he said in desperation, in anger, in relief, "I'm shitting!"

The barber, oblivious, began to shave his cheeks.

And Mitchell began to move. Already knowing that he would regret this moment for a long time, maybe for the rest of his life, and yet unable to resist the sweet impulse that ran through his every nerve, Mitchell headed to the front of the home, right past Matthew 25:40, and up the steps to the bright, fallen world above.

The street was thick with pilgrims. Inside the Kali temple, where they were still killing goats, he heard cymbals clashing. They built to crescendos and then went silent. Mitchell headed toward the bus stop, going against the flow of pedestrians. He looked behind him to see if he was being followed, if the beekeeper was pursuing him to bring him back. But no one had seen him leave.

The sooty bus that arrived was even more crowded than usual. Mitchell had to climb up on the back bumper with a squad of young men and hang on for dear life. A few minutes later, when the bus paused in traffic, he clambered up to the luggage rack. The passengers there, also young, smiled at him, amused to see a foreigner riding on the roof. As the bus rumbled toward the central district, Mitchell surveyed the city passing below. Bands of street urchins were begging on corners. Stray dogs with ugly snouts picked over garbage or slept on their sides in the midday sun. In the outlying districts, the storefronts and habitations were humble, but as they neared the center of town the apartment buildings grew grander. Their plaster facades were flaking off, the iron grilles on the balconies broken or missing. Mitchell was high enough to see into living rooms. A few were furnished with velvet drapes and ornately carved furniture. But most were bare, nothing in them but a mat on the floor where an entire family sat, eating their lunch.

He got off near the Indian Railways office. In the underlit interior, presided over by a black-and-white portrait of Gandhi, Mitchell waited in line to buy his ticket. The line moved slowly, giving him plenty of time to scan the departures board and decide where he was going. South to Madras? Up to the Hill Country in Darjeeling? Why not all the way up to Nepal?

The man behind him was saying to his wife, "As I explained before, if we travel by bus we must make three deviations. Much better to travel by train."

There was a train leaving for Benares at 8:24 that evening from Howrah Station. It arrived at the holy city on the Ganges the next day at noon. A second-class ticket with a couchette would cost Mitchell about eight dollars.

The speed with which he left the railways office and went about buying provisions for his trip was like that of someone making a getaway. He bought bottled water, mandarins, a chocolate bar, a package of biscuits, and a hunk of strangely crumbly cheese. He still hadn't had lunch, so he stopped at a restaurant for a bowl of vegetable curry and *paratha*. After that, he managed to find a *Herald Tribune* and went into a café to read it. Still with time to kill, he took a valedictory stroll around the neighborhood, stopping to sit by a lime green *bagh* that reflected the clouds passing over his head. It was after four by the time he got back to the Guest House.

Packing up took a minute and a half. He threw his extra T-shirt and shorts into his duffel bag, along with his toiletry case, his pocket New Testament, and his journal. While he was doing this, Rüdiger came into the lodge, carrying a roll of something under one arm.

"Today," he announced with satisfaction, "I find the leather ghetto. There is a ghetto for *everything* in this city. I am walking and I find this ghetto and I have the idea to make myself a super leather pouch to carry my passport."

"A pouch for your passport," Mitchell said.

"Yes, you need a passport to prove to the world that you exist. The people at passport control, they cannot look at you and *see* you are a person. No! They have to look at a little photograph of you. *Then* they believe you exist." He showed Mitchell the roll of tanned leather. "Maybe I make you one too."

"Too late. I'm leaving," Mitchell said.

"So, you are feeling frisky, eh? Where are you going?"

"Benares."

"You should stay at the Yogi Lodge there. Best place."

"O.K. I will."

With a sense of formality, Rüdiger extended his hand.

"When I first see you," he said, "I think to myself, 'I don't know about this one. But he is open.'"

He looked into Mitchell's eyes as if validating him and wishing him well. Mitchell turned and left.

He was crossing the courtyard when he ran into Mike.

"You checking out?" Mike said, noticing the duffel bag.

"Decided to do some traveling," Mitchell said. "But hey, before I go, do you remember that lassi shop you told me about? With the bhang lassi? Can you show me where it is?"

Mike was happy to oblige. They went out the front gate and across Sudder Street, past the chai stand on the other side, and into the warren of narrower streets beyond. As they were walking, a beggar came up, holding his hand out and crying, "Baksheesh! Baksheesh!"

Mike kept on going but Mitchell stopped. Digging into his pocket, he pulled out twenty paise and placed it in the beggar's dirty hand.

Mike said, "I used to give to beggars when I first came here. But then I realized, it's hopeless. It never stops."

"Jesus said you should give to whoever asks you," Mitchell said.

"Yeah, well," Mike said, "obviously Jesus was never in Calcutta."

The lassi shop turned out not to be a shop at all but a cart parked against a pockmarked wall. Three pitchers sat on its top, towels over the mouths to keep out flies.

The vendor explained what was in each, pointing. "Salt lassi. Sweet lassi. Bhang lassi."

"We're here for the bhang lassi," Mike said.

This provoked merriment from the two men loafing against the wall, the vendor's friends, presumably.

"Bhang lassi!" they cried out. "Bhang!"

The vendor poured two tall glasses. The bhang lassi was a greenish brown. There were visible chunks in it.

"This stuff will get you fucked up," Mike said, lifting the glass to his mouth.

Mitchell took a sip. It tasted like pond scum. "Speaking of fucked up," he said. "Can I see that picture of that girl you met in Thailand?"

Mike grinned lecherously, fishing it out of his wallet. He handed it to Mitchell. Without looking at it, Mitchell promptly tore it in half and threw it on the ground.

"Hey!"

"All gone," Mitchell said.

"You ripped my photo! Why did you do that?"

"I'm helping you out. It's pathetic."

"Screw you!" Mike said, his teeth bared, rat-like. "Fucking Jesus freak!"

"Let's see, what's worse? Being a Jesus freak or buying underage prostitutes?"

"Ooooh, here comes a beggar," Mike said derisively. "I think I'll give him some money. I'm so holy! I'm going to save the world!"

"Ooooh, here comes a Thai bar girl. I think she likes me! I'm going to marry her! I'm going to take her home to cook and clean for me. I can't get a woman in my own country because I'm a fat, unemployed slob. So I'll get a Thai girl."

"You know what? Fuck you *and* Mother Teresa! So long, asshole. Have fun with your nuns. I hope they jerk you off, because you need it."

This little interchange of ideas with Mike had put Mitchell in a terrific mood. After finishing the bhang lassi, he returned once again to the Salvation Army. The veranda was closed but the library was still open. In the back corner, sitting on the floor and using the Francis Schaeffer as a writing surface, he began filling up a new aerogram.

Dear Madeleine,

In the words of Dustin Hoffman, let me say it loud and clear:

Don't marry that guy!!! He's no good for you.

Thank you for your nice long letter. I got it in Athens about a month ago. I'm sorry I haven't written back until now. I've been doing my best to keep you out of my thoughts.

I just drank a bhang lassi. A lassi, in case you've never had one, is a cool and refreshing Indian drink made from yogurt. Bhang is weed. I ordered this drink from a street vendor, five minutes ago, which is just another of the many wonders of the subcontinent.

Now here's the thing. When we used to talk about marriage (I mean in the abstract) you had a theory that people got married in one of three stages. Stage One are the traditional people who marry their college sweethearts, usually the summer after graduation. People in Stage Two get married around 28. And then there are the people in Stage Three who get married in a final wave, with a sense of desperation, around 36, 37, or even 39.

You said you would never get married straight out of college. You planned to wait until your "career" was settled and get married in your thirties. Secretly, I always thought you were a Stage Two, but when I saw you, at graduation, I realized you were decidedly, and incorrigibly, Stage One. Then came your letter. The more I read it, the more aware I became of what you weren't saying. Underneath your tiny handwriting is a repressed wish. Maybe that's what your tiny handwriting has been doing all your life, trying to keep your crazy wishes from exploding your life.

How do I know this? Let's just say that during my travels I've become acquainted with interior states that collapse the distance between people. Sometimes, despite how far apart we are physically, I have drawn very close to you, right up into your innermost chamber. I can feel what you're feeling. From <u>here</u>.

I've got to make this quick. I've got a night train to catch and I just noticed that my vision is getting a little sparkly around the edges.

Now, it wouldn't be fair of me to tell you all this without giving you something else to think about. An offer, you could call it. The nature of this offer, however, isn't something a young gentleman (even one like me, who's given up wearing underwear) could very well entrust to a letter. This is something I'll have to tell you in person.

When that will be I'm not sure. I've been in India three weeks and all I've seen is Calcutta. I want to see the Ganges and that's where I'm headed next. I want to visit New Delhi and Goa (where they have the incorruptible corpse of St. Francis Xavier on display in a cathedral). I'm keen on visiting Rajasthan and Kashmir. Larry is still planning to meet me in March (wait until I tell you about Larry!) to do our internship with Prof. Hughes. In short, I'm writing this letter because, if you are indeed a Stage One, there may not be enough time for me to personally disrupt the proceedings. I'm too far away to speed across the Bay Bridge in my sportscar and crash the ceremony (and I would never jam the door with a crucifix).

I don't know if this letter will reach you. I'll have to trust to faith, in other words, which is something I've been trying to do lately with limited success.

This bhang lassi is pretty strong, actually. I've been looking for the ultimate reality but right now there are a few mundane realities I'd settle for. I'm not saying anything. But there is an English graduate program at Princeton. And Yale and Harvard have divinity schools. There are crappy little apartments in New Jersey and New Haven where two studious people could be studious together.

But nothing of that. Not yet. Not now. Please attribute anything untoward that I've written here to the power of the Bengali smoothie. I really only meant to write you a short note. It could have been a postcard. I just wanted to say one thing.

Don't marry that guy.

Don't do it, Mad. Just don't.

By the time he got downstairs, evening had fallen. Crowds of people were walking down the center of the street, the yellow bulbs strung over their heads like lights at a carnival. Music vendors were tooting their wooden flutes and plastic trombones, trying to entice customers, and the restaurants were open.

Mitchell walked beneath the vast trees, his mind humming. The air felt soft against his face. In a sense, the bhang was superfluous. The amount of sensations bombarding Mitchell as he reached the corner— the incessant honking of the taxis, the chugging of the truck engines, the shouts of the ant-like men pushing carts piled with turnips or scrap metal—would have made Mitchell dizzy even if he were completely straight in the middle of the day. This was like a contact buzz on top of a buzz. Mitchell was so absorbed that he forgot where he was going. He might have stayed on the corner all night, watching the traffic move another three feet forward. But suddenly, swooping in from his peripheral vision, a rickshaw stopped beside him. The rickshaw wallah, a gaunt dark man with a green towel wrapped around his head, beckoned to Mitchell, gesturing toward the empty seat. Mitchell looked back at the impenetrable wall of traffic. He looked at the seat. And the next thing he knew he was climbing up into it.

The rickshaw wallah bent down to pick up the long wooden handles of the rickshaw. As quickly as a runner at the starting gun, he darted into traffic.

For a long time they moved sideways through the jam. The rickshaw wallah snaked his way between the vehicles. Whenever he found a seam alongside a bus or a truck he plunged forward until he was forced to cut back again against the grain. The rickshaw stopped and started, swerved, sped up, and abruptly halted, like a bumper-car ride.

The rickshaw seat was throne-like, upholstered in bright red vinyl and decorated with a portrait of Ganesh. The awning was down, so that Mitchell could see the big wooden wheels on either side. Every now and then they came abreast of another rickshaw, and Mitchell looked across at his fellow exploiters. A Brahmin woman, her sari exposing the roll of fat on her stomach. Three schoolgirls doing their homework.

The honking and shouting seemed to be happening in Mitchell's mind. He clutched his duffel bag, putting his trust in the rickshaw wallah to get him where he was going. The driver's dark-skinned back gleamed with perspiration, the muscles and sinews working beneath it as taut as piano strings. After fifteen minutes of zigzagging, they left the main thoroughfare and picked up speed, passing through a neighborhood largely without lights.

The red vinyl seat squeaked like a diner booth. Elephant-headed Ganesh had the sooty eyelashes of a Bollywood idol. Suddenly the sky brightened and Mitchell gazed up to see the steel supports of a bridge. It rose into the air like a Ferris wheel, ringed with colored bulbs. Down below was the Hooghly River, pitch black, reflecting the red neon sign of the train station on the far bank. Mitchell leaned out of his seat to look down at the water. If he fell out of the rickshaw now, he would plunge straight down hundreds of feet. No one would ever know.

But he didn't fall. Mitchell remained upright in the rickshaw, carried along like a sahib. He planned to give the rickshaw wallah an enormous tip when they reached the station. A week's salary at least. Meanwhile, he enjoyed the ride. He felt ecstatic. He was being carried away, a vessel in a vessel. He understood the Jesus Prayer now. Understood *mercy.* Understood *sinner,* for sure. As he passed over the bridge Mitchell's lips weren't moving. He wasn't thinking a thing. It was as if, just as Franny had promised, the prayer had taken over and was saying itself in his heart.

Lord Jesus Christ, have mercy on me, a sinner.
Lord Jesus Christ, have mercy on me, a sinner.
Lord Jesus Christ, have mercy on me, a sinner.
Lord Jesus Christ, have mercy on me, a sinner.
Lord Jesus Christ, have mercy on me, a sinner.
Lord Jesus Christ, have mercy on me, a sinner.
Lord Jesus Christ, have mercy on me, a sinner.
Lord Jesus Christ, have mercy on me, a sinner.
Lord Jesus Christ, have mercy on me, a sinner.
Lord Jesus Christ, have mercy on me, a sinner.
Lord Jesus Christ, have mercy on me, a sinner.
Lord Jesus Christ, have mercy on me, a sinner.
Lord Jesus Christ, have mercy on me, a sinner.

And Sometimes They Were Very Sad

When Alton Hanna had become president of Baxter College in the mid-sixties, leaving his position as dean of faculty at Connecticut College to move to New Jersey, his daughters hadn't come along willingly. On their maiden voyage to the Garden State, the girls had begun holding their noses and shrieking as soon as they saw the "Welcome to New Jersey" sign, long before the car passed any actual oil refineries. Once they were installed in Prettybrook, their homesickness increased. Alwyn complained about missing her old schoolmates. Madeleine found the new house creepy and underheated. She was scared to sleep in her big bedroom. Alton had moved his daughters to Prettybrook thinking they would enjoy the spacious house and the verdant backyard. The news that they preferred the family's cramped town house in New London, a place that was basically all stairs, hadn't been what he wanted to hear.

But there had been little nice to hear in that turbulent decade. Alton had come to Baxter at a time when the school's endowment was shrinking and its student body in florid revolt. His first year in the job, student protesters had staged a sit-in of the administration building. Armed with a comprehensive list of demands—for the elimination of academic requirements, the establishment of a department of Afro-American Studies, the banning of ROTC recruiters on campus, and the divestment of endowment funds from corporations involved with military or oil production—they had camped out on the Oriental runners of Alton's outer office. While Alton met with the student leader, Ira Carmichael, a clearly brilliant kid dressed in army fatigues with his fly ostentatiously open, fifty hirsute undergrads chanted slogans outside the door. Partly to send a signal that this kind of thing wouldn't be tolerated on his watch, and partly because he was a Republican who supported the war in Vietnam, Alton finally had the borough police remove the students forcibly from the building. This had the predictable effect of further inflaming tensions. Soon an effigy of "Hiroshima Hanna" was burning on the college green, his bald head hideously enlarged into the shape of a mushroom cloud. Beneath Alton's office window a swarm of protesters formed each day, baying for his blood. At six o'clock, when the students dispersed (their commitment to the cause didn't extend to skipping dinner), Alton made his nightly escape. Crossing the green, where the charred remnants of his effigy still dangled from an elm, he hurried to his car in the administration parking lot and drove home to Prettybrook to find his daughters still loudly protesting the move to New Jersey.

With Alwyn and Madeleine, Alton was willing to negotiate. He bought Alwyn off with riding lessons at the Prettybrook Country Club. Soon she was sporting jodhpurs and a riding jacket, had formed a near-sexual attachment to a chestnut mare named Riviera Red, and never mentioned New London again. Madeleine was swayed by interior decorating. One weekend, Phyllida took Madeleine into New York. Arriving home on Sunday night, she told Madeleine there was a surprise for her in her room. Madeleine ran up the stairs to find the walls of her bedroom covered by reproductions from her favorite book in the world at the time, Ludwig Bemelmans's *Madeline*. While she'd been in Manhattan, a wallpaper installer had steamed off the old design to replace it with this new one, which Phyllida had had custom-printed at a wallpaper manufacturer in Trenton. Stepping into her bedroom was like entering the pages of *Madeline* itself. On one wall was the austere dining room of Madeleine's convent school, on another, the girls' echoing dormitory. All around the room multiple Madelines were doing brave things, one making a face ("and to the lion in the zoo Madeline just said 'poo poo'"), another balancing like a daredevil on a bridge over the Seine, still another lifting her nightgown to show off her appendicitis scar. The deep, squiggly greens of Parisian parks, the repeated motif of Nurse Clavel "hurrying faster and faster," steadying her wimple with one hand, her shadow elongating with her premonition that "something is not right," and, over by the light socket, the one-legged soldier, on crutches, beneath the caption that said, "And sometimes they were very sad"—the sense conveyed, by the illustrations, of Paris, a city as orderly as the girls' "two straight lines," as colorful as Bemelmans's pastel palette, a world of civic institutions and statues of military heroes, of cosmopolitan acquaintances like the Spanish ambassador's son (a dashing figure, to Maddy, at six), the storybook Paris that wasn't without hints of adult error or misfortune, that didn't candy-coat reality but faced nobly up to it, the singular victory for humanity a great city represented, and which, though vast, didn't scare Madeline, who was so small—somehow all of this had communicated itself to Madeleine as a little girl. And then there was her name, so similar, and the familiar signs of class, and the sense she had of herself, then and now, as being the one in a troop of girls a writer might write a book about.

Nobody had wallpaper like hers. Which was why, as she grew up on Wilson Lane, Madeleine had never torn it down.

It was sun-faded now, and peeling along the seams. One panel, showing a Bouvier in the Luxembourg Gardens, was stained yellow from a roof leak. If moving back in with her parents didn't feel regressive enough already, waking up in her old bedroom, surrounded by the storybook wallpaper, completed the process. Therefore Madeleine did the most adult thing she could do now, under the circumstances: she reached across the bed with her left hand—the one bearing the gold wedding band—and patted the bed to see if her husband was lying next to her.

Lately, Leonard had been coming up to bed around one or two in the morning. He found it difficult to sleep in the double bed, however—he was having insomnia again—and often moved to one of the guest rooms, which was probably where he was now. The space beside her was empty.

Madeleine and Leonard were living with Madeleine's parents because they had nowhere else to go. Leonard's fellowship at Pilgrim Lake had ended in April, a week before the wedding. They'd lined up a sublet in Provincetown for the summer, but after Leonard had been hospitalized, in Monte Carlo, in early May, they'd had to give the place up. Returning to the States, two weeks later, Madeleine and Leonard had moved down to Prettybrook, which, in addition to being a peaceful place for Leonard to recuperate, was within reach of top psychiatric care in

Philadelphia and New York. It was also a good base from which to start looking for a Manhattan apartment. In mid-April, while Madeleine had been honeymooning in Europe, letters from graduate admissions programs had made their way, via the Pilgrim Lake post office, to Wilson Lane. Harvard and Chicago rejected her, but Columbia and Yale sent letters of acceptance. Having been turned down by Yale the year before, Madeleine took pleasure in returning the favor. She didn't want to live in New Haven; she wanted to live in New York. The sooner she and Leonard found a place there, the sooner they could begin putting their life—and their eight-week-old marriage—back together.

With that end in mind, Madeleine got out of bed to call Kelly Traub. She used the phone in Alton's upstairs office, a small beige room, at once cluttered and highly organized, that looked down on the back garden. The room smelled like her father, even more so with the June humidity, and she didn't like to stay in there long; it was almost like pressing her nose into one of Alton's old bathrobes. As she dialed Kelly's office, Madeleine looked down at the gardener, who was spraying a bush with a bottle of something the color of iced tea.

The secretary at Kelly's office said that "Ms. Traub" was on the other line and asked if Madeleine wanted to be put on hold. Madeleine said she'd wait.

In the year since graduation, while Madeleine had been on the Cape, Kelly had been pursuing an acting career with limited success. She'd had a small part in an original one-act, staged over a single weekend in a church basement in Hell's Kitchen, and had also appeared in an outdoor performance piece by a Norwegian artist that involved semi-nudity and paid nothing. In order to support herself, Kelly had gone to work at her father's real estate company on the Upper West Side. The job was flexible, paid reasonably well, and allowed her plenty of time to get to auditions. It also made her the perfect person to call if you needed an apartment near Columbia.

After another minute, Kelly's voice came on the line.

"It's me," Madeleine said.

"Maddy, hi! I'm glad you called."

"I call every day."

"Yeah, but today I've got the perfect place for you. Are you ready? 'Riverside Drive. Prewar one-bedroom. Hudson River view. Office possible second bedroom. Available August first.' You have to come see it today or it'll be gone."

"Today?" Madeleine said doubtfully.

"It's not my listing. I made the agent promise not to show it until tomorrow."

Madeleine wasn't sure she could do it. She'd gone apartment-hunting in the city three times in the past week already. Since it wasn't a good idea to leave Leonard alone, she'd had to ask Phyllida to stay with him each time. Phyllida claimed she didn't mind this, but Madeleine knew that it made her mother nervous.

On the other hand, the apartment sounded ideal. "What's the cross street?" she asked.

"Seventy-seventh," Kelly said. "You're five blocks from Central Park. Five stops to Columbia. Easy to get to Penn Station, too, which you said you wanted."

"That's perfect."

"Plus, if you come up today, I'll take you to a party."

"A party?" Madeleine said. "I remember parties."

"It's at Dan Schneider's. Right by my office. There'll be a ton of Brown people, so you can reconnect."

"First let's see if I can even come up."

The potential obstacle was no mystery to either of them. After a moment Kelly asked in a quieter voice, "How's Leonard?"

This was difficult to answer. Madeleine sat in Alton's desk chair, casting her eyes to the white pines at the end of the yard. According to Leonard's latest doctor—not the French psychiatrist, Dr. Lamartine, who'd taken care of him in Monaco, but the new specialist at Penn, Dr. Wilkins—Leonard didn't have a "pronounced risk of suicidality." This didn't mean that he wasn't suicidal, only that his risk was relatively low. Low enough, anyway, not to warrant his being hospitalized (though this was subject to change). The previous week, on a rainy Wednesday afternoon, Alton and Madeleine had driven down to Philadelphia to meet with Wilkins alone, in his office at the Penn Medical Center. Madeleine had come away from the experience feeling that Wilkins was like any other knowledgeable, well-intentioned expert, an economist, for example, who made predictions based on available data, but whose conclusions were by no means definitive. She'd asked every question she could think of about possible warning signs and preventative measures. She'd listened to Wilkins's judicious but unsatisfactory answers. And then she'd driven back to Prettybrook and resumed living and sleeping with her new husband, wondering every time he left the room if he was going to do violence to himself.

"Leonard's the same," she said finally.

"Well, you should come up and see this apartment," Kelly said. "Come at six and then we can go to this party. Just come for an hour. It'll cheer you up."

"I'll see. I'll call you later."

In the bathroom, a fresh-mown-grass smell drifted through the screens as she brushed her teeth. She looked at herself in the mirror. Her skin was dry, and slightly purplish under her eyes. Nothing much in the way of deterioration—she was still only twenty-three—but different even from a year ago. There were shadows on her face from which Madeleine could extrapolate what her older face would look like.

Downstairs, she found Phyllida arranging flowers at the laundry room sink. The sliding glass doors to the deck were open, a yellow butterfly fluttering above the bushes.

"Good morning," Phyllida said. "How did you sleep?"

"Badly."

"There are English muffins by the toaster."

Madeleine padded sleepily across the kitchen. She took a muffin from the package and began trying to split it with her fingers.

"Use a fork, dear," Phyllida said.

But it was too late: the muffin top ripped off unevenly. Madeleine dropped the uneven sides into the toaster and pressed down the lever.

While the muffin toasted, she poured herself a cup of coffee and sat at the kitchen table. Suitably roused, she said, "Mummy, I have to go into the city tonight to see an apartment."

"Tonight?"

Madeleine nodded.

"Your father and I have a cocktail party tonight." Phyllida meant that they wouldn't be able to stay with Leonard.

The muffin popped up. "But Mummy?" Madeleine persisted. "This apartment sounds perfect. It's on Riverside Drive. With a view."

"I'm sorry, dear, but I've had this party in my book for three months."

"Kelly says it won't last. I have to come today." She felt bad for pressing. Phyllida and Alton had been so good about everything, so helpful to Leonard in his distress, that Madeleine didn't want to burden them further. On the other hand, if she didn't find an apartment, she and Leonard couldn't move out.

"Maybe Leonard will go with you," Phyllida suggested.

Madeleine fished the bigger half of her muffin out of the toaster, saying nothing. She had taken Leonard to the city just last week, and it hadn't gone well. In the crowds at Penn Station he'd begun to hyperventilate and they'd had to take the next train back to Prettybrook.

"Maybe I won't go," she said finally.

"You might as well ask Leonard if he'd like to go," Phyllida said.

"I will when he gets up."

"He *is* up. He's been up for a while. He's out on the deck."

This surprised Madeleine. Leonard had been sleeping late into the mornings. Standing up, she took her coffee and muffin out to the sunny deck.

Leonard was on the lower level, in the shade, sitting in the Adirondack chair where he'd been spending most of his days. He looked large and shaggy, like a Sendak creature. He had on a black T-shirt and baggy black shorts. His feet, clad in old basketball sneakers, were propped up on the porch railing. Plumes of smoke were rising from the area in front of his face.

"Hi," Madeleine said, coming up beside his chair.

Leonard croaked out a greeting and continued smoking.

"How are you doing?" she asked.

"I'm exhausted. Couldn't sleep so I took a sleeping pill around two. Then I woke up about five and came out here."

"Did you get some breakfast?"

Leonard held up his pack of cigarettes.

A lawn mower started up in an adjoining yard. Madeleine sat down on the wide arm of the chair. "Kelly called," she said. "What do you think about coming into the city with me tonight? Around four-thirty?"

"Not a good idea," Leonard said again in his croaking voice.

"There's a one-bedroom on Riverside Drive."

"You go."

"I want you to come with me."

"Not a good idea," he repeated.

The sound of the lawn mower was getting closer. It came right up to the other side of the fence before moving away again.

"Mummy's going to a cocktail party," Madeleine said.

"You can leave me alone, Madeleine."

"I know."

"If I wanted to kill myself, I could do it at night, when you're sleeping. I could drown myself in the swimming pool. I could have done that this morning."

"You're not making me feel better about going into the city," Madeleine said.

"Look. Mad. I'm not feeling too good. I'm exhausted and my nerves are all jangled. I don't think I can handle another trip into New York. But I'm O.K. here on the porch. You can leave me."

Madeleine squeezed her eyes shut. "How are we going to live in New York if you won't even go look at an apartment?"

"That is a paradox," Leonard said. He stubbed out his cigarette, flicked the butt into the bushes, and lit another. "I'm self-monitoring, Madeleine. That's all I can do. I've gotten better at self-monitoring lately. And I'm not ready to go cram into a subway with a bunch of hot, sweaty New Yorkers—"

"We'll take a cab."

"—Or ride around in a hot cab, in the heat. What I *can* do, though, is take care of myself perfectly fine here. I don't need a babysitter. I've been telling you that. My doctor's been telling you that."

She waited for him to finish before bringing the conversation back to the topic at hand. "The thing is, if this place is good, we're going to have to decide right away. I could call you from a pay phone after I see it."

"You can decide without me. It's *your* apartment."

"It's both of ours."

"You're the one paying for it," Leonard said. "You're the one who needs a place in New York."

"You want a place in New York too."

"Not anymore."

"You *said* you did."

Leonard turned and looked at her for the first time. These moments, oddly enough, were the ones she dreaded: when he looked at her. Leonard's eyes had an emptiness to them. It was like looking into a deep, dry well.

"Why don't you just divorce me?" he said.

"Stop."

"I wouldn't blame you. I'd understand completely." His expression softened and became thoughtful. "Do you know what they do in Islam when they want a divorce? The husband repeats three times, 'I divorce thee, I divorce thee, I divorce thee.' And that's it. Men marry prostitutes and divorce them right afterwards. To avoid committing adultery."

"Are you trying to make me sad?" Madeleine said.

"Sorry," Leonard said. He reached out and took her hand. "Sorry, sorry."

It was almost eleven by the time Madeleine went back inside. She told Phyllida that she'd decided not to go into the city. Back in Alton's office, she called Kelly, thinking that maybe Kelly could go see the apartment and describe it to her over the phone, and that she could decide based on that. Kelly was out with another client, however, so Madeleine left a message. While she was waiting for Kelly to call back, Leonard came up the back stairs, calling her name. She went out to find him standing in the hall, holding on to the stair railing with both hands.

"I changed my mind," he said. "I'll go."

Madeleine had married Leonard in the grip of a force much like mania. From the day when Leonard began experimenting with his lithium dosages, to the moment, in December, when he stormed into the apartment with his wild proposal, Madeleine had ridden a similarly cascading wave of emotion. She, too, had been insanely happy. She, too, had been hypersexual. She'd been feeling grandiose, invincible, and unafraid of risk. Hearing a beautiful music in her head, she hadn't listened to anything anyone else was saying.

In fact, the comparison extended even further because, before becoming manic, Madeleine had been nearly as depressed as Leonard. The things she liked about Pilgrim Lake when they first arrived—the landscape, the exclusive atmosphere—didn't compensate for the unpleasantness of the social environment. As the months passed, she didn't really make any friends. The few women scientists at the lab either were much older than Madeleine or treated her with the same condescension as the male scientists did. The only bedfellow Madeleine got along with was Vikram Jaitly's girlfriend, Alicia, but she came up only one or two weekends per month. Leonard's obsession with keeping his condition secret wasn't conducive to having much of a social life, anyway. He didn't like being around people. He ate dinner as quickly as possible and never wanted to hang out in the bar afterward. Sometimes he insisted on eating pasta at home, even though the lab employed a professional chef. Whenever Madeleine went to the bar without Leonard, or played tennis with Greta Malkiel, she couldn't relax. She got paranoid if anybody asked about Leonard, particularly if they asked how he was "feeling." She couldn't be herself, and always left early, returning to the apartment and closing the door, drawing the shades. It turned out that Madeleine had a madwoman in the attic: it was her six-foot-three boyfriend.

And then, in October, Alwyn found Leonard's lithium and things became even more complicated. After Phyllida flew back to Boston, and from Boston back to New Jersey, Madeleine waited for the inevitable phone call. A week later, in early November, it came.

"I'm so glad I had a chance to visit the famous Pilgrim Lake Laboratory! It was terribly impressive."

It was the excessive cheer in Phyllida's voice that was worrisome. Madeleine braced herself.

"And it was so nice of Leonard to take time out of his schedule to show us around his lab. I've been giving a little tutorial down here to all my friends. I call it 'Everything You Ever Wanted to Know About Yeast but Were Afraid to Ask.'" Phyllida tittered with pleasure. Then, clearing her throat, she changed the topic. "I thought you might want to be apprised of developments chez Higgins."

"I don't."

"Things are much better, I'm happy to report. Ally has moved *out* of the Ritz and back home with Blake. Thanks to the new nanny— which your father and I are paying for—there has been a cessation of hostilities."

"I said I don't care," Madeleine said.

"Oh, Maddy," Phyllida lightly scolded.

"Well, I don't. Ally can get divorced for all I care."

"I know you're angry with your sister. And you have every right to be."

"Ally and Blake don't even like each other."

"I don't think that's true," Phyllida said. "They have their differences, like any married couple. But they're from the same background, fundamentally, and they understand each other. Ally's lucky to have Blake. He's a very stable person."

"What do you mean by that?"

"Just that."

"It's an interesting choice of words, though."

Phyllida sighed over the line. "We need to have this talk but I don't know if now is the right time."

"Why not?"

"Well, it's a serious discussion."

"This is only happening because Ally's a snoop. Otherwise, you wouldn't know anything."

"That's true. But the fact is I *do* know."

"Didn't you like Leonard? Wasn't he nice?"

"He was very nice."

"Did he seem like there was something wrong with him?"

"Not exactly, no. But I've been learning a lot about manic-depressive illness in the past week. You know the Turners' daughter, Lily?"

"Lily Turner is a druggie."

"Well, she's certainly on drugs now. And will be for the rest of her life."

"Meaning?"

"Meaning that manic depression is a *chronic* condition. People have it their *entire* lives. There's no cure. People go in and out of the hospital, they have breakdowns, they can't hold a job. And their families go along for the ride. Sweetheart? Madeleine? Are you there?"

"Yes," Madeleine said.

"I know you know all this. But I want you to think about what it would mean to marry a person with a . . . with a mental illness. Not to mention raise a family with him."

"Who says I'm going to marry Leonard?"

"Well, I don't know. But I'm just saying, if you are."

"Say Leonard had another disease, Mummy. Say he had diabetes or something. Would you be acting the same way about that?"

"Diabetes is a dreadful disease!" Phyllida cried.

"But you wouldn't *care* if my boyfriend needed insulin to stay healthy. That would be O.K., right? It wouldn't seem like some kind of *moral failing.*"

"I didn't say anything about morality."

"You didn't have to!"

"I know you think I'm being unfair. But I'm just trying to protect you. It's a very difficult thing to spend your life with someone unstable like that. I read an article by a woman who was married to a manic-depressive, and it literally curled my hair. I'm going to send it to you."

"Don't."

"I'm going to!"

"I'll throw it away!"

"Which amounts to sticking your head in the sand."

"Is this why you're calling?" Madeleine said. "To lecture me?"

"No," Phyllida said. "Actually, I was calling about Thanksgiving. I was wondering what your plans were."

"I don't know," Madeleine said, tight-lipped with anger.

"Ally and Blake are coming here with Richard the Lionhearted. We'd love to have you and Leonard too. It won't be a big do this year. Alice has the weekend off and I can't seem to manage the oven the way she does. It's really getting to be an antique. But of course your father thinks it works just fine. He who never cooks so much as oatmeal."

"You don't cook much either."

"Well, I try. Or I did when you were young."

"You never cooked," Madeleine said, trying to be mean.

Phyllida remained unprovoked. "I think I can still manage a turkey," she said. "So, if you and Leonard would like to come, we'd love to have you."

"I don't know," Madeleine said.

"Don't be angry with me, Maddy."

"I'm not. I've got to go. Bye."

She didn't call her mother for a week. Whenever the phone rang at a Phyllida-like time, she didn't answer. The following Monday, however, a letter from Phyllida arrived in the mail. Inside was an article titled "Married to Manic Depression."

I met my husband, Bill, three years after graduating from college in Ohio. My first impression of him was that he was tall, good-looking, and a little bit shy.

Bill and I have been married for twenty years now. During that time, he has been committed to a psychiatric ward three times. That's not to mention the many, many times he has voluntarily admitted himself.

When his illness is under control, Bill is the same confident, caring man I fell in love with and married. He is a wonderful dentist, very much beloved and respected by his patients. Of course, it has been difficult for him to maintain a steady practice, and even harder for him to join a practice with other dentists. For this reason, we have often had to move to new locations around the country, where Bill felt there was a need for dental services. Our children have gone to five different schools and this has been hard on them.

It hasn't been easy for our boys, Terry and Mike, to grow up with a dad who might be cheering them from the sidelines at their baseball games one day, and the next, talking nonstop nonsense and acting inappropriately to strangers, or shutting himself up in our bedroom and refusing to come out for days.

I know that the divorce rate for people married to manic-depressives is very high. There have been many times when I thought I would become just another statistic. But my family and my faith in God always told me to hold on for a day longer, and then a day after that. I have to remember that Bill has a disease, and that the person who does these crazy things is not really him but his disease taking control.

Bill didn't tell me about his condition before we were engaged. Previous relationships of his had broken up when his girlfriends (and in one case, his fiancée) learned about his illness. Bill says that he didn't want to lose me the same way. No one in his family told me, either, even though I became quite close to Bill's sister. But this was in 1959 and the subject of mental illness was pretty much taboo.

In all honesty, I'm not sure that it would have mattered. We were so young when we met and so in love that I think I may have looked the other way, even if Bill had told me about his manic depression on our first date (to the Ohio State Fair, if you'd like to know). Of course, I didn't know then what I know now about this terrible disease, or the strain it can put on children and families. Still, I think I would have married Bill anyway, knowing everything—because he was "the one" for me.

But, as I joked with Bill at our wedding, "From now on, you better not keep any secrets from me!"

The article continued, but Madeleine read no further. In fact, she crumpled it into a ball. To ensure that Leonard wouldn't find it, she stuffed the crumpled pages into an empty milk carton and buried the carton at the bottom of the trash can.

Part of her anger had to do with Phyllida's closed-mindedness. Another part had to do with the fear that she might be right. A long, hot summer with Leonard in his un-air-conditioned apartment, followed by two months in their unit at Pilgrim Lake, had given Madeleine a good idea of what it would be like to be "married to manic depression." At first, the drama of their reconciliation had overshadowed any difficulties. It was a rush to be needed the way Leonard needed her. As the summer wore on, however, and Leonard didn't noticeably improve—and especially after they moved to Cape Cod and he seemed, if anything, worse—Madeleine began to feel suffocated. It was as if Leonard had brought his hot, stuffy little studio apartment with him, as though that was where he lived, emotionally, and anyone who wanted to be with him had to squeeze into that hot psychic space too. It was as if, in order to love Leonard fully, Madeleine had to wander into the same dark forest where he was lost.

There comes a moment, when you get lost in the woods, when the woods begin to feel like home. The further Leonard receded from other people, the more he relied on Madeleine, and the more he relied on her, the deeper she was willing to follow. She stopped playing tennis with Greta Malkiel. She didn't even make a pretense of having drinks with the other bedfellows. In order to punish Phyllida, Madeleine turned down her invitation to come home for Thanksgiving dinner. Instead, she and Leonard celebrated at Pilgrim Lake, eating in the dining hall with the skeleton crew of people who stayed around. The rest of the holiday weekend, Leonard didn't want to leave the apartment. Madeleine suggested driving to Boston, but he wouldn't budge.

The long winter months stacked up ahead of Madeleine like the frozen dunes above Pilgrim Lake. Day after day, she sat in her desk chair, trying to work. She ate cookies or corn chips, hoping this would give her the energy to write, but the junk food made her lethargic, and she ended up napping. Then came days when she didn't think she could stand it anymore, when she lay on the bed deciding that she wasn't such a good person, that she was too selfish to devote her life to taking care of someone else. She fantasized about breaking up with Leonard, moving to New York, about getting an athletic boyfriend who was simple and happy.

Finally, when things got very grim, Madeleine broke down and told her troubles to her mother. Phyllida listened without much comment. She knew that Madeleine's call indicated a significant shift in policy, and so she just murmured on the other end of the line, happy with the territory won. When Madeleine spoke about her plans for the future, the grad schools she was applying to, Phyllida discussed the various options without referring to Leonard. She didn't ask what Leonard might do or whether he would like moving to Chicago or New York. She just didn't mention him. And Madeleine mentioned him less and less, trying to see what it might feel like if he were no longer in her life. Sometimes this seemed like a betrayal of him, but it was just words, so far.

And then, at the beginning of December, with a magic that resembled their first days together, things began to change. The first sign that Leonard's side effects were lessening was that his hands stopped shaking. During the day, he was no longer running to the bathroom every ten minutes, or drinking water constantly. His ankles looked less swollen, and his breath sweetened.

The next thing she knew, Leonard was working out. He began using the gym, lifting weights and riding a stationary bicycle. His disposition became more cheerful. He started smiling and making jokes. He even moved more quickly, as if his limbs no longer felt so heavy.

The experience of watching Leonard get better was like reading certain difficult books. It was like plowing through late James, or the pages about agrarian reform in *Anna Karenina*, until you suddenly got to a good part again, which kept on getting better and better until you were so enthralled that you were almost *grateful* for the previous dull stretch because it increased your eventual pleasure. All of a sudden, Leonard was his old self again, extroverted, energetic, charismatic, and spontaneous. One Friday evening, he told Madeleine to put on her worst clothes and some rubber boots. He led her out to the beach, carrying a bushel basket and two garden trowels. The tide was out, the exposed seabed glistening in the moonlight.

"Where are you taking me?" she said.

"This is kind of a Moses deal," Leonard said. "This is kind of a Red Sea deal."

They walked far out in the muck, their boots sinking. The smell was strong, fishy, clammy, half rotten: the smell of the primordial ooze. They bent their faces close to the seabed, digging and sliding around. When Madeleine looked back at the beach, she was frightened to see how far out they were. In less than a half hour they'd filled the bushel.

"Since when do you know about digging for oysters?" Madeleine asked.

"I used to do this in Oregon," Leonard said. "Excellent oyster country where I come from."

"I thought all you did growing up was smoke pot and sit in your bedroom."

"I got out into nature once or twice."

After they'd lugged the now-heavy bushel back to shore, Leonard declared his intention of throwing an oyster-eating party. He knocked on people's doors, inviting them over, and soon he was at the kitchen sink, cleaning and shucking oysters, as the apartment filled up. It didn't matter if he made a mess; the rough floorboards of the barn had seen worse. All night, plates of oysters flowed from the kitchen. People slurped the jiggling, opalescent blobs straight from the shells, drinking beer. Around midnight, when the party began to thin, Leonard started talking about this Indian casino at Sagamore Beach. Did anybody feel like gambling? Playing a little blackjack? It wasn't that late yet. It was Friday night! A group of people piled into Madeleine's Saab, the girls sitting on the guys' laps. While Madeleine drove out Highway 6, Leonard rolled a joint on the door of the glove box and explained the intricacies of counting cards. "The dealers at a place like this'll probably only use one deck. It's easy." The two guys, being Poindexters, got caught up in the mathematical details. By the time they arrived at the casino, they were fired up to give it a try, and headed off to different tables.

Madeleine had never been to a casino before. She was slightly horrified by the clientele, liver-spotted white men in baseball caps and hefty women, in track suits, parked in front of slot machines. Not a Native American in sight. Madeleine followed the other two bedfellows into the bar, where at least the drinks were cheap. Around three o'clock, the two guys came back, both telling the same story. They'd been up a few hundred dollars when the dealer changed decks, messing up their count, and they lost it all. Leonard appeared sometime after that, looking equally glum, before smiling and pulling fifteen hundred dollars out of his pocket.

He claimed he could have won more if the dealer hadn't got suspicious. The dealer called the pit boss over, who watched Leonard win a few more times before suggesting that he might want to quit while he was ahead. Leonard took the hint, but he wasn't done for the night. Out in the parking lot, he had a new idea. "It's too late to drive back to Pilgrim Lake now. We're too wasted. Come on, we've got the whole weekend!" The next thing Madeleine knew, they were checking into a hotel in Boston. Leonard bought each couple a double room with his winnings. The next afternoon, they reconvened in the hotel bar, and the party continued. They went to dinner in Back Bay and bar-hopping afterward. Leonard kept peeling bills from his diminishing wad, giving tips, buying food and drinks.

When Madeleine asked if he knew what he was doing, Leonard said, "This is play money. How many times are we going to be able to do something like this in our lives? I say, 'Go for it.'"

The weekend was already becoming legendary. The guys kept chanting, "Leonard! Leonard!" and slapping each other's hands. The hotel rooms had Jacuzzis, minibars, twenty-four-hour room service, and really big beds. By Sunday morning the girls were mock-complaining about being too sore to walk.

Madeleine wasn't walking so well by then, either. Their first night at the hotel, Leonard had come out of the bathroom, naked and grinning.

"Look at this thing," he said, staring down at himself. "You could hang a coat on it."

Indeed you could. If they needed a sure sign that Leonard was feeling better, there was none more obvious. Leonard was back in action. "I'm making up for lost time," he said, after the third time they had sex. As good as it felt, as wonderful as it was to be properly serviced after months of going without, Madeleine noted that the clock now read 10:08 a.m. It was broad daylight outside. She kissed Leonard and begged him to *please* let her go to sleep.

He did, but as soon as she woke up he wanted her again. He kept telling her how beautiful her body was. He couldn't get enough of her, not that weekend and not in the weeks that followed. Madeleine had always thought that she and Leonard had great sex, but to her amazement it got better, deepened, became both more physical and more emotional. And noisier. They said things to each other now. They kept their eyes open and left the lights on. Leonard asked Madeleine what she wanted him to do and, for the first time in her life, she wasn't too inhibited to answer.

One night in their unit Leonard asked, "What's your most secret sexual fantasy?"

"I don't know."

"Come on. Tell."

"I don't have one."

"Do you want to know mine?"

"No."

"Tell me yours, then."

To placate him, Madeleine thought for a moment. "This'll sound weird, but I guess it would be to be pampered."

"Pampered?"

"Like to be really pampered, at the hairdresser's, getting your hair washed, getting a facial, a pedicure, a massage, and then, you know, little by little . . ."

"That would never have occurred to me as a fantasy," Leonard said.

"I told you it was stupid."

"Hey, it's your *fantasy*. Stupid doesn't apply."

And for the next hour or so, Leonard went about fulfilling it. While Madeleine protested, he carried one of the chairs from the living room into the bedroom. He ran the bath. Under the kitchen sink he found two utility candles, brought them into the bathroom, and lit them. Tying his hair back and rolling up his sleeves, he came over as though waiting on her. In what was presumably his idea of a hairdresser's voice—a straight hairdresser—he said, "Miss? Your bath is ready."

Madeleine wanted to laugh. But Leonard remained serious. He led her into the candlelit bathroom. He turned his back, with professional courtesy, while she took off her clothes and got into the warm scented water. Leonard knelt beside the tub and, using a cup, began to wet her hair. By this point Madeleine was going along with it. She imagined that Leonard's hands belonged to a handsome stranger. Exactly twice, his hands strayed to the sides of her breasts, as if testing boundaries. Madeleine thought Leonard might go further. She thought Leonard might end up in the bath, but he disappeared, returning with her terry-cloth robe. Wrapping her in it, leading her to the chair and putting her feet up, he placed a warm towel over her face and, for what seemed like the next hour (but was probably twenty minutes), he gave her a massage. He started with her shoulders, moved to her feet and calves, came up her thighs, stopping just short of her you-know-what, and started on her arms. Finally, opening her robe, and pressing harder now, as if taking charge, he rubbed moisturizer into her stomach and chest.

The towel was still over her eyes as Leonard lifted her out of the chair and onto the bed. By this point, Madeleine felt totally clean, totally desirable. The moisturizer smelled like apricots. When Leonard, naked now himself, undid the belt of her robe and opened it, when he pushed into her slowly, he was himself and not himself. He was a strange man taking possession of her and her familiar safey-safe boyfriend, all in one.

She was frightened to ask Leonard what his secret fantasy was. But in a spirit of reciprocity, a day or so later, she did ask. Leonard's fantasy was the inverse of hers. He wanted a sleeping girl, a sleeping beauty. He wanted her to pretend to be asleep when he snuck in her room and climbed into bed. He wanted her to be limp and bed-warmed while he pulled off her nightclothes and to not even fully come to consciousness until he was inside her, at which point he was so excited he didn't seem to care what she did.

"Well, that was easy," she said afterward.

"You got off lucky. It could have been a slave-master sort of deal."

"Right."

"It could have involved enemas."

"Enough!"

The spirit of exploration that now dominated their bedroom had a strong effect on Madeleine. It led her, a little while later, to confess to Leonard one night, when he wanted to repeat the hairdresser scenario, that being pampered wasn't really her secret fantasy. Her *secret* secret fantasy was something she'd never told anyone and could barely admit to herself. It was this: whenever Madeleine masturbated (this was hard in itself to confess to) she pictured herself as a little girl, being spanked. She didn't know why she did this. She had no memory of being spanked as a girl. Her parents hadn't believed in spanking. And it wasn't really a fantasy of hers; that is, she didn't want Leonard to spank her. But, for some reason, thinking about herself as a little girl being spanked had always helped her to have an orgasm when she was touching herself.

Well, there it was: the most embarrassing thing she could tell another person. A weird thing about herself that upset her if she thought about it much, which was why she didn't. She had no control over it, but felt guilty about it nonetheless.

Leonard didn't see it that way. He knew what to do with this information. First, he went to the kitchen and poured Madeleine a big glass of wine. He made her drink it. Next he pulled off her clothes, turned her over on her stomach, and started having sex with her. While he did this, he spanked her, and she hated it. She kept telling him to stop. She said she didn't like it. It was just something she *thought* about sometimes; she didn't really want it to happen. Stop it! Now! But Leonard didn't. He kept it up. He held Madeleine down, and spanked her again. He put his fingers in her and spanked her some more. She was furious with him now. She struggled to get up. And right then it happened. Something broke open inside her. Madeleine forgot who she was, and what was nice. She just started moaning, her face pressed into the pillow, and when she finally came she came harder than she'd ever come before, and cried out, spasms still running through her for minutes after.

She wouldn't let him do it again. It didn't become a habit. Whenever she thought about it later, she was scalded with shame. But the potential of doing it again was always there now. The expectation that Leonard would take over like that, and not listen to her, and do what he wanted, forcing her to admit what she really wanted—that was there now between them.

After that, they went back to regular sex, and it was even better for their time away. They did it multiple times a day, in every room of the apartment (the bedroom, the living room, the kitchen). They did it in the Saab while the engine idled. Good old straight no-frills sex, as the Creator intended. The pounds were melting off Leonard, leaving him lean again. He had so much energy, he worked out two hours at the gym at a time. Madeleine liked his new muscles. And that wasn't all. One night, she pressed her lips to Leonard's ear and said, as if it were news, "You are so *big!*" And it was true. Mr. Gumby was long gone. Leonard's girth filled Madeleine up in a way that felt not only satisfying, but breathtaking. Every millimeter of movement, in or out, was perceptible along her inner sheath. She wanted him all the time. She'd never thought much about other boys' penises, or noticed much about them, really. But Leonard's was highly particular to her, almost a third presence in the bed. She found herself sometimes judiciously weighing it in her hand. Did it all come down to the physical, in the end? Is that what love was? Life was so unfair. Madeleine felt sorry for all the men who weren't Leonard.

All in all, the rapid improvement, on just about every level, in Madeleine's relationship would have been enough to explain why she accepted Leonard's sudden proposal that December. But it was a convergence of factors that finally pushed her over the edge. The first was how helpful Leonard had been with her grad school applications. Having decided to reapply, Madeleine faced the option of retaking the GRE as well. Leonard encouraged her to do so, tutoring her in math and logic. He read over Madeleine's writing sample (the new essay she was sending to *The Janeite Review*), flagging sections where her argument was weak. The night before the applications were due, he typed up the biographical information and addressed the envelopes. And the next day, after they dropped the applications at the Provincetown post office, Leonard threw Madeleine down on the bed, pulled off her pants, and proceeded to go down on her, despite her protestations that she needed to shower. She kept trying to wriggle free but he held her tight, saying how great she tasted, until she finally believed him. She relaxed in a profound way that wasn't sexual so much as existential. So it was finally true: Leonard equaled maximum relaxation.

A few days later, Leonard proposed to her, and Madeleine said yes. She kept waiting for it to seem like a bad idea. For the next month they didn't tell anybody. At Christmas, she took Leonard home to Prettybrook, daring her parents not to like him. Christmas was always a big deal at the Hannas. They had no fewer than three trees, decorated in different themes, and gave an annual Christmas party for a hundred and fifty guests. Leonard handled these festivities with aplomb, chatting with Alton and Phyllida's friends, joining in on the caroling, and making a good impression all around. In the following days, he proved capable of watching bowl games with Alton and, as the son of an antiques dealer, of saying intelligent things about the Thomas Fairland lithographs in the library. Snow fell the day after Christmas, and Leonard was out early, wearing his slightly absurd hunting cap, shoveling the front walks and sidewalk. Whenever Phyllida took Leonard aside, Madeleine got nervous, but nothing seemed to go amiss. That he was twenty pounds lighter than he'd been in October, and unimpeachably handsome, couldn't fail to register on Phyllida. Madeleine kept the visit short, however, not wanting to push her luck, and they left after three days, spending New Year's in New York before returning to Pilgrim Lake.

Two weeks later, Madeleine called to break the news of her engagement.

Clearly taken off guard, Alton and Phyllida didn't know how to respond. They sounded profoundly surprised, and got off the phone quickly. A few days later, the letter campaign began. Separate handwritten messages arrived from Alton and Phyllida, questioning the wisdom of getting "tied down" so early. Madeleine replied to these missives, which invited further responses. In her second letter, Phyllida got more specific, repeating her warnings against marrying a manic-depressive. Alton repeated what he'd said in his first letter, while making a case for a prenuptial contract to protect Madeleine's "future interests." Madeleine didn't respond, and, a few days later, a third letter from Alton arrived, in which he restated his position in less legalistic language. The only thing the letters accomplished was to reveal how powerless her parents were, like an isolated dictatorship engaged in saber rattling that couldn't follow through on its threats.

Their final move was to engage an intermediary. Alwyn called from Beverly.

"So I hear you're engaged," she said.

"Are you calling to congratulate me?"

"Congratulations. Mummy is *so* pissed."

"Thanks to you," Madeleine said.

"She had to find out sooner or later."

"No, she didn't."

"Well, now she knows." In the acoustical spillover from the earpiece, Madeleine could hear Richard crying. "She keeps calling and asking me to 'talk some sense' into you."

"Is that why you're calling?"

"No," Alwyn said. "I told her if you want to marry him, it's your business."

"Thanks."

"Are you still mad at me about the pills?" Alwyn said.

"Yes," Madeleine said. "But I'll get over it."

"Are you sure you want to marry him?"

"Also yes."

"O.K., then. It's your funeral."

"Hey, that's mean!"

"I'm *joking.*"

Her parents' official surrender, in February, only brought further conflict. Once Alton and Madeleine stopped arguing about the prenuptial agreement, and whether such a document, by its very nature, invalidated the trust any marriage needed to survive, once the document had been drawn up by Roger Pyle, Alton's lawyer in town, and signed by both parties, Phyllida and Madeleine started arguing about the wedding itself. Madeleine wanted something small and intimate. Phyllida, aware of appearances, wanted to throw the kind of grand wedding she would have thrown had Madeleine been marrying somebody more suitable. She proposed holding a traditional wedding ceremony at their local parish, Trinity Episcopal, followed by a reception at the house. Madeleine said no. Alton then suggested an informal ceremony at the Century Club, in New York. Madeleine tentatively agreed to this. A week before the invitations were to go out, however, she and Leonard chanced upon an old mariner's church on the outskirts of Provincetown. And it was there, in a stark, lonely space at the end of a deserted peninsula, a landscape befitting a Bergman film, that Madeleine and Leonard were married. Phyllida and Alton's most loyal friends made the trek from Prettybrook to the Cape. Madeleine's uncles, aunts, and cousins were there, as well as Alwyn,

Blake, and Richard. Leonard's family came, his father, and his mother and sister, all of whom seemed a lot nicer than Leonard's descriptions. The majority of the forty-six guests were Madeleine's and Leonard's friends from college, who treated the ceremony less as a religious rite than as an occasion to cheer and hoot.

At the rehearsal dinner Leonard played a Latvian love song on the kokle, while Kelly Traub, whose grandparents were from Riga, sang along. He made a simple toast at the wedding banquet, alluding to his breakdown so tactfully that only those in the know got the reference, and thanking Madeleine for being his "ministering Victorian angel." At midnight, after changing into their traveling clothes, they took a limousine to the Four Seasons in Boston, where they immediately fell asleep. The next afternoon, they left for Europe.

Looking back, Madeleine thought that she might have picked up the warning signs more quickly if she hadn't been on her honeymoon. She was so excited to be in Paris, at the height of spring, that for the first week everything seemed perfect. They stayed at the same hotel where Phyllida and Alton had spent *their* honeymoon, a three-star place now well past its prime, staffed by white-haired waiters who carried trays at precarious angles. The hotel was thoroughly French, however. (Leonard said he saw a mouse wearing a beret.) There were no other Americans there, and it looked out on the Jardin des Plantes. Leonard had never been to Europe before. It made Madeleine happy to show Leonard around, to be more knowledgeable about something than he was.

The restaurants made him nervous. "We have four different waiters serving our table," he said on their third night in the city, as they dined in a restaurant overlooking the Seine. "Four. I counted. One guy's just for sweeping up bread crumbs."

In passable third-year French, Madeleine did the ordering for both of them. The first course was vichyssoise.

After tasting it, Leonard said, "I'm guessing this is supposed to be cold."

"Yes."

He nodded. "Cold soup. New concept."

The dinner was everything she wanted her honeymoon to be. Leonard looked so handsome, dressed in his wedding suit. Madeleine felt beautiful herself, bare-armed and bare-shouldered, her hair thick on the nape of her neck. They were both as physically perfect as they were ever going to be. They had their whole life together before them, stretching out like the lights along the river. Madeleine could already imagine telling this story to their children, the story of "The First Time Daddy Ate Cold Soup." The wine had gone to her head. She almost said this out loud. She wasn't ready for children! And yet here she was, already thinking about them.

They spent the next days sightseeing. To Madeleine's surprise, Leonard was less interested in museums and churches than in the merchandise in the shop windows. He kept stopping along the Champs-Élysées to admire things he'd never shown interest in before—suits, shirts, cuff links, Hermès neckties. Wandering the narrow streets of the Marais, he stopped outside a tailor shop. In the slightly dusty window was a headless mannequin and on the mannequin was a black opera cloak. Leonard went inside to look at it.

"This is really nice," he said, examining the satin lining.

"It's a *cape*," Madeleine said.

"You'd never find anything like this in the States," Leonard said.

And he bought it, spending way too much (in her opinion) of his last monthly stipend from Pilgrim Lake. The tailor wrapped the garment up and put it in a box, and soon Leonard was carrying it out the door. The cape was an odd thing to want, no question, but it wasn't the first strange souvenir someone had bought in Paris. Madeleine quickly forgot about it.

That night, a rainstorm swept over the city. Around two in the morning, they were awakened by water dripping from the ceiling above the bed. A call to the front desk produced a bellman with a bucket, no apology, and a vague promise about an "*ingénieur*" coming in the morning. By positioning the bucket just so, and lying head to toe, Madeleine and Leonard managed to find a position in which to stay dry, though the dripping kept them awake.

"This is our first marital mishap," Leonard said softly, in the dark. "We're handling it. We're dealing with it."

It wasn't until they left Paris that anything seemed the matter. From the Gare de Lyon they took an overnight train to Marseille, occupying a romantic sleeper cabin that made romance impossible. With its disorder, sense of danger, and mixed population, Marseille seemed like an American city, or merely less French. A Mediterranean-Arabic atmosphere prevailed; the air smelled of fish, motor oil, and verbena. Women in headscarves called to broods of brown-skinned children. At a zinc bar on their first night, sometime past two a.m., Leonard became instant friends with a group of Moroccans in soccer jerseys and flea market jeans. Madeleine was exhausted; she wanted to go back to the hotel, but Leonard insisted that they had to have *café cognac*. He'd been picking up words along the way, deploying them every so often as though this meant that he actually spoke French. When he learned a slang term (the word *branché*, for instance, when applied to persons, meant that they were "plugged in"), Leonard told it to Madeleine as if *he* were the fluent speaker. He corrected her pronunciation. At first, she thought he must be joking, but this didn't seem to be the case.

From Marseille they traveled east along the coast. When a dining-car waiter came to take their order, Leonard insisted on ordering in French. He got the words out, but his pronunciation was atrocious. Madeleine repeated Leonard's request. When she finished, Leonard was glaring at her.

"What?"

"Why did you order for me?"

"Because the waiter didn't understand you."

"He understood me fine," Leonard insisted.

It was evening by the time they reached Nice. After checking into their hotel, they went out to a small restaurant down the street. Throughout dinner, Leonard was conscientiously distant. He drank a lot of house wine. His eyes glittered whenever the young waitress came over to their table. For nearly the entire meal Madeleine and Leonard sat without speaking, like a couple married for twenty years. Returning to their hotel, Madeleine used the bad-smelling communal WC. While she was peeing, she read the sign in French that cautioned against throwing paper of any kind into the toilet. Turning her head, she located the source of the stench: the wastebasket was overflowing with soiled toilet paper.

Gagging, she fled back to their room. "Oh my God!" she said. "That bathroom is so gross!"

"You're just a princess."

"Go in there! You'll see."

Leonard calmly took his toothbrush into the WC and returned, un-ruffled.

"We have to change hotels," Madeleine said.

Leonard smirked. Glassy-eyed, he said in a prim voice, "The prin-cess from Prettybrook is appalled!"

As soon as they went to bed, Leonard grabbed her by the hips and turned her onto her stomach. She knew that she shouldn't let Leonard have sex with her after the way he'd treated her all evening. At the same time, she felt so sad and unwanted that it came as a huge relief to be touched. She was making some awful pact, one that might have conse-quences for her entire married life. But she couldn't say no. She let Leon-ard turn her over and take her, not lovingly, from behind. She wasn't ready and it hurt at first. Leonard paid no attention, blindly thrusting. She could have been anyone. When it was over Madeleine began to cry, at first quietly, then less quietly. She wanted Leonard to hear. But he was asleep, or pretended to be.

When she woke up the next morning, Leonard wasn't in the room. Madeleine wanted to call her mother, but it was the middle of the night on the East Coast. And it was dangerous to go on record about Leonard's behavior. She would never be able to take it back. Instead, she got up and searched his toiletry case for his pill bottles. One was half empty. Leon-ard had refilled the other one before the wedding, so that he wouldn't run out while they were in Europe.

Reassured that he was taking his medicine, Madeleine sat on the edge of the bed and tried to figure out how to handle the situation.

The door opened and Leonard burst in. He was beaming, acting as if nothing had happened.

"I just found us a new hotel," he said. "Much nicer. You'll like it."

The temptation to ignore the previous night was great. But Made-leine didn't want to set a bad precedent. The weight of marriage pressed down on her for the first time. She couldn't just throw a book at Leonard and leave, as she'd done in the past.

"We need to talk," she said.

"O.K.," Leonard said. "How about over breakfast?"

"No. Now."

"O.K.," he said again, somewhat softer. He looked around the room for a place to sit, but there was none, so he remained standing.

"You were so mean to me yesterday," Madeleine said. "First you got mad when I ordered for you. Then you acted like I wasn't even there at dinner. You kept flirting with the waitress—"

"I wasn't flirting with the waitress."

"Yes, you were! You were flirting with her. And then, we came back here and you—you—you just used me like I was a piece of meat!" Saying this made her burst into tears again. Her voice had gone all squeaky and girly in a way she hated but couldn't help. "You acted like you were . . . with that waitress!"

"I don't want to be with the waitress, Madeleine. I want to be with you. I love you. I love you so much."

These were exactly the words Madeleine wanted to hear. Her intelligence told her to distrust them, but another, weaker part of her responded with happiness.

"You can never treat me that way again," she said, still hiccuping with sobs.

"I won't. I never will."

"If you ever do, that's the end."

He put his arms around her, pressing his face into her hair. "It's never going to happen again," he whispered. "I love you. I'm sorry."

They went to a café for breakfast. Leonard was on his best behavior, pulling out her chair, buying her a *Paris Match* from the newsstand, offering her a brioche from the basket.

The next two days went well. The weather in Nice was cloudy, the beaches full of pebbles. Hoping to take full advantage of her prewedding diet, Madeleine had brought along a two-piece swimsuit, modest by the standards of the Côte d'Azur but daring for her. But it was a little too cold to swim. They used the lounge chairs reserved for them by their hotel only once, for a couple of hours, before rain clouds chased them back inside.

Leonard remained attentive, and sweet, and Madeleine hoped that their fighting was over.

The plan was to spend their last two days in Monaco, before taking the train back to Paris for their return flight. On a cloudless late afternoon, the first truly warm, sunny day of their trip, they boarded the train for the twenty-minute ride. One minute they were passing cypresses and glittering coves, the next they were arriving in the overbuilt, overpriced precincts of Monte Carlo.

A Mercedes taxi took them up a corniche to their hotel high above the town and harbor.

The front desk clerk, who wore an ascot, said they were lucky to have come when they did. The Grand Prix was starting the next week and the hotel was completely booked. Now, however, it was relatively peaceful, perfect for a couple on their honeymoon.

"Is Grace Kelly around?" Leonard asked, out of the blue.

Madeleine turned to look at him. He had a big smile, his eyes glassy again.

"The princess passed away last year, monsieur," the desk clerk replied.

"I forgot about that," Leonard said. "My sincere condolences to you and your countrymen."

"Thank you, monsieur."

"This isn't a real country, though, right?"

"Excuse me, monsieur?"

"It's not a kingdom. It's just a principality."

"We are an independent nation, monsieur," the clerk said, stiffening.

"Because I was wondering how much Grace Kelly knew about Monaco when she married Prince Rainier. I mean, she probably figured he was the ruler of a real country."

The clerk's expression was now impassive. He produced their room key. "Madame, monsieur, I hope you enjoy your stay."

As soon as they were in the elevator, Madeleine said, "What's the matter with you?"

"What?"

"That was so rude!"

"I was just playing with him," Leonard said with his antic smile. "Have you ever seen the movies of Grace Kelly's wedding? Prince Rainier's in a military uniform, like he has some great realm to defend. Then you get here and you realize the whole country could fit inside the Superdome. It's a stage set. No wonder he married an actress."

"That was so embarrassing!"

"You know what else is a joke?" Leonard continued, as if he hadn't heard her. "The way they call themselves Monegasques. They had to come up with a special, slightly longer name for themselves because their actual country's so dinky."

Leonard charged into their room, tossing his suitcase on the bed. He went out onto the balcony but in a few seconds came back in. "You want some champagne?" he said.

"No," Madeleine answered.

He went to the phone and dialed room service. He was operating just fine. The qualities he was displaying—extroversion, vitality, boldness—were the qualities that had attracted Madeleine to him in the first place. Only now they were amplified, like a stereo with the volume turned up so loud that the sound was distorted.

When the champagne arrived, Leonard told the waiter to set it on the balcony.

Madeleine walked out to talk to him.

"Since when do you like champagne?" she asked.

"Since I got to Monte Carlo." Leonard raised his hand and pointed. "See that building? I think that's the casino. I can't remember what Bond film it's in. Maybe we should go check it out after dinner."

"Leonard?" Madeleine said in a soft voice. "Sweetie? If I ask you something, promise you won't get mad?"

"What?" he said, already sounding irritated.

"Are you feeling O.K.?"

"I'm dandy."

"Are you taking your pills?"

"Yes, I'm taking my pills. In fact"—he went back inside to get his lithium from his suitcase, then returned—"it's time for my medicine right now." Popping a pill into his mouth, he tossed it back with more champagne. "See? I'm fine and dandy."

"That's not even something you say. 'Fine and dandy.'"

"Apparently, I do say it." He laughed at this.

"Maybe you should call your doctor. Just to check in."

"Who? Perlmann?" Leonard scoffed. "He should call *me*. I could school that guy."

"What are you talking about?"

"Nothing," Leonard said, gazing down at the distant yacht-filled harbor. "Just that I'm making some discoveries a guy like Perlmann could never even *conceive* of making."

The evening got worse from there. After finishing the bottle of champagne mostly by himself, Leonard insisted on ordering another.

When Madeleine refused to let him, he got angry and went down to the bar. He began buying drinks for the other patrons, a group of Swiss bankers and their girlfriends. When Madeleine went to find him an hour later, Leonard acted overjoyed to see her. He hugged and kissed her, overdoing it.

"This is my beautiful bride," he said. He introduced the bankers. "This is Till and Heinrich. And these girls' names I forget, but I'll never forget their pretty faces. Till and Heinrich know a great restaurant they'll take us to. It's the best in town, right, Till?"

"It's very good," the Swiss said. "A local secret."

"Good. Because I don't want to go to a place with any American tourists in it, you know what I mean? Or maybe we should go straight to the casino. Can you eat at the casino?" It was difficult to tell if the Europeans saw how strange he was acting or if they took his excessive familiarity as an American trait. They seemed amused by Leonard.

It was then that Madeleine did something she regretted. Rather than hauling Leonard off to see a doctor (though she had no precise idea how to do this), she went back upstairs to the room. Getting Leonard's pills from where he'd left them, she had the hotel operator place a long-distance call to Dr. Perlmann's number, which was written on the prescription label. Perlmann wasn't in his office, but after Madeleine said it was an emergency, the secretary took the number of Madeleine's hotel and promised that Dr. Perlmann would call her right back.

After fifteen minutes passed with no response, Madeleine went back down to the bar, but Leonard and the Swiss bankers were no longer there. She checked the hotel restaurant and the patio but found no sign of them. With growing alarm, she returned to the room to find that Leonard had been there while she was out. His suitcase was open and clothes were flung on the floor. There was no note from him. At that moment the phone rang. It was Perlmann.

Madeleine told Perlmann everything that had happened in a long rush of words.

"O.K., I need you to calm down," Perlmann said. "Can you do that for me? I'm hearing a lot of anxiety in your voice. I can help you, but you need to calm down, O.K.?"

Madeleine gathered herself. "O.K.," she said.

"Now, do you know where Leonard might be going?"

She thought for a moment. "The casino. He said he wanted to go gambling."

"Listen to me," Perlmann said, his voice steady. "What you need to do is get Leonard to the nearest hospital. He needs to be evaluated by a psychiatrist. Right away. That's the first thing. They'll know how to take care of him at the hospital. Once you get him there, give them my number."

"What if he won't go to the hospital?"

"You need to get him there," Perlmann said.

The taxi driver sped down the corniche with his brights on. The road twisted back and forth. Sometimes the sea was in front of them, black and empty, and it seemed as if they might plunge over the cliff, but then the car swerved, and the lights of the city appeared, ever closer. Madeleine wondered if she should go to the police. She tried to think of how to say "manic-depressive" in French. The only word that came to mind, *maniaque*, sounded too severe.

The taxi entered the densely populated area around the harbor. The traffic grew heavier as they neared the casino. Surrounded by formal gardens and lighted fountains, the Casino de Monte-Carlo was a Beaux Arts construction, with fanciful wedding-cake towers and a domed copper roof. Lamborghinis and Ferraris were parked six deep outside, the lights of the marquee reflecting off their hoods. Madeleine had to show her passport for admission, citizens of Monaco being prohibited by law from entering the casino. She bought a ticket for the main gaming room and made her way inside.

As soon as she entered, she despaired of finding Leonard. The Grand Prix might not have begun, but the casino was packed with tourists. They were clustered around the gaming tables, better dressed than the gamblers she'd seen at the Indian casino, but with the same canine hunger on their faces. Three Saudis, wearing sunglasses, sat around the baccarat table. A six-foot-tall man with a bolo tie was throwing craps. A group of Germans, the men in Bavarian suede-collared jackets, were admiring the frescoed ceiling and stained-glass windows, speaking in trilling tones. It might have been interesting to Madeleine, at another time. But now every aristocrat or high roller was just a person in the way. She felt like shoving them aside. She felt like kicking and hurting them.

Slowly, she made her way into the center of the room, concentrating on tables where cards were being played. It began to seem less likely that Leonard was here. Maybe he'd gone out for dinner with the Swiss bankers. Maybe the best idea was to go back to the hotel and wait. She moved in farther. And there, in a maroon velvet seat at the blackjack table, was Leonard.

He'd done something to his hair—wet it, or gelled it, so that it was plastered back. And he was wearing the black cape.

His stack of chips was smaller than those of the other players. He was leaning forward with concentration, his eyes fixed on the dealer. Madeleine calculated that it would be best not to interrupt him.

Seeing him like this, wild-eyed, antiquely dressed, as slick-haired as a vampire, Madeleine realized that she'd never accepted—had never taken fully on board—the reality of Leonard's illness. In the hospital, when Leonard was recovering from his breakdown, his behavior had been peculiar but understandable. He was like someone dazed after a car crash. This—this mania—was different. Leonard seemed like an actual crazy person, and it scared her senseless.

Maniaque wasn't far from wrong. What did *maniac* refer to, after all, if not to mania?

All her life she'd avoided unbalanced people. She'd stayed away from the weird kids in elementary school. She'd avoided the gloomy, suicidal girls in high school who vomited up pills. What was it about crazy people that made you want to shun them? The futility of reasoning with them, certainly, but also something else, something like a fear of contagion. The casino, with its buzzing, smoke-filled air, seemed like a projection of Leonard's mania, a howling zone full of the nightmare rich, opening their mouths to place bets or cry for alcohol. Madeleine had the urge to turn and flee. Taking one step forward would commit her to a life of doing the same. Of worrying about Leonard, of constantly keeping tabs on him, of wondering what had happened if he was a half hour late coming home. All she had to do was turn and go. No one would blame her.

And then, of course, she took the step. She came up and stood silently behind Leonard's chair.

There were a half dozen other players around the table, all men.

She moved into his field of vision and said, "Sweetie?"

Leonard glanced sideways. He didn't appear surprised to see her.

"Hi, there," he said, returning his focus to the cards. "Sorry for taking off like that. But I was afraid you wouldn't let me gamble. Are you mad at me?"

"No," Madeleine said soothingly. "I'm not mad."

"Good. Because I'm feeling lucky tonight." He winked at her.

"Sweetie, I need you to come with me."

Leonard threw in an ante. Again he leaned forward, concentrating on the dealer. At the same time, he said, "I remembered the Bond flick this place is in. *Never Say Never Again*."

The dealer dealt the first two cards.

"Hit me," Leonard said.

The dealer dealt Leonard one more.

"Again."

The next card broke him. The dealer scooped up Leonard's cards and the croupier took his chips away.

"Let's go," Madeleine said.

Leonard leaned toward her conspiratorially. "He's using two decks. They think I can't handle two, but they're wrong."

He tossed in another ante and the cycle repeated itself. The dealer had seventeen and Leonard thought he could beat it. At thirteen, he asked for one more card, and got a jack.

The croupier swept away the last of Leonard's chips.

"I'm out," Leonard said.

"Let's go, sweetie."

He turned his glassy-eyed gaze on her. "You wouldn't lend me some money, would you?"

"Not now."

"For richer and for poorer," Leonard said.

But he got up from the chair.

Madeleine led Leonard by the arm across the casino. He went willingly. Just as they were nearing the top of the stairs, however, Leonard stopped. He lifted his chin and made a curious face. In an English accent, he said, "The name's Bond. James Bond." Suddenly raising his arms, he wrapped himself in his cape like Dracula. Before Madeleine could react, he bolted away, flapping his cape like wings, his expression mad with delight, playful, confident.

She tried to go after him, but her heels slowed her down. Finally, she took them off, running barefoot out of the casino. But Leonard was nowhere in sight.

He didn't come back the entire night.

He didn't come back the next day either.

By this time she was in touch with Mark Walker at the consulate in Marseille. Through Baxter alumni connections, Alton had managed to speak personally with the American ambassador to France. Ambassador Galbraith had taken down Madeleine's information and forwarded it to Walker, who called Madeleine to say that the authorities in Monaco, France, and Italy had all been informed about the situation and that he would be in touch as soon as he knew more. Meanwhile, Phyllida had gone straight to Newark Airport and caught a night flight for Paris. The following morning, she took a connecting flight to Monaco, arriving at Madeleine's hotel just after noon. During the eighteen hours between the phone call and Phyllida's entering her room, Madeleine went through a range of emotions. There were periods when she was angry with Leonard for running off, and others where she castigated herself for not recognizing sooner that something was wrong. She was furious with the Swiss bankers and, for some reason, with their girlfriends, for enticing Leonard away from the hotel. She was frantic with worry that Leonard might hurt himself, or be arrested. Sometimes she was swamped with self-pity, knowing that she would get only one real honeymoon in her life and that hers had been ruined. She thought about calling Leonard's mother, or his sister, but she didn't have their numbers, and she didn't want to talk to them, anyway, because somehow she blamed them too.

And then Phyllida was there, with a bellman in tow, her clothes neat and her hair in place. Everything Madeleine hated about her mother—her imperturbable rectitude, her lack of visible emotion—was exactly what Madeleine needed at the moment. She broke down, sobbing in her mother's lap. Phyllida responded by ordering lunch brought to the room. She waited until Madeleine had eaten a full meal before she asked the first question about what had happened. Shortly afterward, Mark Walker called with the news that a person matching Leonard's description had been admitted, early that morning, to the Princess Grace Hospital, suffering from psychosis and minor injuries sustained in a fall. The man, who had an American accent, had been found on the beach, shirtless and shoeless, and carrying no identification. Walker offered to come from Marseille and accompany Madeleine and Phyllida to the hospital to see if this person, as seemed likely, was Leonard.

While they waited for Walker, Phyllida told Madeleine to get cleaned up and look presentable, insisting that this would make her feel more in control of herself, which in fact it did. Walker, a model of efficiency and tact, picked them up in a chauffeured consulate car. Grateful for his assistance, Madeleine did her best to appear as though she wasn't falling apart.

The Princess Grace Hospital, renamed in tribute to the former American movie star, was where she'd died the year before, following an automobile accident. Signs of mourning were still visible in the hospital: a black garland draped over the oil portrait of the princess in the main lobby; bulletin boards covered with condolence letters from around the world. Walker introduced them to Dr. Lamartine, a lean, skull-faced psychiatrist, who explained that Leonard was presently under heavy sedation. They were administering an antipsychotic manufactured by Rhône-Poulenc and not available in the States. He had had excellent results with the drug in the past, and saw no reason why the present case would be different. The clinical results of the drug were so out-standing, in fact, that the FDA's refusal to approve it was a mystery—or perhaps not so mysterious, he added in a tone of professional complaint, given that the drug was not American-made. At that point he seemed to remember Leonard. His physical injuries were as follows: chipped teeth, bruises to the face, a broken rib, and other minor abrasions. "He is sleep-ing now," the doctor said. "You can go in and see him, but please let him sleep."

Madeleine went in alone. Before parting the curtain around the bed, she could smell the tobacco vaporizing from Leonard's skin. She almost expected him to be sitting up and smoking in bed, but the person she found was neither the erratic, wild Leonard nor the shaken, withdrawn one, neither manic nor depressive but merely inert, an accident victim. An intravenous tube ran into his arm. The right side of Leonard's face was swollen; his split upper lip had been sutured, the flesh around it deep purple, beginning to crust. The doctor had told her not to wake him, but she bent over him and gently lifted his upper lip. What she saw made her gasp: both of Leonard's front teeth had been cracked off at the root. Pink tongue glistened behind the gap.

What had happened was never entirely clear. Leonard was too out of it to remember the final thirty-six hours. From the Casino de Monte-Carlo he'd gone to the restaurant where the Swiss bankers were having dinner. He had no money, but he convinced them that he had a foolproof method of counting cards. After dinner, they took him to the Loews casino, an American place, and gave him seed money. The agreement was to split the winnings fifty-fifty. This time, either by design or by luck, Leonard did well at first. He went on a little streak. Soon he was up a thousand dollars. At that point the night grew wilder. They left the casino and visited a series of bars. The bankers' girlfriends were still there, or maybe they had left. Or he was with another group of bankers by then. At some point, he returned to Loews. The dealer there used only a single deck. Despite his mania, or because of it, Leonard managed to count cards and keep them straight in his head. He was perhaps insufficiently secretive about what he was up to, however. After an hour, the pit boss arrived and kicked Leonard out of the casino, warning him never to come back. By this time Leonard was up nearly two thousand dollars. And it was here his memory faded out. The rest of the story Madeleine pieced together from police reports. After getting kicked out of Loews the final time, Leonard had been seen at an "establishment" in the same neighborhood. Sometime the next day, he ended up at the Hôtel de Paris with a group of people who may or may not have been the Swiss bankers. At some point, drinking in their adjoining rooms, Leonard had made a bet that he could jump from one balcony to the other next door. This was only on the second floor, fortunately. He'd taken off his shoes to do this, but didn't make it. He slipped, hitting his cheek and mouth against the balcony railing and falling to the ground below. Bleeding, half out of his mind, he'd wandered off down the beach. At one point he'd taken off his shirt and gone for a swim. It was when he came out of the sea and tried to reenter the hotel that the police had picked him up.

The French antipsychotic was indeed a wonder drug. Within two days Leonard was lucid again. He was so full of remorse, so horrified by his behavior and his attempt to alter his medications, that he spent Madeleine's visits either apologizing to her or mute with regret. She told him to forget about it. She said it wasn't his fault.

For the duration of Phyllida's time in Monaco, from the moment she arrived to the moment she left, a week later, she never once said "I told you so." Madeleine loved her mother for this. She was surprised to see how worldly Phyllida was, how unruffled she remained when it became clear what the "establishment" Leonard had visited turned out to be. On learning this, Madeleine had been reduced to tears again. But Phyllida had said with grim humor, "If that's the only thing you have to worry about in your marriage, you'll be lucky." She also said, humanely, "He wasn't in his right mind, Maddy. You have to forget about it. Just forget it and go on." It struck Madeleine that Phyllida was speaking from personal experience, that her parents' marriage was more complicated than she'd ever suspected.

Phyllida's sickroom visits were awkward, however. Phyllida and Leonard still barely knew each other. As soon as Leonard was "out of the woods," she flew home to New Jersey to get the house ready for Madeleine and Leonard's eventual arrival.

Madeleine stayed on at the hotel. With nothing to do but watch French television on the two stations the TV set in her room received, and determined never to set foot in the casino again, Madeleine spent hours in the Musée Océanographique. It soothed her to sit in the underwater light, watching sea creatures glide across their tanks. At first she ate alone, in the dining room of the hotel, but her presence attracted too much male attention. So she stayed in her room, ordering room service and drinking more wine than she was used to.

She felt as if she'd aged twenty years in two weeks. She was no longer a bride or even a young person.

On a clear day in May, Leonard was discharged. Once again, as she had the year before, Madeleine waited outside a hospital while a nurse brought him down in a wheelchair. They took the train back to Paris, staying at a modest hotel on the Left Bank.

On the day before they flew back to the States, Madeleine left Leonard in the room while she went out to buy him cigarettes. The summer weather was lovely, the colors of the flowers in the park so bright they hurt her eyes. Up ahead, she saw an amazing sight, a troop of schoolgirls being led by a nun. They were crossing the street, heading into the courtyard of their school. Smiling for the first time in weeks, Madeleine watched them proceed. Ludwig Bemelmans had written sequels to *Madeline*. In one, Madeline had joined a gypsy circus. In another, she'd been saved from drowning by a dog. But, despite all her adventures, Madeline had never gotten any older than eight. That was too bad. Madeleine could have used some helpful examples, further installments of the series. Madeline passing the *baccalauréat*. Madeline studying at the Sorbonne. ("And to writers like Camus, Madeline just said 'Poo poo.'") Madeline practicing free love, or joining a commune, or traveling to Afghanistan. Madeline taking part in the '68 protests, throwing rocks at the police, or crying out, "Under the pavement, the beach."

Did Madeline marry Pepito, the Spanish ambassador's son? Was her hair still red? Was she still the smallest and the bravest?

Not exactly in two straight lines, but orderly enough, the girls disappeared through the doors of the convent school. Madeleine went back to the hotel, where Leonard, still bandaged up, a casualty of a different kind of war, was waiting.

> They smiled at the good
> and frowned at the bad
> and sometimes they were very sad.

Down the track, the Northeast Corridor train appeared in a haze of soot and heat distortion. Madeleine stood on the platform, behind the yellow line, squinting through her crooked glasses. After two weeks of being lost, the glasses had turned up yesterday at the bottom of her laundry hamper. The prescription was too weak now, the lenses no less scratched and the frames no more in style than they'd been three years ago. She was going to have to break down and get a new pair before grad school began.

As soon as she'd confirmed that the train was approaching, she took off the glasses and shoved them into her purse. She turned around to look for Leonard, who, already complaining about the humidity, had gone inside the meagerly air-conditioned waiting room.

It was a little before five p.m. About two dozen other people were waiting for the train.

Madeleine stuck her head into the waiting room door. Leonard was sitting on a bench, staring at the floor, his eyes dull. He was still wearing the black T-shirt and shorts but he'd tied his hair back into a ponytail. She called his name.

Leonard looked up and slowly got to his feet. He'd taken forever to get out of the house and into the car and Madeleine had worried they might miss their train.

The train doors had already opened before Leonard emerged onto the platform and followed Madeleine into the nearest car. They chose a two-person seat, so they wouldn't have to sit with anyone. Madeleine took a well-thumbed copy of *Daniel Deronda* out of her bag and settled back.

"Did you bring something to read?" she said.

Leonard shook his head. "I'll just stare out at the beautiful landscape of New Jersey."

"There are some nice parts of New Jersey," Madeleine said.

"Legend has it," Leonard said, staring.

The fifty-nine-minute train ride didn't provide much support for this view. When they weren't passing the backyards of subdivisions, they were rolling into another dying city, like Elizabeth, or Newark. The courtyard of a minimum-security prison backed up to the train tracks, the inmates wearing white uniforms like a convention of bakers. Near Secaucus, the pale green marshes began, surprisingly pretty if you didn't raise your eyes to the surrounding smokestacks and loading docks.

They reached Penn Station at rush hour. Madeleine led Leonard away from the packed escalators to a less trafficked stairwell, where they climbed up to the lobby. A few minutes later they stepped into the heat and light of Eighth Avenue. It was just after six.

As they joined the taxi line, Leonard eyed the nearby buildings, as though worried they were going to topple on him.

"'New York,'" he said. "'Just like I pictured it.'"

It was his last little joke. When they got in a cab and were heading uptown, Leonard asked the driver if he could please turn on the air-conditioning. The driver said it was broken. Leonard rolled down the window, hanging his head out like a dog. For a moment, Madeleine regretted bringing him along.

Her premonition in the Casino de Monte-Carlo had been more accurate than she even knew at the time. She'd already become the trembling wife, the ever-watchful custodian. She'd become "married to manic depression." It wasn't news to Madeleine that Leonard could kill himself while she was sleeping. It had already crossed her mind that the swimming pool might invite oblivion. Of the twenty-one signs on the list Wilkins had given her, Madeleine had marked a check next to ten of them: change in sleeping patterns; unwillingness to communicate; neglect of work; neglect of appearance; withdrawal from people/activities; perfectionism; restlessness; extreme boredom; depression; and change in personality. Among the warning signs Leonard didn't exhibit were that he hadn't attempted suicide before (though he'd thought about it), didn't use drugs (at present), wasn't accident prone, didn't talk about wanting to die, and hadn't been giving away his possessions. On the other hand, this morning, when Leonard had said that he no longer wanted to move to New York and referred to the apartment as "hers," he'd sounded a lot like a person giving away his possessions. Leonard didn't seem to care about the future anymore. He didn't know what he was going to do. He didn't want an office. He'd been wearing those black shorts for two weeks.

Ten warning signs out of twenty-one. Not very reassuring. But when she pointed this out to Dr. Wilkins, he'd said, "If Leonard didn't have any warning signs, you wouldn't be here. Our job is to reduce the number, little by little, to three or four. Maybe one or two. Over time I'm confident we can do that."

"What about until then?" Madeleine asked.

"Until then we have to proceed very carefully."

She was trying to proceed carefully, but it wasn't easy. Madeleine had brought Leonard to New York to avoid the danger of leaving him home unsupervised. But now that he was in the city, there was the danger that he might have a panic attack. She'd had the choice between leaving him in Prettybrook, and worrying, and bringing him to New York with her, and worrying. In general, she worried less if she could keep an eye on him.

She was the thing that stood between Leonard and death. That was how it felt to her. Because Madeleine now knew the warning signs, she was constantly alert to their appearance. Worse, she was alert to any change in Leonard's mood that might be a *precursor* of one of the warning signs. She was alert to *warnings* of the warning signs. And this got confusing. For instance, she didn't know if Leonard's being up early constituted a new change in his sleeping pattern, was part of the former change in his sleeping pattern, or indicated a beneficial development.

She didn't know if his perfectionism canceled out his loss of ambition, or if they were two sides of the same coin. When you stood between somebody you loved and death, it was hard to be awake and it was hard to sleep. When Leonard stayed up, watching late-night TV, Madeleine kept tabs on him from her bed. She could never really fall asleep until he came upstairs and climbed in beside her. She listened for the sounds he made downstairs. It was as if her own heart had been surgically removed from her body and was being kept at a remote location, still connected to her and pumping blood through her veins, but exposed to dangers she couldn't see: her heart in a box somewhere, in the open air, unprotected.

They came up Eighth Avenue, veering onto Broadway at Columbus Circle. Leonard pulled his head back inside the car as if to retest the temperature, then leaned out the window again.

The driver made a left at Seventy-second Street. A few minutes later they were rolling up Riverside Drive. Kelly was waiting on the sidewalk outside the building.

"Sorry!" Madeleine said, getting out of the taxi. "The train was late."

"You always say that," Kelly said.

"It's always true."

They hugged, and Kelly asked, "So are you coming to the party?"

"We'll see."

"You have to! I can't go alone."

All this time, the cab was idling at the curb. Finally Leonard climbed out. With heavy steps he made it out of the sunlight to the shade of the awning.

Kelly, who was a pretty good actress, smiled at Leonard as though she hadn't heard anything about his illness and he looked just fine. "Hi, Leonard. How you doing?"

As usual, Leonard treated this like a real question. He sighed, and said, "I'm exhausted."

"*You're* exhausted?" Kelly said. "Think about me! I've shown Maddy like fifteen apartments. This is it. If you guys don't take this one, I'm firing you."

"You can't fire us," Madeleine said. "We're your clients."

"Then I quit." She led them into the cool, paneled lobby. "Seriously, Maddy. I've got one other listing, closer to Columbia, if you want to see it. But I doubt it's as nice as this."

After signing in with the doorman, they took the elevator up to the twelfth floor. Outside the apartment, Kelly hunted in her bag for the right keys, which took a while, but finally she got the door open and ushered them in.

Up until now, Kelly had shown Madeleine apartments that looked onto air shafts, or adjoined SROs, or were tiny and roach-infested, or smelled like cat pee. Even if Madeleine hadn't been desperate to move out of her parents' house, the one-bedroom she now walked into would have dazzled her. It was a classic, with freshly painted white walls, crown moldings, and parquet floors. The bedroom was big enough for a queen bed, the galley kitchen updated, the office usable, the living room undersize but graced by a nonworking fireplace. There was even a dining room. The chief selling point, however, was the views. In rapture, Madeleine opened the living room window and leaned out over the sill. The sun, still a couple of hours from setting, was spangling the chop in the river and turning the usually gray Palisades a light pink. To the north were the transparent peaks of the G. W. Bridge. Traffic noise rose from the West Side Highway. Madeleine looked down at the pavement in front of the building. It was a long way down. Suddenly she got scared.

She pulled her head back in and called Leonard's name. When he didn't answer, she called again, already moving down the hall.

Leonard was in the bedroom with Kelly. The window was closed.

She hid her relief by examining the bedroom closet. "This closet's mine," she said. "I've got more clothes than you do. But you can have the office."

Leonard said nothing.

"Did you see the office?"

"I saw it," he said.

"And?"

"It's fine."

"Not to pressure you or anything," Kelly said, "but you guys need to decide in the next, say, half hour. The other agent in my office wants to start showing this place tonight."

"Tonight?" Madeleine said, unprepared for this. "I thought you said tomorrow?"

"That's what he said. But now he changed his mind. People are desperate for this place."

Madeleine looked at Leonard, trying to read his thoughts. Then she crossed her arms decisively. Absent moving to a prairie state, she was going to have to accept the inherent risks of living with him in Manhattan. "O.K., I want it," she said. "It's perfect. Leonard, we want it, right?"

Leonard turned to Kelly. "Can we have a minute?" he said.

"Sure! No problem. I'll be in the living room."

When she was gone, Leonard went to the window. "How much is this place?" he asked.

"Don't worry about that."

"I could never afford an apartment like this. I'm worried how it's going to make me feel."

This was a reasonable conversation to have once or twice. But they'd had it about a hundred times. They'd had a version of it that morning. The sad truth was that any place that Leonard could afford would be a place that Madeleine would refuse to live in.

"Sweetie," she said. "Don't worry about the rent. Pay as much as you can. I just want us to be happy."

"I'm saying I'm not sure I could be happy here."

"If I were the man, we wouldn't even be talking about this. It would be normal for the husband to pay more rent."

"The fact that I feel like the wife here is sort of the problem."

"Why did you come to see it, then?" Madeleine said, growing frustrated. "What did you expect we were going to do? We can't live with my parents forever. How does *that* make you feel? Living with my parents?"

Leonard's shoulders slumped. "I know," he said, sounding truly sorrowful. "You're right. I'm sorry. It's just hard for me. Do you see how it could be hard for me?"

It seemed best to nod yes.

Leonard stared out the window for what seemed like a half minute. Finally, taking a breath, he said, "O.K. Let's take it."

Madeleine wasted no time. She told Kelly they were taking the apartment and offered to write a check for the deposit. Kelly had a better idea, however. She suggested that they go ahead and sign the lease today, which would save them from making another trip to the city. "You can go have coffee while I draw up the lease. It'll take me about fifteen minutes."

This plan made sense, and so the three of them took the elevator back down to the lobby and reentered the sweltering streets.

As they made their way to Broadway, Kelly pointed out the local services, the dry cleaners, the locksmith, and the corner diner, which was air-conditioned.

"You guys wait in there," Kelly said, pointing at the diner. "I'll be back in fifteen minutes. Half hour tops."

Madeleine and Leonard took a booth by the front window. The diner had Hellenic murals and a twelve-page menu. "This'll be our diner," Madeleine said, looking around approvingly. "We can come here every morning."

The waiter walked over to take their order.

"You know what you like, my friends?"

"Two coffees, please," Madeleine said, smiling. "And my husband would like some apple pie with a slice of cheddar cheese on top."

"You want it, you got it," the waiter said, moving off.

Madeleine expected Leonard to be amused. But to her surprise his eyes filled with tears.

"What's wrong?"

He shook his head, looking away. "I forgot about that," he said in a husky voice. "Seems like a long time ago."

Outside, shadows were lengthening along the pavement. Madeleine stared out at the Broadway traffic, trying to stave off a rising feeling of hopelessness. She didn't know how to cheer Leonard up anymore. Everything she tried brought the same result. She worried that Leonard would never be happy again, that he had lost the ability. Right now, when they should have been excited about the new apartment, or checking out their new neighborhood, they were sitting in a vinyl booth, avoiding each other's eyes and not saying anything. Even worse, Madeleine knew that Leonard understood this. His suffering was sharpened by the knowledge that he was inflicting it on her. But he was unable to stop it. Meanwhile, beyond the plate-glass window, the summer evening was settling over the avenue. Men were coming home from work, their ties loosened, carrying their coats. Madeleine had lost track of the days, but from the relaxed looks on people's faces and the happy-hour crowd spilling out of the bar on the opposite corner, she could tell it was Friday night. The sun would still be up for hours but the night—and the weekend—had officially begun.

The waiter brought the apple pie, with two forks. But neither of them took a bite.

After twenty minutes, Kelly returned, carrying papers. She'd made two amendments to the standard lease, one stipulating approval of subletters, the other prohibiting pets. At the top of the form she'd typed Madeleine's and Leonard's full names, and had filled in the rent and security deposit amounts. Sitting down in the booth, helping herself to pie, she instructed Madeleine to write checks covering the security deposit and the first month's rent. Then she had Madeleine and Leonard sign their names.

"Congratulations. You guys are officially New Yorkers. Now we can celebrate."

Madeleine had almost forgotten. "Leonard," she said. "Do you know Dan Schneider? He's having a party tonight."

"It's like three blocks away," Kelly said.

Leonard was staring into his coffee cup. Madeleine couldn't tell if he was consulting his feelings (self-monitoring) or if his mind had stopped. "I'm not really in a party mood," he said.

This wasn't what Madeleine wanted to hear. She felt like celebrating. She'd just signed the lease on a Manhattan apartment and she didn't feel like getting back on the train to New Jersey. She checked her watch. "Come on. It's only seven-fifteen. Let's just go for a little while."

Leonard didn't say yes but he didn't say no. Madeleine got up to pay the check. While she was at the register, Leonard went outside and lit a cigarette. His smoking was getting greedier. He sucked on the filter as if it were clogged and required extra force. When she came out with Kelly, the nicotine seemed to have mollified him sufficiently that he accompanied them up Broadway without complaint.

He was quiet as they reached Schneider's building, right in front of the Seventy-ninth Street subway station, and as they rode in the elevator up to the seventh floor. But as they came into the apartment, Leonard suddenly balked, and grabbed Madeleine's arm.

"What?" Madeleine said.

He was looking down the hall toward the living room, which was full of people talking loudly over the music.

"I can't deal with this," he said.

Kelly, sensing potential trouble, kept right on going. Madeleine watched her join the knot of lightly clad bodies.

"What do you mean you can't deal with it?"

"Too hot in here. Too many people."

"Do you want to leave?" she said, unable to hide her exasperation.

"No," Leonard said, "we're here now."

She took his hand and led him into the party, and, for a while, everything went reasonably well. People came over to say hello and congratulate them on their wedding. Leonard proved capable of maintaining conversation.

Dan Schneider, bearded and burly, but wearing an apron, approached Madeleine with a drink in his hand. "Hey, I hear we're going to be neighbors," he said. It was early in the evening, but his speech was already slurred. He began telling her about the neighborhood, where to shop and eat. While he was describing his favorite Chinese takeout, Leonard peeled away, disappearing into what looked like a bedroom.

There was something erotic about the atmosphere of the hot apartment. Everybody had given in to sweating visibly. A few girls were wearing tank tops braless, and Adam Vogel, sitting on the couch, was rubbing an ice cube against his neck. Dan told Madeleine to get a drink and lurched away.

Madeleine didn't follow Leonard into the bedroom. She felt like not worrying about him for a few minutes. Instead, she joined Kelly at the drinks table, which was lined with Jim Beam bottles, Oreo cookies, glasses, and ice. "Little Red Corvette" was playing on the stereo.

"There's only bourbon," Kelly said.

"Anything." Madeleine held out a glass. She took an Oreo and began nibbling it.

Before she even turned around, Pookie Ames descended on her from the kitchen.

"Maddy! You're back! How was the Cape?"

"It was great," she lied.

"It wasn't bleak and depressing in the winter?"

Pookie wanted to see her ring, but barely looked at it when Madeleine showed her. "I can't believe you're married," she said. "That is so retrograde."

"I know!" Madeleine said.

"Where's your boyfriend? I mean, husband?"

It was impossible to tell from Pookie's face how much she knew.

"He's here somewhere," Madeleine said.

Other friends elbowed in to see her. She kept hugging people and telling them that she was moving to the city.

Pookie began telling a story. "So I'm waitressing at Dojo's, and last night this customer calls me over and goes, 'I think there's a rat in my sausage.' And I look—and there's a tail sticking out the end. Like, the whole rat was cooked inside."

"Oh, no!"

"And one of the perks of the job is you get to eat there for free, so."

"That is so gross!"

"But wait. After that, I brought the rat sausage over to my manager. Because I didn't know what to do. And he goes, 'Tell the customer, no charge.'"

Madeleine started to enjoy herself. The bourbon was so sweet it tasted like an alcoholic form of Coke. It was nice to be around people she knew. It made her feel that the decision to move to New York was the right one. The isolation at Pilgrim Lake might have been part of the problem. She finished her drink and poured herself another.

As she turned from the bar, she noticed a decent-looking guy checking her out from across the room. She'd been feeling so nurse-like and desexualized lately that this came as a welcome surprise. She met his eyes for a moment before looking away.

Kelly came up and whispered, "Everything O.K.?"

"Leonard's in the bedroom."

"At least he came."

"He's driving me crazy." Immediately, she felt guilty for saying this, and softened it. "He's just really tired. It was sweet of him to come."

Kelly leaned in again. "Dan Schneider is plying me with liquor."

"And?"

"I'm pliable."

For the next half hour Madeleine circulated around the party, catching up with people. She kept expecting Leonard to reappear. After another fifteen minutes, when he still hadn't, she went to check on him.

The bedroom was full of mission furniture and Shakespeare-themed etchings. Leonard was standing by the window, talking to a guy who had his back turned. Madeleine was already through the door before she realized it was Mitchell.

There were probably people it would have been more awkward to run into with Leonard, but at that moment Madeleine couldn't think of who they might be. Mitchell had cut off his hair and gotten even skinnier. It was hard to decide what was more shocking: his suddenly being there, the strange way he looked, or the fact that he was talking to Leonard.

"Mitchell!" she said, trying not to seem thrown. "What did you do to your hair?"

"I got a little haircut," he answered.

"I almost didn't recognize you. When did you get back?"

"Three days ago."

"From India?"

But here Leonard interposed himself. "We're sort of in the middle of a conversation," he said with annoyance.

Madeleine shifted abruptly, as if wrong-footed by a serve. "I just came to see if you were ready to leave," she said quietly.

"I *do* want to leave. But first I want to finish this conversation."

She looked at Mitchell as if he might object. But he seemed eager to have her leave as well. And so she gave a little wave, trying to seem in command of things, and backed out of the room.

Returning to the party, she tried to resume enjoying herself. But she was too preoccupied. She wondered what Leonard and Mitchell were talking about. She worried that they were talking about her. Seeing Mitchell had stirred up an emotion that Madeleine couldn't quite identify. It was as if she was excited and regretful at the same time.

After fifteen minutes, Leonard finally came out of the bedroom, saying he wanted to go. He didn't meet her eyes. When she said she wanted to say goodbye to Kelly, he told her he'd wait for her outside.

Madeleine was acutely aware, as she found Kelly and thanked her again for helping find her a place, that Mitchell was still somewhere at the party. She didn't want to talk to him alone, because her life was already complicated enough. She didn't want to explain her situation or face his recriminations or feel whatever talking to him might make her feel. But as she was just about to leave, she caught sight of him and paused, and he came up to her.

"I guess I should say congratulations," he said.

"Thank you."

"That was kind of sudden. Your wedding."

"It was."

"I guess that makes you a Stage One."

"I guess it does."

Mitchell was wearing flip-flops and jeans with the bottoms rolled up. His feet were very white. "Did you get my letter?" he asked.

"What letter?"

"I sent you a letter. From India. At least I think I did. I was somewhat high at the time. You really didn't get it?"

"No. What did it say?"

He was looking at her as if he didn't believe her. It made her uncomfortable.

"I'm not sure it matters now," he said.

Madeleine glanced toward the front door. "I have to go," she said. "Where are you staying?"

"On Schneider's couch."

They stood smiling at each other for a long moment, and then suddenly Madeleine reached out and rubbed Mitchell's head. "What did you do with your curls!" she groaned. Mitchell kept his head down while she ran her hand over the bristles on his scalp. When she stopped, he lifted his face. With his hair buzzed off, his big eyes looked even more imploring.

"Are you coming into the city again?" he asked.

"I don't know. I might." She glanced toward the door again. "If I do, I'll call you. Maybe we could have lunch or something."

There was nothing left to do but hug him. As she did, Madeleine was startled by Mitchell's pungent smell. It felt almost too intimate to breathe it in.

Leonard was smoking in the corridor when she came out. He looked for some place to toss his cigarette but, finding none, carried it into the elevator. As the car descended, Madeleine leaned against his shoulder. She felt a little drunk. "That was fun," she said. "Did you have a good time?"

Leonard tossed the butt on the floor, crushing it with his shoe.

"Does that mean no?"

The door opened and Leonard walked through the lobby without a word. Madeleine followed him out to the sidewalk, where she finally said, "What's the matter with you?"

Leonard faced her. "What's the matter with me? What do you think? I'm *depressed*, Madeleine. I'm suffering from *depression*."

"I know that."

"Do you? I'm not so sure you do. Otherwise you might not say stupid things like that."

"All I did was ask you if you had a good time! God!"

"Let me tell you what happens when a person's clinically depressed," Leonard began in his infuriating doctorly mode. "What happens is that the brain sends out a signal that it's dying. The depressed brain sends out this signal, and the body receives it, and after a while, the body thinks it's dying too. And then *it* begins to shut down. That's why depression *hurts*, Madeleine. That's why it's physically *painful*. The brain thinks it's dying, and so the body thinks it's dying, and then the brain registers this, and they go back and forth like that in a feedback loop." Leonard leaned toward her. "That's what's happening inside me right now. That's what's happening to me every minute of every day. And that's why I don't answer when you ask me if I had a good time at the party."

He was being hyperarticulate, but his brain was dying. Madeleine tried to take in what Leonard was saying. She felt warm from the bourbon and hot from the city. Now that they were downstairs, back on Broadway, she was disappointed to be heading home. For over a year she'd been taking care of Leonard, hoping for him to get better, and now he was worse than ever. Having just come from a party where everyone else seemed happy and healthy, she found the situation grossly unfair.

"Can't you just go to a party for an hour without acting like you're being tortured?"

"No, I can't, Madeleine. That's the problem."

A stream of people came up the subway stairs. Madeleine and Leonard had to move aside to let them pass.

"I understand you're depressed, Leonard. But you're taking medication for that. Other people take medication and they're fine."

"So you're saying I'm dysfunctional even for a manic-depressive."

"I'm saying that it almost seems like you *like* being depressed sometimes. Like if you weren't depressed you might not get all the attention. I'm saying that just because you're depressed doesn't mean you can yell at me for asking if you had a good time!"

Suddenly Leonard's face took on a strange expression, as if he was darkly amused. "If you and I were yeast cells, you know what we'd do?"

"I don't want to hear about yeast!" Madeleine said. "I'm sick of yeast."

"Given the choice, a yeast cell's ideal state is to be diploid. But if it's in an environment with a lack of nutrients, you know what happens?"

"I don't care!"

"The diploids break into haploids again. Solitary little haploids. Because, in a crisis, it's easier to survive as a single cell."

Madeleine felt tears welling in her eyes. The heat from the bourbon was no longer warm but a burning in her chest. She tried to blink away the tears, but a drop fell down one cheek. She flicked it away with her finger. "Why are you doing this?" she cried. "Do you want to break us up? Is that what you want?"

"I don't want to ruin your life," Leonard said in a gentler tone.

"You're not ruining it."

"The drugs just slow the process down. But the end's inevitable. The question is, how to turn this thing off?" He jabbed at his head with his index finger. "It's cutting me up, and I can't turn it off. Madeleine, listen to me. *Listen*. I'm not going to get better."

Oddly, saying this seemed to satisfy him, as though he was pleased to make the situation clear.

But Madeleine insisted, "Yes you will! You just think that now because you *are* depressed. But that's not what the doctor says."

She reached out and put her hands around his neck. She'd been so happy only a little while ago, feeling that their life was finally turning around. But now it all seemed like a cruel joke, the apartment, Columbia, everything. They stood at the subway entrance, one of those hugging, crying couples in New York, ignored by everyone passing by, granted perfect privacy in the middle of a teeming city on a hot summer night. Madeleine said nothing because she didn't know what to say. Even "I love you" seemed inadequate. She'd said this to Leonard so many times in situations like this that she was worried it was losing its power.

But she should have said it, anyway. She should have kept her arms around Leonard's neck and refused to let go, because, as soon as she stopped hugging him, with swift decisiveness, Leonard turned and fled down the steps of the subway. At first Madeleine was too surprised to react. But then she ran after him. When she reached the bottom of the stairs, she didn't see him. She ran past the token booth toward the other exit. She thought Leonard had climbed back up to the street, until she caught sight of him on the other side of the turnstiles, walking toward the tracks. As she dug into her pocketbook for change to buy a token, she felt the rumble of an approaching train. Wind was moving through the subway tunnel, kicking up pieces of litter. Realizing that Leonard must have jumped the turnstile, Madeleine decided to follow. She ran and leapt over the barrier. Two nearby teenagers laughed, seeing her do this, an Upper-East-Side-looking woman, in a dress. The train's lights appeared in the tunnel. Leonard had reached the edge of the platform. The train was roaring into the station and Madeleine, running, could see that she was too late.

And then the train slowed and stopped. Leonard was still there, waiting for it.

Madeleine reached him. She called his name.

Leonard turned and looked at her, his eyes vacant. He reached out and placed his hands tenderly on her shoulders. In a soft voice edged with pity, with sadness, Leonard said, "I divorce thee, I divorce thee, I divorce thee."

And then he pushed her back, not gently, and jumped onto the train before the doors closed. He didn't turn back to look at her through the window. The train began to move, at first slowly enough that it seemed Madeleine might be able to stop it with her hand—stop everything, what Leonard had just said, his shoving her, and her lack of resistance, her collaboration—but soon accelerating beyond her power to arrest it or to lie to herself; and now all the litter on the platform was swirling and the train wheels were screeching and the lights inside the car were blinking on and off, like the lights on a broken chandelier, or the cells in a dying brain, as the train disappeared into the darkness.

The Bachelorette's Survival Kit

There were a lot of things to admire about the Quakers. They had no clerical hierarchy. They recited no creed, tolerated no sermons. They'd established equality between the sexes in their Meetings as early as the 1600s. Just about every American social movement you could think of had been supported and often spearheaded by the Quakers, from abolition, to women's rights, to temperance (O.K., one mistake), to civil rights, to environmentalism. The Society of Friends met in simple spaces. They sat in silence, waiting for the Light. They were in America but not of America. They refused to fight America's wars. When the U.S. government had interned Japanese citizens during World War II, the Quakers had strongly opposed the move, and had come out to wave goodbye as the Japanese families were boarded onto trains. The Quakers had a saying: "Truth from any source." They were ecumenical and non-judgmental, allowing agnostics and even atheists to attend their Yearly Meetings. It was this spirit of inclusiveness, no doubt, that led the small group of worshippers at the Friends Meeting House, in Prettybrook, to make room for Mitchell when he began to appear on hot July summer mornings.

The Meeting House stood at the end of a gravel road just beyond the Prettybrook Battlefield. A simple structure of hand-laid stones, with a white wooden porch and a single chimney, the building hadn't changed from the date of its construction—1753, according to the plaque—save for the addition of electric lights and a heating system. The bulletin board outside bore a flyer for an antinuke march, a plea to petition the government on behalf of Mumia Abu-Jamal, convicted of murder the previous year, and assorted pamphlets on Quakerism. The oak-paneled interior was filled with wooden benches set in opposing sections, so that worshippers faced one another. Light issued from masked dormers above a beautifully carpentered, curved ceiling of gray wooden slats.

Mitchell liked to sit in the rear set of benches, behind a pillar. He felt less conspicuous there. Depending on the Meeting (there were two First Day Meetings, one at seven a.m., the other at eleven), anywhere from a handful to three dozen Friends took their seats in the cozy, cabin-like room. Most of the time the only sound was the distant hum of Route 1. An entire hour might pass without anyone saying a word. On other days, responding to inner promptings, people spoke up. One morning Clyde Pettengill, who used a cane, stood up to lament the recent accident at the Embalse nuclear plant in Argentina, where there had been a *total loss of coolant*. His wife, Mildred, felt compelled to speak next. Not getting up as her husband had, but remaining seated with her eyes closed, she spoke in a clear voice, her pretty old-woman's face lifted in smiling remembrance. "Maybe because it's summer—I don't know—but I'm put in mind today of going to Meetings when I was a little girl. Summer always seemed like the hardest time to sit still and be quiet. So my grandmother developed a strategy. Before the Meeting began, she used to take a piece of butterscotch candy out of her purse. She'd make sure I saw it. But she wouldn't give it to me. She'd hold it in her hand. And if I was good, and behaved like a proper young lady, my grandmother would give me the candy after forty-five minutes or so. Now I'm eighty-two, almost eighty-three, and do you know what? I feel exactly the same as I did then. I'm still waiting for that piece of butterscotch candy to be placed in my hand. It's not candy that I'm waiting for anymore. It's just a sunny summer day like this, with the sun like a great big butterscotch candy in the sky. I see I'm waxing poetic now. That means I had better stop."

As for Mitchell, he didn't say anything at the Meetings. The Spirit didn't move him to speak. He sat on the bench, enjoying the stillness of the morning and the musty scent of the Meeting House. But he didn't feel entitled to illumination.

The shame he felt for running away from Kalighat hadn't gone away, even with the passage of six months. After leaving Calcutta, Mitchell had traveled around the country with no fixed plan, like a fugitive. In Benares, he'd stayed at the Yogi Lodge, going down to the funeral ghats every morning to see bodies being cremated. He hired a boatman to take him out on the Ganges. After five days, he took the train back to Calcutta, heading south. He went to Madras, to the former French outpost of Pondicherry (home to Sri Aurobindo), and to Madurai. He stayed a single night in Trivandrum, at the southern end of the Malabar Coast, and then began traveling up the western shore. In Kerala the literacy rate soared and Mitchell ate his meals off jungle leaves instead of plates. He kept in touch with Larry, writing him at AmEx in Athens, and, in mid-February, they were reunited in Goa.

Instead of flying to Calcutta, as his ticket originally stipulated, Larry changed his stop to Bombay, and traveled down to Goa by bus. They had arranged to meet at the bus station at noon, but Larry's bus was late. Mitchell came and went three times, scanning the passengers disembarking from different multicolored buses before Larry finally climbed off of one around four in the afternoon. Mitchell was so happy to see him that he couldn't stop smiling and patting Larry on the back.

"My man!" he said. "You made it!"

"What happened, Mitchell?" Larry said. "Get your head caught in a lawn mower?"

For the next week they rented a hut on the beach. It had a tropical-seeming thatch roof and a disagreeably utilitarian concrete floor. The other huts were full of Europeans, most of whom went around without clothes. On the terraced hillside, Goan men clustered amid the palm trees to ogle the immodest Western women below. As for Mitchell, he felt too translucently white to expose himself, and stayed in the shade, but Larry braved sunburn, spending a good portion of each day on the beach with his silk scarf wrapped around his head.

During the serene, zephyr-filled days and coolish nights, they shared stories about their time apart. Larry was impressed by Mitchell's experience at Kalighat. He didn't seem to think that three weeks of volunteering were of no consequence.

"I think it's great you did it," he said. "You worked for Mother Teresa! Not that I would want to do something like that. But for you, Mitchell, that's right up your alley."

Things with Iannis hadn't turned out so well. Almost immediately, he'd begun asking Larry how much money his family had. On learning that Larry's father was a lawyer, Iannis asked if he could help him get a green card. He acted possessive or distant, depending on the circumstances. If they went to a gay bar, Iannis became insanely jealous if Larry so much as looked at another guy. The rest of the time he wouldn't let Larry touch him for fear people would learn their secret. He started calling Larry a "faggot," acting as if he, Iannis, were straight and only experimenting. This got tiresome, as did hanging around Athens for days on end while Iannis went back home to the Peloponnese. And so finally Larry had gone to the travel agent and rebooked his ticket.

It was comforting to learn that homosexual relationships were just as screwed up as straight ones, but Mitchell made no comment. Over the next three months, as they traveled over the subcontinent, Iannis wasn't mentioned again. They visited Mysore, Cochin, Mahabalipuram, staying no more than a night or two in any place, heading back north, reaching Agra in March and making their way to Varanasi (they sometimes used Hindi names now) and back to Calcutta to meet Professor Hughes and begin their job as research assistants. With Hughes they ended up in remote villages without plumbing. They defecated side by side, squatting in open fields. They had adventures, saw holy men walk across hot coals, filmed interviews with great choreographers of masked Indian dance, and met an actual maharaja, who had a palace but no money and used a tattered "brolly" as a parasol. By April, the weather was turning hot. The monsoons were still months away, but Mitchell could already feel the climate growing inhospitable. By the end of May, oppressed by increasing temperatures and feelings of aimlessness, he decided that it was time to go home. Larry wanted to see Nepal, and stayed on a few more weeks.

From Calcutta, Mitchell flew back to Paris, staying a few days in a decent hotel and availing himself of his credit card for the last time. (He wouldn't be able to justify it once he returned to the States.) Just as he was adjusting to the European time zone, he took a charter flight back to JFK. And so he was alone, in New York, when he learned that Madeleine had married Leonard Bankhead.

Mitchell's strategy of waiting out the recession hadn't worked. The unemployment rate was 10.1 percent the month he returned. From the window of his shuttle bus into Manhattan, Mitchell saw shuttered businesses, their windows soaped over. There were more people living on the street, plus a new term for them: the homeless. His own money pouch contained only $270 worth of traveler's checks and a twenty-rupee note he'd kept as a souvenir. Not wanting to shell out for a hotel in New York, he'd called Dan Schneider from Grand Central, asking if he could crash at his place for a few days, and Schneider said yes.

Mitchell took the shuttle to Times Square, then hopped on the 1 train to Seventy-ninth Street. Schneider buzzed him in and was waiting in his doorway when Mitchell reached his floor. They hugged briefly, and Schneider said, "Whoa, Grammaticus. You're a little ripe."

Mitchell averred that he'd stopped using deodorant in India.

"Yeah, well, this is America," Schneider said. "And it's *summertime*. Get yourself some Old Spice, man."

Schneider dressed all in black to match his beard and cowboy boots. His apartment was fussily nice, with built-in bookcases and a collection of iridescent ceramics made by an artist he "collected." He had a decent job grant-writing at the Manhattan Theatre Club, and was happy to buy Mitchell drinks at Dublin House, the bar close to his building. Over pints of Guinness, Schneider filled Mitchell in on all the Brown-related gossip he'd missed while in India. Lollie Ames had moved to Rome and was dating a forty-year-old. Tony Perotti, the campus anarchist, had wimped out and gone to law school. Thurston Meems had made a tape of his own faux-naïf music on which he accompanied himself on a Casio. All this was fairly amusing until Schneider suddenly said, "Oh, shit! I forgot. Your girl Madeleine got married! Sorry, man."

Mitchell made no reaction. The news was so devastating that the only way he could survive it was to pretend that he wasn't surprised. "I knew that was going to happen," he said.

"Yeah, well, Bankhead's lucky. She's sexy. I don't know what she sees in that guy, though. He's like Lurch." Schneider went on complaining about Bankhead, and guys like Bankhead, tall guys with lots of hair, while Mitchell sucked bitter-tasting foam off the top of his stout.

This simulated numbness got him through the next few minutes. And since it worked so well, Mitchell kept it going the next day, until the wages of all this unprocessed emotion woke him up, the next night, at four a.m. with the force of a stab wound. He lay on Schneider's shabby-chic couch, his eyes wide open. Three different car alarms were going off, each seemingly centered in his chest.

The following days were among the most painful in Mitchell's life.

He wandered the baking streets, sweating, fighting off a childish urge to bawl. He felt like a great big boot had come down from the sky and ground him under its heel like the cigarette butts on the pavement. He kept thinking, "I lost. I'm dead. He killed me." It felt almost pleasurable to denigrate himself in this fashion, and so he kept it up. "I'm just a piece of shit. I never had a chance. It's laughable. Look at me. Just look. Ugly baldheaded crazy religious stupid PIECE OF SHIT!"

He despised himself. He decided that his believing that Madeleine would marry him stemmed from the same credulity that had led him to think he could live a saintly life, tending the sick and dying in Calcutta. It was the same credulity that had made him recite the Jesus Prayer, and wear a cross, and think that he could stop Madeleine from marrying Bankhead by sending her a letter. His dreaminess, his swooning—his intelligent stupidity—were responsible for everything that was idiotic about him, for his fantasy of marrying Madeleine and for the self-renunciations that hedged against the fantasy's not coming true.

Two nights later, Schneider threw a party, and everything changed. Mitchell, who hadn't been feeling very festive, had gone out as the party was getting under way. After walking around the block about five or six times, he'd gone back to Schneider's to find the place even more crowded. Ducking into the bedroom, intending to mope, he'd come face to face with his nemesis, Bankhead, who was sitting on the bed, smoking. To Mitchell's further surprise, Bankhead and he had gotten into a serious discussion. Mitchell had been aware, of course, that Bankhead's being at the party meant that Madeleine must be there too. One reason he'd kept talking to Bankhead was that he was too scared to leave the bedroom and run into her. But then Madeleine had appeared on her own. At first, Mitchell pretended not to notice, but finally he'd turned—and it was like it always was. Madeleine's sheer physical presence hit Mitchell with full concussive force. He felt like the guy in the Maxell cassette commercial with his hair blown straight back, even though he didn't have any hair. Things happened quickly after that. Bankhead chased Madeleine away, for some reason. A little while later, he left the party. Mitchell managed to talk to Madeleine before she left too. But twenty-five minutes later, she came back, clearly upset, looking for Kelly. Seeing Mitchell instead, she'd come straight up to him, pressed her face into his chest, and begun to shake.

He and Kelly took Madeleine into the bedroom and closed the door. While the party swirled outside, Madeleine told them what had happened. Later on, after Madeleine had calmed down a little, she called her parents. Together they decided that the best thing to do, for the moment, was for Madeleine to take a car service back to Prettybrook. Since she didn't want to be alone, Mitchell had volunteered to ride with her.

He'd been staying at the Hannas' ever since, for almost a month. They'd put him in the attic bedroom where he'd stayed during Thanksgiving break sophomore year. The room was air-conditioned, but Mitchell had gone Third World and preferred to leave the windows open at night. He liked to smell the pine trees outside and to be awoken by the birds in the morning. He'd been getting up early, prior to anyone else in the house, and often took long walks before coming back to have breakfast with Madeleine around nine.

It was on one of these walks that Mitchell discovered the Friends Meeting House. He'd stopped on the battlefield to read the historical marker beside its only remaining tree. Halfway through the text, Mitchell realized that the "Liberty Oak" the marker commemorated had died of blight years ago, and that the tree growing there now was a mere replacement, a variety more resistant to insect infestation but less beautiful or big. Which was a history lesson in itself. It applied to so many American things. He started walking again, finally following the gravel road into the wooded parking lot of the Quaker compound.

Various fuel-sipping vehicles—two Honda Civics, two VW Rabbits, and a Ford Fiesta—were nosed up against the wall of the cemetery. Aside from the pristine Meeting House, which was set next to the woods, the grounds contained a scruffy playground and a long, many-winged, aluminum-sided building with an asphalt roof that housed the preschool, office, and reception rooms. The bumper stickers on the cars pictured Planet Earth next to the slogan SAVE YOUR MOTHER, or simply, PEACE. The Prettybrook Friends had their share of crunchy, sandal-wearing members, but as Mitchell got to know them better that summer, he saw that the stereotype only went so far. There were older Quakers, like the Pettengills, who were formal in bearing and given to plain dress. There was a gray-bearded, suspenders-wearing man who resembled Burl Ives. Joe Yamamoto, a chemical engineering professor from Rutgers, and his wife, June, were faithful attendees of the eleven o'clock

Meeting. Claire Ruth, a bank manager in town, had gone to Quaker schools; her daughter, Nell, worked with disabled children in Philadelphia. Bob and Eustacia Tavern were retired, Bob an amateur astronomer, Eustacia a former elementary school teacher who now penned fiery letters to the *Prettybrook Packet* and *The Trentonian* about pesticide runoff in the Delaware region water system. There were usually a few visitors, too, American-born Buddhists in town for a conference, or a student from the theological seminary.

Even Voltaire had approved of the Quakers. Goethe counted himself as an admirer. Emerson said, "I am more of a Quaker than anything else. I believe in the still, small voice." Sitting on the back bench, Mitchell tried to do the same. But it was difficult. His mind was too preoccupied with daydreams. The reason he hadn't left Prettybrook yet was because Madeleine didn't want him to. She told him she felt better when he was around. She looked up at him, furrowing her brow adorably, and said, "Don't go. You have to save me from my parents." They spent nearly every minute of every day together. They sat on the deck, reading, or walked into town for coffee or ice cream. With Bankhead gone and Mitchell at least physically taking his place, his chronic credulity began flaring up. In the silence of Quaker Meeting, Mitchell wondered, for instance, if Madeleine's having gotten married to Bankhead might be all part of the plan, a plan that was more complex than he'd originally anticipated. Maybe he had arrived in New York at just the right time.

Every week, when the elders shook hands, signaling that Meeting was over, Mitchell opened his eyes to realize that he hadn't stilled his mind or been moved to speak. He went outside to the picnic table where Claire Ruth was setting out juice and fruit and, after chatting awhile, made his way back to the ongoing drama at the Hannas'.

For the first few days after Leonard had taken off, they'd concentrated on trying to find him. Alton contacted the New York City police and the New York State police, only to be told both times that a husband's abandoning his wife was considered a personal matter and didn't meet the requirements for a missing-person investigation. Next, Alton had called Dr. Wilkins, at Penn. When he asked the psychiatrist if he'd seen Leonard, Wilkins had cited patient confidentiality and declined to answer. This infuriated Alton, who not only had referred Leonard to Wilkins in the first place but also had been paying for his treatment.

Nevertheless, Wilkins's silence on the matter indicated that Leonard was in touch with him and possibly still in the area. It also suggested that Leonard was taking his medicine.

Mitchell then began calling everyone he knew in New York to see if anyone had seen or talked to Bankhead. Within two days, he reached three different people—Jesse Kornblum, Mary Stiles, and Beth Tolliver—who claimed they had. Mary Stiles said that Bankhead was staying in DUMBO, in an unspecified person's loft. Bankhead had phoned Jesse Kornblum at work so often that Kornblum finally had to stop taking his calls. Beth Tolliver had met Bankhead at a diner in Brooklyn Heights, and said that he seemed sad about the demise of his marriage. "I got the feeling that Maddy had dumped *him*," she said. That was how things were left for over a week, until Phyllida thought to call Bankhead's mother, in Portland, and learned from Rita that Leonard had been in Oregon for the past two days.

Phyllida described the phone call as one of the strangest of her life. Rita acted as though the matter was of minor consequence, like a breakup between high schoolers. Her opinion was that Leonard and Madeleine had made a foolish mistake and that Rita and Phyllida, as mothers, should have seen it coming all along. Phyllida would have taken issue with this view if it weren't so obvious that Rita had been drinking. Phyllida stayed on the line long enough to establish that, after staying with his mother for the two nights, Leonard had gone to a cabin in the woods with an old high school friend of his, Godfrey, where they planned to live for the summer.

At that point Phyllida lost her composure. "Mrs. Bankhead," she said, "well, I'm, I'm—I just don't know what to say! Madeleine and Leonard are still married. Leonard is my daughter's husband, *my* son-in-law, and now you tell me he's going off to live in the woods!"

"You asked where he was. I told you."

"Did it occur to you that Madeleine might want to know that information? Did it occur to you that we might be worried about Leonard?"

"He only left yesterday."

"And just when were you going to let us know that?"

"I'm not sure I like your tone."

"My tone is beside the point. The point is that Leonard has told Madeleine that he wants a divorce, after two months of being married. Now, what Madeleine's father and I are trying to ascertain is whether

Leonard is serious about this, and in his right mind, or if this is another aspect of his illness."

"What illness?"

"His manic depression!"

Rita laughed slowly, with rich gurgling in the throat. "Leonard's always been theatrical. He should have been an actor."

"Do you have a telephone number for Leonard?"

"I don't think they have a telephone at that cabin. It's pretty rustic."

"Do you think you'll be hearing from Leonard in the near future?"

"It's hard to say with him. I didn't hear much from him since the wedding until all of a sudden he showed up at my front door."

"Well, if you do, could you please ask him to call Madeleine, who is still his legal wife? This situation has to be clarified one way or another."

"I agree with you there," Rita said.

Once they knew that Bankhead wasn't in immediate danger, and especially that he'd put a continent between himself and his bride and in-laws, Alton and Phyllida began to take a different line. Mitchell saw them talking together in the teahouse, as though they didn't want Madeleine to hear. Once, returning from a morning walk, he surprised them both sitting in the car in the garage. He didn't hear what they were saying, but he had an idea. Then one night, when they had all gone out to the deck for an after-dinner drink, Alton broached the subject that was on their minds.

It was just after nine, twilight turning into darkness. The pump of the swimming pool was laboring behind its fencing, adding a whooshing sound to the omnidirectional buzz of crickets. Alton had opened a bottle of Eiswein. As soon as he'd filled everybody's glass, he sat next to Phyllida on the wicker love seat and said, "I'd like to call a family board meeting."

The neighbors' old Great Dane, hearing activity, barked dutifully three times, then commenced nosing along the bottom of the fence. The air was heavy with garden smells, floral and herbal.

"The subject I'd like to bring before the board is the situation with Leonard. In light of Phyl's conversation with Mrs. Bankhead—"

"The kook," Phyllida said.

"—I think it's time to reassess where we go from here."

"You mean where I go," Madeleine said.

396

At the end of the yard the swimming pool hiccuped. A bird swooped from a branch, just a little blacker than the sky.

"Your mother and I are wondering what you're planning to do."

Madeleine took a sip of wine. "I don't know," she said.

"Fine. Good. That's why I've called this meeting. Now, first, I propose that we define the alternatives. Secondly, I propose that we try to determine the possible outcomes of each alternative. After we've done that, we can compare these outcomes and make a judgment as to the best course of action. Agreed?"

When Madeleine didn't reply, Phyllida said, "Agreed."

"As I see it, Maddy, there are two alternatives," Alton said. "One: you and Leonard reconcile. Two: you don't."

"I don't really feel like talking about this now," Madeleine said.

"Just—Maddy—just bear with me. Let's take reconciliation. Do you think that's a possibility?"

"I guess so," Madeleine said.

"How is that possible?"

"I don't know. Anything's possible."

"Do you think Leonard will come back on his own?"

"I said I don't *know*."

"Are you willing to go out to Portland and find him? Because, if you don't know if Leonard's coming back, and you're not willing to go look for him, I'd say the chances of a reconciliation are pretty slim."

"Maybe I *will* go out there!" Madeleine said, raising her voice.

"O.K. All right," Alton said. "Let's propose that you do. We send you out to Portland tomorrow morning. What then? How do you intend to find Leonard? We don't even know where Leonard is. And suppose you *do* find him. What will you do if he doesn't want to come back?"

"Maddy shouldn't be the one to do anything," Phyllida said, grim-faced. "Leonard should be coming here begging on his hands and knees to have her back."

"I don't want to talk about this," Madeleine repeated.

"Sweetheart, we have to," Phyllida said.

"No, we don't."

"I'm sorry, but we do!" Phyllida insisted.

All this time, Mitchell had sat quietly in his Adirondack chair, drinking wine. The Hannas seemed to have forgotten that he was there, or else they now considered him part of the family and didn't care if he saw them at their most fractious.

But Alton tried to ease the tension. "Let's put reconciliation aside for the moment," he said in a milder tone. "Let's agree to disagree about that. There's another alternative that's a little more clear-cut. Now, suppose you and Leonard don't reconcile. Just suppose. I took the liberty of talking to Roger Pyle—"

"You told *him*?" Madeleine cried.

"In confidence," Alton said. "And Roger's professional opinion is that, in a situation like this, where one party is refusing contact, the best course of action is to get an annulment."

He paused. He settled back. The word had been said. It seemed that voicing it had been Alton's main objective all along, and now that he'd said it he was momentarily at a loss. Madeleine was scowling.

"An annulment is a lot simpler than a divorce," Alton continued. "For a lot of reasons. It represents a voiding of the marriage. It's as though the marriage never was. With an annulment, you're not a divorcée. It's as though you never were married. And the best thing is, you don't need both parties to get an annulment. Roger also looked into the statutes in Massachusetts, and it turns out that annulments are granted for the following reasons." He counted them off with his fingers. "One: bigamy. Two: impotence on the part of the male. Three: mental illness."

Here he stopped. The crickets seemed to get louder and, over the dark backyard, as if this were a lovely summer evening, lightning bugs began magically to flash.

The silence was broken by the sound of Madeleine's wineglass smashing against the deck. She jumped to her feet. "I'm going inside!"

"Maddy, we need to discuss this."

"All you know how to do whenever there's a problem is talk to your lawyer!"

"Well, I'm glad I called Roger about that prenuptial agreement you didn't want to sign," Alton said, unwisely.

"Right!" Madeleine said. "Thank God I didn't lose any money! My whole life is ruined but at least I didn't lose any of my capital! This isn't a board meeting, Daddy. This is my life!" And with that, she fled to her bedroom.

For the next three days, Madeleine refused to eat with her parents.

She seldom came downstairs. This put Mitchell in an awkward position. As the only impartial person in the house, it was up to him to maintain communication among the parties. He felt like Philip Habib, the special Middle East envoy, whom he saw every night on the evening news. Keeping Alton company during the cocktail hour, Mitchell watched Habib meeting with Yassir Arafat, or Hafez al-Assad, or Menachem Begin, going back and forth, bringing messages, cajoling, goading, threatening, flattering, and trying to keep full-scale war from breaking out. After his second gin and tonic Mitchell was inspired to draw comparisons. Barricaded in her bedroom, Madeleine was like a PLO faction hiding out in Beirut, emerging every so often to lob a bomb down the stairs. Alton and Phyllida, occupying the rest of the house, were like the Israelis, unrelenting and better armed, seeking to extend a protectorate over Lebanon and make Madeleine's decisions for her. On his shuttle missions to Madeleine's lair, Mitchell listened to her complaints. She said that Alton and Phyllida had never liked Leonard. They hadn't wanted her to marry him. True, they'd treated him well after his breakdown, and hadn't so much as mentioned the word *divorce* until Leonard had said it first. But now Madeleine felt that her parents were secretly happy that Leonard was gone, and for this she wanted to punish them. After gathering as much information about Madeleine's feelings as possible, Mitchell returned downstairs to confer with Alton and Phyllida. He found them to be far more sympathetic to Madeleine's plight than Madeleine gave them credit for. Phyllida admired her loyalty to Leonard, but thought it was a losing proposition. "Madeleine thinks she can save Leonard," she said. "But the truth is that he either can't be saved or doesn't want to be." Alton put on a stern front, saying that Madeleine had "to cut her losses," but it was clear from his frequent silences, and from the stiff drinks he sipped while Habib limped in plaid slacks across yet another stretch of desert tarmac on TV, how much he was suffering on Madeleine's account.

Following diplomatic example, Mitchell played out his string, letting everyone vent until they finally asked for advice.

"What do you think I should do?" Madeleine asked him, three days after her blowup with Alton. Before Schneider's party, Mitchell's answer would have been easy. He would have said, "Divorce Bankhead and marry me." Even now, given that Bankhead showed no desire to remain married, and had disappeared into the wilds of Oregon, there didn't seem much hope for reconciliation. How could you stay married to someone who didn't want to stay married to you? But Mitchell's feeling about Bankhead had undergone a significant change since talking to him and he was beset now, troublingly, with something resembling empathy and even affection for his onetime rival.

The subject of their long dialogue in Schneider's bedroom had been, surprisingly enough, religion. Even more surprisingly, Bankhead was the one who had initiated the discussion. He'd begun by mentioning the religious studies course they'd taken together. He said that he'd been impressed with a lot of things Mitchell had said in that class. From there, Bankhead began asking Mitchell about his own religious inclinations. He seemed jittery and listless at the same time. There was an air of desperation about his questioning, as strong and acrid as the tobacco from the cigarettes he kept rolling while they talked. Mitchell told him what he could. He provided testimony to his own specific variety of religious experience. Bankhead listened intently, receptively. He appeared eager for any help Mitchell might provide. He asked Mitchell if he meditated. He asked if he went to church. After Mitchell had said everything he could, he asked Bankhead why he was interested. And here Bankhead surprised him yet again. He said, "Can you keep a secret?" Though they didn't know each other, though in some respects Mitchell was the last person Bankhead should have wanted to confide in, he had told Mitchell about an experience he'd had recently, on a trip to Europe, that had changed his attitude about things. He was on a beach, he said, in the middle of the night. He was looking up into the starry sky when suddenly he had the feeling that he could lift off into space, if he wanted to. He hadn't told anybody about this experience because he hadn't been in his right mind at the time, and this tended to discredit the experience. Nonetheless, as soon as the idea had occurred to him, it had happened: he was suddenly in space, floating past the planet Saturn. "It wasn't at all like a hallucination," Bankhead said. "I need to stress that. It felt like the most lucid moment of my life." For a minute, or ten minutes, or an hour—he didn't know—he had drifted by Saturn, examining its rings, feeling the warm glow of the planet on his face, and then he was back on Earth, on the beach, in a world of trouble. Bankhead said that the vision, or whatever it was, was the most awe-inspiring moment of his life. He said that it "felt religious." He wanted to know Mitchell's opinion of what had happened. Was it O.K. to think of the experience as religious, since it felt that way, or was it invalidated by the fact that he was technically insane at the time? And if it was invalid, why did it still bewitch him?

Mitchell had answered that, as far as he understood them, mystical experiences were significant only to the extent that they changed a person's conception of reality, and if that changed conception led to a change in behavior and action, a loss of ego.

At that point, Bankhead lit another cigarette. "This is the deal with me," he said in a quiet, intimate voice. "I'm ready to make the Kierkegaardian leap. My heart's ready. My brain's ready. But my legs won't budge. I can say 'Jump' all day long. Nothing happens."

After that, Bankhead had looked sad and had become instantly distant. He'd said goodbye and left the room.

The conversation changed Mitchell's attitude toward Bankhead. He was no longer able to hate him. The part of Mitchell that would have rejoiced in Bankhead's collapse was no longer operative. Throughout the conversation, Mitchell experienced what so many people had before him, the immensely satisfying embrace of Bankhead's intelligent and complete attention. Mitchell felt that, under other circumstances, he and Leonard Bankhead might have been the best of friends. He understood why Madeleine had fallen in love with him, and why she had married him.

Beyond that, Mitchell couldn't help respecting Bankhead for what he'd done. It was possible that he might recover from his depression; in fact, given time, that was more than likely. Bankhead was a smart guy. He might get his act together. But whatever success he achieved in life wasn't going to come easy. It would always be shadowed by his disease. Bankhead had wanted to save Madeleine from that. He was a long way from working things out and he wanted to do it on his own, with minimum collateral damage.

And so the summer flowed on. Mitchell continued to stay at the Hannas' and to take long walks to the Friends Meeting House. Whenever he suggested that it was time for him to leave, Madeleine asked him to stay a little longer, and he did. Dean and Lillian couldn't understand why he didn't come home right away, but their relief that he was no longer in India gave them the patience to wait a little longer to see his face.

July turned into August and still Bankhead didn't call. One weekend, Kelly Traub came down to Prettybrook, bringing the keys to Madeleine's new apartment. Slowly, doing a little each day, Madeleine began to pack the things she wanted to bring with her to Manhattan. In the hot storage area of the attic, wearing a tennis skirt and bikini top, her back and shoulders glistening, she picked out furniture to have shipped and went through cupboards, looking for glasses and odds and ends. She was barely eating, however. She had crying jags. She wanted to go over the chain of events again and again, beginning with the honeymoon and leading up to the party at Schneider's, as though she might find some moment when, had she acted differently, none of it would have happened. The only times Madeleine brightened were when an old girlfriend of hers came by the house. With her friends—and the earlier made and dippier they were, the better: she was hugely fond of certain ex–Lawrenceville girls with names like Weezie—Madeleine seemed to be able to will herself back to girlhood. She went into town shopping with these friends. She spent hours trying things on. At the house, they lay by the pool, tanning and reading magazines, while Mitchell drew away to the shade of the porch, watching them from afar with desire and revulsion, exactly as *he* had done in high school. Sometimes Madeleine and her friends, growing bored, tried to coax Mitchell to come for a swim, and he put down his Merton and stood poolside, trying not to stare at Madeleine's near-naked body gliding through the water.

"Come on in, Mitchell!" she pleaded with him.

"I don't have a bathing suit."

"Just wear shorts."

"I'm opposed to shorts."

Then the Lawrenceville girls left and Madeleine became intelligent again, as lonely, misfortunate, and inward as a governess. She rejoined Mitchell on the porch, where the sun-warmed paperbacks and iced coffee awaited her.

Every so often, as the days passed, Alton or Phyllida would make an attempt to get Madeleine to decide what she wanted to do. But she kept putting them off.

September approached. Madeleine chose her fall semester seminars, one on the eighteenth-century novel (*Pamela, Clarissa, Tristram Shandy*) and another on triple-deckers, taught from a poststructuralist perspective by Jerome Shilts. Madeleine's arrival at Columbia, it turned out, would coincide with the first class of women being admitted to the university as undergraduates, and she took this as a good omen.

As much as Madeleine wanted Mitchell around, as close as they'd become that summer, she gave no clear sign that her feelings about him had altered in any significant way. She became freer in her actions, changing clothes in front of him, only saying, "Don't look." And he didn't. He averted his eyes, and *listened* to her undressing. Making a move on Madeleine seemed unfair. It would be taking advantage of her sadness. Being pawed by a guy was the last thing she needed right now.

One Saturday night, late, while Mitchell was reading in bed, he heard the door to the attic open. Madeleine came up to his room. Instead of sitting on his bed, however, she just poked her head in and said, "I want to show you something." She disappeared. Mitchell waited while she shuffled around the attic, moving boxes. After a few minutes, she returned, holding a shoe box. In her other hand was an academic journal.

"Ta-da!" Madeleine said, handing the journal to him. "This came in the mail today." It was a copy of *The Janeite Review*, edited by M. Myerson, and containing an essay by one Madeleine Hanna titled "I Thought You'd Never Ask: Some Thoughts on the Marriage Plot." It was a marvelous thing to see, even though a printing error had transposed two pages of the essay. Madeleine looked happier than she'd looked in months. Mitchell congratulated her, whereupon she proceeded to show him the shoe box. It was covered with dust. Madeleine had unearthed it from one of the cupboards as she was packing. The shoe box had been there for close to ten years. On the lid, in black ink, were the words "Bachelorette's Survival Kit." Madeleine explained how Alwyn had given it to her for her fourteenth birthday. She showed Mitchell all the items inside, the Ben Wa balls, the French tickler, the plastic fornicators, and, of course, the dehydrated prick, which was now hard to identify. Mice had nibbled the breadstick. At some point during all this, Mitchell got the courage to do what he'd been too scared to do at nineteen years of age. He said, "You should take that to New York with you. That's just what you need." And when Madeleine looked at him, he reached up and pulled her down onto the bed.

The rush of details that followed overwhelmed Mitchell's ability to take immediate pleasure in them. As he removed Madeleine's clothing, layer by layer, he was confronted by the physical reality of things he had long imagined. An uncomfortable tension existed between the two, with the result that after a while neither felt entirely real. Was this really Madeleine's breast he was taking into his mouth, or was it something he had dreamed, or was he dreaming now? Why, if she was finally there before him in the flesh, did she seem to be so odorless, and vaguely alien? He did his best; he persevered. He put his head between Madeleine's legs and opened his mouth, as though singing, but the space was somehow unwelcoming, and her answering calls sounded far away. He felt very alone. This didn't disappoint Mitchell so much as bewilder him. At one point, while Madeleine was nuzzling his own nipple, she groaned and said, "You really need to start using deodorant, Mitchell." Not long after, she fell asleep.

The birds woke him early, and he realized it was First Day. Dressing quickly, kissing Madeleine on the cheek, he set off for the Friends Meeting House. The way led through the Hannas' neighborhood of large, older houses, through the hopelessly quaint town of Prettybrook itself, with its town square and statue of Washington crossing the Delaware (some fifteen miles distant), and on through a series of leafy streets and alongside a golf course until the town ended and the battlefield began. The scenery rolled past Mitchell as though he were watching it on a screen. He was too happy to be involved in it, and though he was walking, he felt as if he were standing still. He kept bringing his hands to his nose to inhale Madeleine's smell. That, too, was fainter than desirable. Mitchell knew that their lovemaking hadn't been perfect the previous night, or really much good at all, but they had all the time they needed now to get it right.

Therefore, in his first act of fidelity, Mitchell stopped at the drugstore in town and bought a Mennen Speed Stick. He carried the deodorant in a paper bag all the way to the Meeting House, and kept it in his lap after he took a seat.

The day was going to be hot. For this reason, there were more people at the seven a.m. meeting than usual to take advantage of the cooler temperature. Most Friends had already withdrawn into themselves, but Joe and June Yamamoto, who had their eyes open, nodded in greeting.

Mitchell sat down, closed his eyes, and tried to empty his mind. But this was impossible. For the first fifteen minutes, all he thought about was Madeleine. He remembered what she'd felt like in his arms, and the noises she'd made. He wondered if Madeleine would ask him to move in with her on Riverside Drive. Or would it be better for him to get a place of his own, nearby, and take it slowly? No matter what, he had to go back to Detroit to see his parents. But he didn't have to stay there long. He could come back to New York, and find a job, and see what happened.

Whenever he caught himself thinking these things, he gently turned his attention away.

For a while, he went deep. He breathed in and out, and listened, among the other listening bodies. But something was different today. The deeper Mitchell went inside himself, the more troubled he was. Instead of his previous happiness, he felt a creeping unease, as if the floor were about to give way beneath him. He couldn't testify that what he then experienced was an Indwelling of the Light. Though the Quakers believed that Christ revealed himself to every person, without intermediaries, and that each person was able to take part in a continuing revelation, the things Mitchell saw weren't revelations of a universal significance. A still, small voice was speaking to him, but it was saying things he didn't want to hear. Suddenly, as if he was truly in touch with his Deep Self and could view his situation objectively, Mitchell understood why making love with Madeleine had felt as strangely empty as it had. It was because Madeleine hadn't been coming to him; she'd only been leaving Bankhead. After opposing her parents all summer, Madeleine was giving in to the necessity of an annulment. In order to make that clear to herself, she'd come up to Mitchell's bedroom in the attic.

He was her survival kit.

The truth poured into him like light, and if any of the Friends nearby noticed Mitchell wiping his eyes, they gave no sign.

He cried for the last ten minutes, as quietly as he could. At some point, the voice also told Mitchell that, in addition to never living with Madeleine, he would never go to divinity school, either. It was unclear what he was going to do with his life, but he wasn't going to be a monk, or a minister, or even a scholar. The voice was urging him to write Professor Richter to tell him so.

But that was all the understanding the Light brought him, because a minute later Clyde Pettengill shook hands with his wife, Mildred, and then everyone in the Meeting House was shaking hands.

Outside, Claire Ruth had set up muffins and coffee on the picnic table, but Mitchell didn't stay for conversation. He headed along the path, past the Quaker cemetery, where the markers bore no names.

A half hour later, he entered the front door on Wilson Lane. He heard Madeleine moving around in her bedroom, and climbed the stairs.

As he entered her room, Madeleine glanced away, long enough for Mitchell to confirm his intuition.

He didn't let things get any more awkward than they already were, and spoke quickly.

"You know that letter I sent you? From India?"

"That I didn't get?"

"That's the one. My memory of it's a little sketchy, for the reasons I mentioned. But there was one part, at the end, where I said I was going to tell you something, ask you something, but I had to do it in person."

Madeleine waited.

"It's a literary question."

"O.K."

"From the books you read for your thesis, and for your article—the Austen and the James and everything—was there any novel where the heroine gets married to the wrong guy and then realizes it, and then the other suitor shows up, some guy who's always been in love with her, and then *they* get together, but finally the second suitor realizes that the last thing the woman needs is to get married again, that she's got more important things to do with her life? And so finally the guy doesn't propose at all, even though he still loves her? Is there any book that ends like that?"

"No," Madeleine said. "I don't think there's one like that."

"But do you think that would be good? As an ending?"

He looked at Madeleine. She wasn't so special, maybe. She was his ideal, but an early conception of it, and he would get over it in time. Mitchell gave her a slightly goofy smile. He was feeling a lot better about himself, as if he might do some good in the world.

Madeleine sat down on a packing box. Her face looked more drawn than usual, and older. She narrowed her eyes, as if trying to bring him into focus.

A moving van rolled down the street, shaking the house, the arthritic Great Dane next door bellowing hoarsely after it.

And Madeleine kept squinting, as though Mitchell was already far away, until finally, smiling gratefully, she answered, "Yes."